EARTH GIRL

Janet Edwards lives in England. As a child, she read everything she could get her hands on, including a huge amount of science fiction and fantasy. She studied Maths at Oxford, and went on to suffer years of writing unbearably complicated technical documents before deciding to write something that was fun for a change. She has a husband, a son, a lot of books, and an aversion to housework. *Earth Girl* is her first book.

JANET EDWARDS

Earth Girl

HARPER
Voyager

HarperVoyager
An Imprint of HarperCollins*Publishers*
77–85 Fulham Palace Road,
Hammersmith, London W6 8JB

www.harpercollins.co.uk

A Paperback Original 2012
1

Copyright © Janet Edwards 2012

Janet Edwards asserts the moral right to
be identified as the author of this work

A catalogue record for this book
is available from the British Library

ISBN: 978 0 00 744349 9

Set in Meridien by Palimpsest Book Production Limited,
Falkirk, Stirlingshire

Printed and bound in Great Britain by
Clays Ltd, St Ives plc

MIX
Paper from
responsible sources
FSC
www.fsc.org **FSC˙ C007454**

ACKNOWLEDGEMENTS

To my husband, with thanks for all his help and support. I'd also like to thank Chris Morgan for encouraging me to take my writing seriously, as well as my agent Ian Drury, and my editor Amy McCulloch.

1

It was on Wallam-Crane day that I finally decided what I was going to do for my degree course Foundation year. I'd had a mail about it from Issette that morning. It showed her jumping up and down on her bed in her sleep suit, waving a pillow, and singing: 'Make your mind up, Jarra! Do it! Do it! Make up, make up, make up your mind girl!' She was singing it to the tune of the new song by Zen Arrath. Issette is totally powered on him, but I don't think much of his legs.

Issette is my best friend. We're both 17 and we'd been in Nursery together, and had neighbouring rooms all through Home and Next Step. She'd put in her application for the Medical Foundation course months ago. Issette is organized and reliable. I'm not. Most of my other friends had made their decisions too, except for Keon who was planning to do absolutely nothing. He'd been doing that all through school and I had to admit he was good at it.

I didn't fancy being another Keon, so I had to decide what to do, and I had to do it fast. The deadline for applying for courses was the day after the holiday.

Wallam-Crane day is a holiday on Earth, just like on all

the other worlds, but in the circumstances we don't have celebration parties the way they do. Thaddeus Wallam-Crane invented the portal and gave humanity the stars, but we on Earth are the one in a thousand who missed out when he created the ticket to the universe.

One of my private fantasies is inventing a time machine and travelling back in time nearly six hundred and fifty years to 15 November 2142. I would then strangle Wallam-Crane at birth. If it wasn't for him, I'd be normal instead of labelled a nean, a throwback. Yes, I'm one of them. The polite people would call me Handicapped, but you can call me ape girl if you like. The name doesn't change anything. My immune system can't survive anywhere other than Earth. I'm in prison, and it's a life sentence.

If you're still scanning this, I expect it's just out of shock that an ape girl can write. 'Amaz! Totally zan!' you will cry to your friends in disbelief, but you know that I'm just the same as you really. It could have been you here on Earth, and me travelling between worlds, if only the dice had fallen differently. When you have a baby, it could turn out like I did, and have to be portalled to Earth in minutes or it dies.

My psychologist says you people are scared of us. He says that's why you call us names and have your little superstitions. We see it all on the vids. Portalling between worlds late in pregnancy turns the baby into a nean. Don't eat Karanth jelly when you're pregnant or the baby will be an ape. The latest scare is plastered all over the newzies, and everyone throws out their Karanth jelly, and it makes no difference at all.

It's all rubbish. The best scientists have been researching this for hundreds of years and they still don't have a clue. Every other handicap can be screened out or fixed, but not this one. Whether you eat Karanth jelly or not, it can get your baby just the same way it got me. Maybe they'll find

2

a cure one day, but with my luck I bet I'm dead by then. I expect I'll die the day beforehand, so fate can enjoy a last big laugh at my expense.

My psychologist also says I still have a lot of unresolved bitterness and anger. He's right. You've probably already noticed it. I was feeling especially bitter on 15 November 2788. I was due to meet Candace in half an hour and tell her my decision on my course, my career, my whole future life. I still hadn't made up my mind, and really needed to do some hard thinking. Naturally, I was avoiding doing that by watching the vid.

The vid info channels were all packed with special anniversary programmes. Half of them were showing that old footage of the first experiment that everyone has seen a thousand times. Wallam-Crane smirks at the camera and says: 'One small step for a man, one giant leap for humanity.' Do you know he stole that line from the first moon landing? Do you even know that they went to the moon by rocket long before they portalled there? Probably not. Well, that's a fascinating bit of pre-history for you, totally free of education tax.

The rest of the info channels were either showing bits about the first interstellar portals, or the Exodus century that emptied Earth. I switched to the vid ent channels, but they were all showing vid stars getting drunk or powered at huge parties. I spotted the male lead out of that new vid series *Defenders*. Arrack San Domex. Now there's a man with good legs. I'm a big fan of those scenes where he's looking sexy and heroic in his tight-fitting Military uniform, saving humanity from the mythical menacing aliens that we still haven't discovered. I stopped a moment to listen.

'. . . great tragedy that genius Thaddeus Wallam-Crane died so young, before he could even portal to another planet himse . . .'

I turned off the vid before Arrack could demonstrate his stupidity any further. Nice legs, not much on the brain cells. I shouted my frustration at the blank screen. 'Don't you know that the genius was already 64 when he got that first portal working? He didn't die young; he lived to celebrate his hundredth! It took them another hundred years before anyone portalled to another habitable planet. Work out how old he would have needed to be to go there, nardle brain!'

It annoys me so much when people don't know their history. I have a passion for facts and . . .

Yes, I admit it. I'd known what course I'd take all along. You've probably already seen I'm a natural historian. I was just rebelling against it because being a historian is like giving in to what fate has done to me. Everyone knows Earth is for the triple H: Hospital. History. Handicapped. There are other careers you can follow on Earth – we need the entire infrastructure any world has – but our two big speciality areas are medicine and history.

So it boiled down to this. I could be a dutiful stereotype Handicapped and become a historian, or I could rebel by not studying something I loved. Great choice. Then I thought of a third possibility. I could do it if I was crazy enough or angry enough. I was grinning like a maniac as I went out of my room and headed down to the portal in the entrance hall.

I met Candace in the huge tropical bird dome of Zoo Europe. They have an even bigger one in Zoo Africa of course, but cross continent portalling is more expensive than local and you hit time zone problems. You probably didn't know that, since Earth is the only world with more than one inhabited continent. Another tax-free fact for you.

Candace was sitting on the bench by the guppy pool. I

4

sat next to her, and for a moment we just watched the tiny shimmering crimson, electric blue, and emerald tails of the male guppies as they showed off to the drab females. Overhead, there were flashes of iridescent feathers from birds in flight. I loved this place, with its rampaging plants, humid jungle smells, and the constant bird song. Candace and I had been meeting here for years and I still never tired of it.

'So, I suppose you're still thinking things over,' Candace said. 'I hate to nag, but we have to get your application in by tomorrow.'

'You can nag,' I said. 'You're my ProMum. It's your job.'

I bet you've never heard of a ProMum. ProParents are what you get if your real parents don't want to know about a Handicapped baby. In 92 per cent of cases, it takes parents less than a day to register consent to make their embarrassing throwback a ward of Hospital Earth, give notice to dissolve their marriage or other relationship, and head in opposite directions while each screaming the throwback genes belonged to the other party.

My parents were in the 92 per cent. I'd had the right to attempt contact with them when I was 14, but I hadn't bothered. The exos threw me away, and I sure as chaos wasn't chasing after them and begging!

I used the exo word there. Us apes call people like you 'norms' when we're being polite, and 'exos' when we're not. I don't feel I have to be polite about parents who dumped me.

I mentioned that my psychologist thinks I still have a lot of unresolved bitterness and anger, didn't I?

Instead of parents, I have Candace for two hours a week. She is ProMum to ten of us. I don't know who the others are and I don't want to. I also don't want to know about her own kids. She must have experienced at least one serious relationship, and have at least one child of her own, because it's a prerequisite for being a ProParent.

So, I know about all the kids who are my competition, but I prefer to ignore them and think of Candace as being mine and mine alone. She may only be mine for two hours a week, but unlike all the other adults that come and go in my life, Candace is two hours a week for ever. ProParents are for life. She'll be there to advise me when I get into a relationship, or have kids of my own, or strangle Wallam-Crane at birth. I have a ProDad too, and he was great until I got to be about 11. Since then we haven't got on so well.

I've run into a couple of the kids with real parents who moved to Earth to take care of them. I think I prefer ProParents really. They only bother to make you do something if it's really important, and if you're in trouble they're like superheroes. I mean, seriously, they have huge powers. If they suspect one of their kids is being badly treated, ProParents can wade in, claim advocate authority, and get Homes inspected, closed, anything they want. They can walk right into the board meeting of Hospital Earth if they feel it's necessary. Now that really is totally zan!

It's always been nice to know Candace had that sort of power and was on my side. I'd never needed her to use her authority before, but given what I was planning I might need it now.

It was time to break the news to her. I took it by gentle stages. 'I want to go history, so I need to start with Pre-history Foundation Year.'

'Well done,' said Candace. 'You've been working towards it for years, and it's obviously right for you, but the way you've been delaying the decision had me worried. I was afraid you'd have one of your moods and bite off your own nose by choosing something else. I've got your application ready; we just need to submit it.'

'It could be a bit more complicated than that,' I said. 'I want to apply to an off-world university.'

Candace closed her eyes for a few seconds. I swear she even stopped breathing. Finally she opened her eyes again. 'We aren't going back to the denial phase are we? You went through the whole thing about how they must have made a mistake in your case, just like all the kids do. You elected to take up your option to portal off world on your fourteenth birthday. You went into anaphylactic shock, the medical team shipped you back, and you took a week to recover. Surely you remember that.'

'Yes,' I said. I'd been dying. I'd been terrified. It wasn't something I'd ever forget.

'Then you know it's not a mistake. If you go off world, you'll die. You can't go to an off-world university!'

'But I don't have to go off world.' I grinned crazily. 'All Pre-history Foundation Year courses are held on Earth. I can transfer back to University Earth after that for the main degree.'

She tried all the sensible arguments. 'University Earth does exactly the same Foundation course. They use the same facilities, the same dig sites, and the teaching is as good or better.'

I kept grinning. 'I want a course run by an off-world university.'

'You're guaranteed to get a place on a University Earth course. You need the right grades to get on an off-world course.'

'I have great grades, you know that.'

'What about cost? Any education you want is free here but . . .'

Yes, I get educated free. Are you jealous? Being an ape has certain advantages. We get guaranteed places to study anything we want, and we never have to pay education tax at the end of it. We get a guaranteed job in whatever field we like. If we don't want to work we have a guaranteed basic income. That's how my friend Keon was planning to live – by lazing around for the rest of his life. Every inhabited world contributes generously to care for the rejects of humanity. It's guilt money to ease their consciences. You lot pay up, so you can dump your reject babies on Earth and then forget about them.

'Does it actually say anywhere that my free education is limited to University Earth and not any other university?' I asked.

'I'll have to check. No one has ever thought it relevant so . . .' Candace was clearly cracking in the face of my determination. 'You do realize that the other students will be . . . difficult. They may not like you being on their course. Is that the idea? You want to vent your anger?'

'That's not the idea. Not to start with anyway. I don't want them to know what I am. I want them to think I'm one of them. Normal.'

'You *are* normal, Jarra. If you'd been born before the invention of the portal, no one would ever have known there was a problem with your immune system.'

This fact was recited to me regularly. I was normal. I wasn't to think of myself as a reject. I was to value myself. All the irritating repetition achieved was to make me briefly try fantasizing about being born six hundred years ago. Then I remembered all the wars and famines in pre-history, decided I preferred modern civilization, and went back to fantasizing about strangling Wallam-Crane.

I shook my head at Candace. 'People keep saying that to me. My psychologist says it, you say it, but you're Handicapped too so it doesn't help. I need the normal people to say it. I want to go on this course and have the real people think I'm one of them. It doesn't matter if I don't manage it for

8

a whole year, even a few days would work. That would really mean I'm worth something.'

There was more to it than that. At the end, when I'd fooled them all into thinking I was a real person like them, then I was planning to tell them what I was. One of the neans, one of the people whose existence they ignored, had forced herself into their cosy little lives. I could watch the shock and embarrassment in their eyes, when they realized they'd been fooled into thinking a throwback was one of them. I could yell at them, let out all the anger and resentment, and walk away laughing. It didn't seem a bright idea to tell Candace about that bit of my plan though.

'If this would help you value yourself at last . . .' Candace sat there thinking this through. 'It would be hard to fool the other students, Jarra, but you won't even get the chance to try. Your application will come from an Earth school, and they'll know what that means. Children born here without the condition commute to off-world schools, and their applications come from those.'

Yes, I know you're staggering at the thought of the expense of portalling between worlds every day just to go to school. It's true though. Even if both parents are Handicapped, nine out of ten of their kids will be able to portal off world. The guilt money of humanity pays for them to portal to normal schools to aid their assimilation into 'real society'.

Did you know, at one time they tried swapping babies? They took away the normal baby of Handicapped parents and gave them a Handicapped baby from off-world instead. They did it by force. I bet they never taught you that in your off-world school. My psychologist says I should forget about it because it generates hostility, but you shouldn't forget history; you should learn from it.

'The staff may know,' I said, 'but that's my personal data!'

'You're right!' Candace was in ProMum mode now, fighting for her kid's rights. 'Staff can only access personal data for professional purposes. Your school's planet of origin implies your handicap; therefore it has the same protection status as medical data. We can make that clear on your application. The staff may know, but it's professional misconduct if they tell the students. What university do we go for?'

'Errr . . . Asgard.' I picked it at random because it was the home planet of that nardle-brained vid star I had a crush on. Arrack San Domex. The one with the legs.

'Asgard . . .' Candace took her lookup from her pocket and typed a question. Data flooded the screen and she nodded. 'That's a high-rated history department. Good choice.'

It was, was it? 'Are my grades good enough? Will I get in? Should I pick somewhere easier?'

'You have great grades, Jarra, and your relevant experience section can't be beaten. You've visited more history sites in a year than their other applicants will have visited in their life time. I'd bet most of them have never even set foot on Earth. If they turn you down, they had better be able to prove every student on that course has better grades or I'll file a legal challenge from Hospital Earth on behalf of their ward.'

'Yay!' I just love having a ProMum with super powers on my side.

'As for the cost . . . It won't be more than if you go to University Earth. If anyone argues, then I'll take it as high as necessary to get it authorized.'

I got a lot more than my statutory two hours of Candace that day, because we sent off my application. When

University Asgard got back to work after the holiday, they were going to have a shock waiting for them. They were the first off-world university to ever get an application from an ape student, and they were going to have to accept me or Candace would go legal and tear them to shreds.

2

In the end, I didn't tell any of my friends about University Asgard, not even Issette. Asgard might find a way to wriggle out of accepting me, and then I'd look a nardle. I just said I was going history, and they assumed the rest. Anyway, everyone's attention was on Keon's startling news.

Would you believe it? Keon calmly told us he had actually applied for a course in Foundation Art! The other eight of us from our Next Step were stunned that the legendarily lazy Keon Tanaka had applied for a course at all, and totally grazzed that he'd chosen something as commercial as art.

'Well there's lots of money in it . . .' said Ross. 'But you need to be able to paint, or sculpt, or light, or *something* to be an artist. Whatever you make has to be good.'

'You know, there were times in history when that wasn't true,' I told them.

They all groaned. 'No!' said Issette. 'No history lesson. Bad, bad, Jarra!'

'Art mustn't be good,' said Keon. 'It has to be mediocre. That's the whole point. People pay a lot to have real art in their home, something unique that's totally created by human hands. It has to be good enough to look at, but bad enough that it's obviously not one of a hundred thousand manufactured copies of a brilliant original art work.'

'Yes, but can you even manage mediocre?' asked Cathan. He was looking a bit offended, since he was going art himself and took it seriously. He saw it as a secure, high-earning career, and had already researched how Earth artists sold their work via off-world agents to hide the fact it had been created by an ape.

I was tempted to ask if Cathan could manage mediocre either, but I was good and kept quiet. Things were edgy between me and Cathan. We'd got a bit boy and girlish at the beginning of the year, starting at the big Year Day party of course. The relationship only lasted a couple of months and it was mostly arguments. Cathan had nice legs, but was so sensitive. He threw tantrums if I didn't mail him every two hours, and he didn't like the amount of time I spent watching history info vids. I'd lose my temper too, because I had a right to do stuff I liked, and . . . Well, Cathan still had a few grudges about it.

Keon shrugged. 'Maybe I won't even go to the classes. I found out I'd get more money as a student than just on basic maintenance so . . .'

All of us laughed except Cathan.

Everyone forgot about applications then. There wasn't any suspense as far as my friends were concerned, since they were guaranteed places on their chosen courses at University Earth. I was a nervous wreck though. I'd been scanning stuff about University Asgard. There was a lot of competition for places on their courses, especially history, and they'd be trying to find every reason they could to reject an ape girl.

If they rejected me . . . Well, Candace could go legal at them, but forcing my way in with a lot of publicity was no good. Everyone would know what I was, and the whole point was to fool them, and see their faces when they found

13

out the truth. Maybe I should have been sensible and applied to University Earth as well, but it was too late to be thinking of that. I could only hope that if necessary, Candace would throw her ProMum weight around and get me a place there.

We were due to get the mails about our degree courses on 1 December. I spent all day waiting to hear from University Asgard, nerves jumping every time a mail arrived. Mostly I flipped through vid channels, but I couldn't even concentrate on an episode of *Defenders*. By the evening, I was furious. They hadn't even bothered to reject me! I sent Candace a mail telling her exactly what I thought of off-worlders. She sent me a mail back saying the inhabited continent of Asgard was in a time zone eleven hours behind us, and they hadn't had breakfast yet.

Have you ever felt really stupid? I had no excuse at all. We have enough time zones on Earth. The everyday stuff we portal to is all local and in a similar time zone, but some of our school trips had set off in the middle of the night so that we would arrive in daylight at the other end. I'm a nardle brain. Nardle, nardle, nardle . . .

My mail from University Asgard came five hours later. They'd accepted me! They didn't sound ecstatic about it, and there was a special note about how they couldn't make any non-standard arrangements to allow for my disability, but I didn't care. I danced round my room in victory.

The special note was designed to worry me, but it didn't. They couldn't do anything to stop me taking part in all the classes. There was a shakeup in history teaching twenty years ago, because so many historians had never been to Earth at all. That wasn't so bad if they specialized in modern history, but even the leading experts in pre-history had never visited a single site. They didn't want to be contaminated by us apes! Teaching pre-history when you've never been to Earth is like teaching literature when you've never scanned a book.

14

So they cracked down on the whole thing, made the History Foundation course purely about pre-history, and made it compulsory for it to be held on Earth. It makes sense. You can't ignore pre-history. It's the starting point for everything that has happened since the invention of the portal. So, all historians have to learn pre-history and experience Earth dig sites right at the start of their training.

When I finished dancing round the room, I sent a jubilant mail to Candace. She wouldn't read it until next day of course. I had enough sense not to wake up my ProMum at midnight with an emergency-flagged mail unless it really was an emergency. Issette was a totally different matter. She was my best friend and I wanted to tell her this right away!

I dashed next door and stuck my hand on the door plate. I could hear the faint sound of its response from the other side of the door. A musical tone, followed by a voice saying, 'Your friend Jarra is requesting admission.'

I gave it another minute or two and then tried again. The door opened and Issette stood there in a crumpled sleep suit, looking at me with bleary, accusing eyes. 'This better be good! Are you dead or something?' She turned round without waiting for an answer, went across to the bed and flopped on it with a dramatic groan.

I followed her in and the door shut behind us. 'I got the mail about my course. I've been accepted!'

'What? You woke me up at this hour to tell me that!' Issette lifted her head to glare at me.

I grinned back at her. 'I've been accepted by University Asgard.'

'WHAT!' Issette screeched.

A computerized voice interrupted us. 'Please have consideration for others attempting to sleep at this hour and reduce your noise levels.'

Issette threw her pillow at its sensor box. We all hated

having those things in our rooms. Officially they weren't an invasion of privacy, because the units didn't record or pass on information, they just told us off reproachfully. If you kept ignoring them for too long then they started making an annoying noise like a gong being sounded every second until they beat you into submission.

It wasn't just noise they complained about either. They didn't like fire hazards, messy rooms, or you getting too boy and girlish. It does nothing for a romantic moment when a computer voice interrupts saying: 'Your current inter-person intimacy is exceeding that acceptable for your age group.'

There were always rumours going round that people had managed to hot-wire their room sensor to bypass monitoring, but most people just set the tampering alarm off and have to pay for a new unit out of their personal credits. Those things are expensive so I've never tried it myself. Cathan wasn't worth it.

'I can't wait to leave Next Step and get away from that thing,' snarled Issette. She turned back to me. 'You're not serious about University Asgard? You can't be!'

I spent the next hour convincing her I was serious, and explaining what I was planning. The computer complained about our noise level several more times. Eventually Issette started taking me seriously.

'I'd love to see their faces when they find out,' she said. 'You have to promise me to vid it and mail it to me.'

'And you have to promise to keep this secret. Don't tell anyone, none of our friends, no one. Only you and Candace know. If too many people find out about it, then someone will be bound to give it away. I can't fool the other students if they're expecting an ape to join their course.'

Issette pulled a face. 'Don't call yourself that!'

'Please have consideration for others attempting to sleep at this hour and reduce your noise levels,' said the voice.

We both groaned.

'You aren't even telling your psychologist then?' Issette was shocked.

'I'm dumping my psychologist. He's optional after I leave Next Step.' I didn't think much of psychologists, and I felt my sessions with mine were a total waste of time.

'I'd be lost without my psychologist,' said Issette, but she didn't argue any more. She was a believer in psychologists and I wasn't. We'd been round this too many times in the past to bother with it again now.

She got back to the point. 'I don't see how you can manage to fool them even if you do manage to keep it secret. You won't know all their stuff. The right clothes. The way they talk. I know we watch the vids but . . . And the sectors all have their own silly words. Those aren't in the vids we see. We don't see sector only stuff, there's only the odd bit in a comedy when they do it for a joke.'

I nodded. 'Yes, they can all speak Language, but they have dialects too. Alpha sector has the strongest dialect because those are the first planets settled during the Exodus century. Did you know, the newer the sector, the closer the dialect is to standard Language? I saw this info vid about linguistic history mapping and . . .'

Issette had her fingers in her ears. 'No history lesson. Bad, bad, Jarra!'

'Stop doing that.'

She took her fingers out of her ears. 'Well, stop lecturing me on history. You're always doing it.'

'I'm not.'

'Oh yes you are. You're obsessed.'

'I'm not obsessed.'

Issette just gave me her special look. It's a sort of hard stare, which says she's right, I'm wrong, and we both know it. It's very hard to argue with, so I gave in.

17

'Well, if you say so . . . Anyway, if I pretend to be from a sector, there are bound to be some other students from there, and I won't have the accent or know the dialect. My plan is to say that my parents are Military.'

Issette looked suspicious. 'Is that because you're a fan of Arrack San Domex?'

It wasn't, really it wasn't. I'd picked Asgard because of Arrack San Domex, and he plays a Military character in *Defenders*, but my decision was based on logic this time.

'No, it isn't. All the sectors have their dialect, but the Military don't. They stick to Language. When they're on assignment, their kids live in places just like Home and Next Step, and Military kids usually go Military themselves. No chance of running into one in a class of thirty history students.'

'That could work,' Issette admitted. 'That would explain your name too. Hospital Earth and the Military both use stupid old-fashioned names. I mean, "Issette"! Have you ever seen an Issette in the vids who's less than eighty?'

I giggled. Issette has successfully resolved her anger and bitterness over being Handicapped, but her psychologist is still working on her hatred of her name. The only reason she hadn't changed it years ago was that she couldn't make up her mind about a new one.

Issette fell asleep soon after that, so I went back to my own room and started scanning info vids about the Military. You can't totally trust the facts in these things, but it was fascinating all the same.

Well, the ones about Planet First opening up new worlds were fascinating. The ones about running the solar space arrays were interesting too, though I didn't follow all the science in them. The policing stuff was a bit too like sociology in school. Yeah, yeah, we have cross-sector Military so the different sectors don't have their own armies and get tempted to re-invent war. I shouldn't be rude about it – I'm going history and I know we don't want any more wars – but it gets a bit preachy.

As for the alien standby exercises, well that was just funny. Even the Military people taking part in them sometimes started to laugh in the middle. How do you train to fight aliens when you've never met any? The answer is you get someone to imagine mad scenarios, so you find yourself fighting computer-generated bouncing-ball-shaped aliens who can stick to ceilings or eight-legged things that squirt sticky ribbons at you that explode on contact.

All right, it's serious stuff really. We haven't met intelligent aliens yet, but it's been mathematically proven that they must exist, and humanity will at some point meet them. Some of those aliens will be hostile. I may find it hard to believe, but it's a scientific fact. We have to be prepared, and the Military are doing their best.

I scanned vids all night, and made notes of what I needed to study. I had one month to create myself an identity as a kid of Military parents. If I was going to make a success of this, I needed to make Military Jarra into a real person, and know what she would know. The more I found out, the more I realized I had to learn.

The bit about Military schools was a big shock. Since Military kids usually go Military themselves, their schools cover a lot of things to prepare them for that career. Military basic training is for new recruits from the sectors. Military kids skip it because they've already done it at school.

I nearly gave up when I found out all Military kids were trained in unarmed combat. It was only a month until Year Day, and University courses started the day after that. How could I learn unarmed combat in that short a time? Should I pick a different fake background? At least there were info vids I could study on this, and if I didn't know all I should

19

about the Military, it was pretty certain that my fellow students would know a lot less.

In the end, I decided to stick with the Military idea. I started making up career histories for my fake Military parents, details about bases where I would have lived, and mailed Candace asking if she could arrange anything about unarmed combat training.

Candace mailed me back about nine in the morning. The mail showed her holding a glass of frujit and smiling. 'Congratulations, Jarra. I'll find out about the training, but maybe you're taking the Military research a bit too seriously. You do tend to get carried away by things. Why not have breakfast and get some sleep?'

I decided to take her advice.

3

The Year Day party was . . . a bit sad. The nine of us had lived together through Nursery, Home and Next Step, but now we were splitting up. I was heading off on my personal war against University Asgard. The others were all going to University Earth, but would be scattered across different courses and campuses.

Maeth and Ross were doing different courses, but would be on the same campus in Europe Central. Issette, Cathan and Keon would be together on a campus in Europe South. The other four of us would be heading off alone. I'd always known I would be, of course, since Pre-history Foundation classes spent the year working at some of the major dig sites.

Issette was going Foundation Medical. Cathan and Keon were both going Art, but they'd chosen different specialities. Cathan was going Art Paint and Keon was going Art Light. Probably just as well. They'd been asked to send in sample pieces of their work before starting their course, and Keon had been given some sort of award for his.

I'd seen a vid of his piece. A laser sculpture of lights weaving and shimmering through all the colours out of the tropical dome in Zoo Europe. Most of the time it looked totally abstract, but every now and then the colours would sort of fuse together and you saw it was a bird with outstretched wings. Keon called it 'Phoenix Rising'. You'd have to see it to understand, but it was seriously zan. We were all grazzed to discover Keon actually had some talent. Most of us were grazzed in a good way, but Cathan was a simmering heap of resentment just waiting for an excuse to explode.

So, the nine of us were splitting up, and the Year Day party was a bit like a funeral. We were leaving Next Step. We'd meet up, but it would never be quite the same again. You wouldn't understand, living out there with real parents, but the nine of us had been a family. We didn't always like each other (Cathan usually wasn't speaking to someone) but we were all we had to hang on to.

The younger ones were at the party too, sending us off the way we'd sent off the other years ahead of us. We opened all the partition walls in Commons, to make it one big room. We did all the traditional things, singing Old Lang Zine just before midnight. I tried telling the others just how old that song was, the way I did every year, and they all threw cups of Fizzup over me.

Then we put on the big vid wall to show the countdown to midnight, and shouted along in chorus as the numbers flashed on the screen. 'Three! Two! One! Happy Year Day 2789!'

We cheered wildly as we all became a year older. Our Next Step Principal had been lurking in a corner keeping an eye on things, now she stepped forward. 'Congratulations to our new adults. Let's all wish them happiness in the future.'

The younger kids cheered again. I was embarrassed to find I was getting a bit weepy. Issette was unashamedly crying. We were 18, we were adult, we were moving on.

There was a time when people counted ages from the day each person was born, not from Year Day. Must have made things really messy and lonely at times like this.

Eventually the younger ones headed off to bed, the Principal said goodnight, and it was just the nine of us left in Commons. Issette was asleep on the floor. We woke her up because Ross and Maeth wanted to register their first Twoing contract. They'd been waiting months for this. The rest of us watched while they dialled Registry, entered their details, and got the confirmation. Then we all applauded and gave a big cheer.

Ross was planning to work in either a Home or a Next Step one day, so he was going Care and Community Foundation Course. Maeth had picked a random course that was on the same campus. She wasn't bothered what course she did, because she was planning to be a ProMum and you don't need qualifications for that.

'They only allow you to have a three-month contract to start with,' Maeth said, 'but that means we can get on to our second Twoing contract quickly, and qualify for joint student accommodation.'

Ross nodded. 'One more three-month contract, then a six-month contract, and we'll have the minimum three contracts and a year needed to get married. You have to all promise to come to our wedding next Year Day.'

We all promised.

'After that . . .' Ross grinned at Maeth.

She blushed. 'After that, we have our kids. Ideally, I'd like our own kids to be at least two years old before I start being a ProMum when I'm 25.'

They had their whole future lives planned out. Listening to them, I didn't know whether to be jealous or terrified. After a bit, they said goodnight and headed off. The rest of us went a bit quiet after that. I suppose we were all thinking the same thing. Just because a couple start Twoing, it doesn't automatically mean that they . . . On the other hand, Maeth and Ross had been together a long time, so now they were adults they probably would . . . I told myself sternly that it was none of my own business.

Cathan's mind was clearly also considering the options available to adults. He wandered over to sit next to me with horribly fake casualness.

'We should get back together, Jarra,' he said, in a low voice.

'I'm about to spend a year on assorted history dig sites,' I pointed out. 'They're only open to authorized visitors.'

'You could visit me even if I can't visit you.'

'It's not a good idea. You wouldn't be happy unless we spent most of our time together, and that just wouldn't be possible because of my work and the time zones.'

Cathan wasn't accepting the polite brush off. 'We've got a bit of time still before we head off. We can try and work things out. Let's go to my room and talk. We're 18 now, so I could go and buy some wine and . . .'

I got sick of being tactful. 'I know we're adults now and the room sensors won't bother us, but I'm not getting drunk and spending the next thirty-six hours in bed with you.' I stood up and tried to walk away.

'Oh come on. You want to try it too . . .' Cathan came after me, grabbed me, and gave me an incompetent attempt at a masterful kiss.

Just maybe my psychologist is right about my aggression, because I really enjoyed what happened next. I grabbed Cathan's arms, rolled backwards, and threw him over my head. I'd been enjoying doing this sort of thing in unarmed combat lessons every morning for the past month, but doing it for real was totally zan!

I stood up, and looked down at Cathan. Commons had a

nice padded floor, so he wasn't hurt, just absolutely grazzed. So was everyone else. Issette pulled a buggy-eyed, amazed face at me.

'Like I said, Cathan. The answer is no. Good night, everyone.' I made a magnificent exit and headed to my room.

Once inside, with the door safely closed behind me, I fell on my bed and burst out laughing. Cathan's face!

After a bit, I calmed down. I have to admit I put the vid on after that. I'd turned down Cathan's generous offer, but I couldn't resist indulging my curiosity by scanning a few adult vids. Since there was no one under 18 in the room, it gave me access to all the forbidden channels. I knew Beta was the most sexually permissive sector, so I took a look at some of their vids. Hoo eee! I'd never seen so much leg!

I went to bed after that and slept solidly through until early afternoon. When I woke up, I grabbed a quick meal down in Commons and started on the demoralizing task of packing. I'd lived in this room for six years, and it felt like I was dismantling part of myself.

I'd splashed out some credits on a set of luggage with hover pads. I wasn't sure if everything would go in. It's amazing how much stuff you can accumulate in one room. After an hour of sorting, I was quite positive everything wouldn't go in.

A musical tone sounded and my door said, 'Your friend Issette is requesting admission.'

I went over and hit the unlock plate. Yes, I know what you're thinking. We do have voice command doors on Earth, we aren't totally last millennium here, it's just we don't have them in our Next Step. They all got disabled after someone in the year above me hacked the system and started sneaking into girls' rooms. A girl caught him vidding her in the shower, and when they checked his lookup he had vids of two other girls as well. All chaos broke out. It was the most exciting thing that ever happened here. Our Principal had six fuming ProParents in her office, and another forty officially registering concern. After that, the culprit got transferred to Correctional for his last three months in Next Step, and we all had to use unlock plates instead of voice commands.

Issette stood outside, arms full of old toys, her face registering total despair. 'I'll never find space for all this.'

'I'm in trouble too, and I'll be moving dig site several times during the year. I'll have to keep unpacking and repacking it all.' I tried to be practical. 'I suppose we could throw some stuff out.'

'I can't throw them away,' wailed Issette. 'I can't throw out Whoopiz the Zen and all the fluffies.' Issette was very attached to her toys in Nursery, especially the strange skinny purple object that she called Whoopiz the Zen. She didn't seem to have entirely grown out of it.

I didn't want to toss all my old familiar clutter down a waste chute either, so we dragged everything over to a hired storage unit. It was surprisingly hard to close the door on the sad jumbled relics of our years in Nursery, Home and Next Step, and return to a stripped, impersonal room.

I didn't sleep very well, but the next morning I could laze in bed until late. I was due at my course at ten in the morning, but this time I'd remembered to allow for the time zones. The first part of my course was in America North, so I had five spare hours.

My last bit of packing took only a few minutes. I spent a while helping out Issette, and then we both headed down to the entrance hall with our luggage. I just had to press my key fob, and my bags gathered up in a tight group behind me, bouncing up and down slightly in mid air, like obedient but excited puppies. Issette's bags didn't have hover pads, so she had them loaded on a hired hover trolley.

In the entrance hall we met five other hover trolleys, another two sets of hover pad luggage, and their owners. The nine of us stood in an awkward group, with nothing to say except the goodbyes we'd already said, but feeling unable to actually leave. This was the big moment that we'd dreamed of for years. No more Principal giving us orders. No more rules. No more room sensors nagging us. We could go anywhere we liked, and do anything we wanted. We were adults, we were free, and we were scared.

We'd probably have stood there all day, if the Principal hadn't arrived. She did a quick head count, saw we were all ready to go, and put us out of our misery by waving us off.

We dutifully formed an orderly queue for the portal, and took out our lookups to check our destination codes. One by one we dialled, stepped into the portal, and vanished. I let the others go first, because they all had internal Europe destinations, and I was going inter-continent.

I portalled to the closest Europe Transit, wandered past the information signs about inter-continent portal charges, and portalled to America. AIPTH, that's Automated Intercontinental Passenger Traffic Handling, randomly allocated me an American Transit destination, and I popped out in America Transit 2.

That's where I made a really nardle-brained decision. I could have dialled straight to my destination from any local portal in America Transit 2, but I had the bright idea of going via America Off-world since that was where a genuine off-world student would arrive. I felt this would help me get in character as Jarra the Military kid.

It was a seriously bad move. I thought America Off-world would be nice and quiet by now. Around eight in the morning, it would be busy of course, the plaza full of Earth norm kids gathering up ready to portal through on the way to their off-world schools. The authorities generously pay for them to portal off world daily to school, but they aren't completely insane about it. The big cost is establishing the portal, not keeping it open, so they march the kids through in batches of up to a hundred to keep the cost per head down to the minimum.

The mass off-world kiddie commute would be over by now, so I expected things to be peaceful, but I stepped out of the portal into chaos. It was the day after Year Day and every university course was starting. America Off-world was teeming with Handicapped parents sending their normal kids away to off-world universities. There were also off-world history and medical students flooding in. The problem wasn't so much the people, but the quantities of luggage chasing their owners in all directions.

I weaved my way through the mob, avoiding the area with big red information signs about the colossal off-world portal charges, and went to another local portal. Anyone watching would think I was mad, coming here and then just going from one local portal to another. They'd be right too.

I was relieved when I made it without losing myself, let alone my luggage. I entered the code for the dome on New York Dig Site, where our course would be based for the first couple of months, and the portal started talking to me.

'Warning, your destination is a restricted access area,' it told me. 'If your scanned genetic code is not listed as authorized for access, then your portal will not establish but your personal account will still be charged for this journey.'

I hesitated, with last-minute cowardly thoughts running through my head, and an acid voice spoke from behind me.

'You may have all day, but I don't!'

I glanced behind me at an impatient, elderly woman,

who reminded me of my scary science teacher at school, turned back to face the portal and took a deep breath. I was Jarra, a Military kid, trained in unarmed combat. A history lecturer and twenty-nine other history students wouldn't scare me.

I stepped into the portal and a new identity.

4

I arrived in a very basic accommodation dome. There had been no attempt to disguise the curve of the outside wall, or even colour the flexiplas from its depressing natural grey. I hadn't expected anything better, because I'd been to several dig sites before with the school history club.

A harassed looking man of about thirty had been watching a trail of bobbing luggage head out of the door, presumably following its owner. He turned to face me and my own shoal of bags. 'Welcome to University Asgard Pre-history Foundation course at the New York Dig Site. I'm Lecturer Playdon. You are . . .?' He scrolled down a list of names on his lookup.

'Jarra Reeath,' I told him.

He first looked startled, and then as if he'd just noticed a very bad smell. 'You're in room 6,' he said, stabbing his lookup with a vicious finger to check my name off on his list. 'Student greet is in the dining hall in one hour.'

Someone else had just come through the portal. Lecturer Playdon turned to the new arrival, and I led my little procession of bags through the door and went in search of room 6. I'd learnt a few useful things in the one-minute encounter.

Lecturer Playdon obviously knew what I was, and didn't like it, but he was being professional and he wasn't going to tell the other students. That was good news, but even better was the fact he hadn't been able to tell at first glance that I was the ape girl. Rationally, I knew there was no truth in all the exo jokes about the look and smell of apes, but eighteen years of seeing them on the vid channels had still worn away at my confidence.

I tracked down room 6, which for some reason was between room 4 and room 12. It wasn't bad for a room on a dig site. Bed. Storage space. Even a very small wall vid. I unpacked my bags, and then it was time to face the student greet. I'd survived meeting one enemy, and now I was going to meet another twenty-nine. I comforted myself with the fact that Playdon knew what I was, but the other students wouldn't.

I'd already discovered the dining hall while looking for my room, so I headed back there. I found a dozen or so students sitting on grey flexiplas chairs around grey flexiplas tables and looking at the grey flexiplas walls. More were arriving.

I sat near the back, and tried to get in character. For a month, I'd studied Military vids. I'd trained in unarmed combat. I'd built an entire life history and family for Jarra Military kid, or JMK as I'd nicknamed her. By this time, I knew JMK better than I knew myself.

Lecturer Playdon was sitting at the front of the room and looking depressed. After a few minutes, he seemed to decide he had a full class present. He started with exactly the same words he'd said when I arrived.

'Welcome to University Asgard Pre-history Foundation course at the New York Dig Site. I'm Lecturer Playdon.'

After that, he branched out into daring new verbal territory. 'We will be staying at New York for the next two months before moving on to our next dig site. This is the dining hall, used for meals and classes. You'll have noticed all the other rooms in this dome are very small. Has everyone found their rooms, and have you any problems or questions?'

A hand went up, from a blonde girl in a clinging dress of glowing fabric that showed patches of bare skin in unexpected places. None of them were actually over restricted body areas, but they were certainly very close to them. She could have stepped straight out of a wild party scene in a vid.

'I couldn't find the concealed door to the bathroom in my room, or the concealed window,' she said. 'Should I have a special key code?'

There were a few giggles from round the room. I was one of the guilty parties.

Lecturer Playdon broke the bad news to her. 'That's probably because there is no concealed door. There's a bathroom at the end of each corridor. That's one bathroom between ten of you, so no lingering in the shower. There are no windows in the dome. Anyone else?'

Everyone else kept quiet.

'Good. I've one very important warning for you. Don't go outside the dome until instructed to do so. I really mean that. Now I'll let you get on with your meet and greet.'

He went to sit in a corner and ostentatiously started working through some info on his lookup. Apparently we were supposed to run things ourselves now. There was a nervous silence, and then a girl stood up. She looked just like a vid presenter, with glittering rainbow lights flickering randomly through her waist long, straight black hair. Expertly applied makeup emphasized the delicate features of her classically-beautiful dark face, and her clothes must have cost a fortune.

'We'd better start introducing ourselves,' she said, gazing

round at us with a superlatively confident smile. 'I'm Dalmora Rostha.' The slow drawling way she spoke told me her home sector before she said it. 'I'm from Alpha sector. My father is Ventrak Rostha. He's made some info vids, and I'm hoping to make history vids myself some day.'

There was a sort of stunned silence. What got to me was the sweetly modest way she said it. 'Made some info vids' . . . Ventrak Rostha was famous. Just about everyone followed his *History of Humanity* series, each eagerly awaited episode covering another key event of the period since the first colony was set up on an Alpha sector world until the present day.

Ventrak Rostha was a brilliant man. I loved his vids so much that I could even forgive him for being an exo. That didn't stop me hating his daughter though. She was probably a rich and spoilt nardle brain, who thought the rest of humanity should just lie down and be trampled on by her elegant little Alphan feet. It would happen too. She was guaranteed a glistening career ahead of her making vids. It didn't matter how second-rate and incompetent they were, everyone would praise them to the skies because she was the daughter of the incomparable Ventrak Rostha.

Yes, I admit it, I was jealous.

Ventrak Rostha's daughter smiled round at the grazzed class. 'So who next? Anyone else from Alpha?'

There was dead silence.

'Anyone from Beta sector then?' asked our new celebrity leader.

The one in the party dress stood up and gave a theatrical wiggle. Oh yes, of course she was Betan. I'd worked that one out already from her dress.

'I'm Lolia. I see we have sixteen men and fourteen women, so I know you won't think I'm greedy when I say I'm looking out for a trio with two of you gorgeous boys.'

There were a few startled giggles. The sixteen gorgeous boys seemed a bit nervous as Lolia gave them each a predatory look of assessment. All except one, who was lounging back in his chair advertising the fact he didn't care. He spotted me looking at him, and gave me what I could best describe as a leer.

I remembered I was Jarra the Military kid, gave him a long cold look in return, and then turned away. I hoped the general effect was that I'd considered him and was unimpressed. I made a mental bet that he was Betan too. I was right. He was the next one to stand up and introduce himself.

After that, we had a whole mob from Gamma sector, who talked with a slightly lilting quality to their sentences. The number of Gammans made sense since Asgard was in Gamma sector. I grudgingly had to admit they seemed a quiet and inoffensive bunch. The thought occurred to me that my random selection of University could have landed me on a Beta sector course. I shuddered, and mentally thanked Arrack San Domex for being from Asgard.

Miss Celebrity took us through the people from sectors Delta through Kappa after that. There were a few from Delta, a solitary girl from Epsilon, and no one from Kappa. That was hardly surprising. Epsilon sector is still busy building everything on its colony worlds, but Kappa is even newer so it's still mostly in Planet First or Colony Ten phase.

Dalmora smiled at me. 'I'm really sorry, but if you aren't from Kappa then we seem to have missed you out somehow.' She was a good actress, because she actually sounded like she cared.

I stood up. I noticed Playdon abandon his lookup to watch this, but I refused to let him intimidate me. 'I'm Jarra,' I said. 'My family is Military.'

'Interest!' Celebrity Dalmora gazed at me in what appeared to be absolute delight and fascination. 'A Military doing history! Are you going to go Military later?'

'Unsure.' I smiled. 'I love history, but it's difficult to combine it with a Military career.'

The boy from Beta chipped in. 'I've never met anyone Military before. What does a Military girl do when a man kisses her?'

I gave him the cold stare. 'That depends. If he asks politely first, and I say yes, then I kiss him back. If he doesn't ask politely, or doesn't take no for an answer, then I throw him across the room as a gentle hint to improve his manners.'

There were a few startled expressions round the room.

'Do you do that often?' asked the boy from Beta.

'The last time was yesterday,' I said, quite truthfully.

Everyone laughed.

I sat down again. I could see Lecturer Playdon looking at me with a raised eyebrow. I turned my head to give him a wide smile. He knew I was telling a pack of lies, but he couldn't do anything about it. He wasn't allowed to tell the others my confidential data.

Celebrity Dalmora started splitting us into little social groups next, like the perfect hostess that she was. She annexed me, two lads from Delta and the quiet girl from Epsilon for her own group. I had a feeling she picked us out as the ones who were most likely to need help socially.

She smiled round at us and decided to honour me with her attention first. 'Jarra, it's just totally zan being on a course with someone like you. Military! I chose to come on a Gamman university course because I wanted to meet people from other sectors, but this is even better than I'd hoped for.'

Part of me wondered what the great Dalmora would say if she knew she was wasting her charm on an ape girl, but most of me was busy being Jarra Military kid. I gave a politely modest shrug.

'I hope you don't mind me asking something personal,' she said, with the confidence of someone who could always get away with asking anything she liked. 'Both your parents are on active service? You went to residential schools rather than living with your family? That must be hard.'

Both the real me and the fake me could answer that one. 'The residences are separate from the schools, but yes. We spend a lot of time living with other kids. They become almost like a family to us. I wouldn't say it's that hard . . .'

'Interest!' cried Dalmora.

Incredible the way she could sound as if she really cared. She turned the spotlight on one of the boys from Delta next. She remembered his name too, and the couple of sentences he'd said to the class. How did she do that? I'd only managed to remember a couple from the avalanche of names that had buried me in the last hour. Everything else was a blur.

'Fian, you said you wanted to be a pre-history specialist. You're sure about that already? I find all of history totally fascinate. I know I can't study everything but it's so hard to choose.' Dalmora bestowed her professional smile upon Fian, just like an interviewer in a news vid.

Fian obviously had some strength of character, because he didn't blush or act overwhelmed by Dalmora gazing at him. 'Pre-history is where everything starts. People may feel modern history is more relevant, but it's only a few hundred years out of millions. That's a very thin skin on the surface of time. The minute you dig deeply into the reasons behind something in modern history, you find yourself back in pre-history. That's where the blood and the bones are. The real problem is where to specialise within pre-history. You've got everything back to the dino-saurs to choose from.'

'One day, I'd love to have you say exactly that in a vid, Fian,' said Dalmora. 'I hope I get the chance to do it. People casually dismiss so much in pre-history as no longer relevant. Getting people to really stop and think is the true achieve-ment in an info vid.'

I wanted to scream. Dalmora was being so insufferably nice even if it was all an act. Fian actually sounded intelli-gent. I didn't want these people to be nice or intelligent. I hated them for being norms when I was Handicapped, for being able to travel to other worlds when I was locked in a cage. I wanted them to be awful, horrible people, so I could think I was quite right to loathe exos.

I was in luck. Our group contained the celebrity, and the Betans weren't going to be left out of it for long. The boy came over first, and gave me ample excuse to detest him. He looked Dalmora over first, blatantly examining her body, his attention lingering on the more private areas as if she was on offer for him to take. I hated Dalmora, but I found myself resenting that gloating assessment on her behalf. Even she, with her polished society manner, seemed rather disturbed by it.

With our hostess clearly disconcerted, there was an awkward silence in the group. The Betan ignored it. He finished enjoying his examination of Dalmora and moved on to the next item on the menu offered to him today. The next item was me. 'Jarra . . .' His eyes started crawling over me. I could almost feel them touching me.

I didn't like it. JMK didn't like it either. I tried not to react, since I had a theory he would get more enjoyment out of studying my body if I showed I objected to it. 'I don't remember your name,' I said, trying to sound bored.

'Lolmack,' he said.

Now the gaze was off her, Dalmora had pulled herself together. 'We have a Lolia and Lolmack from Beta. Very similar names.'

'It's the clan cluster prefix,' said Lolmack. 'Lolia is my half cousin by my father's first triad marriage.'

'Ah yes, Betan naming.' Dalmora still wasn't sounding her confident self.

Lolia oozed her way over to join us next. She exchanged a glance with Lolmack, and then gave the Deltan boys the same sort of lingering examination that Dalmora and I had just suffered. 'Nice butts,' she drooled.

There was a collective gasp from all the non Betans in earshot, including me. Hoo eee! Lolia had said the butt word! I know there were times in pre-history when it was fairly acceptable in polite conversation, and I've heard it used in the more daring Betan vids, but I'd never heard anyone say it in public before. Everyone says legs, and you can tell which bit they mean by the way they say it.

Lecturer Playdon seemed to appear from nowhere. I'd labelled him as one of those teachers who put in the bare minimum of work, but now I realized I was wrong. He'd been sitting on the sidelines, letting Dalmora run things, so he could study us. He spoke in the hard voice of authority.

'I must remind the students from Beta sector that this is a University Asgard course, and monitored under the Gamma sector moral code. You agreed to abide by that code when you accepted a place on this course.'

Lolia looked at him wide eyed, with an expression of exaggerated surprise. 'I only said "butt".'

He gave her a thin smile. 'I have just given you one formal reminder; I now give you an amber warning. That word is not acceptable under the Gamman moral code.'

'I had no idea,' said Lolia. 'It's really not that bad a word. If I'd said . . .'

'You can recite me a list of obscene words if you like,' said Playdon, 'but each one will get you a warning. You can get yourself off this course in less than five minutes, with no refund of fees.'

He paused and looked round the class. 'This seems a good time for me to point out that there are students here from five sectors and twenty different planets. You'll be aware Beta is the most permissive sector, while Delta and Epsilon are the most conservative, but don't depend too much on sector stereotypes. Planetary and individual standards vary within sectors, and the Gamman moral code requires you to treat other students with respect and consideration for their personal boundaries.'

Playdon walked away and sat down in his corner again. The Betans looked at each other and laughed.

'Such a prude,' whispered Lolia.

Despite Dalmora's best efforts, conversation was a little sluggish after that. Everyone was relieved when Lecturer Playdon stood up again.

'I think it's time for lunch.' His eyes turned to me. 'Jarra, I'm sure you won't mind me calling on you to help with your Military skills from time to time. Perhaps you can show the class how to use the food dispensers?'

'Yes, sir.' I stopped myself in mid salute. No, seriously, I wasn't faking it. I'd watched so many info vids, and Jarra Military kid was so real in my head, that the 'yes, sir' and salute came automatically. The pupils at Military schools were cadets, and would salute their officer teachers.

The rest of the class seemed convinced, even impressed, as I marched over to the food dispensers and started demonstrating them. The Military me was in charge, but the real me was lurking somewhere on the mental sidelines and throwing a fit of the panics. I'd been in domes just like this on school history club trips, and I knew the food dispensers, but I'd clearly heard the message in Playdon's words. I'd publicly claimed to be Military. He couldn't call me a liar, but he was going to keep challenging me to prove my Military knowledge. I could get the food dispensers right, I could get a hundred things right, but just one mistake could ruin me. If I once showed that I wasn't Military, everyone would start asking what I really was. I didn't want them to find out the answer to that. Not yet. I wanted them to fully accept me, and to show them I was just as good as they were.

Having got my lunch, I left the choosier students complaining about reconstituted food, sat down at a table and started eating.

'Excuse me,' said a voice.

I looked up and recognised the Deltan boy, Fian. I remembered his name, when most of the others were a blur, because he seemed intelligent about history, and . . .

All right, I admit that was a lie. I could remember Fian's name because he had long blond hair and nice legs, rather like Arrack San Domex.

'I'm asking very politely if I can sit next to you,' Fian said. 'If you say no, then I'll leave quietly. There's absolutely no need for violence.'

I had to grin. 'Of course.'

He put his tray on the table and sat down. 'I'm hoping you'll defend me from Lolia.'

He wasn't the only one. Within thirty seconds, the remaining six seats at the table had been taken by other boys. There was silence for a while as everyone either ate, or prodded the food with a fork in the hope it would make it taste better.

'What are those Betans doing here anyway?' grumbled one of the boys from Gamma. 'Since when did Beta sector have any interest in history?'

I moved on from my unappetizing main course to my

cake. I'd told the class that cake survives the reconstitution process better than most things, so they'd all wisely gone for cake as well.

'If we're lucky they'll leave soon,' I said. 'I doubt they have the faintest idea of what life on a pre-history dig site will be like. I'm just waiting to see if they scream when we go outside.'

One or two of the faces round the table looked worried. 'Is it that bad?' one of the Gamman boys asked. 'I went on a dig last summer. We were excavating the remains of one of the first settlements on Asgard. It's incredibly slow work of course, moving the soil away with tiny brushes, but we spent a lot of time sunbathing and we had picnics and . . .'

His words trailed off as he saw the look on my face. I didn't believe it. I really didn't believe it. By now, I was expecting complete ignorance from the Betans, but this was totally amaz! This lot had signed up for pre-history, and they had absolutely no idea what they were letting themselves in for. I couldn't help myself. I laughed helplessly.

After lunch, Playdon got us to shift the tables out of the way, and set up the chairs in rows ready for our first class. We settled down in our seats and looked expectantly at him.

'I realize you've come from a lot of different time zones,' said Playdon, 'so all I'm doing today is giving my standard introduction to the course. You're here to learn about pre-history. This is a huge and largely neglected subject. Schools tend to focus on modern history, sometimes restricting their view even more narrowly to their own sector and planet history. Pre-history covers the whole of humanity's history until when exactly?'

He looked expectantly at the class. I thought it was best if I kept quiet and didn't attract attention.

Several voices muttered about Wallam-Crane inventing the portal.

'Wrong,' said Playdon.

Someone mentioned the first interstellar portal.

'Wrong again,' said Playdon.

'The opening of the first Alpha sector planets to civilian settlement at the start of the Exodus century,' said a voice from behind me. It sounded like Fian.

'Correct,' said Playdon. 'Until that moment, humanity had effectively existed on only one world. That is the moment when pre-history ends and modern history begins. I normally give a brief introduction to the methods of the Planet First programme now, but since it's a Military operation, I think we should hear about it from Jarra.'

Well, I could obviously forget the tactic of keeping quiet and not attracting attention. Playdon was going to give me every opportunity to make a fool of myself. He took a seat in the front row, and watched as I stood up and went to the front of the hall.

I'd scanned a lot of vids on Planet First in the last month. I summoned up those memories, took a deep breath, and let my Military alter ego take over.

'Planet First Approach, Assessment, Screening, Control and Handover methods began with those used right at the end of pre-history on the Alpha planets. Of course, they've been improved hugely over the centuries, adding things like the Colony Ten phase. Every time something went wrong, the Military tried to build on the experience and make sure it could never happen again. One Thetis was more than enough.'

The whole class nodded at that, even the Betans. The ent vid channels were always showing horror vids, set in the Thetis chaos year, with celebrity casts struggling to survive and dying heroic deaths in ghastly detail.

'The first approach to a new star system is with an unmanned probe sent through a five second, drop portal,' I continued. 'It sits there passively assessing planets and looking for signs of intelligent alien life. Eventually, it tries sending out a whole series of mathematical and other greets. If there's still no sign of intelligence, then it moves in towards the most habitable planet, stops, passively monitors again for a spell, and then starts active sensor scans.'

This was just like lecturing to my class at school. I was starting to enjoy myself. They didn't let me lecture my class at school very often. I always had lots of interesting things to say, but my school friends were reluctant to listen.

Having got over my initial nerves, I risked trying some humour. 'If, at any point, a sign of intelligent alien life is found then the probe sends alarm calls, Alien Contact programme activates, and thousands of specialist people will get an emergency mail calling them up for instant duty. You may know that hasn't happened yet.'

There was encouraging laughter from the class.

'We have however had two near misses, and those worlds are under quarantine to allow those neo-intelligent races to continue their normal evolution. If the issue of intelligent aliens doesn't arise, and the sensor scans show the planet is suitable for human life, the planet moves into Planet First stage 2. We have a lot of conditions on climate and other things, and we want a sizeable continent that satisfies them. There are plenty of planets around and we can afford to be choosy. There are checks for any number of hazards, stellar radiation, solar storm strength. You name it, we check it.

'If the planet still looks good, then it moves into the process people really think of as Planet First. Stage 3 is where the Military go planetside on our chosen continent, and this is where it gets dangerous. Almost every planet capable of sustaining life has already evolved its own eco system. The Military have to find and analyse every form of animal, plant, insect, fish, bacteria or other life. They have to discover and assess every possible threat, or we end up with another Thetis. If any of those life forms cannot either be controlled or eliminated then the planet is abandoned.'

Playdon had an odd expression on his face now. I couldn't work out what it meant, so I tried to ignore it. 'Stage 4 of Planet First is cleansing the continent of anything harmful. Creatures are either culled, or relocated on other land masses to keep the ecologists happy. Finally, we think things are safe. The planet then moves from Planet First into Colony Ten, and is handed over to the first stage colonists. They can't leave for ten years, unless they find something dangerous that the earlier stages missed. That's only happened half a dozen times, but when it did things got nasty. At the end of the ten years, the colonists get paid a fortune, plus bonuses for every child born, and the planet is opened for habitation as part of the newest sector, currently Kappa.'

I looked round at my audience. They still seemed awake, so I added a bit from a Military public information vid I'd seen. 'It's worth remembering that every new planet opened up for humanity costs not only a lot of credits, but is also paid for in human blood. Not a single one of the planets has been opened up without at least one member of the Military dying to make it safe for you.'

I went to sit down, and was startled by a round of applause.

Playdon stood up again. 'Well, thank you for that very eloquent explanation, Jarra. I expect you're all sitting there wondering what that had to do with pre-history. The answer is this. Only one inhabited planet has never been through Planet First screening, and that's Earth. If it had been assessed by Planet First, it would have failed. It suffers from too many solar storms, its moon is too large, it's too close to an asteroid belt. It has five inhabited continents and none of them satisfy the climate conditions for Stage 2. Even if you overlook that, all of them contain plant and animal life that would never be allowed through Stage 3. This planet is dangerous. It was dangerous in pre-history, and it's a lot more dangerous now.'

'But the apes live here without any problems,' a dark haired Gamman boy objected. I was somehow glad Fian hadn't said that.

'The settlements are safe, Krath, protected by shields from wild animals, but those are a very small part of the planet,' said Playdon. I noticed he'd objected to Lolia using the butt word, but didn't comment on the word 'ape'. 'You won't get eaten by anything hostile wandering round a terminal or a shop, but most dig sites are outside the shields in long abandoned areas.'

He gave a grim smile. 'You're here to experience pre-history in a way that you can't by just scanning vids, so you're going to the old ruined cities. They are extremely hazardous. There are animals, plants and insects that can and will kill you given the chance. The ruins you're studying can also be lethal. Humanity had this planet pretty well tamed before Exodus century, but it still had its dangerous areas. Now it's not tame at all. If you didn't realize it before, realize it now.'

He looked round the class. 'I draw your attention one final time to the conditions you agreed to when joining this course. I hope you bothered to scan them. University Asgard will make every effort to ensure your safety, but has absolutely no liability for any death or injury that occurs. This is a legal warning and is on record. If you don't accept the conditions, then portal out now.'

Several of the class looked hopefully at the Betans, but

sadly they showed no sign of leaving. I expect they thought Playdon was exaggerating. Maybe they would think again when they found out he wasn't.

'That's all for today,' said Playdon. 'I suggest you rest and try and get yourselves acclimatized to this time zone. Tomorrow we start work at nine.'

5

I tried to call Issette later on and just got the 'not available' message. Then I tried to send her a mail, but gave up in the end. I couldn't work out what to say about the exos on my course. The Betans were ghastly, Krath was an idiot, and the Alphan girl was too sickeningly perfect, but the others seemed normal. I don't mean normal rather than Handicapped, I mean they were ordinary people.

I was feeling pretty weird to be honest. In amongst the hate thing I felt for the norms, there was some guilt about the lies, and the whole Jarra Military kid fantasy was getting disturbingly real. I went to bed in a bad mood, and had a dream where I really was JMK. I was living her life on a Military base, my Military parents were back on leave and . . .

I woke up early, feeling confused and disoriented after that crazy dream, and found a mail waiting for me from Issette. A long one, where she chattered away with the flushed, happy, excited look that I knew so well, telling me all about how she'd been at her evening student meet and greet when I tried to call her, and how wonderful it had been. I wanted to call her back and talk properly, but she'd be in classes. The five hour time difference between our continents didn't sound much but it was a real communication problem.

Instead, I spent half an hour recording and rerecording a one minute reply. It was difficult, because there was so much I couldn't talk about without seeing Issette face to face, or that I couldn't tell her at all. If I mentioned the dream, she'd start sending me mails full of nardle stuff about talking to a psychologist.

In the end, I just replied with a mail where I said I'd arrived fine, and we'd had a meet and greet too. Then I went off to the dining hall for breakfast. I was peacefully eating, and wishing the food dispensers could supply frujit, when Playdon's voice interrupted me.

'Jarra, given your Military skills, I'd like you to help out this morning. Can you be prepared to demonstrate how to put on an impact suit? You can collect one from the store room.' He looked down at me with a thin smile of pure evil.

'Yes, sir.' I smiled back. Yesterday, he'd tried catching me out on my knowledge of Planet First, and now he was going to try me with an impact suit. He clearly didn't realize how much experience I had of dig sites. He probably thought my application comments about them meant I'd spent time somewhere like Stonehenge or Pompeii, which were nicely sanitized bits of ancient history located safely within protected areas. He was going to get quite a surprise. I'd been wearing impact suits on school history club trips since I was 11.

I finished my breakfast and headed off to the store room. This assignment from Playdon was really zan, because it meant I got first choice of impact suit. Getting the right size of impact suit is the vital thing, but getting one in good condition as well makes life so much more pleasant. You don't want the oldest and smelliest suit in the bunch. I was lucky; there was one in my size that looked almost new.

I popped back to my room, swapped my underwear for my skintight, and put my ordinary clothes back over the top. My skintight was perfectly respectable, covering all the restricted body areas, but I was feeling defensive with those Betans around. I collected my precious, almost new impact suit, and went back to the dining hall. The class were sitting waiting, and looked at me curiously as I walked up to the front carrying the suit.

Playdon nodded towards me. 'Jarra has kindly agreed to demonstrate an impact suit to you. You'll be wearing these every moment you're outside this dome, so pay close attention. Jarra, over to you.'

I'd given this demonstration about ten times before, to new people on history club trips, so I had it pretty well rehearsed.

'Like the dome we're in, and the food dispensers, the impact suits are standard Military issue. They're the cheaper training versions of those used on Planet First missions. They're designed to do their job, not to be pretty or luxurious. You collect one from the store room and keep it while we're at this dome. They're all an identical black, and it's essential to make sure you get the right size. Professionals have their own personal suits, which have a few extra features and can be painted different colours. I expect Lecturer Playdon has his own.'

Playdon nodded. 'Mine is blue, so it'll be easy to recognise me when we're suited up.'

I held up my standard black suit. 'You wear these on the dig site, and they'll keep you alive in most situations. Your first problem is getting one on. It's not easy. Military standard is to be able to suit up inside two minutes in case of a dome breach. If any of you can get a suit on in less than five minutes then you can feel pleased with yourself.'

I was proud of the fact I could put on an impact suit in

Military standard time. The history club had a competition once and spent an entire day practising. Only three of us broke the two minute barrier.

'I recommend wearing a skintight underneath your impact suit. If you haven't got one yet then go for a swimming costume, leotard, or some thick, sensible and close-fitting underwear.'

Lolia interrupted me. 'I never bother with underwear.'

I smiled at her. 'If you prefer being in severe pain then that's your choice. Impact suit material can pinch delicate body areas when it activates, so you want some protection.'

I switched my attention back to the class in general. 'Remember when putting on an impact suit that you do everything slowly and smoothly. No sudden jerks, or you activate the material and it goes solid, exactly the way it's designed to do. It protects you from falling rocks, being stabbed, or bitten. Predators will break their teeth on it.

'There are a lot of controls here on the left arm,' I pointed them out. 'I suggest you don't touch them. You may feel too hot or too cold to start with, but wait a few minutes for your suit to adjust to outside temperatures. If you can't make it to the bathroom then your suit will handle it, but try not to test that. The suit can cope, but it's not good for your underwear.'

The class laughed.

'One control you do touch is the one that sets your iden-tification. You can't see faces through an impact suit, they're designed to let you see out, but people looking in can only see an unidentifiable blur. So we know who you are, set it to your name like this.'

I set my suit so the front and back had my name in large glowing letters. 'Don't mess around using rude words or other peoples' names. It's not original and it's not funny. In an emergency, not knowing who is where can mean someone dies. You'll also need to know about the communication controls, but I expect Lecturer Playdon will take us through how he wants us to use those.'

I started stripping off my clothes and Lolmack whistled. He looked unimpressed when my skintight appeared. 'You could wear something a lot sexier than that.'

'If the audience was better, then I might,' I said. 'This is a skintight, specially made to wear under an impact suit. As you can see, it's similar to a swimming costume, but rather tougher material. They're wonderful things. Take them in the shower with you after you get out of your impact suit, and they'll wash, dry as fast as you during the hot air cycle, and be ready to wear again. You can get them in several different styles and colours, but I'd recommend the standard male or female style in black.'

I looked at Dalmora who was sitting in the front row. 'Shoulder length hair can just be tucked back into your hood, but very long hair is best in a single plait down your back.'

She nodded.

My eyes drifted from her hair to the ornate gold creation that she wore around her neck. 'Your necklace is very lovely.'

Dalmora glanced down at it. 'It's been in my family for over five hundred years. One of my ancestors brought it to Alpha sector with her when she left Jaipur during Exodus century. By tradition it's handed down to the eldest daughter on her eighteenth birthday.'

I'd assumed the necklace was a reproduction made from manufactured gold, but Dalmora Rostha was wearing a genuine historic artefact around her Alphan neck. Typical. Oh well, I'd feel rather petty if I left it to Playdon to warn her about the risks of jewellery. Three years ago, I'd been nardle enough to forget to take off a ring before putting on my impact suit, and lost my left little finger when the suit triggered. I'd had the finger regrown in hospital of course,

51

but the thought of wearing a ring had given me a creepy feeling ever since.

'It can be hazardous to wear jewellery under an impact suit,' I said. 'If the suit material triggers then it can force the metal to cut into you. Talk to Lecturer Playdon if this is an issue. Now, watch closely as I put my suit on. You always start with the feet.'

I demonstrated how to roll the suit gently and smoothly up your legs, and then arms. Pulling up the hood and sealing the front was the easy bit. Just for fun, I checked my time for putting on the suit. One minute, fifty-five seconds! I noticed Playdon giving me another of his odd looks.

'One last thing,' I said. 'When you seal the front of your suit, it runs an automatic self test sequence. If an alarm goes off, then your suit is faulty. Let Lecturer Playdon know, don't just put it back in the store room.'

Playdon stood up. 'Thank you, Jarra. Now everyone, I'll issue you suits from the store room, and you can start practicing suiting up ready for our first trip outside.'

Lolia raised a hand. 'I'll need you to give me some advice on my underwear.' She gazed suggestively at Lecturer Playdon.

'I'm sure you can manage by yourself,' he said.

'I'm entitled to proper teaching, aren't I?' she said, reproachfully.

'I can give you a hand picking something suitable if you like,' I offered.

'Perhaps Jarra could help me out with my underwear too,' said Lolmack.

Lecturer Playdon and I exchanged glances, and changed at least temporarily from adversaries to allies. 'Jarra will advise Lolia,' said Playdon, 'and I'll help you, Lolmack.'

Lolia sighed. 'You people are no fun.'

It wasn't just Lolia and Lolmack who needed advice. Just

about everyone did. Deciding what to wear under the impact suit was easy; actually putting it on was quite another matter. It's hard to stretch a suit over your skin without the material locking up, so I could hardly blame this bunch of exos for needing some help. Playdon and I ended up doing patrols along the corridors, and responding to cries for help from rooms.

Helping novices with an impact suit is always a strange mix of frustration and comedy. If you don't get the bottom half of an impact suit on properly, then it's impossible to get it over your shoulders. I did my best not to laugh, but sometimes the look of despair on their faces when they realized they had to take it off and start all over again . . .

'But I'm so close,' said Fian, looking at me with a tragic expression. 'It's taken me twenty minutes to get this far. If I could just get my left arm in . . .'

'It's the only way,' I said, trying desperately not to giggle.

'I'll never manage this . . .' He sighed and started peeling the suit off again.

'After a few times, you'll get the hang of it.' I realized I was enjoying the view of a semi-clad Arrack San Domex lookalike rather too much, and headed off to respond to a scream from Dalmora.

It took a mere two hours to wedge everyone into a suit. Even then, Lolia seemed to have a slight limp. Maybe she hadn't stretched the suit over her legs properly, or maybe she'd managed to lock the suit material and pinch somewhere painful. I thought it was better not to ask.

'Everyone finally ready?' Playdon's voice had the faint echo that you always get when you hear someone through the suit communication unit as well as in real life. 'I'm talking to you on the team circuit. Answer when I call your name.'

He took us through the roll call slowly. 'Good, everyone

has their comms working on the team circuit. Always remember the importance of talking on the right channel when you're in an impact suit. If you're just talking to someone standing next to you, don't use the comms at all. If you want your whole team to hear, talk on the team circuit. If you want to talk privately to me, there's a private circuit that links you to your team leader. If it's appropriate for every team on New York Main Dig Site to hear you, talk on the broadcast channel. Talking on the wrong channel can obviously be extremely embarrassing. If you're asking a girl standing next to you for a date, then you don't want hundreds of people on dozens of teams to hear it.'

There was an outbreak of nervous giggles.

'For now, use the team circuit if you're in trouble or out of ear shot, and don't play around with the other channels or you'll annoy all the other dig teams in the area. We move outside now.'

I was deeply thankful when we finally lined up and opened the dome door. This lot were worse than any history club group I'd been with. In fairness, they were all totally new to this, while our history club trips always included far more experienced people than novices, but it was still driving me crazy.

The door opened and we saw a grim world waiting for us. It was winter in New York. There were a scattering of trees on the hillside ahead of us, but they were barren of leaves, and the branches were each carefully etched with a layer of ice. I gazed at the winter landscape thoughtfully. I'd only been here in summer and this looked much more intimidating. The cold hit me as I followed Playdon out of the dome and my impact suit felt like ice on my skin. The next two minutes were going to be painful as my suit adjusted itself.

There were squeals of protest from the others as they

followed us. 'I'm freezing! How do we turn up the warmth on these suits?' asked Krath.

'I strongly suggest you don't,' Playdon said, but a few of them tinkered with the temperature controls anyway.

Two minutes later, everyone who had listened to him was nice and comfortable. The ones who had messed with their controls were screaming they were too hot and turning the temperature down. Two minutes after that, they were freezing. I made a mental note of the idiots in the group. The Betans were on the list of course.

The Deltan boy, Fian, who I had rated as at least semi-intelligent, was sticking close to me. With faces entirely invisible through suits, it was hard to be sure, but my impression was that he was watching me and copying my every move. I felt this proved he was intelligent. At least I knew what I was doing just a little bit better than the ones who were currently screaming about being cooked alive for the second time.

Eventually, we had the temperatures sorted out, and Playdon called us all to gather round him. 'We're just going to head up to the top of the hill and get a view of the dig site. Everyone stay together and be careful. If you manage to get yourself lost, ask for help on the team circuit and stay where you are until we find you. Whatever happens, don't take off your impact suit. Bears should be hibernating, but the wolf packs will be hungry this time of year.'

'What's a wolf?' asked Lolia.

'Wild ancestors of dogs,' said Playdon. 'They hunt in packs. The moose and deer herds shelter in the ruins in winter and the wolf packs follow them. I've got a gun, but I'd rather not have to use it. They tend to attack lone targets. If we all stick together, they probably won't bother us.'

'Are they dangerous?' asked a female voice.

I checked the glowing suit name, and saw it was the girl

called Amalie from Epsilon sector. If they all wore glowing name labels when they weren't in suits, I'd find it a lot easier to work out who they all were. Playdon seemed to have us all tagged correctly, while Miss Personality from Alpha had names and life histories down pat, but the rest of us were struggling.

'Without a suit, they would tear you into pieces and eat you,' said Playdon. 'In an impact suit, I doubt they could do you a lot of harm, but you probably wouldn't enjoy them trying. Let's get moving.'

We headed up the slope ahead of us at a very slow walk. I paused to wait for the rest of them to catch up. A suit labelled 'Fian' came up to me.

'Excuse me,' he said, 'but how do you move that fast? My suit keeps jerking me to a stop.'

I noticed he'd been bright enough to set his comms to the right channel while he asked the question, so it wasn't transmitted for the whole class to hear. I checked that I had mine set properly as well before I replied.

'The trick is moving as smoothly as possible,' I explained. 'Sudden movements can trigger the impact suit material and it locks up.'

'Thank you.'

'Do we have to wear these clumsy things?' moaned Lolia loudly from the back of the group.

'Maybe we should let her take it off. The wolves could use a good meal . . .' I muttered to myself.

Fian overheard me and laughed.

Playdon obviously enjoyed the dramatic, because he gathered us up into a group again just before we reached the top of the hill, so everyone got to see New York at once. I'd seen it before, but never in winter. In summer, it's a vast black expanse as far as the eye can see, with the odd patches of green trying to make an impression on the mess. At this time of year, the white of frost and a dusting of powdery snow added an extra bleakness to the mounds of rubble and the blackened skeletal remains of skyscrapers still soaring up into the sky.

'Dear God!' said Lolmack.

'Respect!' chorused a few others automatically. Ever since the physicists found evidence that the universe was created by an unknown entity or entities, there's been a general feeling that it's wise to avoid swear words involving deities.

'Sorry,' he said. 'It was a bit of a shock.'

'I'd no idea,' murmured Fian. 'I've seen some ancient vids, but the sheer scale of this . . .'

'Welcome to New York, once home to twelve million people,' said Playdon. He let us absorb the scene for a few minutes longer. 'Anyone know when in pre-history the last skyscraper was finished?'

I laughed.

'I see Jarra knows that's a trick question,' said Playdon. 'The last skyscraper was built twenty-five years after the exodus started. By the time it was finished, the population of Earth was already plummeting. No one ever lived or worked in it.'

'Why did they let it all get into this mess?' asked Lolia.

'After Exodus century, there weren't enough people left to maintain the cities,' said Playdon. 'For every building in use, there were a hundred empty ones. It was a lot easier for the remaining people to gather together in selected small towns and villages, than to try and maintain a few buildings in the middle of a ruined city.'

Fian knelt cautiously down and scraped his hand along the ground. The struggling grass became smeared with black. 'There were fires here?'

'There were many fires after it was abandoned,' said Playdon. 'There were inflammable materials left in a lot of the buildings, chemicals, even explosives. One massive fire continued burning for nearly two months. Always keep in mind that the ruins themselves are dangerous. It's not just wild beasts, there are vicious pieces of glass and metal, decaying chemicals, and buildings that can collapse if you just breathe on them. Never trust the ground underfoot because it's treacherous. They built downwards as well as up, and you can fall through into underground sewers, cellars, the transport network, even underground waterways. If you ever need to find your own way through the dig site, then look for the marked clearways, or failing that the deer trails. The herds have worked out their own safe routes.'

'But why?' asked Lolmack. 'Why bother going in there?'

'We're looking for lost history, culture, and technology,' said Playdon. 'During Exodus, the new planets were focused on their own immediate problems. They thought humanity's store of knowledge was safe on the home world. They thought Earth would provide all the technology, spare parts, and medicine whenever they needed them in the future, but so many people left so fast that the whole infrastructure of Earth fell apart. They learnt their mistake one night in 2409 when the Earth data net crashed. The few staff left did their best to patch it and get it running again, but there was a second catastrophic failure. Some fool tried to do the regular data backups and he couldn't have done anything worse.'

Playdon paused. 'The Alpha worlds sent back their best experts, and they salvaged what they could from the corrupted backups, but we'd lost half of humanity's data. After that, they took action. They tracked down all the major art and museum collections they could, and shipped them out to the Alpha worlds.'

'Alpha sector is honoured to be the guardians of human culture,' said Dalmora.

Playdon ignored that remark. The other sectors are a bit jealous of all the ancient relics being kept by Alpha.

'Independent data archives were set up at every university, and we constantly run cross checks between them looking for flaws. The idea is we'll never lose data again, but there are huge gaps in what we have. Some of it may still be out there.' He nodded at the ruins.

'It's hard to believe anything can have survived in that,' said Fian.

'You get the odd freak survival by pure chance,' said Playdon. 'Last year they found an entire dry cellar packed with stuff. There were even two real books. More common are the stasis boxes. People were leaving Earth and you couldn't casually portal between worlds then. They were going and never expected to come back. It was the fashion to leave a stasis box behind them, as a sort of memorial. They left them in their abandoned houses, preserving oddments, souvenirs, and records of who had once lived there. They're still out there, we're still finding them, and you never know what treasure trove may be inside the next one we open. In 2310, humanity's science and technology was at its peak. We've now surpassed them in the areas of medicine and portal technology, but we're still painfully regaining the rest.'

'They were the magicians,' I said. 'Think of the glorious cities they built. New York, New Tokyo, London, Moscow, Paris Coeur, Berlin, Eden . . . Now it's all in ruins, and we're scavenging for scraps of their knowledge.'

'Exactly.' Playdon's voice sounded startled, and I saw his head turn to look in my direction. 'Most of this class will suffer their compulsory year on Earth's dig sites, then leave and never come back, but a few of you may be caught by the joy of discovering the past, or even by its financial rewards, and make this your career.'

His emotion was obvious in his voice, and now it was my turn to be startled. Playdon felt the same way that I did about these sprawling ruins of the past, and the people who had lived there, and the discoveries waiting for us. I'd never managed to make Issette or Candace understand, even most of the school history club didn't share my feeling that the past was still alive, but Playdon did. It was strange to recognize my own passion for pre-history in an exo.

We all stood there for a while after that, silently thinking. Finally, Playdon spoke again in a brisk voice. 'Tomorrow, we're working in Sector 22, and we'll be heading out on to the site along the clearway that you can see over there.' He pointed out the path, with its glowing markers, leading off into the ruins.

Playdon had been carrying his lookup with him. Now he worked on it for a moment, and a miniature model of the New York Dig Site appeared in mid air ahead of us. He increased the projection to a huge size that would be quite a drain on the lookup's power, and zoomed in. We could see the clearway now, with ruined buildings either side.

'This is the way we'll be going tomorrow. I'm getting this image from the data mosaic for New York Main. This is how the area looked at the last aerial survey about ten months ago. I can look at it in several ways. Plain image like this one, or hazard rated by grid square.'

The image changed. Now it was coloured in patches of red, amber and green squares.

'As always,' said Playdon, 'green is good, red is bad, and black is access forbidden, but bear in mind that the hazard ratings are only a best guess from the computer. I can add in the information on which grid squares have already been worked and they go blue.'

Some squares changed to blue. Not surprisingly, the blue squares tended to cluster near the clearway.

'Notice some areas are flashing blue.' Playdon pointed at one. 'Those mean they've been partially worked, but still contain something interesting. I can call up further information on those. Usually, people stopped work because they came across an unexpected hazard, but tomorrow we're going to a grid square where they just ran out of time. The team dug out a stasis box from there, and believed there was a second one but didn't have time to reach it. Normally they'd come back for it the next day, but this was just before Year End and their last day at New York Main. Tomorrow, we'll be picking up where they left off, and we hope they were right about that second stasis box.'

Zan, I thought joyfully. Tomorrow we would be digging, and with every chance of finding a stasis box!

Playdon turned off his lookup, and led us all back to the base. 'You've got an idea now of the conditions you'll be facing. This afternoon, I want you all to practise suiting up. I'm sending details of styles and prices of skintights to your lookups. If anyone wants one, let me know this evening. We can get a discount on a group order, and they usually deliver within a day.'

'That's all for now,' he said. 'Tomorrow we start the real work.'

We headed into the dome and there was a race to get out of our suits and be first into the bathroom. I won!

6

The next day we headed out for our first dig. It was another slow start, with people still struggling with impact suits. We finally got outside and Playdon opened up the big doors of the huge sled storage dome that sat next to the accommodation dome like a big brother. He turned on the glows, which slowly beat back the shadows and illuminated the huge space. There must have been nearly twenty hover sleds, in varying sizes, and I couldn't even see some of the ones at the back.

'We have several types of small specialist sleds, as well as the big transport sleds.' Playdon looked round at us. 'Who's had experience driving a hover sled?'

I put my hand up. In an Earth class, just about every hand would have gone up. Here only about half the hands did. I suppose exos don't have as many hover sleds around as we do on Earth. We get more solar storms, so have more portal outages to worry about, and every settlement has its emergency hover sleds.

'Good.' Playdon made notes against names on his lookup. 'If you can't, then it's really simple to learn, but for our first trip we'll stick to giving people jobs they know as far as possible. Now, who can drive a big transport sled?'

I put my hand up again. There were a lot fewer hands going up this time, but even on Earth not many people can drive the big sleds. It would be quite an achievement to get into trouble driving an ordinary hover sled, given the small size, simple controls, and anti collision protection. Large transport sleds are different though, because of their weight and momentum. You have to pass a test to drive one on Earth, so few bother. We have an age restriction too, so I couldn't do my test until I was 16. I hate age restrictions.

'Krath, when have you driven a transport sled?' asked Playdon.

'I've driven my father's transport sleds. He runs a refuse collection and recycling business.'

There were a few giggles from the class.

'Dalmora?'

'I've gone along with my father when he's been making vids,' the daughter of the great Ventrak Rostha told us lesser mortals. 'Some of them need a lot of equipment, props, costumes, so we use the transport sleds.'

'Amalie?'

'Construction work,' said the quiet girl, Amalie. 'I'm from Epsilon, so I've driven them for years.'

Playdon nodded. Everyone knew that planets in Epsilon sector were in the frantic building phase. The standard joke was that if you wanted to go shopping on an Epsilon planet, then first you had to help build the shop.

'Jarra?'

Was it my imagination, or was Playdon's voice suddenly frosty? I didn't like it, but I kept my reply to him calm and Military. 'Training trips, sir. Transporting people and equipment.'

A couple of the Gamman boys had experience driving big transport sleds too. Playdon made more notes on his lookup.

'We'll be taking out four specialist sleds, and two big transports today. I like to have enough sleds that we can cope if one breaks down. It happens very rarely, and there are emergency evac portals, but walking to one in an impact suit can be hard work.'

He looked round and picked the two Gamman boys to drive the transports, then pointed out four of the specialist sleds and allocated drivers to them. We were taking a sensor sled, a tag support sled, and two heavy lifts. Playdon was only planning to run one dig team then. I didn't blame him for that, since it would be hard enough running one team with this bunch of clueless exos. I could blame him for still not picking me as a driver though. Didn't he trust an ape to drive any of his precious sleds, even the little ones?

The drivers carefully manoeuvred the selected sleds out of the storage dome, and the rest of us piled on board the transport sleds. They were the basic ones, with no luxury frills like roofs to keep off the rain, or comfy chairs. At the front, were the controls and driver's seat, behind that was just a huge bare hover platform with rows of bench seats and some clear space for equipment.

Playdon rode on the lead transport sled, the second transport followed, and then four small specialist sleds. We headed off to the edge of the rubble and started moving along the clearway.

Playdon's voice came over the team circuit. Those of us on the same sled could hear him talking without the comms, but he needed to use the team circuit so those on the other sleds could hear.

'We're now entering New York Main Dig Site,' Playdon said. 'I've notified New York Main Dig Site Command of our entry. Dig Site Command monitor all teams on the site. I'm using a comms channel you can't hear when I talk to them.

At the moment, the only channels you should be hearing are the team circuit, your private channel if I want to talk to you without the rest of the team hearing, and the broadcast channel that Dig Site Command uses when they want to broadcast information to all teams.'

It was thrilling to be entering New York Main. I'd worked on New York Fringe Dig Site on summer trips with the school history club. My first trip into Fringe was when I was 11, the next two years we went to other dig sites, but I was back at the Fringe at 13, and again at 17. The Fringe is a nice flat area, with none of the old skyscrapers left standing, so it's relatively safe. That's where the Earth school parties, and the people who work the sites as a weekend hobby, do their digging.

You don't see any exo schools there. It's too dangerous, and they don't want to come to the ape planet. Exo schools stay at home and do sweet little excavations of settlements that are only a few hundred years old. You do get the occasional party from Military schools though, or even the Military Academy. It's a good place for them to practise wearing impact suits and using equipment, while doing something useful at the same time.

I'd decided it was safe to mention my experience on New York Fringe to the class, since it was quite believable that a Military kid had been there. I'd have to keep quiet about some of the details though, especially getting my pilot's licence there last summer, because being a pilot was too unusual. There might be a survey plane tucked at the back of all those hover sleds in the storage dome, but I couldn't fly it while pretending to be Jarra the Military kid.

I sulked briefly about the flying, but entering New York Main was too exciting to waste time in a bad mood. Fringe was just a children's playground compared to this. I'd scanned all the information, and heard all the stories about New York Main. It's a lot more interesting than Fringe, with far more stasis boxes around, but it's also much more dangerous. They don't let you in until you're 18, however much you try, and believe me I tried as hard as I could. It's not for kids, and it's not for amateurs. New York Main is for the professionals. I'd been waiting for this for years, and I was going in!

'We're following the clearway,' said Playdon. 'The clearways are literally clear routes through the dig site. They were made by the first excavation teams a hundred and fifty years ago. The rubble on them has been crushed and sometimes fused together. The ground beneath them is stable and has been checked for hazards. You'll see glowing markers at each side of the clearway guiding you. Remember in emergency that the green arrows always point you to the shortest route off the dig site. They're especially useful if there is sudden snow or fog and visibility is low.'

Everyone looked round at the ruins. We were passing blackened sections of walls, some only head height, others still many storeys high. Broken remnants of floors jutted out. Huge blocks of concrete lay around, as if some giant child had tossed aside his toy building blocks in a tantrum. One huge girder, orange with the rust of the ages, leant against a blackened wall.

'We're stopping here.' Playdon spoke over the team circuit as we reached a flatter area. 'Park the sleds this side of the clearway in case other teams need to drive by.'

I looked round at our work site. The team that had worked it before us had obviously taken down any dangerous buildings. Shame. Blowing up walls was fun. I thought I could guess where they'd found the stasis box. There was a nice cleared area with a central depression, just the way a good tag leader would have dug out a box.

'Now,' said Playdon, 'on a dig team, there are five roles. The team leader is in overall charge, and that's obviously me. The others are tag leader, tag support, sensor, and lift. Tag leader is the dangerous job, because they're the only person who enters the excavation area. They direct operations on the ground, decide how to clear the rubble, tag rocks, and guide the people working the lifting gear.'

I knew all about tag leaders, because I've always been a tag leader for my school history club. Well, not back when I was 11, because my history teacher flatly refused to have an 11-year-old tag leading, and put me on the heavy lifting gear. That was better than nothing of course, but I still hated having to wait around for a couple of years for the job I really wanted. It was so frustrating watching other people tag leading, and having to follow their instructions even when they were wrong. Still, I got to be tag leader when I was 13, and I've done it ever since.

I was determined to be tag leader now as well. I'd worked hard for years to learn the right skills. Even if I was an ape girl, I was a great tag leader, and if I could just get the chance then Playdon would see that. I was worried whether I'd ever get that chance though. A grim truth had occurred to me. He'd shut me out of driving the sleds by not picking me, and he could shut me out of tag leading just as easily. He could even make me sit on a transport sled and watch the others on this and every other trip on to the site. What would I do then? I'd go crazy having to sit and watch day after day.

I couldn't scream abuse at the norms and walk out. The point was to do that when I'd proved I was as good as them. Doing it then would be a success. Doing it now . . . Well, it would be admitting I'd failed.

'Next, we have tag support.' Playdon continued. 'The tag leader is working in dangerous conditions, so tag support's job is to keep them safe. Your impact suits have a tag point at the back. Draw a line between your shoulder blades, and dead centre is the tag point. Tag support have a lift beam locked on the tag point of the tag leader's impact suit. We often call it the lifeline; a term dating back far into pre-history. If the tag leader is going to be hit by a rock, fall into an underground hole, or be eaten by a bear, then tag support uses their lift beam and pulls the tag leader to safety, and sometimes they have to react very fast.'

If I did get my chance at tag leading then I felt that tag support was going to be a problem. When you're tag leading, you want to have confidence in the person on your lifeline, so you can relax and concentrate on your job. I was on my own here with a bunch of exos, and I didn't fancy trusting an exo with my life. I didn't have much choice though. It was that or stand around watching someone else tag lead, and I hate watching.

'You would normally only have one tag leader in an area,' said Playdon, 'since two tag leaders working at cross purposes could be very dangerous. That means one tag support as well. We usually have one person on the sensors, scanning the site for hazards, and hopefully for interesting things like stasis boxes. If they spot anything nasty happening, they hit the alarm and tag support pull out the tag leader fast.'

'Finally we have one or more people manning the heavy lift sleds, using beams to move the tagged rubble. Most of our equipment is Military issue, but the heavy lift sleds are standard construction site ones. Today we'll have two people using heavy lift gear. Any questions?' Playdon asked.

'Erm,' said the hesitant voice of one of the Gamman boys. 'I don't understand . . . I was on a dig on Asgard and . . . It was rather different. We used sensors, teaspoons, and little brushes.'

I was pretty anxious at this point, but I still couldn't help giggling.

'Well,' said Playdon, 'that was a little different. Where you have a very rare and precious site, and plenty of time, you work that way. Earth is different. It has more ruined cities than you could possibly believe. We'd make no impression on New York working with teaspoons and we have limited people and time. Just look at it!'

I didn't need to look at it. I was still giggling at the idea of excavating New York with teaspoons.

'If seven maids with seven mops swept it for half a year, do you suppose, the Walrus said, that they could get it clear?' It was Dalmora's voice, and I didn't know why she was talking about walruses.

I was startled when Lolia responded. 'I doubt it, said the Carpenter, and shed a bitter tear.'

'I'm sorry?' asked Playdon.

'It's an ancient poem,' said Dalmora.

'Lewis Carroll,' said Lolia. 'He's amaz. I specialized in art of language at school.'

'I see.' Playdon sounded no wiser than I was. 'Well, we have no time for teaspoons. Even searching this one city is a colossal task, and we have thousands. Time is running out for buried items, even the stasis boxes have limited power, so we get what we can, as fast as we can, before it's too late.'

'So, let's get searching,' said Playdon, briskly. 'Five of you will be doing things, while the rest sit on the transport sleds and watch carefully. Who fancies the dangerous job of tag leader?'

This was it. I had my hand up instantly, and looked round fast for the competition. There wasn't any. No one else had their hands up at all, so Playdon could hardly ignore me, could he? If he did, then the writing was on the wall. The ape girl would never be given a chance, whatever happened, and I might as well pack my bags and leave.

'All right.' Playdon didn't seem thrilled. 'Jarra will be tag leader.'

Hoo eee! I was tag leader!

Playdon got a tag gun and hover belt out of an equipment box, and handed them to me. 'This is a tag gun, Jarra. It burns an electronic tag into the rocks. Try to choose the . . .'

'I'm familiar with it, sir,' I said. I snapped on the hover belt, checked the settings on the tag gun, and fixed it on the belt.

'Remember the hover belt keeps you a fixed distance above the ground, but when the ground shifts . . .'

'I know, sir,' I said

'You'll need to head over to the tag support sled and wait for your tag support to . . .'

'Lock my tag point. Yes, sir.' I activated my hover belt and zoomed eagerly over to the tag support sled.

One of the fringe benefits of being tag leader is you get a hover belt, and don't have to mess around walking on the clearway. When they made the clearways, they crushed the rubble, but it didn't end up anything like the perfect fused surface you walk around on in settlements. It's hard work to walk on.

After I whooshed off, Playdon gave a heavy sigh, and then carried on talking on the team circuit. 'Do any of you have experience working heavy lifting gear?'

The selection process dragged on, while I waited impatiently to actually do something. I was going crazy listening to the endless chatting. I'd been working New York Fringe when I was 11. I'd waited seven long years to get my chance to work New York Main. Now I was here at last, and I was having to stand around listening to Dalmora explain that she'd used a lot of vid equipment, Fian talk about helping setting up equipment at a solar observatory, and Krath drivel on about lifting containers of garbage.

I felt like shouting aloud to them: *Listen you dim norms, we're standing in a dig site, how about we stop talking and dig?* I didn't though. I desperately wanted to keep the tag leader spot, and I had to behave myself and look good. I knew how this worked. This was my try out. If I messed up, Playdon would swap me for someone else. If I did well, then I'd be a permanent tag leader.

Normally I would have felt confident. I had plenty of experience. The others had none. I was bound to look impressive, but I was still a bag of nerves because of the ape issue. Would Playdon give me a fair chance at this? He'd been challenging me on my Military knowledge ever since I arrived, trying to make a fool of me in front of the class, but we'd been temporary allies when we were training the others on impact suits. Surely, that would count in my favour.

I had something else on my side as well. Playdon might not like apes, but he'd have to be a total fool if he swapped a good tag leader for a bad one. This was only a Foundation class, not a research team, but it was still important to find as many stasis boxes as possible. Each box had a chance of containing vital lost knowledge or artefacts. Any useful discovery helped humanity, but also earned a bounty payment in credits. My school history club had been limited to working Fringe dig sites, but still managed to pay most of its operating costs with the occasional bounty payments. University Asgard courses must have to think about finances as well.

Playdon finally decided to have Amalie and Krath on the lifting gear, a Gamman boy called Joth on my lifeline, and have Dalmora assist him on sensors. Playdon had to cover sensors himself as well as team lead, because learning to read sensors takes a long time.

When he had everyone in the right sleds, Playdon spent another century explaining all the controls to people. Next we set up the sensor net, which also took ages because Playdon demonstrated how to set up the sensor spikes, and placed all four of them himself. All the time, I waited tensely to get on with proving myself.

At long last, Joth locked his lifeline beam on to the tag point on the back of my suit. Whenever a beam locks on to my back, I get a funny feeling between my shoulder blades, like an itch that needs scratching. If I trust my tag support, then it goes away fast. With a novice exo on my lifeline, the itch wasn't going away at all, it was actually getting worse. I'd been waiting a long time to be tag leader on New York Main, I was going to do this, but I was going to have to do it carefully. My itch was telling me that I couldn't depend on my tag support.

I activated my hover belt and swooped across to the sensor sled to take a look at what we had. Playdon was already looking at the sensor displays and explaining them to Dalmora, so I went to stand next to them. First, I glanced at each of the six peripheral displays which signalled major hazards. Fire, electrical, chemical, water, radiation and magnetic. The last two are highly unlikely to record anything, but you have to pay attention fast if they detect anything because impact suits won't help you against that stuff.

All of the hazard displays were clear. In the centre, the main display was weaving complex patterns. I could see the blob that might be a stasis box. The emphasis is on the 'might be' in that sentence. Stasis boxes are designed to preserve their contents for as long as possible while using the minimum power. That means there are no giveaway power signatures for sensors to pick up. It's not so much a case of looking at sensors and seeing where a stasis box is, as a case of seeing all the places where one can't possibly be.

'It looks like it's fairly deep,' I said.

'What is?' asked Playdon.

I pointed to the blob. 'The stasis box. If it is a stasis box.'

'You've experience with sensors?' asked Playdon.

Oh no, I thought. I didn't want the sensor sled job. 'Not really, sir. I just like a quick look to get an idea of the site before tag leading.'

I looked across at the stack of rubble that must be over the possible stasis box. The barely visible remains of a wall ran along at one side. It would probably have some very solid concrete foundations, so it would be tough to shift. Best not even to attempt to move it, because I could use those foundations to my advantage. Normally, you have to clear a wide area and work down layer by layer to keep the rubble nice and stable. In this case, I could save myself some work by only clearing up to the wall and trusting its foundations to stay stable and prevent any cave-in on that side.

There was a nice group of rocks that would be good practice for my novice lift controllers. I activated my hover belt again and swooped across to start work.

'The working team will be speaking on team circuit,' said Playdon. 'The rest of you should keep that set to listen only so you don't distract them with idle chatter. Jarra, you'd better start with . . .'

I tagged the first rock. If you want to get technical, they mostly aren't rocks, but big chunks of concrete, concraz, or whatever. Frankly, I don't really care. They're big heavy lumps of debris that need shifting, and I call them rocks. My main concern is picking a nice solid place to tag them, since sometimes they can break into pieces when the lift

73

beam picks them up. You look a pretty stupid tag leader if the lift beam breaks off a pebble and the main rock just sits there, but after a while you get a feel for the sweet spots to tag.

'Yes, that group,' said Playdon. 'You obviously know what you're doing.'

I tagged the next three rocks, and moved well back in the opposite direction to the wall. As I did so, something jerked at my back. I paused. 'Joth, you don't need to engage the lifeline beam unless I'm in trouble. I need to be free to move.'

'Sorry,' said Joth.

I backed to what should be a safe distance even with the most incompetent novices on the lifting gear.

'I need the lifts to move the rocks directly away from me,' I said. 'In the direction that I'm facing now, beyond the wall, you can see a nice flat area with a hollow in the middle. That's probably where they found the stasis box. No one will want to dig there again, so that's a nice place to put our rubble.'

'Jarra's tagged the first four rocks for you,' said Playdon. 'Amalie, lock your beam on the first and shift it. Once it's moving, then Krath take the next one. Keep alternating.'

They moved the rocks. Very, very slowly, but they moved them. My back was still itching hard.

The hum on my suit communications changed note. Playdon was talking on my private circuit. 'I see you've done this before, Jarra.'

'Yes, sir,' I replied on the private circuit.

'What are you planning to do with that wall?'

'Keep it, sir. Nice stable barrier at that side.'

'Good plan.' The private circuit hum stopped.

I moved back to my group of rocks, using my hover belt to float just above the rubble. This area was an especially nasty mess of jagged lumps of concrete, with spears of broken glass sticking upwards. I had one hand on my hover belt controls, increasing my height to go over a lump of distorted metal that was blocking my path, when I felt another tug from the lifeline. It lifted me wildly high in the air over the distorted metal, and then suddenly dropped me on the other side.

The poor hover belt had cut out when it was out of operating distance of the ground. It cut back in again as it came back in range, but I was falling too fast by then. I hit the ground before it could stop me, and the impact suit triggered. Its material went suddenly rigid, protecting me from the spikes of glass, then the hover belt brought me back up above the ground again.

'Jarra?' Playdon's voice demanded sharply. 'Are you all right?'

'I'm sorry,' wailed Joth. 'I thought the hover belt would lower her when I let go.'

The shock of the impact suit doing a full scale trigger always takes your breath away for a moment. I eventually managed to speak. 'I'm all right.'

The impact suit material relaxed and I could move again. I floated my way across to a safer spot, where I could check myself, my suit, and my hover belt for damage. Hover belts are always vulnerable in a situation like that, but my checks showed this one had been lucky and missed being hit by the glass spikes.

'Joth, you let Jarra go when she was way above the operating limit for the hover belt,' said Playdon. 'Fortunately, there's no serious harm done, but remember that everyone. Hover belts have their limits. If a hole opened up in the ground beneath Jarra, or there was a landslide, she would fall just like she did just then.'

Playdon paused. 'Jarra, check your hover belt and run

suit diagnostics please. Hitting a pointed edge can cause damage.'

'The belt is fine. The suit has already triggered an automatic test, sir,' I said. If there was a grim edge to my Military calm voice when I said that, then it was justified. If the suit was running an automatic diagnostic test, then I'd landed dangerously hard on something sharp. The idea of having someone on tag support was to save me from things like that, not cause them.

'We'll wait a few minutes while that finishes then,' said Playdon.

The hum on my suit comms told me that Playdon was back on my private circuit. 'Sure you're not hurt, Jarra?'

'I'm sure, sir. I expect I'll have the odd bruise from the impact suit triggering.'

'Good, but that was potentially nasty. It wasn't the first mistake either. I felt Joth was generally overeager and intervening too much. Would you agree?'

That was a polite way to say it. I could have said a few strong words about me being a tag leader and not a doll on the end of Joth's beam. A good tag support shouldn't do anything at all until their tag leader is in trouble. That's when they act, and they act fast.

'I'm afraid Joth gives me bad tag point itch, sir. Sorry, what I mean by that is . . .'

'I know tag point itch, Jarra. If you're experienced enough at tag leading to have that, then you'd better pick your own tag support. Who would you like on your lifeline?'

I thought rapidly. I didn't know most of the names of the class. The Betans were no use. The Deltan, Fian, was intelligent and seemed to pay attention to things. I hadn't been listening closely enough to the endless discussions about who knew what to remember if he was experienced with lift gear, but a tag support beam is easy enough to

76

use. The critical qualities for a tag support are that they pay attention to their tag leader's movements, and have the sense to know when they need to use the beam and when they don't.

'Fian, sir.'

'Right,' said Playdon. 'I'll do a little tactful shuffling of the team, to make it less obvious that I'm dropping Joth. I don't like to hammer a student too hard on their first day on a dig site, but he isn't tag support material.'

The hum changed as Playdon swapped back to team circuit. 'While we're waiting for Jarra's suit diagnostic to finish, we'll do a little shuffling. Amalie, hand over your lift sled to Dalmora for a while. Stay with her and make sure she knows how to use the controls. Fian, go on tag support. Joth, hand over tag support to Fian, and then come over to the sensor sled and take a look at the displays.'

People moved around.

'Suit diagnostics have finished,' I said. 'It's fine.'

'Jarra, can you please come over to the tag support sled?' said Fian. 'I need to lock my beam on to your tag point.'

'It should already be locked on,' Playdon interrupted.

'I'm not seeing the green light,' said Fian.

'I disconnected it before I swapped over with Fian,' said Joth.

Right, I thought, bitterly. What nardle brain just disconnects the lifeline of a tag leader in the middle of a danger zone? The answer is an exo who wants to kill her. Honestly, I'd have been a lot safer with Lolia on my lifeline! I bit my lip to stop myself saying something extremely rude.

'Jarra,' said Playdon, 'please pick the safest route back to the clearway and move cautiously.'

I floated my way carefully back to the clearway and headed over to the tag support sled.

Playdon was totally silent until I reached the clearway,

and then he started talking. He didn't shout, but the tone of his voice had everyone frozen and listening. 'Basic site safety rules are that everyone works from the clearway when possible, failing that from a selected safe area. Only tag leaders enter the danger zone. A tag leader must have a lifeline attached, and their tag support sled manned continuously, while they're in a danger zone. You never detach the lifeline from a tag leader in a danger area. You never leave a tag support sled unmanned when a tag leader is in a danger area. Is that clear?'

He paused. 'Please wait everyone.'

Fian locked the lifeline beam on to the tag point of my suit, peered at his arm to check his comms settings, and whispered to me. 'Did I get Joth into trouble?'

I set my team circuit to listen only while I whispered back. 'No, Joth got himself into trouble. You couldn't let me carry on working out there without a lifeline. If there'd been an accident . . .'

We all stood around in silence.

'What are we waiting for?' Fian whispered after a while.

'I think Playdon's talking to Joth on his private circuit,' I said. My theory was that Playdon had changed his mind about hammering a student hard on their first day on site. Joth's first mistake had been bad enough, but disconnecting the lifeline was criminally stupid.

Playdon finally returned to talking on the team circuit. 'Jarra, please continue working when ready.'

I double-checked the green light on the tag support sled, just in case Fian was another homicidal maniac, and then swooped across the rubble to start tagging again. Things went nice and smoothly for a while, and I began to relax a bit. Fian wasn't hampering my movements the way that Joth had done, and didn't seem to be actively trying to kill me.

I was starting to wonder if Fian had fallen asleep, when there was a very minor rubble slippage. I skidded sideways as the hover belt got confused by the ground beneath me moving. The tug on my lifeline that stabilized me was only there for a second, and I was released the moment the hover belt recovered, but it told me that my tag support was alert and doing his job.

Playdon had one brief chat with me on my private circuit, and asked about my tag point itch. I said it was fading nicely, and Fian was a big improvement on Joth.

After a while, I reached the point where everything visible that was sizeable enough to be worth tagging had been shifted, and it was time to get rid of the layer of small debris smothering my working area. 'Drag net time, please.'

I headed back to the clearway. It's not totally necessary to go to the clearway while the heavy lifts do a drag net run, but it's generally safer since things can get messy. After being tossed around like a rag doll on my lifeline earlier, I preferred not to take any chances.

Playdon moved Dalmora back to sit with him for more training on the sensors, and told Joth to take a break for a while. Joth rejoined the rest of the class who were sitting on the two big transport sleds and watching the show. I could imagine what he was thinking. He'd had a chance to make team 1 and blown it entirely. He could think himself lucky if he got a heavy lift spot for team 4, because he could well end up with the rejects in team 5 or 6. I felt a moment of sympathy for him, but only a short one.

Amalie and Krath each had a heavy lift sled to themselves again now. If I was Amalie, I'd be sighing with relief. She must have wondered if Playdon was thinking of giving her spot to Dalmora, but it was probably obvious to her now what had really been going on.

I suddenly realized that I was making too many assumptions here. These were a bunch of clueless exos. They wouldn't have the faintest idea about team selection, or how important it was to be on team 1 or 2, or at worst team 3 or 4. If you got dumped with the dregs in team 5 or 6, then you were doomed to spend most of your dig site time sitting and watching the action rather than taking part in it.

Playdon started explaining the drag net phase to the class. Up until now, we'd been using heavy lift beams focused tightly and locked on a tag point to shift a single heavy object at a time. Now it was time to fan out the heavy lift beams, and drag them across the area to clear away the smaller rubble.

I went across to the tag support sled, which is where a tag leader is expected to be when not working the site, and watched the drag net in operation. Dust clouds swirled in the glow of the heavy lift beams, as the armies of tiny rubble bounced their way over to join the heap of rocks that the heavy lifts had dumped earlier. Most of the rubble was behaving itself, though the odd larger lump was bouncing around a little unpredictably. There are always a few awkward rocks that are too small to bother tagging, but are on the large size for the drag net.

'Am I doing the right thing?' asked Fian, nervously.

'Fine,' I said. 'I even quit itching after a bit.'

'What?' he asked.

I didn't have time to explain tag point itch, since they were ready for me to start tagging again. I headed back out, celebrating the fact that Playdon hadn't taken advantage of my time out of the danger area to replace me and try someone else tag leading. I couldn't underestimate the fact that he knew I was an ape, but surely I was safe as tag leader for at least team 2 or 3.

We made steady progress down through two more layers of rocks, and were nearly at the level of the possible stasis box. I was just tagging a large rock, or chunk of concraz if you're pedantic about these things, when the sensor alarm shrieked. Playdon or Dalmora had hit the panic button.

I instinctively reached for my hover belt controls, but I was already shooting up in the air on the end of the lifeline beam, and swinging across towards the clearway. Something exploded back where I'd been working, sending huge rocks flying across my dig site, but I was already safely out of their reach, hanging high in the air above the tag support sled.

I hung there for a few seconds, before being gently lowered to the clearway next to the tag support sled. 'Thanks for the save,' I said, politely.

'What the chaos was that?' Fian's stunned voice asked on the team circuit.

'Probably a home power storage unit cracking open as the rubble shifted on it,' said Playdon. 'The ruins are full of them, but most have bled out safely over the years. You get the odd one that's still dangerous, so if the sensors show an electrical spike building up you hit the panic button first and ask questions later. We'll do some more scans before continuing.'

That meant a break of at least five minutes. I stretched out on the bench at the back of the tag support sled, as is tag leader's privilege, and relaxed.

'You all right?' asked Fian.

'Fine. You did well.' He might be an exo, but it's good manners to thank your tag support when they save you.

'You're sure you aren't hurt?'

I laughed. 'Not at all. Five minutes break to lie down and relax is blizz. It's hard work out there in an impact suit.'

'Things look clear on the sensors,' said Playdon after a

81

few minutes. 'Jarra, take it cautiously, and see if you can spot the shell of that power unit. Remember there may still be some residual charge.'

I bounced back to my feet, and headed out again. I floated across the area slowly, looking out for the power unit casing. I finally spotted it, some distance away from the crater that marked the explosion. 'Found it,' I reported.

'Don't risk going in close to tag,' warned Playdon.

'Going for a distance shot, sir.' I lined up the tag gun sight on the metal casing, and took a slow and careful shot. I got lucky and scored a direct hit.

'Got it,' I said, joyfully. There's a lot of luck involved in distance shots with a tag gun, but it naturally looks good when you score a hit first time. Normally you go in close and tag things, because it's far more accurate.

I backed well away, and Amalie carefully shifted the remains of the power unit to the far side of our rubbish heap. After that, I inspected how much havoc the explosion had caused on my nicely levelled dig site. It wasn't too bad, and another fifteen minutes of work got us to the exciting moment when a large lump of concraz was lifted away from directly on top of what might be a stasis box. I floated over eagerly to take a look.

There it was, an oddly furry-looking blackness that was hard for the eyes to focus on. 'I can see the side of it,' I shouted. 'We got a stasis box!'

Everyone cheered.

It took several more minutes to finish clearing rubble from the box, and attach the special harness so it could be moved over to one of the transport sleds. You can't tag a stasis box directly. I don't really understand the physics, but a stasis field is made up of lots of nothing. You can't attach a tag to a nothing, you have to attach it to a something.

When we had our precious stasis box safely on the

transport sled, I retrieved our sensor spikes, and we were finished. Fian unlocked my lifeline, and we moved across to a transport sled.

'I don't have to drive the tag support sled back?' he asked.

I shook my head. 'Working team doesn't drive back, we ride.' I stretched out on one of the bench seats. 'We got a stasis box! Totally zan!'

7

We opened the stasis box after lunch. Totally amaz! Normally they're taken away to be opened by experts, and you have to wait for the report on what was inside. We got to open our box ourselves, because Playdon was a Stasis Q!

We were all sitting in the dining hall when Playdon told us he had his licence. I was utterly grazzed. He might be an exo, but if he was Stasis Q then, well . . . respect! Playdon said he'd go back outside for a while to run the pre-checks on the stasis box, and I got my hand up in record time.

'Yes, Jarra?' asked Playdon.

'Sir, requesting permission to come outside and watch.' I held my breath.

'You'll have to stay well clear while I'm working.'

'Understood, sir.' Zan! I thought to myself. A chance to watch a Stasis Q running the pre-checks!

I planned to get my Stasis Qualification licence myself one day, and any previous experience would help me get a course place. You have to grab these chances when they're offered. It's like the flying. I didn't just stroll up to a survey pilot when I was 17 and get him to teach me to fly. I'd started begging rides in the passenger seat when I was 12,

I'd talked pilots into letting me handle the controls when I was 15, so when I was 17 it was just a question of getting my mandatory flying hours and solo licence.

'Anyone else wildly keen to get back in an impact suit and come and watch?' asked Playdon.

Fian was sitting at the same table as me, and gave me a confused look before putting his hand up. Amalie put her hand up too, closely followed by Dalmora, and then a hesitant Krath. The rest of the class just groaned at the thought of getting back into their suits.

I whizzed off to get into my impact suit, got it on in a new personal record time, and waited happily at the dome door for the others. Ten minutes later we were all outside, and Playdon was taking the stasis box well away from the dome and hover sleds to a nice clear area.

'You can all sit on the transport sled and watch,' he said on the team circuit, 'but under no circumstances come any closer to me.'

He opened up an equipment box, took out a micro sensor ring, and began setting it up around the stasis box. I could tell by the speed he was working, that he'd done this a lot of times.

'Excuse me,' Fian whispered, 'but why is it so great to watch this?'

'Yes,' said Krath. 'What's going on? My dad says you should never volunteer for anything, but I wanted to come along with Jarra and . . .'

'This is amaz!' I told them. 'Don't you realize, the stasis boxes are opened by experts, and you don't usually get the chance to watch. I'm aiming to be a Stasis Q myself, so I can open my own boxes.'

'Is it that hard to open a box?' asked Amalie.

'No,' I said, 'it's easy to open them, but you have to check what's inside first. Bad ones are rare, but . . .'

I shut up, because Playdon was talking over the team circuit. 'Right,' he said, 'I've got a sensor ring set up round the box. I'm now putting a limiter on top of the box. That lets me gradually reduce the strength of the stasis field so I can make tests on what's inside. First, I'm taking the field down two tenths and checking for radiation.'

'Radiation?' Dalmora sounded nervous.

'People used these boxes to leave memorials in their old homes,' I whispered, 'but they were also used to store things, usually things that were either valuable or dangerous. Valuable is fine, but dangerous isn't.'

Playdon gradually took the stasis field strength down, making a series of hazard checks. I was making careful mental notes of it all.

'Everything looks clear,' he said, 'I now take the field strength down to just under ten per cent and run a quick sensor scan.'

There was a pause.

'Yes,' he said, 'it looks like a standard memorial box, so I'll pack up now and we can open it inside.'

I offered to help pack the equipment, and Playdon agreed since the box had been cleared as safe. We would find more stasis boxes in future. If I helped him pack up a few more times, he might allow me to help him with the setting up, and from that to helping run the tests was only a short step.

We went back into the dome. I took off my impact suit, did a bit of fast research on my lookup, and went into the dining hall with my head buzzing with plans. I might be able to cover part of the Stasis Q course from vids and working with Playdon, but I'd need to go on a formal course for several weeks, and then there were theory and practical exams. From what I'd hastily read, the tests were tough. Any error meant a complete failure, because opening a real stasis box with a hazard inside might kill you.

Playdon came into the dining hall, and put the stasis box on a table. We all gathered expectantly round, and he held up something to show us. 'This is a stasis box key. It collapses the stasis field and releases the contents. They're easy to use, but you never open a box yourselves. Boxes have to be checked and opened by qualified people, in case there's something like a nuclear warhead inside.'

Krath gulped. 'Have you ever found one of those?'

'Not personally,' said Playdon. 'I have found radioactive materials in a stasis box, and the last aerial survey of New York Main dig site showed up two new radioactive hotspots that probably came from failed stasis boxes releasing their contents. They're well clear of current working areas, but Dig Site Command may need to get them cleared up in the future.'

'Fortunately,' he continued, 'my tests show this looks like a perfectly ordinary memorial box, so let's see what we've got.'

Playdon used the key, and the black stasis field vanished. Inside was what looked like a flexiplas box covered in metallic webbing. Playdon lifted the lid, and took out something soft and white. He held it up.

'A wedding dress,' said Dalmora, looking grazzed. 'An old style wedding dress. How old is that?'

'From the design, I'd guess the box dates from about the middle of Exodus century,' said Playdon. 'The dress looks older than that.'

'Perhaps it had been handed down in the family,' said Dalmora.

The next thing was a clock made partly of real wood. 'This is an old time piece,' said Playdon. 'It would have hung on the wall.'

The final object was a red and blue flexiplas toy. Playdon shook it and it rattled.

'A baby's rattle, for a baby from hundreds of years ago,' said Dalmora. 'How amaz!'

'And most importantly, this,' said Playdon, holding up something very small. 'A data chip.'

'It looks strange,' said Fian.

'It's an old format,' said Playdon, 'but we make special converters to read and translate them.'

He produced a metal cube, inserted the data chip from the stasis box into one of its connections, and a standard data chip into another. A light flashed for a few minutes and then went out. Playdon took the standard chip, and inserted it into the big vid wall at the front of the hall.

The class waited breathless as a totally black image appeared for a few seconds, and then suddenly a man was smiling at us. I'd found stasis boxes before, and when the report came back from the experts I'd watched the images from the data chips inside. It was always special, but this one was totally zan. Before, the experts had already seen them, but this time . . . This time we were the first. That man had been waiting to smile at someone for four hundred years, and he was smiling at us.

'Well,' he said, 'I don't know if anyone will ever bother to watch this. Maybe not, but if you do, I'm Davide and it's the first of June in the year 2363. Today I'm on Earth and tomorrow I'll be on another world. I've been waiting years for this. My wife, my 5-year-old son, and myself are going to one of the Alpha worlds, Demeter. My brother is there already, and my parents hope to join us next year. We've a very limited luggage allowance, so we're leaving the apartment fully furnished. They aren't selling well at the moment, but the price is really low. I hope you like living here.'

His image flickered out, and was replaced by that of a red-headed woman. She was sitting on a chair, with a small boy on her lap. 'I'm Issette and this is Rhyss.'

Another Issette, I thought. I'd better not mention this to my friend, Issette. I could just imagine her wails about being stuck with a four-hundred-year-old name.

The Issette from four hundred years ago was silent for a couple of minutes before she spoke again, and this time her words came out in a rush. 'I don't want to go, but we can't stay. A third of the apartments in this block are empty. It's getting worse every year, and we have to think of our son. He's only 5, and there'll be the new baby in seven months, and . . . The looters have taken over some areas.'

She suddenly stood up and reached forward. The image changed to a recording of some sort of newzie. We watched the news report from four hundred years ago, and then the data recording ended.

'She didn't want to go,' said Amalie. 'Her husband did, but she didn't.'

'They went to Demeter,' said Dalmora. 'She must have liked it there. It's a beautiful world.'

'But she didn't want to go,' said Amalie. 'Poor woman. She went because she was scared to stay, and was frightened for her children. Everyone in Epsilon sector came because they wanted to build up new worlds.'

I didn't know what to think. I'd watched several of these messages before, with people full of excitement about going to a new world. That was the first I'd seen with an exo who hadn't wanted to leave Earth.

'I'll send the artefacts and the data chip off to the experts for preservation and analysis,' said Playdon. 'No more classes today. Our normal daily pattern will be to work the dig site in the morning, and have classes in the afternoon.'

He paused for a second before continuing. 'Jarra, Fian, Dalmora, Amalie and Krath seemed to work effectively together today, so they're our team 1. For the next few days, they'll be working areas while the rest of you watch and learn. After that, we'll gradually start building up our other dig teams.'

I instantly forgot about a long ago Issette who hadn't wanted to leave Earth. I was tag leader for team 1! I was an ape girl, but I'd still made key spot! I contained myself while Playdon collected the artefacts and tools and went out of the dining hall, and then I looked round for the others. Fian was nearest, so I grabbed him and swung him into a jubilant victory dance.

'What?' Fian looked startled, then saw my grin and smiled back.

'You heard him! We're team 1! Hoo eee!' I yelled.

8

It was our third day working New York Main. We'd found nothing on our second day, but team 1 had worked smoothly together and Playdon had given us a few words of praise at the end of it. Heading out again today, there was a feeling of excitement among the class. Working a city dig site was like a treasure hunt. You never knew if you would find a stasis box, or what might be inside it, and even the Betans seemed caught up in the mood and stopped whining about the impact suits.

We'd just reached our working position, and I was on the sensor sled with Dalmora and Playdon. I was sorting out the sensor spikes ready to set up the net when there was a faint rumbling sound. I looked up, a sensor spike still in my hand, and spotted a lump falling from the skeletal remains of the nearest skyscraper.

'Everyone stay on the sleds.' Playdon's urgent voice came across the team circuit. 'Move them back onto the clearway.'

'What's the problem?' asked Lolia.

'This is Asgard Team 6, Sector 22,' said Playdon. I could tell from the different background note he was on the broadcast channel. 'We're seeing tower breakaways at nine o'clock. Either one or two Sectors out.'

A new voice came over the broadcast channel. 'This is Dig Site Command. Thank you Asgard 6. Teams in Sectors 21 through 27 move to safe ground.'

Our six sleds had pulled back at varying speeds, and now formed a ragged line on the clearway.

'So what's the delay?' It was Lolia again. The girl had the patience level of the average 2-year-old in Nursery, but a lot less brain cells.

'Quiet,' said Playdon on the team circuit.

I was watching the suspect skyscraper, looking for more breakaways, but it was the one next to it that folded over sideways. It seemed to happen in slow motion, as the huge mass of concrete and metal finally lost its battle with time and fell with a long drawn out dying scream. A dense cloud of dust billowed up to mark its grave.

Even before it landed, Playdon was on the broadcast channel. 'This is Asgard 6. Tower down! Tower down!'

'This is Dig Site Command. Status check, teams respond please. Sector 21, Earth 19.'

'Earth 19 secure.'

'Sector 22, Asgard 6.'

'Asgard 6 secure.' Playdon called it in.

'Sector 23, Cassandra 2.' Dig Site Command waited and tried again. 'Sector 23, Cassandra 2, respond please.' Still nothing. 'Sector 25, Beowulf 4.'

Beowulf 4 responded, and then the teams in Sectors 26 and 27.

'This is Dig Site Command. We have a team down in Sector 23. Sectors 21, 22 and 25 assist please. Sector 22, Asgard 6, you are first response.'

Dig Site Command was sounding nicely professional and calm when he said it. Me, I was close to panicking.

'What's that mean?' asked Lolia.

'Nuke it, Lolia!' said Playdon on the team circuit.

There was a sort of collective gasp across all our six sleds. Hoo eee! Playdon had said the nuke word! I have to admit it was effective though. With one crude phrase, he shut up Lolia and communicated just how serious things were to the rest of the class.

'Sleds move out. Stay in a close line.' Playdon tapped Dalmora on the shoulder, and she practically leapt out of the driving seat to let him take over our sled.

Playdon started our sled moving and I saw the other sleds tagging on behind. I was anxious to ask something, but I didn't want Playdon swearing at me next, so I had faith and held my tongue.

'This is Asgard 6,' said Playdon, back on the broadcast channel. 'I have a Foundation course team, with only one experienced member. Who is in Sector 24?'

Yes, that was exactly what I'd wanted to ask.

'Sector 24 is allocated to Earth 8, but they had a sled problem and are not on site today,' responded Dig Site Command.

Oh nuke that! I nearly joined Playdon in the profanity club, but fortunately I thought it rather than actually saying it out loud. I knew the system. They deliberately scattered novice teams between experienced ones on sites like this, to try and avoid the situation we were now in. It should have been Earth 8 leading this rescue, not us. Earth was for the triple H, and one of those was History. University Earth had a large number of highly qualified dig teams.

'Team Leaders Asgard 6, Earth 19, Beowulf 4, please utilize emergency channel to co-ordinate rescue,' said Dig Site Command.

Playdon's voice came across our team circuit. 'My team can open emergency channel to listen in, but don't transmit on it unless ordered to.'

I already had the channel open to eavesdrop on it. Dig Site Command were giving out the last known location of team Cassandra 2. They were a research team of ten, and they'd been working close to the tower that collapsed.

'This is Asgard 6 team leader,' said Playdon. 'Our arrival estimate is twelve minutes. Novice team of thirty-one. Six sleds including two heavy lifts.'

Playdon was taking us round by the safe clearway route. I couldn't fault that. We might save five minutes by going in a straight line across the rubble, but we couldn't afford to take the risk.

'This is Earth 19 team leader,' said a woman's voice. 'Our arrival estimate is sixty-six minutes. Experienced team of twenty-nine. Nine sleds including three heavy lifts.'

'This is Beowulf 4 team leader. We have a team of sixteen, and eight sleds including three heavy lifts, but we have a problem,' said a deep voiced man. 'We're the wrong side of that tower group. We need to skirt the remaining two, as well as the fallen one, to reach the rescue zone.'

Dig Site Command cut in, ordering Beowulf 4 to stick to a safe route clear of the remaining towers. That seemed a good call to me. The other towers might well be unstable as well now, and we didn't need a second team in trouble.

'By a safe route,' Beowulf 4 continued like it really hurt him to say it, 'our response time is about 100 minutes. Sorry, that puts us close to the two hour deadline, but we're coming anyway in case the rescue teams hit trouble themselves.'

'This is Asgard 6,' said Playdon. 'Thanks for that Beowulf 4, we'd appreciate you covering our backs.'

Dalmora was whispering to me. 'What's the two hour deadline?'

Playdon heard her. 'I'm busy. Explain things to them, Jarra.'

I spoke on the team circuit, so our class could hear me on the other sleds. 'One of the other teams on the dig site isn't responding. We can assume they got caught in that skyscraper collapsing. There are ten people missing from University Cassandra, probably buried in rubble. Their suits may have kept them alive, but impact suits can only take heavy pressure for about two hours. We need to dig people out by then or suits start failing.'

There was silence. I don't think any of the others dared to say anything on circuit.

I did a few mental calculations. 'After we get there, that gives us about an hour and forty minutes to get people out. Earth 19 will arrive nearly an hour later than us.'

'Will apes be any use?' muttered someone. This was followed by an oops noise, as he realized he was broadcasting to our whole team.

'A lot more use than we are!' said Playdon savagely on the team circuit. 'Earth 19 are the experts, but we have to make what progress we can until they arrive.'

'This is Dig Site Command, we've contacted the Cassandra 2 team. All team members are alive but buried.'

That was good news, though it upped the pressure. Cassandra 2 team were alive and it was our responsibility to reach them and keep them that way. I wondered if Playdon was feeling anything like as panicky as I was.

There were a few minutes of silence as we headed on towards the rescue site. The two remaining towers were getting closer now, and I looked at them nervously. I didn't fancy joining the University Cassandra team under tons of rubble.

'We're heading off the clearway now,' said Playdon on the team circuit. 'Drive slow and careful. Jarra, stand by with sensor spikes. We'll be setting up a sensor net to locate the casualties. Dig Site Command will give you the locations for the spikes.'

Dig Site Command was reeling off sensor positions. I

coded them into four sensor spikes. Our sled had lurched off the clearway across a mound of rubble, and the other five bobbed along in our wake. We were heading directly towards the towers, and I was deeply relieved when Playdon stopped the sled. We were still probably within the fallout zone if one of the other towers fell, but we would stand a chance.

'Team 1 go to your working sleds,' said Playdon. 'Everyone else get on the transport sleds and stay there. I've got the sleds on the flattest, safest looking area I can find in working range of the casualties, but remember this isn't a clearway. Even the transport sleds are in a hazard zone. Jarra, get your lifeline beam locked on, and set up the sensor net. Watch your step out there. That rubble is highly unstable.'

I activated my hover belt, and went across to Fian on the tag support sled. Once my lifeline beam was locked on, I swooped out across a jagged landscape of rubble, carrying my armful of sensor spikes. There were huge twisted lengths of rusted metal, tangles of wire, and fragments of concrete scattered in all sizes from pebbles up to blocks as large as our base dome. Dust was still thick in the air and I was thankful that my impact suit saved me from having to breathe it in.

The first sensor spike bleeped as I reached my correct position, and I thrust it downwards to activate it. Sensor spikes two and three were easy too, but the last one was a problem because a huge block of concrete was in the way.

'Our closest position for sensor 4 is about four metres above optimal,' I reported.

'Compensating for that,' said Playdon. 'Go for it.'

I gained some height to reach the top of the concrete block, and activated the sensor. 'How's that looking?'

'In the green,' said Playdon. He switched from team circuit to the emergency channel. 'This is Asgard 6. We have sensor

96

net in place and I can see ten suit signals. They're buried deep, and they're scattered across a large area, so we need to start shifting rubble. We don't have time to wait for Earth 19.'

Dig Site Command acknowledged that, and Playdon swapped back to team circuit. 'Back to the sensor sled now, Jarra. I want you and Dalmora monitoring the sensors. I'll be tag leading. I'll help you get a good understanding of the sensor images of the site before I start work, then I'll need you both watching out for developing dangers. That rubble's newly fallen and still settling, so keep a look out for underground cavities opening up, power storage units, chemicals, anything strange suddenly showing up. If you think I'm tagging anything that could cause a landslide then you warn me. Amalie and Krath are on heavy lift sleds as usual. Fian you're on my lifeline.'

I was heading back to the sensor sled as ordered, but I had to challenge this. 'With respect, sir,' I interrupted, 'the sensors need a lot more experience than either Dalmora or I have. We've got unstable rubble and people buried down there. We need you watching sensors and guiding the team. I should be tagging the rubble.'

'It's true that I'd be better on the sensors,' said Playdon, 'but it's going to be dangerous down there. It's my responsibility to take the risks not yours. You're sure about this, Jarra?'

Sure? Not really. I was terrified that I'd mess things up and get the Cassandra 2 team killed, but I knew I was far more likely to make mistakes on sensors than on tagging. I reached the sensor sled, and the chaotic images on the displays were enough to convince me I was right. I could see some patterns that had to be rubble sliding, but I didn't have a clue what others were. 'I'm sure, sir.'

'Right,' Playdon said. 'Jarra is tag leader. Fian, you're on her lifeline. If you see any rubble moving round her, or anything you don't like, don't wait or ask questions, pull her up!'

'Yes, sir,' Fian answered, clearly catching the Military response off me.

'Jarra, set your comms to default to broadcast on emergency channel.' Playdon handed me the tag gun. 'Take a look at the sensors before you start. Ignore everything but the buried suit signals and major landmarks.'

I took a look at the screen. The locations of the buried members of the Cassandra team were marked by green dots. I tried to memorize their positions relative to a massive chunk of concrete that was nearby. There were two groups of three, and four solo dots. One of the solos must have had a very narrow escape from being crushed by that concrete. Impact suits could take a lot but they had their limits.

'Ready,' I said, and floated out over the rubble.

There's an old children's game, dating from pre-history. You have a heap of sticks and you have to pull a stick out of the middle without making the others move. Being tag leader was rather like that. I had to tag rubble that could be moved by the lift teams without making other lumps fall. With unstable heaps like this, there could be a major landslide if I got it wrong. There were people down in that rubble who could be killed by my mistakes, but would run out of time if I did nothing. No pressure. No pressure at all.

Before I did anything, I gave myself a couple of minutes to float over the site and work out where to start. Then I took it easy, tagging a few isolated rocks that were unlikely to affect any others. There were occasional random rubble collapses happening in some areas, and I wanted to let things settle down as much as possible before I did anything drastic.

I swooped back out of the way. 'Lifts go! I want the rubble moved over towards sensor 3. You can drop it into that dip.'

It was weirdly embarrassing hearing myself on the emergency circuit. I could imagine the Earth 19 team listening in and hoping like chaos that I didn't do anything terminally stupid before they arrived to help. I was betting their team leader was biting her tongue to stop herself from ordering us just to wait and do nothing. I'd have really liked to do that, but the Cassandra team were buried deep and they were scattered across my work site. The Earth team would only have about forty minutes after they arrived. However expert they were, that wasn't enough time to dig everyone out.

Amalie and Krath started locking lift beams onto my tag markers and shifting lumps of concrete out of the way. The first two lumps moved painfully slowly, the lift operators clearly nervous, but the next few went faster.

That was the easy ones out of the way. Now it got tricky. I'd decided to work across from a hollow in the rubble, clearing a horizontal section across the top of the buried people. It's always safer to keep a level work site, and especially in a situation like this. The buried impact suits were already stressed to their limit. A landslide on top of them could be fatal.

Once I had my area nicely levelled, I could gradually work my way down, layer by layer. I tagged two more lots of rubble and the lift teams moved them away. I was tagging a third when Playdon's voice stopped me.

'Jarra, I could be wrong but that big rock worries me. The one next to it is just as big, and they're leaning against each other with a cavity underneath. If you move one, then the other will fall.'

I took another look at it, and the equally large lump next to it. 'We need to shift it. Can we take the two as twins?'

'We can try. Amalie and Krath, you'll need to lock on to a tag each but don't move them until I give you the word.'

I tagged the second rock and moved back well out of the way.

'Amalie, Krath, you have them locked?' asked Playdon.

'Yes,' said Amalie.

'Locked,' said Krath.

'I'll count you down to moving them. Three, two, one, go!' said Playdon.

The two rocks soared upwards in beautiful unison.

'Nice job!' I moved back to take a look at things. Now I could see the cavity Playdon had warned me about, a massive hole going deep into the rubble. Nearly as deep as the trapped people, but naturally not in the right place to help that much. If anything it made things worse, since everything around it was unstable.

I tagged more lumps of concrete and got them shifted out of the way. 'There's a huge metal girder right across where the people are. I'm trying to get it cleared so we can shift it,' I told my listeners on the emergency channel. 'Oh chaos!' The words slipped out as I floated round the other side and got a better view.

'Problem Jarra?' asked Playdon.

'There's a huge tangle of old wires anchoring it to some of this concrete. We can't shift that lot in one, so I'll need to laser them through.'

Playdon switched to our team circuit. 'Jarra, can you use a laser gun or should I come and do it?'

Good question. I'd never used a laser gun but I'd watched someone do it. 'I think I can do it. It'll be faster if I do. I'll come and collect it.'

'All right.' Playdon sounded nervous. 'Be very careful. The beam can cut through anything, including right through your impact suit.'

'Yes sir,' I said, grimly. 'I'll try not to cut myself in half.'

I tagged a few more rocks at the other side of the area,

and left Amalie and Krath to lift those while I collected the laser gun. Playdon showed me the controls and the safety mechanism, and then I headed back to the girder before I carefully set the safety to off and tried triggering the beam. It shone out with a misleadingly pretty glitter effect. I gave it an experimental waft in the direction of the wires and it cut through them without a blink, and sliced deep into the metal girder as well. I gulped a bit, and finished cutting the girder loose. Then I made very sure I set the safety catch back on the laser gun before attaching the evil little thing to my belt. I might need it again.

'You remembered to put the safety catch on, Jarra?' Playdon asked anxiously. He was on the team circuit again, clearly not wanting to let the rest of the world know just how clueless we were.

'Most definitely on, sir.'

'Good.'

We shifted the rest of the rubble out from around the big girder, and then I tagged both ends of that and moved back. Amalie and Krath each locked beams on to a tag, and Playdon gave them the countdown to lift it in unison. The huge length of metal lifted smoothly up into the air, then suddenly pivoted and went flying sideways. I felt myself being yanked upwards just as the end of the girder crashed down towards me.

'What went wrong?' wailed Krath on the team circuit.

'Jarra! You all right?' Playdon shouted across the emergency channel.

I couldn't move my left arm where the girder had caught it. I couldn't move it . . . I couldn't move it . . . Then the impact material of my suit stopped being rigid. I could wave my left arm again and stopped panicking. 'I'm fine. It only caught my arm for a moment. Thanks Fian. Nice save. I'll just check what happened.'

'I'm sorry,' said Krath. 'I don't know what went wrong.'

I did. The end of the girder with Krath's tag mark had broken off. I had an uncomfortable feeling that was partly my own nardle fault. I'd just accidentally cut part of the way through that beam. I made a mental note not to be so dumb in future. 'Not your fault, Krath. The girder broke. It's fallen clear of the area, so we can carry on working on the other stuff. Drag net next please.'

I retreated while Amalie and Krath dragged the minor rubble out of the area. We shifted another layer of big rocks, and then had another drag net to tidy up the smaller debris. That all went smoothly, which was a good thing because my nerves needed some recovery time.

The calm voice of authority came across the emergency channel. 'This is Dig Site Command. Asgard 6, can we have a progress report please?'

'The site is levelled, and we've cleared two layers of rubble across the key area,' said Playdon. 'We're just over halfway down.'

'Earth 19, how long before you reach the site?' asked Dig Site Command.

'This is Earth 19. We will be with them in about twenty minutes. Nice progress, Asgard 6.'

I tagged more boulders. Amalie and Krath shifted more boulders. Fian yanked me up out of the way of a slight landslide. We cleared out another layer of minor rubbish. It was all going quite beautifully, and I was just about to start tagging the big stuff again when Playdon yelped urgently on the emergency channel.

'I've got an amber light. Suit failing!'

'Which one? Where?' I'd guessed the answer, and was moving there even before Playdon yelled co-ordinates at me. The solo suit nearest that huge hunk of concrete. I could picture it. That suit must have been caught when the concrete

102

fell and bounced aside. It had absorbed the impact but been weakened in the process. Now it was failing. Under the rubble, a suit was failing, and when it failed someone was going to die!

Nuke it! We were so close! I wasn't going to let this happen! I was tagging rocks like a mad thing. Forget keeping my site nice and level, right now I needed to dig a hole down to that suit as fast as possible. 'Amalie, Krath, lift rocks! As fast as you can! No time to be fancy, just throw them over in the direction of sensor 3.'

'Jarra, you should move out of the way,' said Amalie on our team channel.

'Just lift the furthest tags from me. If I have to, I'll dodge, and Fian can yank me out. Someone's dying down there.'

I could hear screams. My over active imagination of course. Dig Site Command had the trapped team on a separate comms channel, so someone could keep chatting encouragingly to them without distracting the rescuers. There might be real screams on that channel as the wearer of the suit below me started to feel the weight of the rocks on top of them, but I couldn't hear them.

'You're close!' said Playdon.

He was right. As the next two rocks swung out of the hole we were digging, I could see a gleam of an impact suit.

'Amber light is flickering red,' said Playdon.

That meant we had perhaps a minute. 'Fian, I'm going down!' I yelled as I broke all the rules and jumped right down the hole. My hover belt cut out for a moment, then back in again, breaking my fall enough to avoid the impact suit locking up. The sides of the hole were already starting to collapse, showering me with lumps of concrete, as I tagged the impact suit arm sticking out from the rubble. 'Fian pull me out! Amalie lock tag and lift hard!'

I flew up in the air, and a black and golden professional

impact suit followed me up. We'd probably just broken someone's arm, but it might have saved their life. Amalie swung the suit carefully over to land it on the clearway.

'Are they alive?' I asked.

There was a pause of about ten seconds or a few years before Dig Site Command responded. 'Alive and in need of urgent medical assistance. Emergency evac portal 3 is activated and Hospital America Casualty is standing by for incoming injured.'

A female voice spoke up. 'This is Earth 19. We just arrived at rescue site. Asgard 6, should one of our sleds ferry casualty to portal?'

'Thank you, Earth 19. Please do that.' Playdon sounded relieved that he didn't need to send novices off on a sled alone.

'Moving our lifting sleds into position to assist, and awaiting tag leader orders,' said the Earth 19 team leader.

That was me. I hesitated. 'Earth 19, do you wish to send in a new tag leader?'

'You are tag leader, Jarra. You're familiar with the site and doing a fine job. Call for our lifts when ready.'

I glowed at the praise for about a microsecond, then got tagging. Things went a lot faster with five sleds lifting, and three of them fast professionals. I stabilized a bit of the havoc around where we'd dug out the person with the failing suit, and then went back to steadily working downwards across the whole area where people were trapped. Progress went abruptly slower as we neared their level, and Playdon guided me as I carefully freed one impact suit after another and tagged them for rescue. One, two, three . . . Finally, we reached number nine and I could relax.

When we had everyone aboard the sleds, we headed off in convoy towards the emergency evac portal. I lay on the bench at the back of the tag support sled, lost in an exhausted daze, as I vaguely listened to the voices chattering away on the broadcast channel.

'This is Beowolf 4 team leader. Smooth work Asgard 6 and Earth 19. Sounds like you have the situation secure so we're returning to base.'

'This is Asgard 6,' said Playdon. 'Thank you for responding in case we ran into trouble.'

'This is Dig Site Command. Patching Cassandra 2 team circuit to broadcast channel.'

'This is Cassandra 2 team leader, Rono Kipkibor,' said a new voice. 'Thank you for your assistance, Asgard 6 and Earth 19. Great job, tag leader, we appreciate it.'

Several other weary voices chorused agreement.

'We hope Stephan is all right,' said Playdon. 'Things got too close when his suit failed. Say something, Jarra.'

Me? I set my comms to speak on broadcast channel for a moment. 'Glad to help, Cassandra 2.'

We reached the portal. It was only an emergency evac one, so it was tiny and had no controls, but was just calibrated to transmit to a specified receiving portal. We strapped each Cassandra 2 team member to a hover stretcher before sliding them through, then there was another round of polite conversation involving the various teams and Dig Site Command on the broadcast channel before things finally went quiet.

Playdon ordered team 1 across to one of the transport sleds, and picked out some of the rest of the class to drive the sleds back. I shifted across from my bench on the tag support sled to a bench on the transport sled, and stretched out again. With the excitement over, I was so tired that I actually fell asleep on the way back to the dome. This wasn't a good idea. I'd never fallen asleep in an impact suit before, and waking up was quite disorienting and scary. In my panic, I hit poor Fian. He had been holding on to me to stop me falling off the bench whenever the sled hit a bump.

'Sorry,' I said, staggered my way to the edge of the sled, and nearly fell off.

Fian and Playdon grabbed me, one on each side, got me off the sled and steered me into the dome ahead of the crowd.

'That was totally amaz!' Dalmora said. 'Jarra, you were just . . .' She broke off. 'I don't know the words to describe it.'

Yay, I thought. I have Miss Alpha lost for words. I tugged my suit hood off and swayed a bit.

Fian caught me for the second time in two minutes. As my tag support, he probably felt it was still his job. 'You all right, Jarra?'

Good question. I had my feet on the solid flexiplas dome floor, but I felt like I was still hovering in mid air.

Dalmora dashed off for a moment, and reappeared with a glass of Fizzup. She passed it to me, and I gulped it down.

'Jarra's just been working very hard saving some lives,' said Playdon. 'The Military are only human like the rest of us. Get her to the bathroom, Fian, and then to her room.'

There was a bathroom. I managed to peel off my impact suit and there was, oh joy, a shower. After that, there was a bed, and I slept in my skintight rather than making the effort to change. After a few hours, I woke up, dressed, and groped my way to the dining room. There didn't seem to be a class in progress, everyone was just sitting round tables and chatting. They all went quiet and watched me as I got some food from the dispensers and started eating.

'We've had a news report from the hospital,' said Playdon.

I stopped eating and looked up.

'Stephan, the tag leader whose suit failed, lost both legs but has no brain damage. A month in a regrowth tank getting new legs and he'll be perfectly fine again. Everyone else just has minor injuries. I'll be heading over to visit them later.' He paused. 'The Cassandra 2 team are very good friends of mine.'

I probably should have asked Playdon to give them a message from me, and wish them a speedy recovery, but I was too exhausted to do more than mutter I was glad Stephan had made it. I finished eating after that and staggered back to bed. I'd helped save some lives. The lives of norms not Handicapped. All through the madness I'd never even thought about that. They'd just been people.

There was something else. Playdon had referred to me as Military. He'd shifted sides, from threat to ally and I didn't just feel safer because of that, I felt . . . I felt good.

I fell asleep again.

9

After sleeping most of the afternoon and evening, I had a restless night with weird panicky dreams. I was the person stuck in the rubble in the failing suit, lying there helpless while my legs were slowly crushed to a pulp. Not nice. Not nice at all.

We had ordinary lectures all the next day. We didn't go on the dig site, or even set foot out of the dome. Playdon must have felt we needed some recovery time before facing the dig site again. I don't know about the others but in my case he was certainly right. My body was stiff and aching, and my mind was a mess.

So, Playdon spent that day taking us through twentieth century history and the birth of the mega cities instead of working the dig site. The twentieth century is the one they summarize as war, war and bore.

Well, of course it's boring in school history lessons. They miss out the space race since it was made irrelevant by portals. They miss out the cold war because it involves the 'nuclear' word too much. All the kids keep sniggering, tell their parents what teacher said, and the school gets swamped with complaints. At least, that's what happens with

ProParents, and I can't imagine real parents are any more sensible about their kids going round saying 'Nuclear bomb, nuclear bomb, I'm allowed to say nuclear bomb because teacher said nuclear bomb.' As far as young kids are concerned, the line between nuclear bomb and the proper nuke word is so thin it might as well not be there.

Playdon wasn't afraid to refer to nuclear bombs with a bunch of allegedly mature 18-year-olds, so we got war, war, cold war and bore. If there was the odd faint snigger in the class when he said the word nuclear, then it could well have been the memory of him swearing at Lolia on the dig site yesterday, rather than pure childishness.

Boring or not, I was deeply thankful to sit in the dining hall and let a couple of world wars drift past my ears. My nerves were still vibrating like tightly strung wires, and the boredom was soothing.

It was worrying to find I was still so wound up. It was all over. Everyone was fine. Why was I still a nervous wreck? At one point, I even found myself wondering if I should talk to my psychologist, but fortunately I returned to sanity ten seconds later.

I comforted myself with the thought that Playdon seemed to be looking a bit ragged too. Yesterday must have been a nightmare for him, landed with a rescue when all he had to work with was a clueless bunch like us. He'd said the buried team were friends of his, so he must have been trying to stay professional while going through personal hell.

Class finished about five, and Playdon grabbed some food and vanished off somewhere. Maybe he was in his room, reliving the rescue and quietly screaming to himself, the same way I'd been last night.

The rest of us lounged around in the dining hall, snacking on whatever we felt was the closest approximation to real food and drink that the food dispensers could produce.

Having discovered that it's more or less impossible to laze comfortably in a flexiplas dining chair, the class dragged in all their pillows and cushions and lounged on the floor instead. They kept making admiring comments about me being tag leader on the rescue. Even Lolia seemed to be rather impressed. It was somehow nice but embarrassing at the same time, so I retreated to a quiet corner by myself.

Fian joined me after a while, and handed me a fresh glass of Fizzup. 'Playdon was talking about some interesting stuff today. My school barely mentioned pre-history. Delta sector isn't exactly keen on any sort of history for that matter. That's why I applied to Asgard rather than a Deltan university.'

I suddenly realized that while making a cross-sector university application wasn't as crazy as an ape pretending to be a norm, it was still quite a brave step. 'Are you finding it hard on this course?'

'I'm coping. Yesterday was a shock of course. How are you feeling today?'

I hit the glass of Fizzup with a finger nail so that it made a ringing musical noise. 'You hear that? That's my nerves still twanging.'

'You did great yesterday.'

'Only because I knew I could depend on you to get me out of trouble.'

There was a pause before he spoke again. 'I wondered if I could ask you something. It's always puzzled me, and you're Military so you probably know all about it.'

Playdon had called me Military in front of the class, and I'd decided that was a message. I'd helped save the lives of his friends, so he'd stop challenging me on my Military knowledge. I'd let myself relax a bit, thinking things would be easier now. I was wrong. Playdon might have stopped deliberately testing me, but my classmates would keep doing

110

it in total innocence, and avoiding talking to people would advertise the fact I had something to hide.

'Yes?' I asked, warily.

'Why did Kappa sector get settled after Epsilon? Shouldn't it have been Zeta?'

I was lucky. I'd wondered about that myself, and worked out the answer years ago. I reached for my lookup, and displayed a standard holo of the three concentric spheres of humanity.

'Alpha sector is the first sphere centred on Earth. Beta, Gamma and Delta cluster round it forming the second sphere. Beyond those, the third frontier sphere has lots of sectors marked out, though we've only started colonising two of them so far. Now, look where Zeta sector is, and you'll see your answer.'

Fian frowned. 'I don't understand.'

'When the Delta sector planets were nearing the end of Planet First, the Military started setting up the portal relay network for the first frontier sectors. What was happening when Delta was being colonized?'

Fian's eyes widened. 'The Second Roman Empire! Zeta sector is right next to Beta sector.'

'Exactly,' I said. 'Beta sector was independent and hostile back then. They're still the most . . . different . . . of the sectors even now. Their clan system. Their class system. Their lack of a nudity taboo. No wonder Lolia and Lolmack don't fit in with the rest of the class.'

Fian and I instinctively glanced across the room at the two Betans, before tacitly abandoning the subject. I'd answered Fian's question and could relax again, but not too much. I'd passed this test, but I knew there'd be another and another and another. I couldn't afford to fail any of them.

Dalmora entered the hall at this point, carrying a guitar. She explained it was an instrument that dated far back into pre-history. There is a natural law of the universe that says someone always brings a guitar along on a history dig. They always play the same songs too. Two people in my school history club had them, though I had to admit Dalmora played better than they did.

We listened to Dalmora singing the song about two boys and one girl. My first year in Next Step, everyone was singing it. The boys keep asking to date the girl, and she can't decide between them, and the chorus has her singing that her mum won't let her go triad so she can only go two. In the last verse, the boys decide to forget her and date each other instead. Dalmora got the words muddled in verse three, but it was a pretty good performance all the same.

'My home planet is Hercules,' said Fian, when things were quieter again. 'Please don't say that I haven't the muscles for Hercules. Half the class already said it.'

I giggled and looked him over. He wasn't exactly a muscle man but . . . 'I've seen worse.'

He looked absurdly pleased at my comment. 'My parents are specialists in solar storm prediction. My older sister is studying multi particle wave expansions.'

'I understand solar storm prediction,' I said, 'but multi particle wave expansions mean nothing to me. Like . . . what?'

He smiled. 'Me too. Delta sector is heavily into science, like Beta sector is heavily into sex, but I can't see the appeal of it.'

I laughed.

'I meant I can't see the appeal of science, not sex. Sex is . . .' Fian shook his head. 'I'm digging myself in deeper here, aren't I?'

I nodded.

'Well, I can't understand the fascination of science, and

112

my family feel much the same about history. It's pretty zan being here with people who I can actually talk to about history without them falling asleep.'

'I know,' I said. 'I was always boring my friends to death, and getting told off for lecturing them, but when I find out something totally amaz about the past I just want to share it with someone.'

'I can imagine history isn't the number one topic of conversation on the average Military base.'

Alarm bells sounded in my head. I'd been off guard again, answering as myself, and I had to remember that I was JMK. 'Not really,' I said.

'Your parents are on assignment?' asked Fian.

'Planet First,' I said.

'Planet First!' He was obviously impressed. 'Whereabouts?'

'Classified.' I made a mental note that this could be a very useful response to difficult questions.

'Sorry.'

'Don't worry. Even if it wasn't classified, the planet still only has a number. It has to pass Planet First to get a name.'

'How long are your parents on assignment?'

I shrugged. 'Could be a year. Could be tomorrow if something too nasty shows up.'

'Scary,' said Fian. 'You have any brothers or sisters?'

'One brother,' I said. 'A year older than me.' I'd given JMK a pretty typical Military background. It was usual for Military families to have either two or three kids, all very close together in age. 'He's training in . . .' I suddenly remembered something. 'Oh chaos!'

'What?'

'I should have called someone, but it's a bit late.'

Fian checked the time. 'It's only seven in the evening.'

'Time zones,' I said. I handed him my glass of Fizzup. 'I'll be back.'

I sprinted to my room. Europe was five hours ahead of our dig site time zone. It was already midnight there. I daren't call Candace at this time of night, but I could call Issette. After yesterday's excitement, I had something I could easily chat about.

Not surprisingly, Issette was slow to answer my call. Eventually the screen responded, and showed her sitting on a bed in a sleep suit, looking tired and reproachful. 'I knew it before I even looked. If someone calls me at midnight, it has to be Jarra . . .'

I grinned. 'Blame the time zones. I had to talk to you.'

'So, how are you? Have the norms found out yet?'

I shook my head. 'Not yet. You'll never guess what happened yesterday. We were just starting a dig when . . .'

Issette covered her ears. 'No history lectures! Not at midnight! Bad Jarra!'

'Listen! There was a tower collapse and it buried ten people.' I told her all about what happened and how I'd been tag leader.

Issette gazed at me in amazement. 'How could you? I'd just have frozen with terror.'

'Jarra of the Military doesn't freeze with terror,' said an unexpected male voice. Keon strolled into view and sat on the bed next to Issette. He was wearing a sleep suit and his short black hair looked even more rumpled than usual. He was . . . He and Issette must be . . . I gaped at them.

'I told Keon,' Issette said. 'I was worried about you and . . . I hope you aren't angry.'

Angry? No. I was too busy being stunned to be angry. Issette and Keon? When had that started? How far had it got? Had they deliberately arranged to be on the same campus? They must be Twoing surely, or were they? If they were spending nights together then Issette would want a contract, on the other hand my mind reeled at the thought

114

of Keon and contracts in the same sentence. You're either a nice respectable contract boy or girl, or you aren't. Issette was, and Keon wasn't.

I pulled myself together. 'I'm not angry. You won't tell anyone, will you Keon?'

He shook his head, and gave me his usual look of lazy amusement. 'Of course not. Too much effort.'

'Anyway, I'm fine. I wanted to tell you about the rescue, but now I'd better let you . . . both . . . sleep.'

I hastily ended the call, and stared blankly at the wall of my room. I couldn't believe this. I knew that lots of kids went a bit wild when they first left Next Step, making the most of their new freedom, but . . . Issette was supposed to be sensible!

10

When I eventually went back to the dining room, Fian was still there guarding my pillow. He handed me back my Fizzup.

I looked down into the glass. 'I could do with something stronger.'

'If you mean alcohol, I don't think the dispensers can help,' he said. 'There's a choice of six flavours of Fizzup, or that brown muddy stuff the Gammans drink. There isn't even any frujit. Something wrong?'

'I'm in shock.'

'Something happened?'

I nodded.

'What could shock you after what you went through yesterday?'

'This is worse than yesterday.'

'What?' He stared at me. 'Don't tell me they found aliens at last. Can't be. If they'd found aliens then every lookup in the place would be screaming.'

At that moment, there was a chorus of chimes, bleeps and dings from around the room. My lookup chimed along with the rest.

'Oh nuke!' Fian gasped and frantically pulled out his

lookup. He stared at it. 'Solar storm warning . . . I'm sorry about the language, but . . .'

I'd collapsed on my pillow, and was clutching it and laughing hysterically. 'Your face when all the lookups bleeped . . .' I giggled madly into my pillow.

Fian looked down at me and gave a reluctant laugh. 'You nearly gave me a heart attack. I thought it really was aliens! I thought you'd got warned ahead of the news announcement because the Alien Contact programme was active and they were calling you in for . . . Can you stop laughing now?'

I shook my head, still giggling. 'Yes, I'm the first person they call when they meet aliens.'

Fian buried his face in his hands with a groan.

I slowly calmed down to the level of the occasional muffled squeak as a new giggle tried to surface.

He glanced warily at me. 'You safe yet?'

I nodded, biting my lip so I wouldn't laugh.

Fian frowned at his look up. 'The solar storm warning says we can expect portals to be off for three hours. That's scary. We had one on Hercules once, but the portals were only out for an hour. Even so, a couple of people died because they couldn't get to hospital.'

'Solar storms hit Earth several times a year,' I told him. 'Anything up to six hours portal outage is quite normal. It can be as long as three days for a really bad storm.'

'Really?' Fian looked suspicious. 'Three days! This is a joke, right?'

I shook my head. 'No, that can really happen on Earth. You remember all that stuff on the first day about Planet First?'

He nodded. 'You were amaz. Playdon called on you out of the blue, and you just calmly stood up and took us through the whole thing.'

I could feel myself blushing. 'Thanks. Actually, I rather enjoy giving lectures. Anyway, as Playdon said, Earth would have failed Planet First because of the level of solar storm activity. They reject planets where storms are bad enough to interfere with portals on a regular basis. I think the acceptable level is about one portal outage in fifteen years. On Earth, it's about once every couple of months.'

He pulled a face. 'How do people cope?'

I shrugged. 'The warning that just came in was a five hour one, which is about the minimum you get. Five hours is enough warning to close schools, send kids home, and get anyone likely to need medical attention into hospital. They have medical buildings in most settlements to deal with emergencies. Once the portals are off, they just wait it out.'

'Sounds a bit primitive,' said Fian.

'I'm sure it's covered in the legal stuff you accepted when you joined the course.'

Fian laughed. 'I should have read all 20,000 words of that instead of skipping it. I really wasn't prepared for the sort of thing that happened yesterday. Please tell me that doesn't happen every three months too.'

'Oh no.' I shuddered. 'That was very, very unusual. I think Playdon, the Earth 19 team, everyone in Dig Site Command . . . . Well, they must have all been throwing fits at a novice team being in the middle of a rescue. I bet there were a lot of private channel discussions going on that we couldn't hear, but they had no choice. They had to send us in, or leave the University Cassandra research team to die.'

I pulled a face. 'One of the experienced University Earth teams should have been in Sector 24 and leading the rescue. With Earth 19 able to arrive an hour later as backup, Dig Site Command would just have ordered us back to our dome. If another tower went down, they wouldn't want to have to nursemaid a Foundation course.'

'Could one of the other towers have fallen?'

I nodded. 'Didn't you realize? That was why Beowulf 4 were coming. They couldn't reach Cassandra 2 in time to help them, but if another tower came down and buried us too then Beowulf 4 would have arrived in time to dig us out.'

'I'm glad I didn't know . . .' muttered Fian.

'The first breakaway that Playdon reported was from tower one in a bunch of three. That labelled it as likely to fall, and that's why Dig Site Command had everyone in the area going to safe ground. Cassandra 2 would have been heading away from the tower cluster when tower three collapsed with no warning and buried them. Fortunately, they were outside the main debris area or the suits might not have coped. The suit closest to the main debris was the one that failed early.'

'Why don't they do something to prevent this?' asked Fian. 'Blow up the remaining towers maybe?'

I grinned. 'We're historians. We're supposed to study the remains of the past not destroy them. If we blow up towers, it wipes out any surviving artefacts in the area, and deeply buries any stasis boxes. Some boxes would be too difficult to ever reach after that, and ones with weakening power supplies would be destroyed by major rubble hits. It's a bit of a trade off. Risk to life against potential loss of history.'

'In theory, I agree history is worth dying for, but when you're actually out there . . .' Fian shook his head.

'You're unlikely to ever be in that situation again,' I reassured him. 'Only specialist research teams like Cassandra 2 are allowed to work on towers.'

'If this solar storm had happened yesterday . . . We couldn't have got people to hospital. The person with the crushed legs . . .' Fian broke off, looking queasy.

'That couldn't happen. Dig Site Command would never

let teams work the site during a portal outage. The minute a solar storm warning comes in, they evacuate the teams.'

'That's a relief.' Despite his words, Fian was still frowning. 'What do they do with off-world Handicapped babies during an Earth portal outage? Do they all die?'

I was pleased he'd said Handicapped babies not ape babies, and he sounded like he felt it would be a bad thing to let people like me die at birth. That put Fian a long way ahead of some off-world people I'd seen on the vids, especially the comedians out for an easy laugh at the expense of us apes.

'Oh no,' I said, 'they don't die. Solar storms mess up portal signals originating on Earth, but they can still receive incoming signals from off world. Remember it's the transmitting portal that does all the work, or we'd get nowhere exploring space. Planet First have special portals that fire through and create their own drop portal at the other end. It's one shot, and only holds the portal open for five seconds because there isn't a proper receiving portal to stabilize it, but that's enough to get a dart ship through.'

I shrugged. 'Earth usually cuts off regular incoming portal traffic during solar storms as a safety precaution, but they still take emergency ones like the incoming Handicapped babies. There's a very small risk of minor ill effects, but if they don't accept them they'll die in minutes.'

'You know an amazing amount of stuff about this,' said Fian. 'I didn't know any of it, and my parents study solar storms! I try not to listen when they talk about it but . . .'

I realized I'd been giving myself away. Only an ape girl would know this much about how they deal with solar storms on Earth. My big mouth! I could never resist the chance to lecture someone. I thought rapidly about the vids I'd watched.

'Remember that the Military run the solar power arrays. Solar storms are dangerous out in space because of the radiation. The crews have to lock down the array, disconnect it from the transmitter, and evacuate until the storm is over.'

'Oh I see. Of course . . .' said Fian. 'Yes, the Military must be even more worried about solar storms than the rest of us.'

I nodded. 'Other planetary arrays aren't so bad, but they have a busy time coping with all the storms Earth has. All the procedures are based on the five Earth arrays, because if they work for Earth, they'll work anywhere that has been through Planet First.'

I told myself sternly to remember not to open my big mouth and show off again. I thought I'd got away with it this time, but Fian was bright. If I did it again he would be bound to get suspicious. Acting my part was going to be a lot harder than I'd realized. I had to remember not only the things JMK should know, but the things she wouldn't.

'Since we got distracted by the alien first contact,' Fian said, 'I never found out what it was that had really shocked you more than yesterday. Your parents are all right?'

'They're fine,' I said. 'I'd called my best friend and . . . Well, she had someone male staying the night.'

Fian laughed.

'Yes, I know it sounds silly, but I wasn't expecting it, and you don't understand the complications.'

'What complications?' he asked.

'You know what they say. Some girls are contract girls and some aren't. Issette, my best friend, she's . . . Well, she's like me about these things. I always thought she'd want a Twoing contract before spending the night with someone.'

'Maybe they have one, and she hasn't told you. It might have only just happened. Did you ask?'

'I was far too embarrassed to ask questions. I'd been telling Issette about yesterday, and he walked into view in his sleep suit. After that, I just ended the call.'

'Well then,' said Fian. 'They could have registered today and your friend hasn't had time to tell you.'

'With anyone else I'd think that, but . . . Well, it's just that Keon isn't a contract boy.'

'Oh, you know the other party as well. You're sure he isn't the contract type? How well do you know him?'

I glibly wrote Keon into JMK's background story. He was the same age as me of course, but the odd year didn't matter, and it would help explain why I was so bothered by this. 'He's my brother.'

Fian frowned at his empty glass. 'I suddenly see why you're worried. Your best friend is a nice contract girl. Evil non-contract boy takes advantage of her. Evil non-contract boy being your brother makes life difficult. This needs more than Fizzup. I tell you what. I've a bottle of wine in my room. It's not enough to go round everyone, but we could sneak off, watch a vid together, and share the wine.'

I hesitated. Back in Next Step, we'd watch vids together in our rooms all the time. Sometimes all nine of us would wedge into one room, but Fian wasn't one of us. He wasn't even a friend from outside Next Step. He was a norm. Treating a norm like a real friend . . . On the other hand, after the strain of the rescue, and the shock of finding Keon was spending the night with Issette . . . Well, it was tempting to relax, and watching vids should be a lot safer than talking.

'Don't worry,' said Fian. 'I got the message. You're a nice contract girl. I promise to behave myself. I have two good reasons for that. One is that I'm a nice contract boy from ultra conservative Delta sector. The other is that I know you can throw me across the room.'

I giggled. For a norm, Fian wasn't bad. 'What vid do we watch?'

'What's your favourite series?'

'*Defenders*,' I admitted.

'I don't know it.'

'What's yours then?'

'*Stalea of the Jungle*.' Fian definitely blushed.

'Never heard of it.'

'Well,' said Fian. 'You show me an episode of *Defenders*. I'll show you an episode of *Stalea of the Jungle*. We both promise not to laugh too much. Deal?'

'Deal.'

We headed off, remembering to take our pillows and a couple of empty glasses with us. Fian's room was just as tiny as mine of course. I sat on the bed. Since there wasn't a chair, Fian tactfully settled himself on the floor. I set up the vid to play one of my favourite episodes of *Defenders*, while Fian poured out wine and passed me a glass.

I sipped at the wine. It's just about impossible to get alcohol when you live on Earth and in a Next Step, so this was my first try at it. I'd had all the school lectures about using alcohol sensibly of course, and I wasn't going to do anything silly. I'd turned down the offer of getting drunk and going to bed with Cathan, and it would be even more stupid to do it with Fian. For a norm, Fian wasn't bad, but he was a norm and I was an ape. Even if I hadn't told him a pack of lies about being Military, the complications didn't bear thinking about.

'So, what do I need to know about *Defenders*?' asked Fian.

The opening credits were rolling. 'Well, the story is that humanity has met hostile aliens. *Defenders* is set on a Military base in the forefront of the war.'

Fian laughed. 'You're Military and you like watching this? Doesn't it all seem a bit unrealistic to you?'

'It's fun,' I defended myself.

'You don't get irritated by them getting facts wrong?'

I shook my head. 'You aren't supposed to take it seriously.'

I pointed at the screen. 'This is the hero, played by Arrack San Domex.'

Fian went quiet and we watched the vid for a bit. It was the usual sort of plot for a *Defenders* episode. The base received an alert about an attack on a nearby planet and sent out a team to assist. As always, it was the same team that went out, led by the hero.

I glanced furtively between the hero and Fian. There was a definite resemblance. Fian had similar long straight blond hair, slim build, and fine features. Issette said she preferred men to have a rugged type of face. I couldn't see how Keon fitted into that. He definitely wasn't rugged, and I didn't think he was particularly handsome, but I knew him too well to be objective. When I looked at Keon, I just saw Keon.

The hero was now wrestling a green alien with tentacles. Fian made a choking noise. 'Is taking on aliens bare handed a standard Military tactic? Don't you normally wear impact suits and carry guns?'

I grinned. 'There's something silly in the plot to explain it, but really it's just an excuse for the hero to get his clothes shredded. Look!'

On screen, our hero's jacket was in tatters from the green tentacles. He threw the remains aside.

'His top goes next,' I grinned, unashamedly drooling.

Fian laughed as the hero's top was wrecked and thrown aside, and the hero continued to fight bare-chested. 'Don't the aliens shred his skin now?'

'Ah well,' I giggled. 'The touch of human skin wounds aliens.'

Fian blinked. 'How much more clothing does the hero lose? Logically, his best tactic fighting them would be . . .'

I grinned. 'It's not a Beta sector vid. The aliens only attack him above the waist.'

'How considerate of them. It's good the way they attack in such small numbers as well.'

I nodded. The hero slew the last alien, rescued his team member who had been about to be dissected, and the team went back to base.

'Best bit comes now,' I said.

'It does? I thought they'd won and it was over.'

'They always do a last scene of the hero back at his quarters in the evening,' I said.

'Aliens only attack in the daytime on this Military base so they can sleep nights?'

'Of course. All the planets are conveniently in the same time zone.' I grinned. 'Now we get the scene where the hero goes out on his balcony, dressed in a really skimpy sleep suit, and gazes soulfully at the stars.'

On the screen, Arrack San Domex gazed soulfully at the stars and the vid ended.

Fian laughed. 'Do Military bases have balconies?'

'No,' I said, happily, 'but that's not the point.'

'Well this has given me a whole new view of Military life,' said Fian. 'It also means I'm going to be much less embarrassed while you watch *Stalea of the Jungle*. Would you like another glass of wine?'

'I'd better not. I've never had it before, and I don't want to get totally powered. You go ahead though.'

Fian shook his head. 'My parents don't like alcohol, so I'm not used to it either. The first thing I did when I was 18 at Year End was to go out and buy a bottle of wine. It's a traditional thing on Hercules, but I was so busy getting ready to come to my course I never had time to actually drink it.'

I remembered something and went pink.

Fian looked at me suspiciously. 'What was the first thing you did when you were 18?'

I went pinker.

He shook his head. 'You didn't? You're a nice contract girl!'

'No!' I giggled. 'Cathan wanted to, but I threw him across the room. I just watched a Beta vid. I was curious . . .'

'Cathan and you are?'

'Not are, were. Definitely past tense. And we weren't very much to start with.'

'Good.' Fian set up the vid. 'Now the plot of this is that a world got into Colony Ten phase. The colonists did their ten years but the portal failed, people had forgotten about them, and they were just stuck there.'

'Yes.' I giggled. 'The Military forget planets all the time. I suppose they also forgot the mandatory daily contact with the colonists, and to give them a backup portal.'

'Exactly,' said Fian. 'The colony survived as best they could, cut off from civilization. It's now two hundred years later, and Stalea is a heroic girl who defends her village from the hostile beasts in the jungle.'

'These are the hostile beasts that the incompetent Planet First team didn't notice before they cleared the planet for Colony Ten?'

'You've got the idea.'

'And Stalea fights them off single handed? That's a big job isn't it?'

'Stalea is quite a girl,' said Fian. 'You remind me of her a bit. She has a male friend who helps her out. They're sort of Twoing, but they argue a lot. Ready?'

'I can't wait.'

Stalea of the Jungle started. Stalea had a limited wardrobe of strategically placed fake animal skins. I examined her closely, trying to see why I reminded Fian of her. I was fairly tall, but not as tall as Stalea. Our hair was a different colour. I didn't wear animal skins. I really couldn't see it.

Stalea and her lover beat off a couple of savage creatures

that had been threatening their village. The lover also favoured the minimal animal skin sort of wardrobe. Nice legs, but not really my type.

Stalea and her lover now had an argument. I didn't quite follow what it was about.

'There's this other girl in the village that keeps being friendly to him, and Stalea is possessive,' Fian helpfully explained. 'He's not interested in the other girl, but Stalea keeps thinking he is.'

'I see.' I watched as they had another fight with a beast and then another argument with each other. The row seemed to be building up to something.

'This is the good bit,' said Fian, leaning forward and watching eagerly. 'It happens just about every episode.'

Stalea appeared to lose patience totally, grabbed her lover, threw him across the jungle clearing and pinned him to the ground.

I blinked and realized something. 'I remind you of her because of the throwing him around!'

Fian nodded.

'I don't do it very often,' I defended myself.

'Stalea does,' said Fian, 'and I'm a nice contract boy from Delta who gets a bit powered at the thought of a beautiful girl throwing him across the room, pinning him down and . . .'

I watched Stalea and her lover demonstrating the unfinished 'and' part of the sentence. The credits rolled and the vid ended just as things were getting really interesting.

I looked at Fian, and burst out laughing. 'Throwing men across the room . . .'

He grinned back at me. 'Aliens ripping off the hero's clothes . . .'

'True.' I stood up and collected my pillow. 'I'd better say good night. We'll be working the site again tomorrow.'

'Yes, you may have more lives to save so you'd better get your sleep.' Fian opened the door. 'I enjoyed *Defenders*, so thank you.'

'*Stalea* wasn't that bad either, so thank you too.'

As I went out, I could see Fian was watching for me to pause and give him the opening for a kiss, or maybe he was hoping I'd throw him across the room and leap on him. Either way, he was out of luck. I walked down the corridor to my own room and I didn't look back.

Fian was great. He loved history. He could laugh at himself instead of sulk the way Cathan had always done. He even looked a bit like Arrack San Domex. Fian was the man of my dreams, but he was a norm and I was only an ape. He liked JMK, not me, and JMK didn't even exist. When he found out the truth, he was going to hate me.

11

Team 1 sat together at breakfast the next morning, and Fian suggested that he and I could spend another evening sharing the rest of the wine and watching history vids together. It sounded nice, but I remembered the norm and ape thing, and just shrugged my shoulders. I then ignored Fian completely and made myself smile and look interested while a delighted Krath took his chance to babble idiocies at me and suggest that I watch vids with him instead. Out of the corner of my eye, I could see Fian's face change expression from disappointment to confusion, and on through annoyance into grim resignation. He'd got the message.

Dalmora wasn't her usual calm and confident self that morning. Krath finally paused for breath long enough for me to ask her what was wrong. I discovered she'd stayed up specially to see the dome portal go into lockdown mode as the solar storm hit. Half the other norms had done the same. They sat around in the dining room for the following three hours, having panicky chats about the fact they were totally cut off from the rest of the universe, until the portal was back on.

Amaz! Totally amaz! Why would anyone deliberately stay awake for hours so they could panic about not being able to use a portal? If they hadn't got the solar storm warning, they'd have been fast asleep and never have known the portal was out of action.

Dalmora could tell I was completely grazzed. 'It must seem silly to you, but most of us just aren't able to cope with things the way you do. We don't have your confidence, and when the portal wasn't working we felt so isolated. I've never been anywhere without a working portal before.'

That grazzed me too. Dalmora Rostha, daughter of Ventrak Rostha, felt she didn't have as much self confidence as me.

'If we really got cut off in a place like this, if the portal was damaged by the solar storm and didn't start working again, what could we do?' she asked.

She was genuinely scared, so I tried to be reassuring without showing I thought she was an idiot. 'Portals automatically lock down during a storm to prevent damage to themselves or anyone trying to travel. Even if there was some freak damage to the portal, we could still call for help. The comms system is totally separate from the portal network.'

'I don't know that sort of thing,' Dalmora said shakily. 'We don't get solar storms back home on Danae.'

I tried to explain. 'Well, comms portals are tiny, low power things. They stay open all the time, even in solar storms. The odd bit of interference on a mail message doesn't matter. When a proper portal sends out a signal to transmit a person, that's very different. It's far more complicated and it has to be perfect or what arrives the other end is . . . unpleasant.

'So,' I continued, 'if our portal didn't work, we'd just call for help. Someone would bring a new portal to us, or we

130

could go to another portal ourselves. There are several dozen other domes round the New York Dig Site, all with their own portals. We've plenty of hover sleds, they aren't fast but we could get to another dome easily. It would probably only take half an hour or so. We could even get across country to the nearest settlement, though that would take hours. There's really nothing to worry about.'

I discovered my audience wasn't just Dalmora. Most of the class were listening to me with anxious faces. They seemed to gradually relax as the sense of my words sunk in.

We spent a frustrating morning on the dig site, where we dug out two underground cavities that might have contained stasis boxes but didn't, and ended up covered in some weird reddish brown dust that clung lovingly to our impact suits. Playdon spent at least fifteen minutes running sensor tests on the stuff, before announcing that it didn't seem in any way hazardous but he was still putting the lot of us through decontamination before letting us enter the dome or open our suits.

'But isn't this a waste of time?' Joth asked, as we all queued up outside our dome.

'No,' I chorused in unison with Playdon, Fian, and what sounded like Krath. My head snapped round to check, and I saw Playdon looking in Krath's direction as well. Yes, it really had been him.

Playdon had been attaching a decontamination hose to a bulky gray tank set against our dome wall, but now he stopped. 'I really have to ask . . . Fian, why did you say that?'

'The dust is metallic and attracted to our impact suits,' said Fian. 'You gave us all the safety lectures about magnetic hazards being dangerous because they mess up the low level magnetic field in the impact suit material. My guess is the dust is being attracted to that low level magnetic field, and if it gets inside the suit then it could damage it, make the material trigger unpredictably, or fail to trigger at all.'

'Very good,' said Playdon. 'Even if the metallic dust didn't actually damage the suit, it would be hard to remove and make it hideously uncomfortable to wear. I don't want to have to send all our suits off for reconditioning. Krath, what was your reason?'

'I've seen ordinary rubbish heaps with dangerous stuff in them. Those ruins are extra big rubbish heaps, so there could be extra dangerous stuff.'

'I'd never thought of it quite that way before,' said Playdon, 'but your conclusion is correct.' He turned to me. 'Jarra?'

'Dig site rule 1. If you don't understand what's happening, be extra careful,' I said.

'Exactly,' said Playdon.

He finished attaching the hose and sprayed everyone, and we all trooped into the dome. The disinfectant smell of the decontaminant haunted us all through lunch and the afternoon lectures, so we picked strongly flavoured food at dinner and drowned out the disinfectant with the odours of spices from five different sectors. I didn't recognise half of them, including the bright blue sauce that Krath was eagerly shovelling down his throat, but I didn't risk advertising my ignorance by asking about them.

After dinner, I saw Fian approaching me, so I headed for my room on the pretext of getting a cushion. When I got back to the hall, I saw him sitting by one wall with another Deltan boy, so I went to sit by the opposite wall and chat to Amalie.

'Dalmora's amaz,' she said, nodding at where the Alphan was sitting and softly strumming her guitar.

'She's really good,' I said. 'Someone tried to teach me to play once. We were on London Fringe, and it rained for three solid days. By the end of it, everyone made me promise never to try and learn to play the guitar ever again. I'm not even remotely musical.'

'You seem to have spent a lot of time on dig sites,' said Amalie.

I realized I'd opened my big mouth again, and hastily tried to divert the conversation away from my past. 'Guitar playing is a tradition on dig sites, like light bulb jokes.'

'What's a light bulb joke?' asked Amalie.

'A light bulb was part of ancient glows used back in the twentieth century. I think they were some sort of primitive power cell. Anyway, a dig team found an ancient book of jokes about changing light bulbs, and ever since then people on dig sites have made light bulb jokes. Changing a light bulb was apparently very easy to do, and the jokes . . . Well, it's easiest to explain by giving an example.'

I paused and thought for a moment. 'How many Military does it take to change a light bulb? This is where you say that you don't know, and repeat the question.'

Amalie looked confused. 'I don't know. How many Military does it take to change a light bulb?'

'Under Military regulations section 39, subsection 8.1, one officer, or two cadets in training, should be an adequate personnel allocation to change a light bulb.'

She thought about it for a moment, and then started laughing. Fian had been watching us thoughtfully and now stood up and wandered over.

'What's the joke?' he asked.

I explained the light bulb thing, and repeated the joke. After that, the whole class got interested, and I had to say the whole thing a third time in a louder voice.

'How many Alphans does it take to change a light bulb?' asked Dalmora.

We all told her that we didn't know.

'Alphans don't change light bulbs,' she said. 'Light bulbs

133

are irreplaceable relics of our cultural history, and Alpha sector is honoured to care for them on behalf of humanity.'

Everyone laughed.

'How many Betans does it take to change a light bulb?' asked Lolmack.

We warily admitted that we didn't know.

'One to change the light bulb, two to have sex with it, and three to make the vid,' said Lolmack.

I hadn't even realized that Playdon was in the room, so I was startled to hear his voice from behind me.

'How many Gammans does it take to change a light bulb?'

We gave the ritual response.

'One to change the light bulb, and two to check if being too friendly with it is against the Gamman moral code,' said Playdon in a pointed voice.

We weren't too sure whether we should be laughing at that one. Fian helpfully spoke on behalf of Delta sector.

'How many Deltans does it take to change a light bulb?'

We gave the required response.

'Ten to research a new improved light bulb and one to change it.'

It was definitely safe to laugh at that, so it got a good audience reaction.

'How many Epsilons does it take to change a light bulb?' asked Amalie.

Joth decided to speed things up. 'We don't know,' he yelled solo.

'Planets in Epsilon sector don't have light bulbs yet, but they're in the five-year development plan,' she said, with a perfectly serious face that got us all laughing helplessly.

I thought we'd finished then but Krath decided to take a hand.

'How many apes does it take to change a light bulb?'

I froze and sat silently cursing the exo. Around me, I could hear several people calling out that they didn't know. Nuke Krath, and nuke the rest of them as well. What were they going to say now? I'd heard plenty of ape jokes on the sector vid channels, and some of them were really . . .

'If you start giving apes light bulbs,' said Krath, 'they'll want the vote next.'

It could have been much worse, the joke wasn't about how ugly apes were, or how they smelled bad, but I'd no idea what was coming next. If this was a vid, then I'd turn it off and walk away, but it wasn't. This was happening right here in front of me, and these were my classmates not strangers.

There seemed to be quite a few people laughing. I bent over, pretending I had a problem with my shoe, so I could hide my face and avoid seeing theirs while I tried to think what to do. This was my moment. I could keep up my pretence of being JMK and make a calmly reasoned argument on behalf of the Handicapped, or I could openly tell the class what I was and scream abuse at them just the way that I'd planned.

'Don't they get to vote?' asked Joth. 'I know every planet has its own system, and voting age can vary between 16 and 25, but . . .'

'Of course apes don't vote,' said Krath. 'Why would Earth need a representative in Parliament of Planets, let alone Sector High Congress?'

'To take care of their interests,' said Joth.

'Hospital Earth does all that,' said Krath. 'It's not as if apes are capable of understanding sector politics, and they're perfectly well cared for. My dad says the funding for Hospital Earth is ridiculously generous. Apes should be adequately housed and fed, but treating them like real humans is . . .'

I still hadn't worked out what I was going to say, but I couldn't sit here silently listening to Krath dismiss me as not really human. I raised my head, and opened my mouth, but the cool, sarcastic voice of Lolmack cut in ahead of me.

'The Handicapped are legally human,' he said, 'but the rules on that certainly need to be tightened up. It's shocking what qualifies as human. Krath does, for example, and you only need to look at him to know he's really a Cassandrian skunk that's been trained to walk on two legs.'

'What?' Krath gazed at Lolmack in shock. 'Why you nuking Betan, I'll . . .'

He scrambled to his feet and raised his fists to attack. I saw Lolmack stand up as well, shed his usual carefully negligent pose, and suddenly appear taller and far more dangerous as he laughed at Krath.

'Am I supposed to be scared of you, infant?'

Playdon was suddenly standing between the pair of them. 'Stop this, both of you!'

Krath hesitated for a second before letting his hands drop. 'But he called me a . . .'

'You were making jokes about who was and wasn't human,' said Lolmack, with an expression of wide eyed innocence, 'and I just joined in. Don't you have a sense of humour, Krath?'

Krath turned to Playdon. 'Are you going to let him get away with that?'

Playdon had an angry line to his mouth as he looked back at him. 'I have a choice here. I can accept this as one of the genuine misunderstandings that arise between students raised in different cultures, or I can treat it as a deliberate insult from Lolmack and an attempted physical attack by you. The second option means you both get official conduct warnings. Which would you prefer, Krath?'

136

Krath opened his mouth, shut it again, and stood there in frustrated silence. Playdon watched him for a few seconds, before nodding and speaking again.

'In that case, I'll just say that everyone should be careful what jokes they make, and that particularly includes jokes about the Handicapped.'

I'd been sitting there like an idiot, feeling embarrassingly relieved that Lolmack had chosen this particular moment to cause trouble again, but now I had a flash of panic. Was Playdon going to tell them . . .?

'You should remember we're all guests of the Handicapped while we're on this dig site and this planet,' he continued. 'Now I suggest Lolmack and Krath should both go to their rooms.'

Lolmack shrugged. 'As you wish.'

He strolled out of the hall, and Krath followed him a moment later, his face and body language reminding me of a sulking toddler. Playdon went after them, presumably to make sure they didn't have a fight in the corridor, and there was an awkward silence before Dalmora stood up.

'Lecturer Playdon is right. We are guests here on Earth and it's discourteous to mock our hosts.' She paused. 'It's late, so I'm going to bed now.'

She headed for the door, and Lolia went after her, then a procession of students that included Amalie and Fian. A few of the Gammans clustered together in a tight knit group, talking in words that were loud enough for me to hear but didn't make any sense. They had to be talking in Gamman dialect rather than Language.

I forced myself to stand up, escaped from the hall, ignored an attempt at conversation from Amalie, and went straight to the refuge of my room.

I lay awake in bed for long hours that night, caught up in burning fury and an odd sense of shame. Why hadn't I screamed my anger at Krath instead of sitting there, like a good little ape, meekly accepting whatever the superior humans chose to say about me? Of course, I hadn't been expecting the conversation. If I'd had time to think, then I could have said . . .

I spent a long time pointlessly trying to work out what I should have said and when, and failing. I was feeling confused. I'd always assumed all exos despised apes, and hated them indiscriminately for it. Now Lolmack had proved he was different, and Dalmora had made her little protest, and a lot of the class had walked out of the door after her.

It was hard to judge Playdon's position on this. He'd made that speech about the Handicapped, but he was our lecturer and his actions could have been forced on him by the Gamman moral code. I remembered the Cassandra 2 rescue. When someone had asked if the apes of Earth 19 would be any help, Playdon had replied with a savage note in his voice. I didn't know if his anger was at the question, or at the fact he needed the help of apes.

I rubbed my forehead, as if the physical action could somehow help me think straight. Was I in the right or the wrong here? Krath had said some rude things about apes, but I'd only heard him because I'd deliberately come here and told the class a whole lot of cold blooded lies. I'd treated them badly, and some of those people deserved it, but some didn't.

I felt . . . I didn't know how I felt. I've always been good at physical things, and bad at dealing with emotions, and it hurt to think about this stuff. This wasn't just about what the norms thought of apes, it was also about how I thought about myself, and . . .

I dragged myself out of bed in the morning, ate breakfast

with an oddly subdued and silent class, and forced myself into my impact suit and outside with the others. It was when we reached our work site, that Playdon took my tag leader spot away.

12

I couldn't believe it. I was just looking at the rubble, assessing the hazards, when Playdon told me to take over Amalie's heavy lift sled, gave her my tag gun and hover belt, and started instructing her in how to use them. He'd replaced me without a word of warning or explanation. I stood there watching them for one shocked moment, and then hurried over to take my place on the heavy lift sled. I wasn't in a rush to do what I was told, but I sure as chaos didn't want to stand around and give anyone the chance to talk to me.

Once I was safely alone on the sled, the pain and hurt hit me like a falling tower. Why had Playdon done this? I'd learned to respect the man, and it felt like he'd stabbed me in the back. I'd thought I was on good terms with him now. I knew he still didn't understand what an ape girl was doing on his course, but I'd got the idea he trusted me to have decent reasons. I'd actually felt a bit ashamed about that, but now . . .

I hadn't done anything stupid on the dig site, so Playdon had to be punishing me for last night. Nuke that for justice! I might have been the one to start the light bulb jokes, but I was the victim, not the criminal here. I'd been a great tag leader, helped train the rest of the class to use impact suits, done every single thing Playdon asked of me, even risked my life for Cassandra 2, but none of that mattered. Nothing could change the fact I was an ape, so he'd used me to help train the class and now he was dumping me. I was getting shuffled away from key spot and on to a heavy lift sled. In a few days, or weeks, I'd probably be shuffled again, to get me away from team 1 entirely.

I was white hot with anger now, as I sat there watching Amalie shooting tags at rocks. This was completely unfair and I wasn't going to meekly accept it. I'd come on this class to make a point. I'd planned to fool the exos, scream abuse at them, and walk away. It was time to do exactly that, but I had enough control left to realize I'd make a complete nardle of myself if I did it here in the middle of a dig site. How would I get out of here afterwards? Walking all the way back to the dome on the uneven clearway surface would be killingly hard work in an impact suit, and the class would probably overtake me on the way past, sitting on their sleds and jeering at the ape trudging behind them.

There wasn't any other way to leave. Playdon wouldn't stand there watching while I stole a sled, and Dig Site Command wouldn't activate an emergency evac portal just because a Foundation course student was throwing a tantrum.

All right, I told myself. I'll sit here like a well behaved, downtrodden ape and do as I'm told, but when we get back to the dome . . . I pictured it, trying to plan exactly what I'd say, but there was no glow of satisfaction as I did it. Things had changed since I started my war against the exos. I'd planned to vent my fury and frustration on a bunch of strangers, and now I knew these people. I didn't want to shout insults at them. Krath might deserve it, but could I really yell abuse at Fian, Dalmora and Amalie, walk away, and feel good about myself afterwards?

No, I decided, it wasn't going to be the exit I'd planned when I was back in Next Step. When the class were back at the dome, I'd pack and I'd leave, but I'd do it with dignity. I'd slip away to the portal when everyone was at dinner, or when they were asleep.

I heard Amalie calling me to shift some rocks, and carefully moved them as instructed, then started to calculate time zones. I was in Earth America, so I could portal out in the middle of the night and arrive in Earth Europe in the early morning. I'd have to find somewhere to stay, contact Candace, and . . .

'It's not working, is it?'

Playdon's voice made me jump twice. Firstly, when I heard it. Secondly, when I realized he wasn't talking over the comms link, but was standing right next to me.

'No, it isn't,' he answered his own question. 'I can hear the stress in her voice. Pity. Amalie has the abilities I need in my team 2 tag leader, but she's not comfortable taking a leading role on the dig site and I daren't push her. She's under enough strain trying to keep up with the academic side of the course after her very patchy schooling in Epsilon. I'll just have to let her stay in her familiar territory of working a heavy lift sled.'

I didn't say a word. I couldn't even make a noise. Playdon was testing Amalie for his team 2 tag leader spot. I should have known that. I would have known that if I hadn't been a paranoid ape, with her nerves on edge, and her brain stupid with fatigue after a sleepless night.

'So, you get to keep your current team, Jarra,' continued Playdon. 'Krath's reliable on a heavy lift, but he's not an option as tag leader because he never stops to think before doing things. Dalmora hasn't the physical strength needed for tag leading, and Fian has just calmly told me that being tag leader wouldn't suit him but he might consider having my job as team leader. Fortunately, the lad realizes he needs a few years experience before he can do that.'

I gave a startled laugh.

'It's certainly not impossible. Team leaders usually start their careers as either tag leader or tag support, and Fian's the right type to . . .'

Playdon let that sentence trail off, tapped his lookup, and an array of small disembodied heads suddenly appeared in front of me. With a flick of his fingers, he sent a group of five of them off to the left. I automatically looked at those faces and saw they were team 1. Fian was looking worried about something, I was wrinkling my nose in concentration, and Dalmora's hair was filled with glowing lights. My guess was the holos had been taken on our first day on the course, maybe during our meet and greet.

'What made you pick Fian for your tag support?' asked Playdon.

I was still a bit of a mess from my panic earlier, but I'd regained enough sense not to mention Fian's resemblance to Arrack San Domex. 'He seemed sensible and intelligent, sir.'

'He is. Any suggestions for team 2 members?'

I pointed out a couple of Deltans, and Kai from Gamma.

'Interesting,' said Playdon. 'I'd considered two of them myself, but I hadn't thought of Kai.'

'She's quiet, but very bright. I was thinking she might be good on sensors,' I said.

Playdon nodded. 'I'll add them to my list and see if your instinct is right again.'

He went off and collected a group of impact suit clad figures together. There were ten of them, so Playdon was obviously trying to fill places on both team 2 and team 3. He spent a long time talking to them, and I was glad of the chance to sit in peace and recover from my emotional overload.

Team 1 spent the rest of that morning training Playdon's candidates for teams 2 and 3. My job was to teach four of them how to use tag guns and hover belts. Playdon must be unsure which of the four had the makings of a tag leader, or possibly thinking ahead to teams 4 and 5. Teaching a novice how to point and fire a tag gun is straightforward, apart from the constant hazard of ricochets from badly aimed tags, but I was still relieved when it was time to head back to the dome. I'd been very tired when we set out for the dig site, and after my panic attack over losing key spot, and the usual strain of working in an impact suit for several hours, I felt on the point of collapse.

I actually lay down on the transport sled for the trip back, which helped a bit, but I clearly still didn't look too good when I took off my suit, because I found Dalmora lying in wait for me when I came out of the shower.

'Jarra, are you ill?'

I just wanted to be left alone, but I could see she was genuinely concerned, so I could hardly tell her to nuke off. 'I'm just tired,' I said. 'I didn't sleep well.'

I regretted my words the minute I'd said them. I was an utter nardle. I'd just told Dalmora that I'd had a sleepless night after Krath's ape joke. I might just as well put up a banner telling people I was an ape. I hastily came out with an excuse.

'I was caught by a few rocks when that wall collapsed yesterday morning. I've got impact suit bruising, and it's very sore.'

Dalmora frowned. 'You should go to Hospital Earth America Casualty and get it checked.'

'It's only bruising,' I said, heading down the corridor to my room.

She followed me, not just down the corridor but into my room, and stood there silently with folded arms.

144

I sighed. 'Dalmora, it's only a bruise. Look.'

I tugged aside the edge of my skintight to show part of a deep black and blue bruise on my left side, which had the distinctive crosshatched lines left by impact suit material triggering hard. It wasn't particularly significant or painful. I was a tag leader, so I just about always had at least one major impact suit bruise, as well as a scattering of the small brown circular bruises left by ricocheting tags, but Dalmora had obviously never seen anything like it before.

'That looks awful. You should get it treated.'

There was no real need to make a fuss about it, impact suit bruises always look more dramatic than they are, but since it was the perfect explanation for anything odd in my behaviour . . .

'There's no need for me to go to casualty, but it does hurt, so could you do me a favour and ask Playdon for a size 7 fluid patch.'

'A size 7 fluid patch.' Dalmora repeated the words.

She vanished off out of the door. There was no point in getting dressed, so I tugged on a robe, sat on my bed, and waited. After a few minutes, Dalmora came back, and I was startled to see she'd brought Playdon with her.

'Dalmora tells me you were hurt yesterday, Jarra,' he said. 'You should have told me at once.'

Chaos take it, my simple excuse was getting out of hand. Fortunately . . . 'It's only an impact suit bruise, sir, just one of the sore ones. I'd show you, but it's under my skintight so . . .'

I swear the man actually blushed. 'I didn't mean to imply . . . You're sure you haven't cracked a rib?'

'Perfectly sure, sir. I've cracked a rib once, and I know how it feels. This is just a bad bruise.'

He handed over the sealed packet containing the fluid patch. 'You know how to put this in place and activate it?'

I nodded.

'If you're still in any pain after the treatment cycle completes, then you're going straight to casualty. I have a duty of care towards my students. Understand?'

'Yes, sir.'

Playdon left, but Dalmora hesitated. 'Do you need any help with the patch?' she asked.

'No, thank you,' I said. 'I've done this before, and since it's somewhere a bit private . . .'

My hint at my statutory right to personal modesty worked its magic as well with Dalmora as it had with Playdon. Dalmora instantly retreated, and I was left alone in my room feeling the worst kind of fraud. Playdon was concerned about me. Dalmora had been so dreadfully nice.

I really and truly hate to admit I'm wrong, but sometimes I have to. Dalmora Rostha, the gifted daughter of Ventrak Rostha, born to be an adored Alphan vid personality of the future, and a living embodiment of everything I envied, was nice. I'd fought the idea for as long as I could, but she really was. It was truly sickening that someone so perfect should actually be nice as well, but . . .

I sighed, stripped off my robe and skintight, and went over to the mirror. I didn't really need the patch, but it seemed vaguely more honest to use it. I ripped open the packet, unfolded the patch, and positioned it carefully over my bruise. When I was sure it was right, I pulled the activation loop, and gasped as the edges of the patch fastened to my skin and the icy chill of the fluid hit me.

'One, two, three . . .' I dutifully followed the instructions and counted up to twenty before getting dressed. As always, the feel of the fluid felt disturbingly cold and alien under normal clothes. I picked up my lookup and checked the time. We'd returned to our dome a little earlier than usual so I could afford to rest a while in my room.

I lay back on my bed, and messed around with my lookup, checking my mail and credit balance, and then setting it to bring up a holo gallery like the one Playdon had shown me on the dig site. I wasn't showing the heads of my classmates of course, but of my friends from Next Step and school. Candace, and assorted other adults who'd been important in my life, were there as well. I was alone among the exos, confused about whether they were the villains or I was, and in a mood to even feel nostalgic about the Principal of my Next Step.

I'd just set the holo heads to drift randomly around the room, when there was a tap on the door.

'It's unlocked,' I yelled.

As the door opened, I reached for my lookup to turn off the holos, but realized there was no need. Who could tell the heads of civilians from Military?

'Playdon wondered if we should bring you some food.'

I'd expected it to be Dalmora again, but it was Fian, his eyes hesitating between me and the drifting holo heads.

'No need,' I said. 'I'll come to the hall and eat there. Dalmora rather overreacted. The bruising isn't that bad, it just kept me awake last night.'

Fian frowned. 'If I'd been faster, got you out of the way of that collapsing wall . . .'

Now I felt really guilty. 'It's not your fault. I'd tagged my rocks, was backing out of the way to let the heavy lifts shift them, and got too close to a wall that wasn't as stable as it looked. I made a nardle mistake, and you were very fast and stopped me getting buried.'

Fian appeared unconvinced, but nodded and dropped the issue. He gestured at the heads. 'Is Issette one of these?'

'Yes.' I pointed to Issette.

'And Keon?'

I pointed to Keon.

Fian looked puzzled. 'There isn't much of a family resemblance.'

I was a nardle. I'd forgotten I'd said Keon was my brother. You only had to look at him to know we couldn't possibly be related. The shape of the eyes was . . .

'He's adopted.' I added yet another lie to the hundreds I'd already told. 'His parents were close friends of mine, so when they were killed . . .'

'Oh, I see.'

I grabbed my lookup, turned off the holo display, and stood up. 'Let's go and eat.'

13

Lunch was a hideously embarrassing affair. Playdon asked if the pain was easing. Fian brought my food over for me. Dalmora told everyone how terribly bruised I was. Amalie offered to make me some strange herbal drink from her home planet, Miranda, that was supposed to counteract fatigue and hangovers. Even the evil Krath insisted on bringing me more glasses of Fizzup than either norm or ape could possibly drink.

I was relieved when lunch was over and everyone, except poor injured Jarra who was only allowed to sit and watch, shuffled the tables and chairs ready for the afternoon lectures. Playdon was sticking to the wise approach of us working the site for a few hours in the morning, and having classes in the afternoon. Just being in an impact suit is tiring, every movement takes extra effort, and after a few hours of it you're going to make more mistakes than usual.

I have no idea what Playdon talked about for the first hour of the afternoon. It could have been pre-history sex for all I know. I wasn't in pain, but I was very tired and embarrassed about making all this fuss over a simple bruise, and I couldn't seem to keep my own head under control.

My brain was totally distracted, replaying all the events since I'd joined the class. Why in chaos had I got myself into this mess, and how was I going to get out of it? It was only when the entire class seemed to bounce with excitement that I came out of my private world and rejoined them.

'That would be totally zan!' said Fian, alive with enthusiasm.

'Just totally!' Everyone cried out.

What the chaos was going on? I sat up, paid attention, and tried to pick up clues on what I'd missed.

'I think so too,' said Lecturer Playdon. 'I know we're supposed to be covering pre-history, and this is much later than that, but I can't resist it either. I've been waiting for this just as impatiently as any of you. So, Dalmora, please go ahead. You have an eager audience waiting.'

Everyone sat up straight in their flexiplas chairs, eyes on Dalmora as she stood up and went to the front of the hall. She turned on the big vid wall, inserted a chip, and started it playing. The wall flashed with some strange white symbols for a moment.

'This is a copy taken straight after final editing,' said Dalmora, 'and those are the edit codes. The vid itself will start in a minute.'

She went and sat down. I'd worked out what was going on now. Dalmora must have an early copy of one of her father's vids. With the class so excited, this had to be . . . I was grazzed!

It was! The familiar amazing graphic sequence started running, showing the history time line. Then the words appeared. 'Ventrak Rostha presents . . .' Those faded and were replaced by ones in larger letters. *'History of Humanity.'*

People living everywhere from Alpha to the first Kappa colony worlds know Ventrak Rostha's series on the history of humanity. The critics love it for its excellence, the historians love it for its accuracy, and ordinary people just love watching the way it brings history to life. Everyone waits eagerly for the next vid in the series. The next one was due out in three weeks, but we were getting to see it early. My tiredness was banished by excitement.

I waited, breathless, as the twisting timeline with its background of stars returned. The view zoomed in and focused on it, and we could hear the famous voice of Ventrak Rostha setting the scene. 'Exodus,' he said, 'the century that emptied Earth.'

The time line passed by, then a date flashed suddenly bright. '2409, the Earth data net failed,' said Ventrak Rostha. 'So much history, science, medicine, and technology lost in a jumble of data corruption. The mother planet had been bled to death by the effort of seeding the new worlds, and those new worlds were barely strong enough to cope alone. We did too much, and we did it too fast. Alpha, Beta and the beginning of Gamma sector in one century was too great an effort. Humanity even came close to losing portal technology. Vital components had only been made on Earth. We were close to a return to barbarism.'

The time line was moving on again now. 'Exodus was followed by two centuries when humanity struggled to survive and rebuild,' Ventrak Rostha continued. 'Few portals could handle the distance between sectors, and they were reserved for priority traffic only. Current messaging technology was yet to be invented. Sector culture began to diverge. Humanity was fragmenting.'

We could watch the time line moving on as he spoke, with its thousands of tiny flickering pictures of the past. Another date flashed brightly. '2605,' said Ventrak Rostha. 'Beta sector declares the Second Roman Empire under its first Emperor, Haran Augustus. Military personnel, together with Alphan and Gamman civilians, are asked to leave Betan territory. Military personnel on the space solar arrays supplying power to the Betan planets are allowed to remain for five years to complete transfer to Betan personnel.'

The timeline moved on a little to another flashing date. '2610. The last Military personnel leave Beta sector and the Second Roman Empire stands alone. Humanity is divided. The spectre of mass warfare had been left behind in pre-history, but now it looms again.'

It was emotional and dramatic, but that's why everyone watches this series. Ventrak Rostha brings history alive and makes you care about it. Even Issette is a fan. If Ventrak Rostha can make Issette voluntarily watch a history vid, then he's really good. She never wants to listen to a word of the stuff I try and tell her.

The timeline moved on to another date. 'It is now 2658. The second Emperor, Kyath Augustus, dies suddenly. His elder son, Faron Augustus, becomes the third Emperor of the Second Roman Empire and is crowned with laurels on Zeus, but the younger brother Ceron mounts a challenge.

'The year is 2658,' repeated Ventrak Rostha.

That was the end of the introduction. The series timeline vanished, and the vid individual title appeared. 'Artemis.'

Ventrak Rostha took us through it all, and I couldn't spot a single factual error. The third Emperor sending troops to capture his rival brother, and the brother taking refuge on the Artemis solar power array and holding the whole planet hostage.

'It's not a solar power array,' muttered Krath. 'Sol is Earth's star, not the star Artemis orbits.'

We all told the class pedant to shut up. Yes, Sol is Earth's star, but I really can't see the point in whining about phrases like solar power and solar storm. Language moved on when we portalled to other worlds. People looked up at the sky and still said the sun is hot today, they didn't start giving technical star names. Every planet has their great sail arrays in space that collect their power, and they all call it solar power. Language evolves, and people like Krath should just shut up and accept it.

We all concentrated on the vid as it built up to the turning point. We looked at pictures of the big sails, with their attendant transmitter, and the great power beam going down to the receiving station on the planet below.

Ventrak Rostha was talking on the vid again. 'Emperor Faron Augustus refuses to step down. His brother Ceron unlocks the power supply beam from its receiving station on the planet surface. He turns it against the inhabited continent of Artemis in a brutal demonstration.'

The graphics were horrific, but I'm sure every molten rock was realistic as the beam carved through a swathe of the Artemis settlements and 47,000 people died.

'Emperor Faron Augustus still refuses to stand down as Emperor, and is overthrown by the population of Zeus. They declare Ceron Augustus the fourth Emperor, but secretly send an appeal to the Military for aid. The Military respond by using Planet First technology to simultaneously open an unprecedented twelve drop portals in space around the Artemis solar array.'

Then came the thrilling moment. We watched as the twelve ephemeral, five second, drop portals opened, and a tiny two man dart ship appeared from each. The power beam turned and fried two of them, but the rest made it through to the solar array.

That was the end of the action. Ventrak Rostha's voice spoke as the picture changed to show a modern day view of Artemis from space. 'Ceron died resisting capture. The control of all the Beta planet solar arrays was returned to the Military. Beta sector declared the end of the Second Roman Empire and rejoined humanity. The scars on the surface of Artemis remain clearly visible from space to this day, but humanity is once more united.'

The end of the vid showed a memorial on Artemis that listed the names of the destroyed settlements. The second it came up on the screen, Lolia and Lolmack were on their feet and saluting the vid. I gaped at them in shock, and then I remembered I was Jarra Military kid. I wasn't sure if Military kids would normally stand and salute at something like this in a vid, but I was pretty sure they wouldn't stay sitting around while civilians were doing it. I bounced to my feet, stood to attention and saluted.

The rest of the class, startled, looked at each other. Fian and Dalmora stood up and joined the salute. Others were hesitantly standing up as the Artemis memorial faded and was followed by the faces and names of each of the four Military casualties in turn. Each face was full screen for a moment, and then shrank off to be in twin screen with a tiny clip from the appropriate Honour Ceremony. Number four just got a picture of a plaque on the wall of the Military Academy. I suppose they didn't have relatives, so there wasn't an Honour Ceremony.

By the end of it, Playdon and all of the class except one was saluting. We held the salute until the last picture faded from the screen.

'That was blatant Military propaganda,' said Krath, class cynic and the only one still sitting down.

Lolia turned on him. 'Shut up! Our clans are from Artemis!'

At this point, Krath badly misread the situation, assuming that in a battle between him and Lolia the rest of the class would be on his side against the common enemy from Beta, but he was wrong.

People are strange in some ways. A couple of days ago,

Playdon had been giving us classes on the twentieth century. War, war and bore. Those wars killed millions of people. They destroyed more lives than you can possibly imagine, and it had left us unmoved. It wasn't just that it was hundreds of years ago; it was that the scale was too big to comprehend. Millions of people died, but they were faceless millions in a war that had no personal meaning to us.

The crisis on Artemis was a hundred and thirty years ago. Thousands of people on the planet had been killed by the power beam, and obviously that didn't mean quite as much to us as it did to Lolia and Lolmack, but we all felt how awful it was. All the planets got their power from their solar arrays up in space. All the planets had their giant beam that was their power lifeline. Earth had five of them, one for each continent. Every one of us could picture exactly what a giant power beam from space would do if it ran wild on our home world, and it was terrifying. I, for one, was really glad to know the Military were up there guarding the arrays from any madman like Ceron.

So, we could all imagine what it was like being there on Artemis. Those Military ships had arrived to save the rest of the population, and the class were pretty emotional about the four who died. They weren't faceless millions from some ancient war. They weren't even like the 47,000, who we cared about but were anonymous because of the sheer number of them. There were only four of the Military, we'd seen each face and we knew each name. We'd just seen their nephew, their niece, their grandson at their Honour Ceremony, and these were real people to us. Krath was on dangerous ground.

Instead of backing off and apologizing, Krath started digging the hole even deeper. 'Oh come on, be realistic. That end bit was ridiculous including the Honour Ceremonies like it did. My dad says it's all rubbish anyway because actually it never happened and . . .'

That did it. When Lolia stepped forward, the class was united against Krath.

'If you wish to remain capable of fathering children, clanless one, you will show respect!' Lolia ordered.

The rest of us probably wouldn't have used those exact words, but we were right behind the spirit of them. We weren't at all happy when Krath reacted by thrusting a defensive hand out to ward off Lolia, gave her a shove backwards, and she nearly fell over.

Lolmack wasn't just unhappy, he was furious. 'Leave my wife alone!' he shouted and leapt forward to put himself between Krath and Lolia.

There was a second of pure confusion. Lolmack seemed intent on throttling Krath, so three of us grabbed him, while another two held on to Krath. Nobody was that keen to hold on to Lolia, since her clothes featured a lot of gaps and she might take it as a sexual advance, but I had my eye on her.

After a couple of minutes, we judged Lolmack and Krath had calmed down enough for us to let go, and then Playdon waded in with a full blown red warning for breach of the Gamman moral code.

Krath didn't seem to believe it was him, a Gamman, getting the warning rather than the Betans. 'Why me?' he asked.

'You physically attacked another student,' said Playdon. 'That is an automatic red warning.'

'She provoked me!'

'You provoked her first,' said Playdon. 'Your conduct breached section 8 of the Gamman moral code on respect. Lolia and Lolmack had just watched a re-enactment of the deaths of 47,000 people on their home world. Memorials were being shown. You failed to show appropriate respect for the natural high emotion of your fellow students.'

Krath seemed about to challenge this, but then backed down. He probably realized it would only earn him another warning for breach of respect.

'Your personal beliefs are not my concern,' said Playdon, 'but your conduct is. Members of this class are from a variety of backgrounds with cultural differences. You will be living together in cramped and difficult accommodation for a year, and working in dangerous conditions where one person's actions could put the lives of others at risk. Anyone deliberately generating conflict among the class will be dealt with.'

Playdon looked round sternly at everyone. 'I won't allow the Betans to amuse themselves by using sexual terms unacceptable to other members of the class. I equally will not allow anyone to be offensive about the Betans honouring their dead. I hope that everyone understands now that they should treat their fellow students with appropriate respect, and I won't have to issue any more warnings. Classes are over for today.'

Krath made his first sensible decision and sloped off to his room. That left the rest of us free to make enquiries about a very interesting point. Naturally, it was Dalmora who first advanced towards the Betans.

'I'm sure I speak for everyone,' she said, 'when I apologise for Krath's behaviour. I also have an apology to make on my own behalf. I had no idea that you were from Artemis. If I'd known, then I would have asked you how you felt before offering to show the class my father's latest vid. I can assure you that both he and I fully appreciate the scale of tragedy that happened on your world.'

The Betans nodded.

'The vid was very sensitive,' said Lolia. 'We have no complaint about it.'

'I should also apologize for any inadvertent offence I may have caused by my conduct to either of you. I didn't realize you were married,' said Dalmora.

We waited hopefully to see what the Betans would say, but they just nodded again. To the disappointment of the class, Dalmora collected her data chip and went off to her room without asking any more questions. The Alphan obviously lacked a decent sense of curiosity.

The Betans stood talking together in low voices for a moment, and then Lolmack put his arm around Lolia and led her off. Playdon trailed discreetly after them, to check they were going to one or other of their rooms rather than to launch another murder attempt on Krath. The rest of us were left in the dining hall.

I got myself a glass of Fizzup from the dispensers, and went over to the side of the room to drag out a table. Of course, it might have been brighter to move a table out from the stack before I was holding a brim full glass of Fizzup. This was a basic dome, and the flexiplas tables weren't going to obligingly move themselves in response to voice commands. Before I managed to spill anything, Fian came over to help.

'You shouldn't try and move tables,' he said. 'You'll hurt your injured side.'

'I'd forgotten all about it,' I said, perfectly truthfully. 'The fluid treatment cycle has finished and it doesn't hurt at all now. There probably won't even be a mark when I take the patch off.'

'I don't understand why you didn't treat it straightaway.'

I shrugged. 'It didn't seem too bad yesterday, and I don't like making a fuss about impact suit bruises. I'm a tag leader, so I get a lot of them, and using a fluid patch sometimes causes more problems than it fixes, because skin can be sensitive after a regen.'

Fian got the table in position and gave me a worried look. 'Will it hurt you wearing an impact suit tomorrow?'

I shook my head. 'The area is covered by my skintight, so it shouldn't be a problem.'

He was from Delta sector, so he blushed at the implied mention of a personal area of the body, and didn't say any more on the subject.

I put my glass on the table and brought a chair over. Fian fetched a chair too and sat down beside me. Well, I couldn't exactly avoid him, and it was important to keep on good terms with my regular tag support. Fian was the person I trusted most among this group to watch my back, so I needed to walk the fine line of being polite and friendly, but giving him absolutely no encouragement at all.

'I was really grazzed that the Betans are married,' said Fian. 'I thought they didn't even like each other.'

This seemed a pretty safe topic of conversation, and I was feeling nosy about the Betans too. 'If they're married, then I suppose they must be older than us.'

'I've no idea,' said Fian. 'Betan marriage rules are very different to ours, and the whole Betan clan system just bewilders me. Lolia and Lolmack do look a bit older than us, but Betans have this . . . sophisticated look. It's hard to tell how old they really are.'

I nodded.

'I never understood why they were on this course to start with,' said Fian. 'They hate the dig sites and they're bored by history. The vid this afternoon was the first time I've seen them take a real interest, and since they're from Artemis . . .'

I nodded again. I was trying to think of a good excuse to leave but there are few convincing excuses you can make in a dig site dome. I decided I'd better try alternative tactics.

I couldn't walk off and leave Fian, but I could get other people to join us.

We'd only been on this course for a few days, and a lot of the class still had a lost, lonely and confused look. I remembered feeling that way myself on my first school history club trip. I was 11 years old, I hadn't known the other people, the place was strange, I didn't know how anything worked, and I wasn't sure what I should be doing. It had been rather scary.

It only took an encouraging smile and wave to get a nervous looking Gamman boy to come in our direction, and Joth instantly followed him over. Within five minutes, I had a full table of people, and Fian was wearing a resigned expression while everyone happily discussed Ventrak Rostha's vids.

Time flew by. I'd dragged Dalmora over, and we were all interrogating her about her father's future plans for the *History of Humanity* series, when my fatigue finally overcame my excitement.

'I'm sorry,' I said, getting up. 'I have to get to bed. I hardly slept last night, and I need to be up before six tomorrow.'

Joth looked panicky. 'Is there something special happening tomorrow that I don't know about?'

I shook my head and grinned. 'No, no. I've just got my two-hour slot booked to talk with my . . .' I broke off. I'd nearly wrecked everything by saying the word ProMum. I tried more carefully. 'With my mum. Given the difference between time zones, before breakfast was the best option.' That was safe enough. Parents off on Planet First could be in any time zone.

'You have to book a slot to talk to your mother?' Joth seemed even more confused.

'I suppose you can't just call up and chat when someone is on Planet First,' said Fian.

Joth started to laugh. 'Oh yes. Just imagine it. They're fighting a giant, man eating, whatever, and ask it to wait a minute because their daughter just called for a chat.'

I headed off before I said something else that was stupid and gave myself away.

14

My lookup woke me punctually at twenty-to-six the next morning, and I groaned before struggling out of bed. I would have loved to sleep for another hour, or six, but it was vital that I called Candace.

Since I'd joined the course, I'd only made one proper call to anyone, and that was the one to Issette. I'd had my lookup set to reject incoming calls with a message saying I wasn't currently available. I couldn't accept calls when I was outside in an impact suit. I couldn't accept them when I was in class or asleep. The rest of the time, I could accept them, but I daren't. If a call came in on my lookup when I was lounging around in the hall, then people might overhear something that gave away I was a smelly ape girl.

So, I hadn't been making or receiving calls. I'd just sent a few recorded mail messages, and Candace was getting edgy about it. Her last mail to me had been pretty strongly phrased. I'd deliberately put myself into a very difficult situation. She wanted to know how I was, and recorded mail was not enough. She insisted on a person to person call, or she would be over to check on me personally.

I was 18 now, and I didn't think Candace could use her

ProMum authority to force her way through a secure portal into a dig site dome being used by University Asgard, but I wasn't prepared to bet on it. An Earth ProMum muscling her way into the dome would totally ruin my Military kid act. Anyway, I didn't want to upset Candace. She wasn't like my ProDad. Candace really cared about me and I cared about her.

So, I washed, dressed, and called Candace exactly at six. It was eleven in the morning in her time zone, and from the speed she answered it was clear she had been sitting waiting for me.

'Jarra,' she said, as she appeared on the screen. 'I was beginning to think you were avoiding me.' She was sitting in her study at home. I'd never been to her house of course, but she'd called me from her study lots of times.

'There's been a lot happening,' I said, 'you don't get much privacy in these domes, and the time difference is difficult.'

'I understand that,' said Candace, 'but I've been worried about you. It's not just this crazy masquerade of yours, but your physical safety as well. I've always felt that working on a dig site was very hazardous. I know you're with an official university pre-history class, but do people from Asgard really know about dig site safety?'

'Well, Lecturer Playdon seems to know what he's doing. The class are novices, but they're coming on well. I'm tag leading of course, and for team 1!' I added jubilantly.

'Congratulations,' said Candace with a smile. 'I know you'd want key spot.'

'I've got Fian on my lifeline. He's from Delta, and he's good.' I grinned. 'I don't get tag point itch when he's watching my back.'

Candace laughed. She'd had to endure many hours of me talking about my dig site experiences, and knew all about tag point itch. 'I know a good tag support is important.'

163

'Absolutely vital,' I said. 'New York Main is a lot tougher than the Fringe. I really had doubts about the other students to start with, but you'll never believe what happened on our third trip on site.'

I told her every thrilling detail about the tower collapse, and how I'd been the tag leader for the rescue of Cassandra 2. Of course, I didn't explain exactly how dangerous it had been when I dived down to get the person in the failing suit. It's never wise to scare your ProMum into fits.

'Fian was on my lifeline, of course, Dalmora on sensors, and Amalie and Krath on heavy lifts. Playdon was helping with sensors too, because Dalmora is doing well but there's a lot to learn about sensor displays. Playdon was going to tag lead, but I said we needed him on sensors and I should be tag leader.'

She laughed again.

'What's funny?' I asked.

Candace shook her head. 'I just feel a little sorry for Lecturer Playdon. I can just imagine you taking over his class.'

'I wasn't taking over. I was just trying to help,' I said. 'Oh, I don't think I've told you. Dalmora is Ventrak Rostha's daughter!'

'Really?' Candace looked impressed.

I nodded. 'It was totally amaz yesterday, because she showed us the new *History of Humanity* vid. It won't be out officially for weeks yet, but she had special permission from her father to show it to our class. It's about Artemis.'

I told Candace all about the vid. 'Dalmora says that her father isn't sure how much closer to the present day he can go with the *History of Humanity* series, because people get more sensitive about recent events, but he's planning a follow up series on pre-history. Dalmora says she wants to specialize in pre-history so she can work with her father on it. He specializes more in history than pre-history himself.'

Candace raised a hand. 'Permission to speak.'

'Sorry,' I said. Candace often complains that when I'm excited about something she never gets a chance to say a word.

She smiled. 'I just wanted to say that you should have explained Ventrak Rostha's daughter was going to do pre-history at University Asgard. I'd have been a lot less worried about agreeing to your crazy plan if I'd known that Ventrak Rostha was part of the reason for it.'

She looked thoughtful. 'I know some of the University Asgard staff are advisers on the *History of Humanity* series. I've seen them listed in the credits. If the real motive for going on this course was to meet Dalmora Rostha, and you're hoping to be an adviser yourself one day for Ventrak Rostha and his daughter when they make a pre-history series, well . . .'

She shook her head. 'You could have told me. I think it's a little over ambitious, but I wouldn't put anything past you. You've achieved some amazing things in the past, like getting your pilot's licence. I certainly wouldn't have laughed at you, Jarra.'

I blushed. I'd picked Asgard because of a vid series, but the series hadn't been *History of Humanity*, it had been *Defenders*. I'd picked Asgard because of an off-world hero of mine, but the hero was Arrack San Domex, not Ventrak Rostha.

'I'm much happier now,' said Candace. 'I know you had a lot of hostility towards people who aren't Handicapped. I've been listening to you talk for two hours, and I think it's the first time I've ever heard you talk that long without saying the "exo" word. You talked about that rescue, and I wasn't hearing any hostility in your voice when you mentioned the other people involved. You've overcome your bitterness towards them to go on this course, and I'm proud of you, Jarra.'

She paused for a moment before continuing. 'I'm proud of you, Jarra, but I've got to warn you too. They'll find out you're Handicapped eventually, and you may get a very bad reaction from some of them when they do. I'd like you to bear that in mind, and try and be prepared to face it. You've proved what you wanted. You've been accepted by the finest off-world historians. If they have any silly prejudices, then it doesn't change anything. Don't let it upset you.'

Candace had got the wrong idea, but if it kept her happy that was fine. She'd mentioned how long I'd been talking. I checked the time and realized I'd used my two hours. 'I'm sorry. I didn't notice my time was up.'

'That's all right, Jarra. This is important, and I can talk some more if there's anything else I should know.'

I shook my head. 'I'd better go. I don't want to steal anyone else's time. I should go and get breakfast anyway.'

I hastily ended the call. I'm sensitive about stealing some other kid's time with Candace. There've been a few occasions when she's arrived late for a meeting with me because one of the others has had a crisis. I try and be polite about it, but underneath I really hate it. Candace is mine for two hours a week and they can keep their thieving hands off my time. Equally, I shouldn't be stealing part of their two hours.

For one or two things, like my application for my Foundation course, I know she has extra time arranged for me. That's Candace being generous to me, giving up her own free time, and that's different. It's a gift to me from Candace that I value, not something I'm taking from anyone else.

166

I was hungry, but I didn't go into breakfast for a few minutes. Instead, I sat there brooding on what Candace had said. She had the wrong idea about some of it. She often did have the wrong idea, because I like to keep some things to myself.

She was wrong, but she was right too. I had to prepare myself for when my classmates found out what I really was. I'd made a lot of mistakes already, I was bound to make more, and eventually I wouldn't be able to think of a lie to cover things up. I'd be in real trouble then. Playdon already knew, and one or two of the others might react like decent people, but I could be hit by a barrage of ape insults.

When I applied for this course, I'd planned what to do when they found out I was a nean. That was the moment when I'd turn round and laugh in their faces. That was the moment when I'd call them exos and scream out my anger. I'd already discovered I didn't want to do that anymore. I couldn't yell abuse at Fian, who'd been on my lifeline and saved my neck several times, and then walk away and feel proud of myself. In fact, I didn't really want to scream insults at any of them any longer, not even the Betans. Maybe Krath deserved it, but . . .

Unfortunately, having given up on my original idea of screaming my fury, I didn't really have an alternate plan. I certainly didn't want to do anything stupid, like bursting into tears and running away. I already had a lot of anger and bitterness to deal with; I didn't want to add a mountain of humiliation to it. I was going to have to calmly listen to all the abuse they could throw at me and then make a dignified exit with my pride intact. I could do that. Maybe.

I pulled myself together, and went to have breakfast. We spent the morning on a dig site as usual. I was a bit distracted

167

by my worries and I made a true beginner's mistake going in close to tag a rock that obviously wasn't stable. Fian pulled me out of trouble. I don't think either he or the rest of the class realized how stupid I'd been, but I got Playdon talking to me on my private channel.

'Jarra?' he said.

I cringed and waited for him to yell at me. He knew I was just a dumb ape, and this was his chance to say so.

'Are you all right today? You don't seem quite your usual self.'

'I realize I made a silly mistake, sir.'

'Everyone does sometimes. Don't take it to heart. No one can be perfect all the time.'

I forced myself to pay attention after that, and I didn't make another mistake, but I was relieved when we went back to the dome. After lunch, Playdon talked about New York. First, he showed us some graphics of New York, showing the city at ten year intervals. They ran from the nineteenth century up to Exodus. He showed us detailed pictures of some of the skyscrapers when they were originally built, and talked about construction methods through the years, and the materials used.

In theory this was useful, because it helps to know what you're working with, but I find in reality that after a few hundred years it's hard to tell the concrete from the concraz, the plas has gone brittle, and the metal is corroded to the point where it's completely unpredictable.

'Why did they build so high?' asked Krath. 'Seventy storeys is insane. Even the most populated Alpha planets only go three or four storeys high.'

'They wanted to get as much into the area of land as possible,' said Playdon.

'But surely they had plenty of land.' Krath was still bewildered.

'Yes,' said Playdon, 'but the problem was a combined one of land and transport. With all the sector worlds having only one inhabited continent, it doesn't matter where you live on that world. You need to live in a settlement to have access to community portal, power and water services, but which one doesn't matter. Whatever settlement you pick, portalling to work will cost you exactly the same. There will be a portal close to your home, and your journey will take a maximum of five minutes.'

He nodded at the picture of a skyscraper on the big vid screen. 'When they built this city, they had no portals, they travelled everywhere by land or air transport. If you lived a long way from New York, it would take you hours, and cost a lot of money to get there. So you wanted to live close, and they built high to pack people and offices into the space.

'Now let's look at what happened to New York after Exodus.' Playdon showed more pictures on the vid. 'They were still doing massive construction there even at the beginning of Exodus, but then people started leaving at ever increasing speed. It was abandoned entirely by the end of Exodus, and ignored for two hundred years because humanity had a lot of other things to worry about.'

'In 2603,' Playdon continued, 'a team of historians began a little minor exploration here at New York. They found enough interesting things in stasis boxes to keep coming back. In 2630, one of the first proper dig sites was set up here. Gradually they built the clearways.'

Playdon used his lookup to project a big image of New York Main dig site, with its green, amber and red hazard warnings. 'This is New York Main dig site as it is today, or at least as each section was at the time of its last aerial survey. All the skyscrapers still standing, or partially standing, are in red hazard areas. Best estimates are there were twelve thousand of them at the start of Exodus, but the number depends on your definition of a skyscraper. Even ten storeys is high enough when it decides to land on your head.'

It might have been a joke if he'd said it differently, but his voice was too grim for anyone to laugh. Besides, the memory of the Cassandra 2 team being buried was still raw in our minds.

'Now, let's add the clearways.' Playdon tapped his lookup and a network of white lines appeared on the projection. 'The clearways mostly head straight into the dig site until they hit either the Grand Circle or the Loop. This is the Grand Circle, and as you can see, it's roughly circular.' Some lines flashed brightly for a moment. 'This is the Loop, and it's more like a tangle of string than anything else.' More lines flashed. 'You must be on either the Grand Circle or the Loop if you want to cross the water.'

'Why can't we portal onto the site?' asked Joth.

'We need heavy equipment,' said Playdon. 'We need the sleds to carry it. Ask Krath or Amalie and they'd tell you how expensive freight size portals are. Just think about the huge area we're dealing with. How many portals would we need to make a difference? Remember, there's no point in keeping working the same spot over and over, we're moving all the time.'

Playdon shook his head. 'A decision was taken in the early days to work from scattered domes. Each dome works a nearby sector. Teams sometimes set up mobile domes at safe points within the dig sites and work from those. Obviously, we have a network of cheap evac portals to get people out in emergencies.'

He gave us his evil smile that meant bad news. 'You're probably wondering why I'm covering New York and the dig site clearways in such detail. In a couple of weeks, we'll be heading deep into New York Main with a mobile dome, and camping out on the Grand Circle to work there for a few days. Before then, I want you to spend time getting familiar with the clearway network. That's all for today.'

The class were still in their seats, just starting to talk nervously about the prospect of camping out on the dig site, when the Betans stood up and marched to the front of the room. Normally their every movement projected an air of sexuality, but now that had vanished and been replaced by something more militant. Playdon had been walking away, but he stopped to watch the situation.

'We wish to speak to people,' said Lolia.

'We've decided that since you people will hate us whatever we do, you might as well know the truth,' said Lolmack.

'We aren't here because we like history,' said Lolia.

Well that wasn't really a surprise to anyone. I wondered what was coming next. Playdon was obviously prepared for trouble, because he was moving to take up an unobtrusive position near the Betans.

'This dome is primitive and the dig site . . .' Lolia gave a delicate shudder of disgust. 'We were forced into this.' She gave a complex hand gesture that probably meant something significant in Beta sector but communicated nothing to the rest of us. 'Three months ago, we were happy. We had a triad marriage. I was about to have our first child. Lolmack was the father, and we planned that a second child fathered by our other partner would soon follow.'

I stared at the Betans in disbelief. Surely not . . .

'Our baby was born Handicapped. Our partner instantly divorced us.' Lolia's face twisted with remembered pain, but she made herself carry on speaking. 'Hospital Earth insisted we must spend most of our time on Earth, or lose our child.

171

Our clans feared the effects if it was known that we had had a Handicapped birth. It would cause the loss of much hard won status.'

Lolia shook her head. 'Clan alliance council met and we were told to keep the child secret or become clanless. We had to find a convincing reason for being on Earth, and the only possible ones were to study history or medicine. Our grades were in arts so it had to be history. Our clans make vids, and we thought to make vids set in history, but this course is . . .'

'It is for the lowlife and clanless,' said Lolmack. 'We exist in barbaric conditions.'

'And we cannot see our child,' said Lolia. 'Lolette can't be with us here, and when it's evening here, it's night at her Nursery. Hospital Earth say she can't move Nursery each time we change dig site to a different time zone.'

'So, despise us,' said Lolmack, 'but you despised us anyway, and we have suffered too much to care.'

I was utterly grazzed. The Betans were here because of their baby. I wasn't sure they were really doing the child a favour. Growing up having Betan parents was going to be difficult, and if their clan made vids . . . Well, everyone knew what Betan vids were like. Still, at least they were trying. No, not just trying, but going through hell to do the right thing.

Nuke it. I daren't speak up in favour of them and their ape baby. If I seemed too emotional, then people might get suspicious, but . . . respect!

I could depend upon Dalmora to do the talking anyway. Before I'd even finished thinking things through, she was on her feet. 'I'm sure that I speak for the whole class, when I say how impressed I am. I think you're doing something wonderful. I don't know that I would have as much courage in your situation, but I admire you and if I can do anything to help . . .'

I hastily made noises of agreement.

The rest of the stunned class gradually nodded, except for Krath of course. 'You're doing this for some . . .' He glanced at Playdon, broke off for a second, and started a new sentence. 'Well, if that's what you want, that's fine of course.'

Playdon strolled over to the Betans. 'It would have helped if you'd explained the situation at the start. I've a strong objection to anyone who appears to be coming on courses just to disrupt them, but I'm always willing to help a genuine student with their problems.'

Playdon's eyes turned away from the Betans for a moment and I realized he was looking at me. It was only for a second, and then his attention was back on the Betans. 'Clearly, you've no long term interest in practical history, so it would make sense if I excuse you from some of the morning sessions on compassionate grounds. That should give you time to visit your child in the daytime. You can start by visiting her tomorrow morning.'

The Betans looked grazzed. 'You would really do that?' asked Lolmack.

Playdon nodded. 'It may affect your practical grade for the course, but it doesn't sound as if that would worry you. I'll make sure you still do enough dig site work to get the pass grade that you need to continue on to do a full history degree. Next year, I'm running a specialist pre-history degree course, but that's going to be heavily practical. I think it would be best if you transferred to a University Earth specialist pre-history degree course at that point. They run several and you could choose a pure theory one with no time on dig sites. University Earth would give you married accommodation and you could have your baby with you.'

'We cannot study at University Earth,' said Lolia. 'If

173

we are known to be students at University Earth, then it will be clear our child is Handicapped. Our clans would disown us.'

'I could arrange to have you study at University Earth but get you accredited via University Asgard so you're technically our students,' said Playdon. 'University Earth will co-operate to assist the parents of a Handicapped child.'

'We would be very grateful if you can do that,' said Lolmack. 'After we have our degree, our time on Earth can be explained as researching our clans' pre-history vids.'

'You're planning to make history vids like Ventrak Rostha?' asked Playdon, warily.

'Yes,' said Lolia, 'but of course with more physical relationships. Sector audiences are hypocritical about sex. They wish to watch our vids, but are embarrassed that they concentrate on physical relationships. We feel there would be a good market for vids that also feature historical events so the viewer can excuse themselves by claiming they are educational.'

Playdon laughed. 'You could be right.'

The Betans headed off, eagerly talking to each other. Playdon got some food and went off to his room. The rest of the class settled down to gossip about the shock news.

'They're doing the right thing. I admire them for it. I don't know if I'd have the courage,' said Dalmora.

'I wouldn't do it,' said Krath. 'Anyway, I don't think it's necessarily the right thing. An ape baby is better off being raised by its own kind.'

I felt a strong urge to throw Krath across the room, but I had to control myself. I was supposed to be Military, so I shouldn't be getting overexcited about some Handicapped baby. I thought it was safest to go back to my room at this point, but I did manage to 'accidentally' tread on Krath's foot as I went past him. I left him hopping on one leg.

I sat in my room rethinking the whole situation. I'd realized earlier that I no longer wanted my time on this course to end in a dramatic scene where I shouted my anger at the exos. I'd shifted my ground to picturing a dignified exit, and now I was admitting something else. I didn't actually want to leave at all.

For the first time, I considered staying on when the class knew I was an ape. Was it remotely possible? Playdon had given me a look when he was talking to the Betans. He'd never spoken to me about my Handicap, I realized he wouldn't unless I opened the subject myself, but what he'd said to the Betans was meant for me too. Playdon had thought I'd come on this course to disrupt it, so he hadn't been welcoming. He'd been quite right about my motives too.

Now he'd changed his mind, and decided I was a genuine student with a problem. I'd changed my mind too, so he was right again. When the day came that the class found out I was an ape, Playdon would be willing to help. He wouldn't allow them to openly abuse me but exactly how many subtle insults could I handle without losing my temper?

The class would naturally be angry with me. Some of them would despise me for being an ape, and the rest would resent all the lies I'd told them. That lying hadn't felt bad when they were the hated exos, but it did now.

I'd have to think about this. I didn't want to leave. I hadn't thought through the consequences before I decided to come on this course, but now they were becoming obvious. Moving to another course in mid year would be a mess, and all their good team spots would be filled. I was a tag leader for team 1 here. Fian was a great tag support. Playdon was a Stasis Q. The class might be exos, but they weren't a bad bunch. I'd taken an instant dislike to the Betans, but now they'd turned out to be being pretty noble in their way. Krath was an idiot, who kept mindlessly repeating his dad's ideas, but . . .

I'd come to terms with the rest of the class being exos. The question was, could they come to terms with me being Handicapped?

15

The following evening, I called a special Registry number. I didn't say anything, just entered a code, put my hand on my lookup screen to verify my identity, and ended the call. That doesn't sound very important, but it was a huge step for me to make. Nothing would happen immediately, because Hospital Earth wants to avoid people asking on a whim when drunk or powered and then regretting it, but in three days time I'd get a mail that gave me access to my parents' details.

After I'd made the call, I sat there, physically shaking, wondering why I'd done it. I could have made it any day since I was 14 years old, and I'd always sworn I never would. My exo parents threw me away at birth, and I sure as chaos was never going to chase after them and beg for acceptance. It was a matter of pride.

So what had happened to change that? Had I lost my pride or just gone totally mad? Maybe both, but it was really because of my crazy masquerade in this class. My norm classmates had accepted me as one of them. Playdon trusted me. Fian was someone that I could have loved if the genetic dice hadn't fallen the wrong way. Dalmora, born to be a celebrity of Alpha sector, was a genuinely caring person. I'd helped save the lives of ten strangers, and it hadn't mattered whether they were exo or ape. They were just people in trouble, and I knew they would have done exactly the same for me.

On the surface, none of that seemed to have the slightest connection to my unknown parents, but of course it did. Everything did. Everything in my life was because of them and their decision. Everything kept coming back to the shadowy figures who'd handed their ape kid over to Hospital Earth and walked away. If they hadn't done that, my entire life would have been different, and I wouldn't be telling a bunch of lies to an off-world class.

I'd tried not to admit it to myself, but I'd known the truth all along. I might have claimed that I'd joined this class to prove I was as good as any norm and yell abuse at them, but the class were just substitutes for my parents. I'd been just as obsessed as all my friends in Next Step. They'd been desperate for acceptance, while I'd been desperate for revenge, but it was just two sides of the same coin.

It's not totally true that all my friends in Next Step were obsessed with their parents. Keon wasn't. He was maddeningly lazy, irritatingly smug, and annoyingly intelligent, but I'd always admired one thing about him. When he was 14 years old, he'd said that it was far too much effort to be bothered about parents he'd never known, and he really meant it!

I lay back on my bed and sighed. There might not seem to be any logic in it, but I knew that the first step towards facing my class as an ape, was facing up to the issue of my parents. I was finally doing what my friends had done four years ago. I was 18 years old, I was at least theoretically an adult, but that wasn't going to help me very much. The only advantage I had over the average naive 14-year-old, was that I'd seen what happened to my friends. I knew from bitter experience that this was going to be an utter disaster.

All of us, except Keon, had gone through difficult times when we hit that big Year Day that meant we were 14 and had two options offered to us. We could ask for information about our parents and attempt to make contact. We could also make one attempt to portal off world. We'd all been thinking about it for years beforehand of course.

I was the only one crazy enough to take up the portal option. Everyone told me not to do it. Issette must have said it a hundred times. The others said it about thirty times each. Candace said it about fifteen times. The Principal of my Next Step said it three times. The teacher who ran my school history club said it eight times. My ProDad insisted on our first meeting in over a year so that he could go on record as saying it.

Even Keon made the supreme effort to comment it was a bad idea. He pointed out that Hospital Earth didn't make mistakes. The last confirmed case of someone being diagnosed as Handicapped in error was over a hundred years ago.

I knew that.

Keon pointed out it was going to be unpleasant. There'd be a medical team standing by off world to grab me on arrival as I went into anaphylactic shock. They'd then portal me back to Hospital Earth Casualty, who would have another medical team standing by to treat me. He said they probably wouldn't let me die, but it was likely to be painful.

Keon came the closest to convincing me. I still went ahead anyway. I knew Hospital Earth hadn't made a mistake. I knew what would happen, and that there was no chance at all, but I had to try. So I had ten seconds on another world and a week in hospital.

I only really needed a day in hospital, but Hospital Earth tend to be a bit neurotic because in very rare cases there can be some lingering after effects. I wasn't a rare case, so there were no after effects. I was just a perfectly average ape girl cursed by a malignant fate. Everyone came to see me, brought grapes, and told me how stupid I'd been. Keon came too, but he just sat there eating the grapes.

I didn't care if they all thought I was stupid. It was still worth it. I hadn't just given in and been a passive victim. I'd tried to fight fate, and experienced the inevitable defeat, but I was proud that I'd tried. The only bad thing was that my psychologist didn't say I was stupid. He said it had been a positive experience for me, and I said he could take his opinions and nuke them!

The others might have thought I was stupid taking up the portal option, but I thought they were totally out of their minds taking up the parental information one. My decision gave me one physically unpleasant day, but they went through mental agony with emotional after effects that lasted for years.

Issette was my best friend, so I was most involved with what happened to her. When she accessed the records, it was obvious that Issette's parents had done the standard thing. Dump the ape kid, blame the neanderthal genes on each other, and head in opposite directions. They'd been from Beowulf, in Gamma sector. Their divorce had been initiated the day after Issette was born. They'd both changed their names. Issette's father was now on a frontier planet in Epsilon. Issette's mother had moved too, but only as far as another planet in Gamma sector.

I thought that made things pretty clear. A throwback baby had shattered her parents' comfortable norm lives, and they had done everything they could to turn their backs on it, but fluffy-headed, romantic Issette was sure that they would feel differently now. She tried to contact them. Her father replied with an impersonal written one line mail. It was polite but basically it could be summed up in two words. Nuke off! Her mother sent a long emotional mail, kept promising to visit then changing her mind, and finally shut the door completely.

Issette was a mess and took years to get over it. Her ProParents got her extra psychotherapy for a year, which Issette thinks helped her immensely, but I think made things worse. Issette is very different to me. She likes sharing everything with people, while I get really angry about a psychologist trying to poke around in my head and tell me which of my feelings get a pass grade and which fail and need correcting.

Seven of my friends took up their parental information option at 14. They went through a lot of pain and only Ross got anything out of it in the end. His real father calls him every few weeks, and even visits a couple of times a year. I met him myself once, when he came to our Next Step. For an exo, he wasn't that bad. He didn't wrinkle up his nose as if I smelled.

So, I knew from my friends' experiences exactly how slim the chances were that I'd end up having a relationship with either of my real parents. My call to Registry was going to lead to catastrophe, but in the end it was like my attempt to portal off world. It was going to fail, it was going to hurt, but afterwards I could be proud that I'd tried, and if I could face the issue of my parents then facing my class should be simple.

That was the point when I made another decision. I'd keep up the lies until I'd dealt with the parent nightmare, but then I wouldn't wait for the class to spot the flaws in my deception. I'd do what the Betans had done. I'd march up to the front of the hall, and tell everyone the truth.

16

I knew that surviving the next three days would be hard. I'm good at doing things, not sitting around and waiting for them to happen. There was an extra complication as well. At breakfast the next morning, Playdon called Fian and me away from the rest of the class for a quiet word.

'I'm going to swap your two roles,' he said, with his most evil smile. 'Fian, you're going to tag lead, and Jarra will act as your tag support.'

I felt an instinctive surge of anger, but caught myself. I'd made this mistake before, and wasn't going to repeat it. Playdon knew what he was doing and I should trust him. It was Fian who objected.

'I don't want to be tag leader.'

Playdon laughed. 'It's only for a few days.'

Fian developed a stubborn look. 'Then why bother? I want to get better at my own job.'

'Because this will help you both to get better at your jobs.' Playdon turned to me. 'Jarra, for a Foundation course tag leader, you're outstanding, but you can be better still. It's my job to help you achieve that. It's perfectly obvious you've worked as a heavy lift operator, but never on tag support.'

'It is?'

He nodded. 'I've talked to Earth 19 about your work during the rescue of Cassandra 2, and they said exactly what I was thinking. You're a dream tag leader for a heavy lift operator; you don't just tag any stable point on a rock, but go for somewhere convenient for the heavy lift beams.'

I flushed with pleasure, but of course he followed the compliment with a criticism.

'You're a dream for the heavy lift operators, but a nightmare for your tag support. A few days changing roles with Fian will fix that. You'll learn about blind spots and awkward beam angles that can make it hard for your tag support to pull you out of trouble. You'll learn to avoid putting yourself in those places, and that will make the second or two of difference which might save your life one day.'

I was going to hate doing this, but I trusted him so . . . 'Yes, sir.'

'Fian, this is your chance to see things through a tag leader's eyes. What they need to do, how they need to do it, the decisions they need to make. It'll help you anticipate Jarra's movements on a dig site, so you see the dangers coming before they actually happen.'

Fian reluctantly nodded.

'And when team 1 aren't working, I'll try and get both of you spending some time watching sensors with me,' Playdon continued. 'If either of you progress to be a research or teaching team leader one day, you must be experts on sensors. That may be five or ten years away, but learning sensors takes time.'

So for the next three days I spent my dig site time doing things I hated, and couldn't even resent it because I soon realized Playdon was right. I hadn't known just how difficult the tag support job was. I sat tensely watching Fian tagging rocks, waiting for him to get into trouble, hardly daring to blink in case that cost a vital second that was the difference between Fian being unscathed and Fian being strapped to a hover stretcher on his way to hospital. In its way, this was much harder than my own job of tagging rocks, and Fian had handled the strain so casually and so competently even as a total novice. Well . . . respect!

Watching the ever changing swirl of sensor readings was a different sort of strain. Playdon wanted much more from us than just a casual check of where a stasis box might be. Fian's scientific background might have helped him, but I was definitely struggling.

And all the time, sitting on the tag support sled, watching the sensors, listening to lectures or chatting to my classmates, part of my mind was always on that call to Registry. The reply would come exactly three days later. I knew the time down to the hour, the minute, and practically the second. I'd studied the instructions until I could recite them by heart. I just had to wait, and wait and wait.

Finally, the three days had crawled past, and I sat in my room with my lookup in my hand, its display already linked in to the wall vid. 'Come on. Come on.' I told it. 'It's got to be time . . .'

I broke off my complaint as I heard the soft chime of arriving mail. I tapped the look up, my fingers clumsy with haste, saw the code number I needed and entered it. It took me two attempts to get it right, and then I took a deep breath and looked nervously at the wall vid screen. I'd planned how to do this. I could ask for as much or as little information as I wanted. The first step was to query my parents' birth sector. If it was Beta, I might have to think for a bit, but anywhere else . . .

And the answer flashed up on the wall in front of me. It was the same for both parents. 'Not Applicable.'

What?

I sat there for a full minute. What the chaos? No sector? They must have been born on Earth, but in that case why dump me?

Well, all right, I obviously hadn't thought of this, but I couldn't leave it with 'Not Applicable'. I queried my parents' birth planets.

Instantly the answer flashed up. Again it was the same for both parents. 'Not Applicable.'

'Oh nuke that!' I told my lookup. This was just total rubbish. What was going on? Did fate hate me that much? Had I wound myself up to face this, only to find Hospital Earth had lost my parental records? Had the maternity ward where I was born just thrown the nean baby through the portal and not bothered to send any medical records after her?

I glared at the lookup. 'All right . . .' I queried my parents' exact place of birth.

The answers flashed up. Two different answers this time. Two Military bases. 'Oh nuke . . . Oh zan . . .'

I sat there in shock. I didn't know where these Military bases had been. They probably weren't there any longer, it must have been more than 40 years since my parents were born and Military bases relocated sometimes. It didn't matter anyway. My parents were born Military. I'd made up a lie; I'd been living a lie, and guess what?

So, they were born Military. The odds were that they were Military themselves. If they were, then I could see things in a whole new light. Most people, if they really tried, could move to Earth and still follow their career in some way. The Military couldn't. I'd made JMK so real, I'd even been dreaming I was her, and I could picture how much it would hurt to give up everything to care for a Handicapped baby on Earth.

I asked myself a couple of questions. If I was a norm

185

would I want to be combat Military? Yes, I would. If I was combat Military, could I give up the life I loved to move to Earth? It might be the right thing to do, but I couldn't honestly be sure I would do it.

So, I tried another query. My parents' exact location was restricted to Military access only, but they were currently on active duty with Planet First, Kappa sector.

I was still staring at that, absorbing that, when there was another musical chime from my lookup to tell me I had mail. I mechanically checked who it was from. The sender was Military Support.

The Military are incredibly efficient. Hospital Earth discovered in the early days that norm parents could really mess their ape kids about. They'd dump us, and then they'd change their minds and move to Earth and want us back. Then they'd decide they couldn't cope and dump us again. Parents coming and going, having contact one minute and ignoring them the next, drove the kids crazy. Hospital Earth brought in strict rules to protect us. No half measures. Either you were a parent and on Earth regularly, or your ape kid was made a ward of Hospital Earth and no contact was allowed unless the kid requested it after they reached the age of 14.

So, I had to admire Military Support. I'd just requested information that told me my parents had been Military. That meant Military Support were now free to contact me, my record on their system had been flagged, and bing I had mail!

It was formal written mail, not a vid. The document was version two. I'm betting version one of it had been sitting on the Military Support system waiting to be sent since I was 14. When I was 18 it was changed and became version two.

I read it. The first part said that since I had at least one Military parent I was entitled to a Military education scholarship for the duration of my studies. As I was a ward of Hospital Earth, the fee element was not relevant as my education fees would be automatically paid by Hospital Earth. I was, however, entitled to the maintenance element in addition to any provision by Hospital Earth, and that would be regularly credited to my account including any arrears due.

It wasn't the most important thing at that moment, but my income had suddenly doubled.

The second section of the mail drove everything else out of my head. I was the Honour Child for my grandmother, Jarra Tell Morrath. As I was now 18, the Honour Ceremony would be carried out if I was ready to take part. Military Support would be happy to supply any information, assistance, or advice I required on these or any other issues.

I was grazzed. I was a Military Honour Child, and named Jarra after my grandmother. How the chaos did that happen? The system just didn't work that way. Hospital Earth chose the names of its wards to prevent us getting ones that labelled us as cast offs from one sector or another. That was for obvious reasons. Just imagine what a kid with a Betan name would suffer at school.

Hospital Earth shouldn't have let me keep my original first name, but they'd broken the rules in my case. They were up against a Military family tradition that even civilians respect. When one of a Military family dies on active service, the next child born in the family is given their name to honour them. Sometimes, they deliberately have an extra child to carry the name. I'd been the Honour Child for my grandmother. I was a girl, so I was Jarra. A boy would have been Jarrack.

When I turned out to be Handicapped . . . Well, I suppose my parents must have discussed it. I could imagine the frantic debates. I was the next-born child, so tradition insisted I bore the name. I was Handicapped, so I could never be Military, but of course not every Honour Child becomes Military themselves. They probably did a lot of thinking, but they'd gone ahead with it in the end rather than have a replacement Honour Child later.

I used my lookup to request more information. Military families usually have two or three kids, very close together in age, because that works best for active assignments. I had a brother and sister who were only a year apart in age, but then there was a gap of twelve years before my birth. I checked my grandmother's details. Yes, she'd died in 2769. I was a deliberately planned Honour Child.

I sat there for a bit. I'd expected to have to make one decision, but now there were two. Did I try to contact my parents? Did I agree to take part in the Honour Ceremony? The second one was much easier, because it only concerned myself and my grandmother. I had no grudge against a Military hero who'd died before I was born, and being Handicapped didn't change the fact I had a duty to perform. My grandmother wouldn't be left with just the mandatory plaque on the Military Academy wall. She would have her Honour Ceremony.

I mailed Military Support saying it would be a privilege to take part in the ceremony, and then I went to bed and had the dream where I was JMK again, but it was even more confusing this time. I was on a Military base that looked just like the one in *Defenders*. My parents were with me, and Fian was there too. We were all sitting round a table drinking frujit, and Fian kept talking about aliens.

17

The next morning, Playdon swapped Fian and I back to our regular roles, and took the class to a new area of the dig site where we found a stasis box. When we got back to the dome, there was the usual suspense as we waited to see what we'd found. Playdon opened it as we stood around. This time it was a child's toy. A lover of fluffy toys from hundreds of years ago, a twenty-fourth century Issette, had left a green furry object in a stasis box. That wasn't all they'd left though. There was a recording of a nervous and excited family about to head off to a new world, and there was a real treasure trove. They'd left us an ancient newzie! Not one from the day they left. This was far older, from before Language was adopted as a common tongue. It wasn't recorded but actually printed on paper.

Playdon used his lookup, while we waited in suspense. 'This is totally new. It's from one of the lost years.'

We cheered wildly. We'd found history!

We all watched while Playdon scanned the precious paper pages with slow and painstaking care and put the results through data translation. The scanned images and data were sent off to researchers and all the University data archives for safe keeping. After that was done, the toy, the family recording, and the newzie itself were packed and sent off. With them secure, we could all scan the data on our lookups.

While we ate lunch, we gloated over fragments from the past. Some of it was trivial, a story about one of their vid stars for example, but it was all part of the patchwork quilt of lost information that humanity was rebuilding.

'What was Formula One?' asked Dalmora.

'It's a report about a land vehicle race,' Playdon explained.

'But they went so fast . . . These speeds can't be right.' Krath was doing calculations on his look up. 'There must have been an error during the translation into Language.'

'Their vehicles could travel much faster than ours can,' said Playdon. 'Speed isn't a priority for us, because we can portal long distances instantly. They had to travel everywhere on foot or in vehicles, like we do when we go places on the hover sleds. Huge amounts of their resources had to be invested in transport systems, vehicles, tracks, roads, ships, aircraft. It was crippling.' Playdon gave us his evil look. 'As it happens, this afternoon we study twentieth century economics.'

I groaned. When they refer to the twentieth century as war, war and bore, its economics is definitely part of the bore.

We were in the middle of the 1930s recession, when Playdon's lookup bleeped. He frowned and checked it. Stared. Checked it again, looked grazzed, then panicky. 'Jarra, I have a mail from the Military. Their team will arrive in one hour.'

I was a bit startled too. I'd only given the Military the go ahead last night. Presumably they'd already done the ceremonies for the other Honour Children who had turned 18 on Year Day, and could tidy up unusual cases like mine very quickly.

'Yes, sir,' I said.

'You know how to do this?' Playdon looked frantically round the all purpose dining room and classroom. 'We need to clear this place up. I'm sorry we don't have a more appropriate venue.'

'Sir, with respect, this is a Military issue training dome. There could be no more appropriate venue for the ceremony. Most of them are held in places like this.'

I realized the rest of the class were listening avidly with fascinated but confused faces. Whatever was going on was a welcome respite from 1930s economics, but they didn't understand it.

Playdon turned to them, and let them in on the secret. 'Jarra is a Military Honour Child. She's 18 and that was the call for the Honour Ceremony.'

The end of his sentence got drowned out by collective class excitement.

'Amaz!' said Dalmora. 'The ceremony comes to the name! We actually get to see . . .'

'If only they'd shown up on the dig site this morning,' wailed Krath. 'An Honour Ceremony with everyone in impact suits. The flag flying in the middle of ruined New York. We'd have made all the newzies!'

'They'd surely have sent us back to the dome to do it,' objected Lolmack.

'You know the rules,' Krath argued. 'The ceremony has to come to the name, wherever they are, whatever they're doing. Remember that boy who was in prison, and they held the Honour Ceremony in his cell. They've held ceremonies in impact suits before too. I remember there was one on a solar power array.'

'And the one last Year Day,' Dalmora said with shining eyes. 'That cadet who'd passed top of his year and won the right to be among the Year Day ceremonial Military at the opening of Parliament. The Honour Guard marched right in to Parliament, and everything stopped in mid-speech, while all the members stood for the Honour Ceremony. It was utterly, utterly zan!'

Yes, I know the Honour Ceremony at the opening of Parliament was probably specially set up for the great publicity, but I agreed with Dalmora. It had still been amaz to watch it.

'It's not too late,' said Krath. 'If we move fast, we could get out to the dig site before they arrive, and they'd have to come to us. Mind you, the vids wouldn't show our faces then, so maybe it would be a better plan to . . .'

'Quiet!' yelled Playdon. 'Let me make one thing absolutely clear. This ceremony is not being used to get anyone on the newzies. I insist on respect during this. Not a word or a squeak out of place from any of you. This is like Remembrance Day but more so. I'm not having any disruption. Understand?'

The class nodded, wide eyed.

'Understand?' repeated Playdon, looking pointedly at Krath.

Krath remembered he already had one red warning, gulped, and nodded.

'Good.' Playdon looked round. 'Now, everyone, move! We have to clear the chairs and tables and clean up this room.'

It wasn't really necessary, but Playdon insisted on hiding the chairs and tables away in peoples' rooms to make the dining hall look more respectable. I left the others to sort it out, because I wanted to cheat just a little bit by changing clothes. I hadn't got a uniform to wear, but quite a few Honour Children wouldn't. I chose trousers and jacket in a suitably Military navy-blue colour, dragged a comb through my hair, studied my reflection in the mirror, and decided that was the best I could do.

I headed back to the dining hall, with a nervous flutter in my stomach. I'd seen plenty of vids of Honour

Ceremonies, and I only had a few words to say, so hopefully I'd get them right. Playdon had the class standing lined up in rows with an aisle left free in the middle. It was like people waiting for Remembrance Day service at school. I walked down the aisle to the front of the hall and tried to stay calm.

Playdon checked the time, dashed off to the portal room, then came back into the hall and took his place in line. 'Class, attention!'

We all came to attention. The class weren't very good at it, but it was the thought that counted. I watched Krath out of the corner of my eye. If there was so much as one snigger from him, then he wouldn't have to worry about getting a warning from Playdon afterwards, because I'd personally kill him! Krath might think these ceremonies pompous and funny, but my grandmother had died to give humanity new worlds, and he'd sure as chaos better respect her and all the others like her. Remembrance dates all the way back into pre-history, because some things are worth remembering.

The Honour Guard entered the hall on time to the second. The Military like to do these things right. In the lead was a white-haired man, in dress uniform, with a slim case under his arm. I'd learned enough to understand the uniform insignia. They'd sent a full Colonel! Amaz!

Behind him were his two aides, also in full dress uniform, and between them floated something small and black. The anthem started to play as they came down the aisle. The Colonel stood to one side with me, while the other two stood by the front wall with the small black square floating between them.

The square unfolded itself, unfolded again, and again, until there was the full size flag of humanity floating at the front of the hall. The music changed from anthem to hymn.

One of the two aides must be controlling the music, and the other the flag, but they were good. I couldn't spot a single movement to give it away.

The hymn hit the high note and ended, and the class recognised their cue. In reasonably good unison, we all saluted the flag.

The Colonel marched centre stage and turned to face me. 'On 12 November 2769 Jarra Tell Morrath died to offer new worlds to humanity.' He recited an incredibly long list of awards, including the Thetis Military medal, and then paused. 'For the honour of Jarra Tell Morrath.'

I gave him my best salute. He presented me with the slim black case, with the flag of humanity engraved on the lid. I held it flat out in front of me, like I'd seen in the vids, and spoke my line. I hope my voice didn't sound shaky. 'For the name and the honour of Jarra Tell Morrath.' That was my name now. The Military would have the name change recorded with Registry at this very moment. That's the sort of detail they do well.

The anthem started playing again; the two aides turned to the flag, and with well practised movements removed the hover tags and folded it. One of them presented the flag to the Colonel, who turned to me and placed it on top of the black case.

A full Military Colonel, his two aides, and a pre-history class of norms all saluted an ape girl. The aides might not have known what I was, but the Colonel must have done. Still, I couldn't detect a single flicker of distaste in his eyes. Of course, he wasn't saluting me, none of them were. They were saluting my grandmother. I was just standing there as a symbol of the honour of the Military being passed on down through the generations.

I know this symbolic stuff is all hopelessly soppy, but like most things there is a point to it. The Military have control of all the weapons of humanity to stop us fighting each other. The Military have control of all the solar power arrays in space. The only things stopping the Military overthrowing the government and ordering us all around are those silly idealistic things: Honour. Trust. Loyalty. All the soppy stuff out of the publicity vids.

Everyone held the salute until the last note of the hymn ended and the ceremony was over, then they relaxed. I expected the Military to just march off, but the Colonel paused for a quick chat while his aides collected the vid bee that had been hovering recording the ceremony for the Military archives.

'I served with your grandmother on Planet First, Jarra. I was rather younger then of course. These days I have a quiet desk job in charge of Earth's solar arrays up in space. Nice view of the home planet of course, but not nearly as exciting.'

I gulped and nodded. I didn't know what to say. I was grazzed that a Military Colonel was speaking to me.

'I saw the commendation. Your grandmother would have been proud of you,' he concluded.

Commendation? What commendation?

The Colonel gave Playdon a friendly nod, and headed off with the two aides trailing after him. I stood there with a black case, a flag of humanity, and a confused expression.

The class clustered round me. Believe it or not, Dalmora was crying. 'Jarra, that was just zan! The symbology. Handing down the honour of the fallen hero to the . . .' She was too emotional to say any more. I expect she was already planning a vid about Military traditions.

Fian spoke up hesitantly. 'Have I got it right? Jarra Tell Morrath is your name now?'

I nodded.

'What's in the box?' asked Krath. 'It's not her ashes, is it?'

'Oh no. Just copies of her medals,' I said. 'Her closest relative would have got the originals when she died.'

I headed off to the door, meaning to take the flag and the medals to my room, but Playdon stopped me. 'This seems an appropriate point to mention something else. University Cassandra formally requested that our help in saving their research team should be recorded. That was still being processed when I checked this morning, but has now gone through. The whole class should find they have a note of commendation on their official record. I'll leave you to read the exact wording yourselves.'

There was a collective gasp, and people all reached for their lookups.

'A few of you will have an extra bit detailing your individual contribution.' Playdon continued. 'Jarra, you have a courage commendation for entering a deep area of collapsing debris to prevent certain loss of life at serious risk of your own.'

The class applauded and I went pink.

Playdon waited for the applause to die down. 'Jarra, you also have a mandatory official reprimand for disobeying dig site safety rules by deliberately entering a deep area of collapsing debris at wanton risk to safety of your life and equipment.'

'That's not fair,' protested Fian.

Playdon actually gave a genuine smile. 'I can't help that. It's mandatory, but coupled with a commendation it won't do her any harm. Consider yourself reprimanded, Jarra.'

'Thank you, sir,' I said.

It was another ten minutes before I managed to escape. Once I was finally alone in my room, I opened the box to take a look inside. There were rows of engraved metal discs. One for each planet my grandmother served on for Planet First. I'd study them, and their planet numbers later, try and work out if any of the new worlds in Epsilon or Kappa sector were there.

There was a set of medals and Military insignia too. No wonder they'd sent a full Colonel. My grandmother had been a Colonel too and they couldn't honour her with a lower rank than her own. I was grazzed.

18

The next day, I woke up and found a mail message from my parents. It was text only, an agonisingly carefully worded few lines. They had been notified the Honour Ceremony had taken place and had watched the recording. They understood it was wholly up to me whether I decided to have contact with them, but they hoped I would.

I read it about five times, with my nerves as tight as Dalmora's guitar strings, and then I called them.

There was no answer of course. I was a nardle to think there would be. My parents weren't just in a different time zone, but on Planet First assignment. I remembered what Joth had said. People fighting a giant, man-eating, whatever, can't ask it to wait because their daughter just called for a chat. The words were silly, but there was a core of truth in them. My parents would be unavailable for calls a lot of the time.

So, I left a message. I asked them to call me when they could, and set my lookup to accept their call as emergency priority. Then I went into breakfast, and ate with my eyes constantly fixed on my lookup. There was still no call when it was time to get into my impact suit, no call when we arrived at our dig site location and it was time for me to start doing my job.

I stared down at the silent lookup. If my parents called and I didn't answer, they might change their minds like Issette's mother and never call again. Even if they did, I'd have to wait for hours or days. I'd already waited eighteen years and . . .

I went over to the tag support sled so Fian could lock the lifeline beam onto my suit. 'Fian, can you do something for me?'

'Yes?'

I handed him my lookup. 'I can't take my lookup with me when I'm tag leading, but if a call comes in then tell me so I can come and answer it.'

'You want me to drag you out of tag leading to answer your mail?' Fian sounded utterly grazzed. 'You really mean it? Playdon will throw a fit.'

'Playdon can throw all the fits he likes,' I said. 'This is . . . This is really important. You'll know the right call, because it'll be flagged as emergency.'

I started work, trying to concentrate on what I was doing. It was two hours later, when I was tagging the last rocks covering what we hoped was a stasis box, that I heard Fian's embarrassed voice on the team circuit.

'Jarra, there's a call on your lookup.'

'What?' asked Playdon. 'You should all have your lookups set to . . .'

I ignored him, dropping my tag gun and setting my hover belt to send me skimming back to Fian's tag support sled. 'Fian, answer the call. Tell them I'm coming.'

'Right . . .' he said.

'Jarra,' said Playdon. 'You can't . . .'

'Sir, this is an emergency.'

'Uh, I've got two Military officers calling from Planet First,' said Fian.

I don't know whether it was because of the desperation in my voice, or Fian's comment, but Playdon backed down. 'All right, Jarra answer your call. Team 1 take a break. Team 2 take over.' He paused. 'I want to make it perfectly clear that nobody is to take this as a precedent. Making personal calls in the middle of a dig site is quite unacceptable.'

I barely heard him. I reached the tag support sled, grabbed my lookup from Fian, and hovered a short distance along the clearway to give myself some privacy before taking the call off standby. I stared for a moment at the two faces on the lookup screen. I'd imagined various fantasies of my parents over the years, and these were nothing like any of them. They were strangers, they looked true combat Military, they were . . . I finally managed to speak.

'Hello.'

They didn't react for a couple of seconds, and I was panicking like a nardle before I remembered this call was being routed through the dedicated comms portal network all the way between Earth and distant Kappa sector, so of course there'd be relay lag. I saw their faces change as they heard me speak.

'Jarra?' asked the woman.

Her hair was almost like mine, though a little longer, and the man . . . Was there a resemblance between our faces, or was I imagining that? I realized that all they could see of me was an anonymous impact suit. I unsealed my hood and tugged it down. 'Yes.'

'We weren't expecting impact suits,' said the man. 'Where are you?'

'I'm on the main New York Dig Site.' I held up the lookup for a moment so they could get a view of the ruins. 'This is what I do. This . . .'

I went all nardle and emotional for a while after that.

Later, I got coherent again, and we talked about what had happened when I was born. My parents were honest about that. They'd had a tough decision to make. It hadn't just been about me and them. They had to think about my older brother and sister as well. I'm not saying that I didn't still feel hurt that they'd dumped me, but I didn't yell any insults, and I don't think I said the exo word.

And eventually my parents had to go and do something Military, and my class had found their stasis box and were preparing to head back to the dome, so we said goodbye. I was both reluctant and relieved to do that. This call had been unbelievable, wonderful beyond anything that amaz or zan or any other words could describe, but I couldn't handle any more emotion.

'In theory, we're on this assignment for at least another three months,' said my mother, 'but things are getting messy on this planet so we may have to pull out. If we do, then perhaps you'll let us visit you on Earth.'

'That would be . . . That would be utterly zan.'

I ended the call and headed back to the waiting sleds. I saw Playdon's distinctive impact suit coming to meet me. I'd broken every rule on the dig site. He was going to kill me, and I didn't care.

'Jarra,' said Playdon, very gently. 'Was that bad news?'

I didn't understand his reaction for a moment, then I realized what I must look like. I was shaking, and my face was . . . I scrubbed the back of my hand across my wet eyes. 'No sir. At least, I don't think . . . It's just . . . I can't explain at the moment, but I appreciate that personal calls are out of place on a dig site. It won't happen again.'

Incredibly, he didn't yell at me about that, or my hood being down, or wandering off alone down the clearway. He just accepted it with a nod of acknowledgement.

As we headed back to the sleds, I pulled up my hood

201

and sealed it to hide my face from the class. I'd explain this to them later, I'd tell them the whole truth, but not now. I needed to give myself a few days to recover before facing that ordeal. It wouldn't be hard to keep up the lies for that long. After the Honour Ceremony, and calls from Planet First, even Playdon believed I was really a norm Military kid who for some incomprehensible reason had sent in her application via an Earth school.

19

It was three days later, during the evening meal, when my lookup chimed to signal emergency mail. I eagerly hurried out of the hall and answered it. I thought it was my parents, calling to tell me they were coming to Earth. I was already celebrating, planning how I could take them to the places that were special to me, like the tropical bird dome of Zoo Europe, and picturing them meeting Candace. But it wasn't my parents. It was a Military General, with a solemn, compassionate expression on his face.

I listened numbly as he described how the Planet First team on K19448 had been forced to abandon the planet and make an emergency withdrawal. They'd held a defensive perimeter while people portalled out. The final group holding the line had suffered casualties as they pulled back to the portals. The General said the words I knew from every Remembrance Day. My parents had lost their lives giving new worlds to humanity.

I held myself together until the call ended, but then I went crazy, pounding the dismal grey flexiplas walls of the corridor with my fists. After so many years of bitterness, I'd finally wound up my nerves to breaking point and contacted my parents. They hadn't told the ape kid to nuke off. They'd called me and talked to me. They'd actually wanted to meet me. It had been . . . It had been like all the happy endings that ape kids hoped for, and it had ended with a Military General saying . . .

And then my anger vanished leaving just a feeling of emptiness. I let my hands drop to my sides, because hitting the walls wouldn't help. Nothing would help now. Fate had finally won, and I didn't care what happened anymore.

I would have just stood there forever, my life in stasis, but someone else wouldn't let me. Jarra Military kid instinctively responded to a civilian in trouble. She took charge, protecting me from reality by taking me into her perfect world. I was her now. I was JMK. I was living the dream, and had everything, and could do anything I wanted, anything at all. My parents were still alive, I could portal to the stars, I could be Military, and I could have Fian.

20

Several of my classmates looked at me anxiously as I came back into the hall, and Playdon came over. 'Everything all right, Jarra?'

That was my second emergency call from Planet First. No wonder these civilians were concerned, and had been treating me like a fragile glass ornament for days. 'Yes. Things had got messy on K19 . . . I mean on the planet where my parents are assigned.'

'I'm assuming that messy is Military language for extremely dangerous,' said Playdon. 'If they'd hit something bad, like the chimera of Thetis, then I can see . . .'

'Exactly. It looked like they might have to pull out while under attack, and that can get nasty, but the situation is back under control. That's great, though it means I won't see them for another few months.'

Playdon nodded and wandered off, but Fian was still hovering nearby, obviously uncertain whether to talk to me or not. I smiled at the way his long blond hair flopped round his shoulders. It was longer than mine. Of course, civilian hair fashions were long at the moment, while the Military tended to be rather more practical.

Fian clearly noticed the smile, because he came over. I'd frozen him off several times, but it looked like he'd decided to make yet another approach. I wondered why I'd kept giving him the cold shoulder. Nerves I suppose, both about the Honour Ceremony, and about possible complications if I got involved with a civilian. Fian was clearly never going to be combat Military, but I might end up just a historian myself.

I really had to make a decision here. Either I kept all men at arm's length for at least four years, or I decided I was open to having relationships and dealt with any problems about how they affected a Military career when and if that happened. If I was going to get involved with anyone, then Fian appealed to me far more than anyone else in the class. He was intelligent, fun, and looked enough like Arrack San Domex for me to get a bit powered just looking at him and that blond hair.

Yes, I know it's a bit silly for a Military Honour Child to drool over the star of a silly vid series like *Defenders*, but I happen to enjoy watching a man with the face, hair, and legs of Arrack San Domex having his clothes torn off by tentacled green aliens.

I'd made my mind up, and it was time to make my move. When you're Military, and you've decided to attack a target, you go for it. No point in a delay that might mean Fian wandering off and turning his attention to one of the other girls. I was tag leader and I was going to tag Fian as mine.

My mind had a naughty moment, as I considered which bit of Fian to tag, and I gave a huge grin. Fian looked a bit puzzled, but grinned hopefully back.

'I've been horribly stressed lately, because of the Honour Ceremony and things getting dangerous on my parents' assignment, but everything is all right now,' I said. 'I can finally relax. Maybe we could watch those history vids you mentioned.'

206

Fian nodded eagerly. 'I could get another bottle of wine as well, though the only place I know to buy wine is back on Hercules.'

I laughed. These civilians were so helpless. With my parents away on assignment most of the time, I'd learnt to manage things for myself. 'Delta sector is a bit far to portal for a bottle of wine. Let's find somewhere closer.'

I took out my lookup and did some rapid checking. 'The nearest settlement to us is . . . a place called Woodstock. They have shops for clothes, furniture, food, and drinks! Let's go!'

I looked round. Lecturer Playdon had been being interrogated by Dalmora about something, but had now escaped to a table by himself. I headed over with Fian following me. 'Permission to use the portal, sir?'

He nodded. 'Remember to check out and back in, so we know who is in the dome in case of emergency.'

'We're allowed to portal?' asked Krath.

Playdon sighed heavily. 'Of course you are. This is a history class, not a jail sentence, but don't come back drunk or powered. I'm not taking people with hangovers out on a high risk dig site.'

Krath frowned. 'On the other hand, I've no idea where to go on Earth, unless . . .' He gazed hopefully at me.

'No,' said Fian. 'You aren't invited on this trip.'

'Jarra could invite me,' said Krath.

I laughed. 'Jarra could,' I said, 'but she isn't going to.'

Fian caught my arm and we ran off to the portal room, dutifully checked out of the dome, and portalled to Woodstock.

'Freedom!' cried Fian, and he dropped to his knees and kissed the ground. We were in the middle of a paved square surrounded by shops, and a few of the shoppers gave Fian funny looks.

I looked round to see what sort of shops they had on

Earth. It looked pretty similar to all the other small shopping squares I'd seen. Well, the Handicapped need the same shops as anyone. 'Wine and drinks!' I pointed out the shop, tugged Fian back up on his feet, and we headed over.

'Any idea what sort of wine?' asked Fian.

I shook my head. 'It's all new to me. With my parents away a lot, I've mostly lived in Residences. It's not easy getting drunk when you're living in a Residence. Getting things past the Military Police is a lot easier than getting things past the Principal of a Residence. There are room sensors monitoring you all the time as well. If the sensor decides what's going on in your room is inappropriate for your age group then a horrible computer voice starts lecturing you.'

'Really?' Fian looked appalled. 'They spy on you in your rooms? You get no privacy?'

'Well, no real people can see what you're doing. It's just sensors, but even just a computer commenting on your behaviour is off-putting at times, and of course they block the adult vid channels.'

'I bet it's a bit limiting,' said Fian. He suddenly laughed. 'No wonder you're a nice contract girl. My home planet is very conservative even by Deltan standards, but even I managed to sneak off with a few friends occasionally and watch vids.'

'Beta sector vids?' I saw him blush and laughed. 'Anyway, I've escaped the evil sensors now. My room here may not have a nice bathroom like my old one, but the only sensor is to detect fires.'

'Yes,' said Fian, grinning back at me. 'It opens up a lot of possibilities.'

I blushed this time. 'Getting back to the subject of wine, let's apply Keon's law of shopping and buy a couple of bottles that are cheap but not the very cheapest.'

'That's your brother?'

'Yes. He has a low effort approach to life, but he says taking it too far tends to be counterproductive. I'm applying the same logic to buying cheap wine. Really cheap might mean really bad.'

Fian laughed as we examined prices of bottles. 'Keon sounds a bit of a strange person to be in the Military.'

I grinned. 'Keon is a strange person to be in anything.'

'What does he do?' Fian picked up two bottles. 'Let's have a red one and a white one. That should keep us going for a few days.'

'He's a laser specialist.'

Fian pulled a face. 'Like that laser gun you used in the rescue? Scary. Is Keon good with them?'

'We all expected him to be hopeless, but then he won an award. My brother seems to have surprising depths, but he keeps them well hidden most of the time.'

Fian scanned out the wine. 'Shall we head back?'

I grinned. 'One more stop. I spotted a takeaway food place.'

'Real food! Lead on!'

I looked at the menu in the takeaway food shop, listed a huge order, and entered my credit code to pay.

Fian watched wide-eyed. 'You have an extremely healthy appetite. Is this normal for the Military?'

'I want to treat the class to a decent meal. I feel like celebrating.'

He laughed. 'You're suddenly very happy today. That call on the dig site . . . You must have been really worried.'

'Of course I was, but they've got everything back under control now.'

We staggered back to the portal, struggling to hold on to all the boxes and bags. Back in the dome, we just about made it to the dining hall without dropping anything. The class stared at us.

'We brought real food,' I told them. 'Eat!'

They cheered wildly and dived for the boxes.

'How much do we owe you?' asked Krath.

'My treat,' I said. 'I'm celebrating my courage commendation.'

'You're sure?' asked Dalmora.

'Yes. I'm on a Military scholarship, remember.' I grinned. 'Next time, you buy your own.'

Krath started loading a plate with food. 'Where is this takeaway?'

I'd prepared for the helplessness of civilians by picking up a stack of leaflets from Woodstock shopping square. I handed them round to eager hands. Everyone ate while reading through the delights that Woodstock had to offer the desperate history student.

'Alcohol!' cried the Betans.

'Hairdresser!' rejoiced Dalmora.

I'd noticed that Dalmora had been getting steadily less well-groomed with every day that went by. Her long black hair no longer had the glittering light ornaments, and was usually hanging down her back in an inexpert plait.

Fian and I collected some food, and our bottles of wine, and went out the door. After a second, I popped my head back into the hall. 'The portal code for Woodstock Shopping Square is on the back of the leaflet,' I told them.

'I'd been wondering where it was,' said Lolia.

Honestly, civilians! I left them to do the next logical step of losing the leaflet, or forgetting to check in or out of the dome.

Fian and I had a great time watching history vids, had a big argument about the Second Roman Empire which I won, and another about the First Roman Empire which I lost, and then watched an episode of *Stalea of the Jungle*.

As in the last episode I'd seen, the vid ended with Stalea

throwing her lover across a jungle clearing and then pinning him down.

Fian looked hopefully up at me from his cushion on the floor. 'I suppose there's no chance of you throwing me across the room?'

I looked round the room, and shook my head. 'Far too dangerous. My unarmed combat tutor would have a fit. We'd need somewhere bigger with a padded floor.'

Fian sighed. 'Pity. I have these dreams . . .'

I stood up. 'Well, time to say goodnight.'

He sighed again.

Oh well, I thought. Why not give Fian a treat. After all, he did look very like Arrack San Domex. I grinned, jumped on him, pinned him to the floor, and gave him a long and thorough kiss before leaving.

As I went out the door, Fian was lying on the floor and muttering. 'Totally, totally, totally zan!'

21

The next day, I started suffering from some sort of mailing error. I got mails from Issette and Keon, but also several from total strangers. They seemed to be for a girl called Jarra Reeath. I fired off a complaint to Message Services, and they said they'd investigate, but the things kept coming.

I'd never had a problem with my mail in all my years living on Military bases, but the minute I moved into civilian territory it all went haywire. Typical. Fortunately, I was much too happy during the next two weeks to let myself get annoyed about trivial mailing errors.

It will sound completely nardle, but I'd never felt like this before. I wasn't just happy, I was blissfully relaxed. Fian and I were really special together. At least, I felt that way, and he seemed to feel the same. We hit our first problem on the day I had a dig site accident. Something deep underground suddenly gave way, and there was a major cave-in. Fian reacted quickly, but he couldn't get me entirely clear of it. I got carried down among tumbling rocks, and buried by them.

That was scary of course. My suit triggered so hard it stunned me, and when I woke up I couldn't move or see.

The suit material was clamped tight round me making it hard to breathe. It had registered a major incident, so my comms had gone to emergency mode. My suit was squawking Mayday codes, Playdon was calling me on the team circuit, and Dig Site Command was talking to me on auto distress channel.

'I'm fine,' I said, getting over the initial shock rapidly. I'd been buried a couple of times on school trips so I knew the routine, but it's always reassuring to hear the voices of rescuers. 'Team all right? How deep am I?'

'The team were safe on the clearway,' said Playdon. 'You're only under a few rocks, but they're big ones.'

'This is Dig Site Command. Do you require assistance, Asgard 6?'

'This is Asgard 6,' said Playdon. 'We should be able to handle this within fifteen minutes. I'm already tagging rocks myself.'

'Don't mess up my tidy dig site,' I said, and lay there waiting.

It was probably only ten minutes before I was back on the tag support sled with Fian and running my suit diagnostics. It was a really minor dig site accident, but Fian was very shaken by it. I assured him that he'd done really well, keeping me clear of the main cave-in, but he was in a filthy mood for the rest of the day.

That evening, we were watching a vid in my room, and suddenly . . . Well, up until then, we'd had our boundaries nicely established. Details about what a nice contract boy and girl do, or don't do, vary between people. Fian and I had worked out our personal rules for boy and girling, but now he went a bit crazy. I fought him off, and he came back to his senses, apologized, and retreated to his room. I wasn't quite sure where that left us, and I didn't sleep too well.

The next morning, I sat in my room and waited nervously

to see if he showed up as usual. He had a routine of bringing our breakfasts on a tray, and we'd eat them and chat. I reflected that last night had made one thing clear at least. Fian might get a bit powered at the idea of a girl pinning him down and kissing him, but he was quite capable of taking the initiative himself.

There was a knock on my door, and Fian came in, carrying the usual breakfast tray. He settled himself on the floor, and started eating. I decided he looked reasonably sane and safe today, sat next to him and started eating too.

'Sorry about yesterday,' he said. 'It was the effect of seeing you get buried. I'd been so scared and . . .'

'It really wasn't a dangerous situation. I wasn't far down, and there were plenty of people at the site to dig me out. It's when everyone gets buried, like the situation with Cassandra 2, that you're in real trouble.'

'Well, I couldn't help being scared,' said Fian, 'I thought I'd lost you, I realized how much I cared, and when we got back here I got a bit carried away . . .'

I giggled. 'I noticed you getting carried away.'

'We need to do some serious talking. I'm a nice contract boy, and if you're planning to get yourself buried like that again . . . Well, we need to go legal before I'm shocked by my own behaviour.' He gave me the look that was all his own, serious and funny at the same time.

I wasn't sure how much of that he meant as a joke. It was still early days for us to be thinking of Twoing contracts. 'Well, we can't do serious talking now. We're going to be late.'

We met up with the others at the dome door. This morning we had a special training session. Tomorrow we had a whole day off. The day after that we were heading deep into New York Main to spend three days out on the Grand Circle. Well, all of us except the Betans. Playdon had excused them from the trip so they could spend more time with Lolette.

We went outside, opened up the sled storage dome, and started doing some complicated shuffling of sleds. The special transport sled with the mobile dome parts was near the back since we hadn't used it yet. When that moved outside, I spotted something much smaller that had been hidden behind it.

'Amaz!' I said, heading over to look.

Fian followed me. 'What is it?'

'Survey plane for aerial surveys. Maybe they have one at every dome here. On New York Fringe they only had two for the whole site.'

Playdon's voice came over the team circuit. 'Team 1, I need you over here now. You get first try at assembling the mobile dome.'

'That's us,' said Fian, and we headed outside.

Fian, Dalmora, Krath, Amalie and I were still team 1. I was happy with that. I had total faith in Fian as my tag support. The girls were both reliable. Krath was a bit of an idiot as a person, but he was great as a heavy lift operator. Playdon had been gradually grouping the rest of the class into teams that worked together as well.

Team 1 tended to be working most of the time, since Playdon was often running dual teams now. He trusted team 1 to be reasonably sensible, so he could give most of his attention to supervising the other team that was working. Team 2 were pretty good given their lack of experience. Teams 3 and 4 were adequate, but you wouldn't want to let them loose anywhere too dangerous.

Team 5 had ten people, but that included Lolia and Lolmack who were only on site occasionally now. They were the leftovers who were planning to be purely theoretical historians and were just enduring the practical sessions on dig sites as a compulsory evil. They had an amicable arrangement going on with Playdon. If they made an effort to do the few things he asked of them as well as they could, then he would get them their minimum practical pass grade with as little work and danger as possible.

My team started working on the mobile dome while the others watched. Mobile domes come in nicely labelled pieces, and it's really easy to assemble them if the previous users packed the bits in the proper sequence, and haven't broken or lost anything. Of course you can't depend on that, which was why Playdon was getting us to do some dome building training today. It was obviously better to find out any problems before we were stuck hours away out on the Grand Circle. Emergency evac portals are intended for emergencies, not for teams who are missing some mobile dome locking pins.

It turned out that we had all the right pieces, though the previous team had helpfully packed them with the dome segments on top of the base pieces. This is a bad idea, because obviously you have to start with the dome base.

We packed things up properly, and team 2 had their turn at dome building. It was easier for them because they had the pieces in the right order.

I watched them for a few minutes, and then couldn't resist calling Playdon on the private circuit. 'Permission to speak, sir?'

'Yes, Jarra?'

'I saw there was a survey plane at the back of the storage dome, sir. I wondered if there was any chance of us flying it.'

'I'm afraid not. I haven't got a pilot's licence.'

'Actually, sir,' I said. 'I happen to have one.'

'You've got a pilot's licence?' Playdon sounded startled. 'How did you manage that? I thought Military pilots

216

started their training at the Military Academy rather than at school.'

'I got my pilot's licence at New York Fringe, sir. I was with a school trip there seven months ago, and Fringe was doing a complete new site survey. I'd managed to cadge rides on survey planes before, but this time I was 17 so the pilot could get me through my mandatory hours and qualified to solo.'

'I see,' said Playdon thoughtfully. 'So you picked up your tag leader knowledge on the Fringe. When did you start going there?'

'Well, Fringe and other places too, sir. I've had three trips to Fringe. The first was when I was 11.'

'11! The University only works on New York Main of course. The Fringe is much safer, so I knew they didn't insist on the minimum age of 18, but I'd no idea they let people in that young. The site rules must surely still apply to a Military school party.'

'Fringe minimum requirement isn't age related, but having your gold safety award. You need qualified adult team leaders of course.'

'Amazing,' he murmured. 'I wish I'd known this before the Cassandra 2 rescue. I'd have felt slightly less guilty about letting you take the risks of tag leading it. You were right that it was safer for everyone if I was on sensors and watching the team, but I still nearly had a heart attack when that girder fell, not to mention when you dived down that hole to tag the failing suit.'

He paused for a moment. 'I'll ask Dig Site Command about the survey plane.'

There were several minutes of silence while he talked on another channel, then he was back again. 'Dig Site Command are delighted to help a new pilot keep up their practice time, and would like you to run a few survey legs to update their dig site mosaic while you're up there. Make sure you run full diagnostics and power checks pre launch, because the plane may have been gathering dust a while.'

'Thank you, sir.' I grinned joyously inside my impact suit. 'Would you like to come along for the ride?'

'No thank you,' said Playdon hastily. 'I'm sure you're a competent pilot, but . . . Don't spread this around, but I'm scared of heights. Take one of the others if you like.'

'Thank you, sir.' I dashed off to where Fian was standing watching team 2 work on the dome. 'Fian, this is zan, Playdon is letting me take up the survey plane.'

'What?' Fian gasped.

'Would you like a ride?'

'Me? Go up there?' He pointed at the sky. 'If something goes wrong, how do you get down? Does it have portals?'

'No,' I admitted. 'You have to jump out.'

'Jump?' He gulped.

'You wear a special hover tunic, which would slow your fall, and the impact suit protects you when you hit the ground, but you shouldn't have to jump. I'm a qualified pilot.'

'I'm sure you are . . .' He sounded terrified.

'It was only an offer, and you don't have to accept,' I reassured him. 'If you don't fancy it, I can take one of the others.'

'Oh no,' said Fian. 'I'm not staying on the ground worrying about Krath or Joth being up there with you.'

I laughed and headed into the sled storage dome. It took several minutes to get Fian and me into our tunics and settled into our seats in the survey plane, and then I ran two sets of in depth diagnostic and power checks. The system log said the plane hadn't moved in nearly a year, so I was taking no chances.

Finally, I engaged hovers and started the plane moving

out through the double doors. By now team 3 were building the mobile dome, but when the class saw the plane they abandoned work and came over to take a look. Planes aren't left open like sleds, they have closed cockpits, so I could only hear what they were saying on the team circuit.

'Is that a plane?' asked Krath.

'Yes,' said Playdon. 'Jarra has a pilot's licence. She's going to fly a little survey.'

'Zan!' said Krath. 'Can I have a ride?'

'Only one passenger seat,' said Fian smugly, 'and I'm in it!'

'That's unfair,' complained Krath. 'We should draw lots to decide who goes up.'

'I don't want to go up there,' said Amalie.

'Nor me,' said Joth.

'It's pilot's choice,' said Playdon.

'I need my tag support,' I said.

'Everyone over to one side out of the way, please,' said Playdon. 'Jarra, let Dig Site Command know you're ready. Use broadcast channel. We always use that for plane launches so people aren't taken by surprise when a plane goes over.'

I positioned the plane to have a nice clear run ahead of me, and nervously opened broadcast channel. Painfully aware that the whole of New York Main would hear me, I tried to sound calm and professional. 'This is Asgard 6 survey plane. Requesting link up to mosaic feed, and clearance to launch.'

'This is Dig Site Command. Opening link to mosaic data feed now. Asgard 6, you are clear to launch survey plane.'

Fian gulped and hung on to his seat.

I closed broadcast channel, hit the thrusters, and we shot forward. 'Hoo eee!' I shouted joyously as I pulled back on the stick. We soared upwards and then banked left to circle over the domes and our class below. I gave them a wave.

'It's a long way down,' said Fian in a shaky voice. 'A long, long way down.'

'We're still lower than some of the ruined towers.' I climbed for more height and did one more circle over the domes.

'They look like ants down there,' said Fian.

I banked right now, flying over the dig site to the survey start location that was flashing on one of my screens, and spoke on broadcast channel again. 'This is Asgard 6 survey plane. Approaching survey start point and opening image transmission now. Are we green?'

'This is Dig Site Command. Image transmission is green.'

I closed broadcast channel as I went through my survey start point and started flying the first leg across the site.

'What are we doing exactly?' asked Fian.

'Taking aerial images and scans. They go into Dig Site Command's system and get patched together to make the dig site map mosaic.'

'That's the thing Playdon uses to project site models and decide where we should work?'

'That's right,' I said. 'They need to update it every now and then because of things like buildings collapsing or being demolished. Danger levels change when buildings come down.'

'Amaz,' said Fian. 'It's really weird being up here, and actually collecting the data for that. I'd never even seen a plane before.'

'They had much bigger planes than this back in prehistory,' I said happily. 'Until they invented the portal, people used planes for long distance transport. They had planes that could carry hundreds of people at a time, and went faster than the speed of sound. Once they invented the portal, of course they didn't need them anymore. Now we only have a few specialist aircraft for jobs like this and the emergency services.'

Fian didn't say anything.

'They used satellites out in space to do surveys like this back then. They used them for communications, and to monitor the weather too. Once they had portals, and created the comms network, those gradually all fell apart. Now we only have the Solar Watch satellites.'

Fian still didn't say anything.

I turned the plane to fly the second survey leg. I hoped Fian wasn't going to be air sick. The pilot who taught me to fly said people can sometimes be sick, and being sick in an impact suit is nasty. The suit takes care of it enough to stop you choking but . . .

'How are you feeling, Fian?'

'I was absolutely terrified, but now I'm just incredibly scared.'

I laughed. 'I was a bit scared the first time I got a ride in a plane. I was really relieved to be back on the ground again. The next time was much more fun.'

'I think this trip is enough for me to cope with at the moment, without worrying about another one,' said Fian. 'Promise me that we stay at ground level tomorrow. We are spending tomorrow together, aren't we? If you go off with Krath, I'll sulk.'

I sighed. 'Why do you keep saying things like that? You can't seriously think I'm interested in the idiot, Krath.'

'Of course not,' Fian said. 'I just keep mentioning him in the hope that you'll say something about me being more intelligent and handsome than he is. That's not asking for much. A Herculean marsh crawler is brighter and better looking than Krath. You could even say a few more affectionate things to me. I'm a nice contract boy from Hercules, but I promise I wouldn't be shocked if things got a little personal.'

I giggled. 'I'm not good at saying emotional stuff.'

221

'I'd noticed that,' said Fian. 'Of course, you might improve with practice, and I'm perfectly willing to let you practice on me. What are we doing tomorrow?'

'I thought we could go to the zoo.'

'They have zoos here?'

'They have zoos everywhere.'

'But why?' said Fian. 'I mean Hercules has a zoo with Earth animals because it's part of our cultural heritage, but why do they need one on Earth?'

'How many Earth animals have you seen here?'

'Some wolves and some deer. I see what you mean.'

'We can go somewhere else if you prefer,' I offered.

'No, I like zoos,' said Fian. 'I belong to Zoolink.'

'Me too,' I said. 'America is a big continent, so I thought we should go to Zoo America South. It will be a lot warmer there.'

'I'm looking forward to it,' said Fian. 'Almost as much as I'm looking forward to being on the ground again.'

'Once we've finished our survey we can land. Or we could stop up a bit longer and give you flying lessons.'

'No, thank you,' said Fian, hastily. 'Perhaps next time.'

When we landed, he did his kissing the ground act again. It didn't work so well when he was wearing an impact suit.

22

'This is going to be a romantic day,' said Fian, as we entered the dining hall next morning. 'Just you, me, and twenty-six members of the class.'

I giggled.

'Only Lolia and Lolmack have gone somewhere by themselves, and that's to see Lolette.'

'Civilians,' I said, sadly. 'No initiative.'

Fian pulled a face of long suffering martyrdom. 'So I have to spend all day watching the lowlife, Krath, make advances towards you, and listening to him repeat his dad's stupid ideas?'

I gave him a suspicious look. 'Are you really upset, or just pretending?'

'I'm a bit disappointed,' he said. 'Our first chance to spend a whole day together alone, and we have twenty-six gate crashers tagging along.'

'Look on the bright side, with twenty-eight of us portalling together, the portal price per head is so low that they practically owe us money for travelling. Anyway, I have a plan.' I lowered my voice to a whisper. 'When we get to the zoo, I send them all for ice cream and we run and hide. They must be capable of portalling back on their own.'

Fian brightened up.

I clapped my hands loudly. 'Zoo time!' I shouted, and led the mob to the portal room. I entered the code for Zoo America South, and the portal started talking to us.

'Warning,' it said, 'your destination has an admission charge that will be debited from your personal account together with the charge for this journey.' It listed the admission charges. 'Members of Zoolink Federation are admitted free,' it concluded. The portal appeared and the 28 of us went through in an orderly line.'

'Warmth,' said Dalmora happily. 'Utter blizz.'

There was bright sunshine here, with a gentle breeze blowing. It was a complete contrast to the icy, bleak landscape back at the dig site.

'Oh, I like this,' said Amalie, looking round at the lawns, flowerbeds, and huge clear domes that showed more plants inside. 'I've never been to a zoo. We haven't got one at home yet, but it's on the planetary development plan for five years time.'

Since Amalie was from Epsilon, we were getting used to that sort of remark from her. It was just like all the jokes about Epsilon. Her first month at school had been spent helping to build it. The Epsilon planets would be really great places in about ten years time, but right now most things were still in flexiplas sections waiting to be assembled.

'First of all,' I said, 'let's get ice cream. There must be ice cream dispensers near the portals.'

Everybody looked round. 'Over there,' said Krath. 'What would you like, Jarra?'

'Chocolate, please.'

Krath's eyes flickered towards Fian, as if he was expecting to get a protest from him. 'Coming right up.'

He led a massed charge towards the ice cream supplies.

Fian and I waited ten seconds, then ran down a path past a dome and hid behind a large bush.

'Did we lose them?' asked Fian.

'I think so,' I said. 'Do you realize, I just made the ultimate sacrifice for you. Chocolate ice cream!'

'I'm worth it,' said Fian. 'Some things can be even better than chocolate ice cream. Allow me to demonstrate.'

We shared an embrace that was interrupted by my lookup chiming for an emergency call. I hastily pulled it out, rather worried. 'If that's Krath messing about trying to find us, I'll strangle him.'

'I hope your family are all right,' said Fian.

'It's a call from Issette.' I accepted the call.

I was relieved to see Issette grinning away on the screen. 'Jarra! Jarra! News!' She waved her left hand, showing a ring. 'We're Twoing.'

'What!' I matched her grin. 'You and Keon? That's wonderful. However did you get him to make the effort?'

Keon's head bobbed into view. 'Issette's much less effort if you keep her happy. They only let you have three months on the first contract. Next time, I want a year contract to save having to bother for a bit.'

Issette spotted Fian standing next to me, and her eyebrows went up. 'Who's the Arrack San Domex look alike?' she whispered.

I put a finger to my lips. 'Shhh.'

I was too late of course. Issette always did have a penetrating whisper. She used to get in trouble at school, when the teachers overheard her using their unflattering nicknames. I was usually the one she was talking to when she did it, so I got in trouble too.

'I'm Fian,' said Arrack San Domex's stand in.

Issette's eyes went from him to me, and back again, in eager speculation, then her face suddenly changed. 'He's not one of them, is he?' Her hand shot to her mouth, and she gave an apologetic look at Fian. 'Sorry.'

That was typical of Issette too. Speak first, think later.

'I quite understand.' Fian grinned. 'I am indeed, as you phrase it, one of them.'

'I didn't mean any harm,' said Issette. 'It was just a shock. Jarra has always been rather critical about you . . . people.'

I groaned, but had to admit it was true. I can be a bit withering about civilians.

'I know,' said Fian. 'On our first day on the dig site, it was quite clear that Jarra knew everything and felt the rest of us were completely incompetent. She even orders Lecturer Playdon around.'

Issette giggled. 'Jarra knows everything about history and dig sites because she's obsessive. She's always trying to lecture me, and she can be really pushy. You have to be firm with her.'

'I wouldn't dare,' said Fian. 'She warned us on the first day that if anyone got out of line, she'd throw them across the room. I wouldn't have gone anywhere near her, but I needed protecting from a Betan girl who was making comments about my legs.'

Issette had another giggling fit. 'Jarra threw Cathan across the room on Year Day. It was totally zan! He's still sulking about it.'

'She hasn't thrown me across the room yet,' said Fian, 'but I live in hope.'

'You want to be thrown across rooms?' Keon was intrigued enough to make the effort to ask a question.

'Only gently,' said Fian. 'I don't want broken bones, but I'm a *Stalea of the Jungle* fan. You know it?'

'Yes,' said Keon, 'but Stalea's not my type. Dominating women are too much effort for me, but if you like that kind of girl then Jarra is ideal for you.'

I sighed heavily. 'I'm not that bad.'

'Oh yes you are,' chorused the other three in unison.

'I think you two are great together, but . . .' Issette hesitated. 'You've talked through the potential future problems?'

We hadn't of course. I'd briefly considered the complications if I got involved with a civilian, but I hadn't talked about it with Fian. 'It's a bit early days for that,' I said.

'Oh no it isn't,' said Fian. 'I'm a nice contract boy from Delta sector, and Jarra's intentions had better be honourable. I expect Twoing contracts, and marriage one day, as well as being thrown gently across rooms and pinned to the floor!'

I went pink, but Issette and Keon were loving this.

'We're both planning to do a practical pre-history degree, but I realize I may have to make a few compromises after that,' said Fian, cheerfully. 'I'm sure we can work things out. My main worry at the moment is that Jarra is planning to teach me to fly.'

'What!' Issette shook her head. 'Don't tell me she got her hands on a plane again. If you don't want to fly then just say no.'

'I've already flown,' said Fian, with his best fake martyred air. 'I had no choice. If I hadn't got in that plane, the snake Krath would have been in there making advances to Jarra. He follows her everywhere. So does everyone for that matter. Twenty-six of the class followed us to this zoo. We had to send them for ice cream and then run away.'

Issette grinned. 'Jarra is mad about zoos.' She glanced sideways, apparently listening to something. 'I'm afraid I've got to go now, some of my classmates are waiting for us, but it was nice to meet you, Fian.'

'Do I have to come?' asked Keon.

'Yes!' ordered Issette.

Keon groaned. 'Women are so much work. Lasers are much less demanding.'

The screen went blank.

Fian laughed. 'Keon's just how you described him. So, Issette got her contract. I expect that's made you a lot happier.'

'It's wonderful,' I said. 'There's only one dark cloud on the horizon.'

'Which is?'

I peered through the branches of our bush. 'Krath is coming this way.'

We ran down some more paths, and reached the tropical bird dome. We went inside, and hid ourselves away on a nice private bench behind a mass of huge palm leaves, while birds flew around overhead like feathered jewels.

'Alone at last in a jungle clearing,' said Fian. 'This seems a good time to grant you permission to intrude on my restricted body areas.'

I frowned at him. 'I've been looking things up. According to the social guidelines, Deltans are supposed to be terribly strict about respecting that boundary until they're actually married.'

He grinned. 'We aren't in Delta sector, and this particular Deltan is very adaptable.'

23

The next day we were back in impact suits, and heading out to face winter in the New York ruins. The class drove a whole convoy of hover sleds along the clearway into the dig site. Fian and I were riding at the back of the lead transport sled. The rest of team 1 and Playdon were sitting nearer the front.

When we were at the zoo, Issette had raised that tricky question about future problems. Since then, I'd been trying to avoid discussing it, but Fian was insisting. Despite all the jokes about me ordering him around, Fian was extremely stubborn about getting his own way when he wanted something, and he had me cornered on this sled. I finally sighed and gave in.

'All right,' I said in a low voice, 'if we must . . . I know quite well that you aren't the Military type. I'm still torn between Military and history. Once I've got my pre-history degree then I really have to make a choice. If I'm committed to a relationship with a civilian at that point, then that would affect the decision.'

Fian shook his head. 'I could make some compromises.'

'Military couples are normally sent on the same active

assignment. That can hinder their career a bit, but it's much better for the relationship. Civilian partners of Military personnel can't go on active assignment, and can have a tough time. They spend too much of their lives waiting around for their partner to be on leave for a few weeks. I wouldn't want things to be like that.'

For some reason, I felt uncomfortable talking about this. I couldn't work out why, but my head really didn't want to debate this issue. Maybe it was all the jokes Issette and Keon had made about me being dominating. I didn't want to push Fian into contracts and commitments. 'I think it's silly to worry too much about something four years away. Can't we just leave it that we would both be willing to make compromises?'

'All right,' said Fian.

We sat in silence for a while. Playdon had been sitting scanning something on his lookup, and occasionally glancing round to check on the other sleds, now he suddenly burst out laughing.

'What's so funny?' asked Krath.

'I was just scanning something for Lolia and Lolmack,' said Playdon. 'They've come up with their first attempt at a vid script. I promised to check their history facts for them, on condition that they don't credit me as an adviser. They kindly offered to, but I'm not sure it would help my professional career.'

Everyone in hearing distance laughed.

'It's the twentieth century, the evening of the Cuban missile crisis,' continued Playdon. 'Two lovers are facing the fact that the world is on the brink of nuclear war and this might be their last night alive. The historical background is quite authentic, until the lovers portal to an isolated cottage where they can surrender to their mutual passion.'

'So what's wrong with . . . oh,' said Krath.

'Yes, it's a terribly easy mistake to make,' said Playdon. 'Other than that, it's not bad. The viewers might actually learn some history from the first half of the script. The second half is the mutual passion, and I'm assuming the Betans know what they're doing in that area.'

The sleds drove on. The class had been cheerfully chatting for the first hour, but now everyone was getting quiet. Out here the ruins were higher, and blacker, and grimly threatening. At least, they seemed that way when we were so far from our base. We turned left on to the Grand Circle and drove a lot further. The ruins didn't get any better.

'I know this will make me sound like a cowardly panicking civilian, but I can't help feeling the ruins are a bit menacing out here,' said Fian.

'Judging from how quiet everyone is, I think a lot of other people are feeling that way too,' I said. 'It feels a bit lonely this far into the ruins, and of course they really are a lot higher here than near the edge.'

'That's not my imagination then?'

'Oh no. As a rule, the further in you are, the taller the buildings were when they were originally built. They're also more likely to have dangerous underground areas.' I glanced round to check no one else would be able to hear me and whispered. 'I find it a bit scary here too.'

'I'm not sure whether I should be glad to hear that or totally terrified,' said Fian.

I giggled.

The sleds finally stopped at a wide point in the Grand Circle clearway, and Playdon got us all to gather round. 'We'll be setting up the dome at the edge here. It's wide enough that we'll have space to drive the sleds past it. Ahead and left of the clearway is where we'll be excavating. A little further beyond that is an emergency evac portal if we have any problems.'

Everyone brightened up noticeably at this news. I have to admit that I found it comforting too.

'First, we set up the dome,' Playdon told us, 'and then we can all have a little break from wearing impact suits. Team 1, please assemble the dome.'

We had the dome up and equipped in half an hour, piled inside with our luggage, and switched on the heat panels and the glows. Playdon had only allowed one bag each in addition to our sleep sacks, though Dalmora got a special dispensation to bring her guitar, but things were still crowded. I dashed over to the furthest point from the door, and unrolled my sleep sack to claim one of the coveted positions by the dome wall and near a heat panel.

Fian sprinted after me, and unrolled his sleep sack next to mine. 'I take it this is one of the best spots.'

I nodded. 'Near the wall is best, because of the heat panels, and because less people tread on you when they decide to go to the bathroom at night. Away from the door is best, because every time it opens people near it will freeze.'

There was a chaotic few minutes, as everyone peeled off impact suits and fought to be first in line for the two minis-cule bathrooms. I took off my impact suit, but I didn't join the rush. Instead, I dug a packet of moisturizing wipes out of my bag.

'We don't want the bathrooms?' Fian asked.

I handed him another packet of wipes. 'I'm planning to wait until they discover there isn't a shower. The queue will die down fast.'

Even without a shower, it felt good just to be out of my restrictive impact suit. I stretched blissfully, and pulled on a robe over my skintight.

Playdon wandered over carrying a box. 'We have a choice of three flavours of soup.'

'I'll take the red one,' I said.

'What flavour is that?' asked Fian.

I grinned. 'Hard to say what it's supposed to be, but it's possible tomato is in there. All I know is that it's a lot better than the yellow or the green.'

'I'll have red, please,' said Fian.

Playdon handed us a couple of squeezy bags and headed off. I showed Fian the tab that heated the soup, and we sat sucking the glorious, tomatoish warmth.

Playdon allowed us an hour to complain about the packaged soup and lack of showers, before ordering us back into impact suits. We headed outside to the hover sleds.

'We'll take a sensor sled, a tag support sled, and the transports,' said Playdon. 'We're just doing some preparation work for tomorrow.'

Our excavation area was only about three minutes along the clearway. The inner core of a building was to one side of it. All four walls had collapsed long ago, but a central spine still stood with some floors clinging drunkenly to it. You could see the remains of what might once have been furniture on one floor.

Playdon looked at it for a minute or two before speaking on the team circuit. 'As you can see, that building is very dangerous. Our first job is to clear the hazard by blowing it up.'

Hoo eee! I thought happily. Blowing things up was fun.

'Are you familiar with placing explosives, Jarra?' asked Playdon.

I set my comms to reply on the team circuit. 'No, sir. They wouldn't let you do that unless you were 18.'

'Excellent,' said Playdon. 'Class, pay very close attention to this moment. We've actually discovered something that Jarra doesn't know how to do.'

The class seemed to find this extremely funny for some reason, but eventually the laughter died down and Playdon could continue talking.

'Unfortunately, for the explosives to do a clean job of demolition, we need them placed on the base of that central post.'

'You mean, Jarra goes under that lot?' asked Fian's anxious voice.

Playdon shook his head. 'No. Manually placing charges is more accurate, but too dangerous in this situation. We'll use the charge rifle.'

He went over to the transport sled, unlocked a secure storage box, and took out a sort of giant gun. He attached a green cylinder to it, and handed it to me. I held the charge rifle for a second, getting a feel for the balance and weight, and rested the end experimentally against my shoulder.

'It's loaded with dummy charges at the moment,' said Playdon, 'so you can pick a target and have a few practice shots. It's firing sizeable solid objects, so very different from using a tag gun. Always make sure you're standing on something solid, and brace yourself before firing. If you use it when you're hovering in mid air, then the recoil sends you flying.'

I braced myself against the side of a sled, and chose a target rock at about the same distance away as the building central post but well clear of it. I squinted through the rifle sights, aimed and fired. The rifle kicked back into my shoulder, triggering the impact suit. I was frozen in position for a moment as the suit material locked.

'Nice shot,' said Playdon, looking at where the dummy charge was stuck to the rock.

I laughed. 'When the rifle recoils into my shoulder, the impact suit locks up.'

'Yes, you have to wait a few seconds between shots. Keep

going with the dummy charges for a while. Even when you're used to a charge rifle, it's always best to have a few goes with those before using the explosive ones. A misplaced charge is bound to happen now and then, it's not a disaster, but it can be inconvenient.'

I took nine more shots and then Playdon seemed happy. 'Jarra, you witness the counts.' He unlocked the storage box again, and swapped the green charge cylinder on the rifle for a red one. 'You see that the live charge cylinder is red and so are the charges. That's to prevent any risk of confusing live and dummy charges.'

He counted out four objects. 'I have four live charges.'

I confirmed that, and Playdon loaded the four charges into the cylinder. 'Rifle is loaded with four live charges.'

I confirmed that again for the record. Playdon handed me the rifle and locked the secure box again.

'That building is really only held up by the central column,' he said, 'but we need to take down the remains of two other columns as well. Jarra, try and place two charges on the central column, and one on each of the others. We'll get more charges if we need them.'

I decided to try for the easier targets first, and used my hover belt to skim across the clearway to get a good angle on one of the isolated columns. I dropped down to stand on the rubble, positioned myself, and fired.

'It didn't go bang,' complained Krath. 'What went wrong?'

'We set off the charges later,' said Playdon. 'That one looks good. Next target, Jarra.'

I headed back along the clearway to get a clean shot at the second column. That went well too, but I couldn't find a good place on the clearway to fire at the central column. The only possible spot had a tree blocking my line of sight. 'I think I'll have to move over to that big lump of concrete to shoot the last charges.'

'I agree,' said Playdon. 'Fian, sort out Jarra's lifeline. She may only be out there for two minutes, but accidents can happen in seconds. That building could collapse just from having a charge shot at it.'

So there was a brief delay while we sorted out the lifeline, and then I swooped over to my chosen block of concrete. It gave me the good view I'd hoped for, so I took my two slow and careful shots at the central column.

'How do they look, Jarra?' Playdon asked. 'I can't see from here.'

'I think they're fine, sir.' I headed back to the sleds and gave the rifle to Playdon.

'All four charges fired,' said Playdon. He detached the cylinder and opened it. 'I've checked the cylinder is empty.'

I confirmed this, as safety protocols required. You really don't want to miscount live explosives.

Playdon then locked away the rifle, took out the explosive trigger controls, and called Dig Site Command on the broadcast channel. 'This is Asgard 6 in Sector 46. Requesting permission to fire charges.'

We waited for a few minutes, while a nearby team withdrew to safe ground, and then Dig Site Command cleared us to fire charges.

'This is Asgard 6. Firing first charge.' Playdon pushed a button and one of the isolated pillars folded in on itself and crumpled neatly to the ground. 'This is Asgard 6. Firing second charge.' The second pillar went down nicely too, and a large chunk of sagging floor broke away from the building and crashed downwards in sympathy. For a moment, I thought all the rest would follow, but that central column was stubborn.

'This is Asgard 6. Firing charges 3 and 4.' Playdon hit the buttons, and this time the building couldn't resist any longer.

It crashed down into a mass of rubble and twisted girders, and our class cheered in victory.

'This is Asgard 6. Firing complete,' Playdon reported, and Dig Site Command cleared the other team to go back to work.

We headed back to our mobile dome after that, leaving the mound of rubble to settle overnight before we started work clearing it. We stopped on the way, to collect fallen branches from a group of trees.

'Why do we want tree branches?' several confused voices asked.

'Dig site tradition,' said Playdon. 'We're cooking dinner outside over a camp fire tonight.'

'He's joking surely?' Fian whispered in my ear.

I laughed. 'No, he isn't. I've done camp fire cooking several times on dig sites. It's traditional, like the guitar playing.'

There is this story that you can light a camp fire by rubbing two dry sticks together, but I'd tried it several times and failed. It's a whole lot easier to cheat and use something like a laser gun to give yourself an instant cheerful camp fire.

Amalie volunteered to be in charge of the cooking. She'd done this a lot back home, and clearly thought the rest of us would just burn the food. She showed us how to wrap potatoes in foil and put them in the heart of the fire, and how to stab the saus on cooking spears and hold them in the flames. Since it was bitterly cold, we were all wearing our impact suits for warmth, with only the hoods pulled back to show our faces.

Fian was fascinated by the camp fire cooking. 'I'd no idea raw potatoes looked like that.'

'We seem to have a lot of food,' I commented.

Playdon laughed. 'I'm allowing for you burning a lot, and also we have guests coming.'

'Guests?' half the class chorused the word in amazement.

'He must mean ghosts,' said Krath, in a spooky voice. 'The ghosts of all the people who died in the ruins. They've haunted them for centuries, and they're out there in the blackness, filled with hatred for those who come and destroy their old homes.'

It's surprising how fast people sitting round a camp fire, in the darkness of a winter night, surrounded by vast expanses of ancient ruins, can go from cheerful to terrified. Or maybe it isn't surprising. Anyway, Krath's words reduced the class to near panic.

'There aren't ghosts are there?' asked Amalie. 'We don't have ruins back home . . .'

Normally, someone would have made a joke about ruins being on the planetary development plan for ten years time, but there was just silence.

'The people of New York didn't die,' said Playdon calmly, 'they left for Alpha sector. Our guests are ten members of a research team that are camped half an hour away on the Grand Circle. Dig Site Command doesn't let Foundation course teams out here without some experienced people close at hand to nursemaid them when necessary. Be nice and polite to our visitors, and don't let me down by telling them you're scared of ghosts.'

We put more potatoes and saus on to cook. Amalie had just declared the first batch fit to eat, when we saw the lights of hover sleds approaching between the twin lines of the glowing clearway markers.

'Nice timing,' I said.

'They're experienced enough to know when dinner is likely to be ready,' said Playdon.

Three hover sleds pulled up, and ten people in impact suits jumped off and lowered their suit hoods. There was a babble of names.

238

'So, who is Jarra?' asked the leader of the visiting team. 'We were listening in during the rescue of Cassandra 2.'

I stepped forward. Playdon introduced me, and the rest of team 1.

'Nice work,' the visitors chorused.

'I'd had some experience on New York Fringe and other sites,' I explained.

'Well, it became clear that you weren't exactly a novice when Asgard 6 launched a survey plane.' The visiting team leader laughed. 'The entire dig site was grazzed. That was you, wasn't it? We thought it was the same voice.'

'Yes, that was Jarra,' said Playdon.

'And we all knew you weren't just going along for the ride with Playdon flying it since you'd never get him in a plane . . .'

Playdon groaned. 'Thank you, Graw. Go ahead and tell my whole class I'm afraid of heights.'

'Well, most people are,' said Graw. 'I know I am. If the deity meant us to fly, we'd have been born with wings. No one is ever getting me in a plane. Dig Site Command can send as many mails as they like about the pilot shortages, and asking people to volunteer to learn, but they aren't getting anywhere with me.'

He grinned at me. 'If you want a job, Jarra, then New York Dig Site's professional pilot retired at Year End, and Dig Site Command are still looking for a new one. They'll probably be sending you and Playdon mails about it.'

I laughed. 'Thanks, but I want to get my pre-history degree, and I can't do that as a full time professional pilot. I'd be happy to fly a few more survey legs for them though. I'm hoping to teach Fian to fly, and that depends on us getting some more time in planes. We'll be changing dig site a lot during the year, so we probably won't get very far.'

'Just talk to Dig Site Command when you arrive at any of the big sites,' said Graw. 'They'll all be happy for you to have flying time to train a new pilot. Keeping up pilot numbers is a major concern for the entire Dig Site Federation. If your dome doesn't have a plane, you can always fly one in from a dome that does.'

'That would be zan!' I said.

'Yes,' said Fian in a dubious voice. 'Totally zan . . .'

I felt suddenly guilty. 'Of course, you don't have to, Fian.'

'Oh yes I do,' he said in his best fake martyr voice. 'I'm not having anyone else go up in a plane with you.'

Everyone laughed.

We started eating after that, and then two of the visitors produced guitars and demanded to know who our guitar players were. We pointed at Dalmora, and the visitors started teaching her some new songs, and gave her a data chip with hundreds more.

Playdon eventually brought the evening to a close by announcing that our visitors probably wanted to get back to their own dome.

'What Playdon means,' said Graw, 'is that he's a slave driver. He doesn't want us keeping you up late when he'll be working you to death tomorrow.'

The visitors headed off on their sleds, and we threw rubble on the fire and went into our dome. I went across to my sleep sack in its place by the wall, began taking off my impact suit, and was disconcerted to find Krath next to me.

'That's my spot,' complained Fian.

'No it isn't,' said Krath. 'My sleep sack and my spot.'

'You swapped sleep sacks!' Fian accused him, outraged.

I noticed Playdon drifting in our direction, clearly ready for trouble.

'Doesn't matter,' said Krath, happily. 'What matters is my stuff is here now.'

'Fian claimed that spot,' I said. 'I suggest you give it back.'

'I want to be close at hand to defend you from the ghosts, Jarra' said Krath.

'I can defend myself,' I said. 'Now move!'

'Oh come on . . .' said Krath. 'I could be much more fun than some prudish Deltan . . .'

He stopped at this point. Possibly that was because my left hand had his arm twisted up behind his back, while my right arm was round his neck.

'I asked nicely,' I said. 'Now, take a hint, and tell Fian he can have his spot back.'

Fian wasn't waiting to be told. He'd tracked down his belongings and brought them over, and now evicted Krath's invading possessions, banishing them to the cold centre of the dome.

I released Krath and waved him a gentle farewell, before changing into my fleecy sleep suit.

'That's not fair,' grumbled Krath.

'Yes it is,' said Playdon, who appeared quite amused by the whole thing. 'You were in breach of three rules there, Krath. First, dig site custom. Second, social etiquette. Third, plain common sense. You're just lucky that Jarra didn't throw you across the dome.'

I looked at Fian's face and laughed.

We settled down for the night eventually. It was a disturbed night as usual in these conditions. There's always someone restlessly moving about, and there's always someone who snores.

Sometime in the early hours of the morning, Fian whispered in my ear. 'Our first night together. This is so romantic.'

'Yes,' I said, 'just you, me, and twenty-seven other

people. It reminds me of that joke about the Betans and the . . .'

'If you start making Betan sex jokes,' said Fian in a stern voice, 'I'll have to give you warnings under the Gamman moral code.'

I had to pull my sleep sack over my head to muffle my giggles.

24

Next day, we realized that the visitor's jokes about Playdon being a slave-driver weren't jokes at all. The man was truly heartless. He woke us up when it was still dark outside, allowed us a brief breakfast of packaged food, and had us outside loading the sleds at the crack of dawn.

'I didn't know days could start this early,' said Fian. 'It's practically still yesterday.'

I laughed at the civilians' agonized faces, but even I was feeling it was a bit excessive starting work at this hour. It wasn't easy work either. I first discovered what was in store for us when we'd set up the sensor net and I went across to the sensor sled. Dalmora was staring at the screen with a panicky expression. 'I don't understand this . . .'

Playdon was looking over Dalmora's shoulder at the screen. 'What do you make of it, Jarra?'

I glanced at the screen, and was grazzed. Convinced I had to be wrong, I took a closer look. 'Underground . . . Is that part of the underground transport system?'

'Correct,' said Playdon. 'One of the subway lines runs under our dig area and we're going to excavate it. You can consider yourselves flattered. Dig Site Command doesn't usually let novices try that, but we did well in that rescue, and we have Earth 3 just down the clearway from us if we get in trouble, so they're letting us have a go.'

As we were the working team, we were talking on the team circuit, so the whole class could hear us. In a way, it was handy having Krath around, because people could always depend on him to ask the tactless questions for them. He did it now. 'Earth 3 . . . Those were the people who visited us last night?'

'That's right,' said Playdon.

'Then they were apes?' Krath seemed grazzed. 'But . . . my dad wouldn't like me sharing food with people like that.'

'I see,' said Playdon. 'If your dad would object to you having your life saved by people like that, then please tell me now. I'll make a note that in case of accidents, I should ask Earth 3 to leave you buried in the rubble until your suit fails and you get slowly crushed to death. Anything to make your dad happy.'

There was a gulping noise from Krath. 'I didn't mean . . .'

'I have a strong personal dislike of hearing remarks like that about the Earth dig teams,' said Playdon. 'They're people I respect, and they've saved my life several times. Now, I don't hand out warnings just because a student offends me, but the Betans have a Handicapped child. I hope I've already made it clear that making comments like that in front of them will earn you warnings under the Gamman moral code.'

He paused, and there was a nervous affirmative noise from Krath.

'Good,' said Playdon. 'Let me make something else clear. I'm prepared to give warnings for comments made on a dig site, no matter who is present, because I don't want all the Asgard teams to be embarrassed by one of our students

244

saying something offensive about the Handicapped on the wrong comms channel.'

He paused for a moment. 'All of you should bear in mind a few facts. Earth teams opened this dig site a hundred and fifty years ago. Earth teams made the clearways. Earth teams taught the first teams from off world. They were the experts and we were clueless. We got into trouble and they dug us out. I know that was a hundred years ago, but teams from new universities still keep showing up and making all the novice mistakes, and the Earth teams patiently help them out.'

'It's still the old joke,' Playdon continued. 'Expert apes and clueless exos. That's the only phrase I ever want to hear on a dig site that includes the word ape. The Earth teams are professionals, Krath. If you said something rude about them on the broadcast channel, they would still come and dig you out from under rubble at the risk of their own lives, but frankly the rest of us exo teams would then quietly take you back out and bury you again ourselves.'

There wasn't another squeak out of Krath, and the rest of us were very quiet as we continued our preparations.

When I arrived at the tag support sled, Fian locked the beam on to the tag point on my suit. Then he very carefully checked he wasn't transmitting on the team circuit or any other comms channels before daring to speak. 'What's an exo?'

I carefully set my comms to listen only. 'Rude term for people not from Earth,' I explained. 'It comes from people running off during Exodus.'

'I see,' said Fian. 'I hate to admit this, but I think my mother would feel exactly the same as Krath's dad. She wasn't keen on me coming to Earth in case it means my kids are born Handicapped.'

I giggled. 'You can't catch it. Your kids don't get it because you visited Earth.'

'I know,' said Fian. 'Whatever you do, it makes no difference. It's triple ten. One in ten risk if both parents are Handicapped themselves. One in a hundred if one parent is Handicapped. One in a thousand if neither parent is. My mother still follows all the superstitions though.'

'So, she didn't eat Karanth jelly?'

Fian laughed. 'She wouldn't even go in a shop that sold it. But don't worry; you'll like my mother when you meet her. She isn't really silly. She admits herself that she got a bit paranoid when she was pregnant with my sister. Her one month scan showed my sister had a potential heart condition. They did preventative treatment immediately of course.'

'Everyone ready?' asked Playdon. 'Jarra?'

I hastily set my comms back to speak on team circuit. 'Yes, sir.'

I used my hover belt to skim forward over the first bit of rubble. The conversation I'd just had with Fian was bothering me a little. I suppose it was that comment about meeting his mother. Meeting parents was . . . well it was a bit serious.

'Everyone, be aware that Jarra is working over a large underground void,' said Playdon, 'so we have to react fast if there's a cave-in.'

I dismissed worries about meeting parents and concentrated on what I was doing. The first thing needed, obviously, was to level out the site a bit. I started shifting some of the unstable heaps that had been left after we blew up the building yesterday. There were some large girders involved, one of which was so long that I decided I'd better chop it into three sections.

The laser gun made short work of that. I'd just turned it off, and was tagging the pieces when two things happened simultaneously. One was that I felt myself being yanked upwards, and the other was something hitting me in the back. The impact suit triggered as I headed on upwards, and I dangled in midair, frozen like a statue for a moment before I could move again.

'What happened?' I asked, thoroughly confused. There hadn't been anything behind me that could have hit me.

'A rather young and clueless wolf decided to have you for lunch,' said Playdon. 'He knocked himself silly on your impact suit. The rest of the pack is skulking over behind that wall.'

I looked down. A stunned wolf got uncertainly to his feet, whined, and then limped off rapidly to rejoin the pack.

'There goes a sadder and wiser wolf,' said Playdon. 'He'll know to leave dig teams alone in future.'

'Poor thing,' I said.

'Serves him right,' said Fian. 'They're still hanging round behind that wall. Should we shoot them?'

'I think throwing a large rock in their direction might be enough,' said Playdon. 'Amalie, pick something big up and throw it their way.'

Amalie locked her beam on to a large section of girder, and sent it flying forcefully towards the wolf pack. They instantly turned and fled.

'That seems to have convinced them,' said Playdon. 'I think you can put Jarra down again now, Fian.'

I was lowered back towards the ground and my hover belt engaged. I carried on shifting rocks and girders. There was an awful lot to move, but after a couple of hours the site was nice and stable and we were gradually working our way downwards. Playdon brought team 2 in to take over for a while, and sent team 1 back to the dome for a two hour break. I was reluctant to hand over my nice tidy dig site to someone else, in case they messed it up, but a break from being in my impact suit was very welcome.

There were just the five of us back at the dome, so we

could make the most of the limited facilities of the bathrooms, and pick out the best of the packaged food. Fian still seemed unnerved by the wolf.

'I didn't know they were there until that one suddenly ran out and leapt at you,' he said. 'Scared me to death.'

'It wasn't going to be able to bite through my impact suit,' I reassured him.

'If it had jumped at you when you were using the laser . . .' Fian let the sentence trail off into grim silence.

I hadn't thought of that. A wolf knocking me over while I had the laser beam active could have been very nasty. I pictured it, and instantly wished that I hadn't.

We headed back to our work site after our break, and found team 2 had worked their way down through several more layers of rubble. We took over again, and team 2 went happily off on their break.

Progress continued steadily. Just after team 2 rejoined us, we reached what appeared to be solid ground, and Playdon spent a while working on the sensors and deciding where we should place charges. We could place the charges manually this time, rather than using a charge gun, which kept things simple. Playdon called in for clearance, he fired the charges, and a huge circular crater appeared in the ground.

'I think we're through to the subway,' said Playdon. 'Tag support and heavy lift sleds will need to move closer and use the hoist extensions so we can have beams working vertically down the hole. Team 2, we need your tag support sled over here as well.'

There was a delay while Playdon went round the lift and tag support sleds, checking the hoist extensions were set correctly. I took my chance to do a bit of watching and listening, since I'd never used a hoist extension.

'Team 2 tag support, you'll be lowering the sensor probe into the hole,' said Playdon. 'It has glows, vid, and sensors, so we get to see what's down there. Sensor probes are expensive, and unfortunately are easily damaged, so treat it just as carefully as if it was your tag leader. Pull it out fast if anything nasty happens.'

The sensor probe went down and Playdon projected the image from it above the crater, so we could all see. Even with the glows, it was still a bit gloomy down the hole. There was a heap of rubble at the bottom obviously, and a tunnel went off at either side into darkness. Playdon sent a beam of light first one way, and then the other.

'One direction seems to be blocked by a cave-in,' he said. 'Possibly an old one, or possibly triggered by us blowing up that building. The other way seems clear but we aren't playing around far from the hole. If someone got buried in another cave-in along that tunnel, then we'd never get them dug out in time. I'll run some sensor scans now to see if there's anything interesting.'

I went over to the sensor sled to take a look. Images from the sensor probe were appearing on a secondary bank of displays. I couldn't entirely figure them out.

'These displays aren't the same as the ones from the usual sensor net,' said Dalmora. She was sounding a bit over-whelmed, and I could sympathize. Standard sensors are complicated enough, without having a whole new secondary bank added to them.

'They're similar,' said Playdon, 'but with several key differences. The sensor probes are Military issue, and designed for a rather different specialist job than the one we use them for. Hmmm, I wonder . . .'

He was silent for a moment. 'I can't be sure, but there might be something interesting down there. There's a lot of luck involved in subway excavations. It was a transport system, and whole stretches of it are empty tunnels, but it was abandoned just after halfway through Exodus century.

The people of New York were rapidly leaving, they gave up using the subway, and the looters moved in. Gangs had their headquarters down here, and sometimes they left things behind when they left or got killed by police or rival gangs.'

I peered at the displays from the probe. There might be something. 'If that's a stasis box, then it's big, and a very strange shape.'

'Yes,' said Playdon. 'If it's a stasis box, it's definitely not one of the standard home memorials. Well, only one way to find out. It's under the edge of the heap of rubble, so we have some digging to do. Fian, you'll have to lower Jarra down carefully, so she can take a look and tag things. We get her and the sensor probe out before anyone tries lifting any rubble. Then the sensor probe and Jarra go back down again, and we keep repeating that. Slow, but safe.'

Fian lifted me up in the air with the lifeline, and dangled me over the hole. 'Jarra, I'll be watching the sensor probe image,' he said, 'but that's not the same as being able to see you myself. If there's a problem, then just scream "pull".'

'I'll do that,' I promised. Fian sounded nervous, and I was a bit nervous too as I got lowered into the hole. I'd never deliberately gone underground on a dig site before. Once I was down in the hole and tagging rocks, I was very aware my only escape route was that circular hole above my head. It was out of my reach using a hover belt, but I trusted Fian. Lifeline beams are designed to be completely reliable, and Fian wouldn't do anything insane like detaching it from my tag point. I concentrated on tagging as many rocks as was sensible.

'This batch is tagged. Lift me up please,' I said.

I soared up through the hole to safety. The sensor probe came up next, and Amalie and Krath shifted the first lot of rocks. Then the probe went down again and checked the situation before I joined it to tag more rocks.

We went round that loop about four times. The messiest bit was trying to shift the small scale rubble out of the way. You couldn't drag net in the usual way, Amalie and Krath had to lift out batches, and that only worked for little stuff. I learnt that I had to individually tag smaller rocks than usual.

'If there was a whole lot of interesting stuff down there,' Playdon said, 'we'd approach this differently and blow out the roof along a whole stretch of subway so we were working on a giant open trench. That's a large scale operation though, usually involving several teams working together.'

Finally, I was down to the last level of rubble. I was getting used to the strange working conditions, and relaxing a bit now. I examined the rocks closely, and found some of them weren't rocks at all. 'There are a few old metal containers here. Most have fallen apart, and whatever was inside is dust or rotted.'

'I'm getting some chemical signals from the sensor probe,' said Playdon. 'It's low level, degraded by time, and won't hurt you in an impact suit. We'll have to decontaminate you before you take that suit off though.'

'Oh nice,' I said. 'I'm a skunk.'

The class gave confused giggles.

'That's dig site terminology,' said Playdon. 'It means that Jarra's suit is contaminated, so the rest of you don't touch her or you need decontaminating too.'

'I can see two intact metal containers, and I think . . .' I peered closely. 'I can only see through a tiny gap in the rocks, but I think it really is a stasis box.'

The class cheered.

'We'll dig out and retrieve the two intact containers and the stasis box,' said Playdon, 'but I'm really suspicious of them. We'll put them on the clearway, and I'm running

Stasis Q tests on them right here before we risk transporting them on sleds.'

We lifted another batch of rocks, and I went down the hole again. The containers and the stasis box were clear of rubble now. 'The containers look intact, and the stasis box is . . . Well, I've never seen one like this. It's a big long cylinder.'

'Does the stasis field look stable?' asked Playdon.

'Solid black fuzz, no flickering, it looks fine.' I tagged the metal containers for lifting, and got a tag harness on the stasis box. 'It's a bit tricky getting the harness on one this shape, but I think I've got it. Lift me out.'

I was lifted back into daylight and across to the clearway. The sensor probe followed, and then came the stasis box in its harness and the two metal containers. Playdon ordered them lowered on to an area of clearway away from the sleds.

After that, Playdon sprayed me with decontaminant, and checked me with sensors. 'Jarra is no longer a skunk,' he reported.

'Yay for that,' I said.

He started getting out his Stasis Q equipment.

'Can I help set up?' I asked hopefully. 'I've helped pack a few times and . . .'

Playdon sighed. 'I suppose you can, but don't think I haven't guessed what you're aiming at. I can't get you Stasis Q qualified. It's not like getting your pilot's licence. Stasis Q involves a residential course, and tests.'

'I know,' I said. 'I can get some practical experience on dig sites, study the theory, and even do the theory tests. That would give me a lot of credits, but I'd still need the minimum residential course and practical exam to get my licence.'

Playdon laughed. 'Well, you've obviously researched it, and realize what's involved. It'll take you at least a year to get to the point where you need the residential course, so we don't need to worry about that for a while. If you're serious, then I'll help you as much as I can, but if I say it isn't working out then you have to accept that. Stasis Q isn't something you can just teach, and it's not entirely to do with intelligence or hard work, there's some instinct involved.'

'You need the nose,' I said.

Playdon laughed again. 'Yes, you need the Stasis Q nose.'

So I helped Playdon set up the sensor ring. We dealt with one of the metal containers first.

'This is easier than a real stasis box of course,' said Playdon. 'We're just running intensive sensor scans, and there's no stasis field blocking our view of the contents. What have we got, Jarra?'

'We got a skunk,' I said. 'Chemicals inside.'

'I thought it would be, but it was worth checking,' said Playdon. 'Probably illegal medications, heavily degraded by time.'

He collected the sensor ring and Amalie used her heavy lift beam to throw the container back down into the subway. We moved on to the second container. Playdon paused before turning on the sensor ring.

'What's your guess, Jarra?'

'Logically, it should be the same as the other one, but . . .'

'But?'

'I feel more hopeful.'

'So do I,' said Playdon. 'Let's see if we're both disappointed.' He turned on the sensor ring. 'What have we got, Jarra?'

I stared at the displays. 'It's not a skunk. Dense metal, stones . . . It's jewellery.'

'I think we can cut this one open.' Playdon cut round the lid with a fine laser beam, and tipped out the contents into a storage box before throwing the container away. He took the storage box over to show the rest of the class.

253

'Ancient jewellery,' Dalmora admired it in delight.

'The gold and diamonds must have been worth a fortune before we could make them,' said Playdon. 'They still have value as historic artefacts, so there could be a small bounty payment.'

'How much?' asked Krath.

Playdon laughed. 'Not that much. It's a percentage of the commercial market value. The Dig Site Federation and University Asgard each get a share, and the rest is divided between us. There's a whole formula for calculating each team member's share.'

'I was on heavy lift,' said Krath, 'so I get more than if I was just watching.'

'Yes, you do,' said Playdon. 'Incidentally, the Betans aren't on site with us, but I'd prefer that the whole class get their base share. It's rather unfair if someone misses out through illness or injury, and the Betans were excused this trip on compassionate grounds. Any objections to that?'

'Well, they wanted to go off and see the apelette,' said Krath, 'but why not.'

'Krath!' Playdon's voice was suddenly icy.

'Sorry,' said Krath hastily. 'I'll stick to saying Lolette in future.'

Playdon nodded. 'See that you do. Now the Stasis box. Any feelings, Jarra?'

'Just that this is important,' I said. 'Not sure if it's important in a good or bad way.'

'Yes,' said Playdon. 'All the guidelines say we treat this stasis box with extreme caution, so I'm afraid you watch this one from the sleds with the rest of the class. I'll let you help me with the next standard memorial type box we find, but this one is too unknown.'

I know when arguing may get me somewhere and when it won't. 'Thank you. I look forward to that.' I retreated to the sleds with good grace.

'I have to call this in to Dig Site Command,' said Playdon. 'If anything nasty happens when I'm working on this stasis box, the rest of you head for the emergency evac portal and get through it as fast as possible. Don't ask questions, just go. Jarra, you would tell Dig Site Command what was happening.'

'Yes, sir,' I said.

'This is Asgard 6,' said Playdon on the broadcast channel. 'We have a non-standard, suspect stasis box. I wish to investigate in situ rather than risk transport. Request clearance to perform on site Stasis Q analysis.'

'This is Dig Site Command. Activating your nearest emergency evac portal now. You are cleared to test.'

Playdon set up his sensor ring round the strange stasis box, and started work. The rest of us waited nervously, talking in whispers with our comms set to listen only.

'How bad could it be in that box?' asked Fian.

'No limit,' I said. 'Poison. Explosives. Unstable radioactive materials. Anything really.' I had one very specific worry in my head, given the size and shape of the box, and that was missiles, but I didn't want to tempt fate by saying it.

'I hope Playdon knows what he's doing,' muttered Krath.

'He's full Stasis Q licensed,' I told them, 'and that's special.'

'You're really aiming to get a licence?' asked Fian. 'It sounds dangerous.'

'I'm going to try,' I said, 'but you have to be really good.'

We waited in silence after that, while Playdon gave occasional updates saying the box was clear of various hazards. He was obviously taking this very slowly and cautiously. Finally, he nodded. 'I can't see any hazards at all, so I'm taking the field strength down to just under ten per cent and running a quick sensor scan.'

We held our breath.

'It looks fine in there,' said Playdon, in an odd sort of

255

voice. 'I can see five separate cylinders. I'm going to collapse the stasis field and open it for a very quick look.'

We held our breath again.

'It's paintings,' said Playdon. 'Five paintings. This is amaz. I think this is a stolen art gallery storage box. I daren't unroll the paintings to look at them. We're getting this straight to the experts.'

'A gallery box,' said Dalmora, shakily. 'We lost so many ancient paintings in Exodus . . .'

'If we've found the Mona Lisa,' said Krath, 'we'll all be rich.'

Playdon spoke on the broadcast channel. 'This is Asgard 6. We have what looks like a stolen art gallery storage box with five paintings. Requesting instructions.'

'This is Dig Site Command. Head for the emergency evac portal and send them through. Dispatching evaluation team now to receive them.'

Our sled convoy headed to the portal, and Playdon allowed us one quick glimpse of the precious canvas rolls inside the storage box before they went through the small circle into the hands of the waiting experts. It was only then that I realized how many hours I'd spent working in an impact suit, and how tired I was.

25

That evening I was truly exhausted. I headed straight into the mobile dome, and there was a moment of pure blizz when I changed into my sleep suit and crawled into my sleep sack. I lay there whimpering.

Fian appeared after a while, in his impact suit with the hood down. 'They're starting the cooking outside.'

'I don't care,' I said.

'Dalmora's singing.'

'I don't care. Every muscle in my body is screaming.'

Fian looked worried. 'It must have been tough out there. The rest of us were mostly just sitting around watching and I know it's a huge physical effort being tag leader.'

'You have no idea,' I moaned. 'Let me quietly die.'

Fian looked really worried now. 'I'd better get Playdon. There's an evac portal nearby and you can be in hospital in . . .'

'No!' I said hastily. I'd obviously overdone the complaining. 'I'm just exhausted, that's all.'

'I'm not used to *Stalea of the Jungle* getting worn out.'

I giggled.

'You stay there, and I'll bring some food when it's ready,' Fian said.

'That sounds wonderful.'

He came back later, bearing baked potatoes and cheezit. 'Food!' I cried, and started eating greedily.

Fian changed out of his impact suit. I furtively admired the view of him in his skintight while still munching my cheezit. He looked good in his sleep suit too.

'I was thinking,' he said.

It's the sort of phrase that tends to be a bad sign. 'Yes?' I asked warily.

He picked up his plate of food. 'When we leave New York to move to a new dig site, we get a few days break, and I'm supposed to be going home to Hercules. I thought maybe you'd like to come with me. Meet my parents.'

That sounded serious.

'It might be a nice time to register a Twoing contract,' Fian continued.

That sounded incredibly serious. 'Wouldn't that be rushing things a little?'

'Not if we're both sure that it's what we want.' He gave me one of his earnest looks. 'I know it's what I want. How do you feel?'

I hesitated. 'Well, I hadn't expected us to move on to contracts quite this fast.'

Fian shook his head, and gave an overacted sigh of depression. 'I'm shocked by your behaviour, Jarra. We've just spent the night together, and I'm a nice contract boy. I'm in exactly the same situation as your poor friend Issette. You have to do the honourable thing, like your brother did, and give me my Twoing contract.'

I laughed. 'It's hardly the same thing. We haven't . . .' I broke off and frowned suspiciously at him. 'Fian Andrej Eklund, are you thinking that if we have a Twoing contract you'll get to tumble me?'

He managed to grin and blush, both at the same time.

'Well, I'm assuming there'd be an . . . adjustment of some physical boundaries.' He gave me a cautious look of assessment, before putting on a fake martyred expression. 'Things are pretty strict back on Hercules, but I'm perfectly willing to adjust to whatever you feel is appropriate behaviour for a couple with a Twoing contract. It'll be a sacrifice of course, but I care about you a great deal, so I'm prepared to suffer.'

I giggled. 'I can't demand such a sacrifice from a well-behaved Deltan.'

He dropped the martyr act and grinned shamelessly. 'You must have noticed by now that I'm a very badly-behaved Deltan. I get bored by science, I like history, and I'm a fan of a suggestive vid series. Incidentally, I'm thinking that when we've got our Twoing contract, you'll need to explain the new arrangements to me. The best way to do that might be if you throw me across the jungle clearing, pin me down and . . . demonstrate.'

I was giggling helplessly by now, but our solitude was suddenly invaded. The rest of the class had had enough of impact suits and had decided to follow our example and eat inside the dome. Things got a bit noisy and confused, so Fian let the subject of meeting his parents and signing up for Twoing contracts drop for the moment.

Krath seemed to have abandoned hopes of me, correctly decided that Dalmora was totally out of his sector, and was now trying to ingratiate himself with Amalie. She was unimpressed.

'I may be an old maid,' she said, 'but I'm not that desperate.'

'What's an old maid?' asked Krath.

Dalmora explained. 'A woman who is still unmarried at an age when most women would be.'

Krath looked suspiciously at Amalie. 'How old are you then? You don't look that old.'

'I'm 18,' said Amalie, 'but Epsilon is the frontier. Most

people leave school at 15. You can have Twoing contracts at 16, and marry at 17. Just about all the girls from my year at school are married.' She shrugged. 'Don't think I haven't had offers either. I've had over twenty men ask me to marry them, and only one of them was drunk.'

'What?' Krath looked utterly grazzed.

I was giggling by now. 'Most people moving to Epsilon sector are male, so there are about ten unmarried men for every unmarried woman. Amalie can take her pick any time she wants a man, or two for that matter.'

'Two?' Krath frowned.

'Triad marriage is legal in Epsilon,' said Amalie, 'but only for one woman and two men because of the imbalance of the sexes. I'm not married yet, because I stayed on at school and I'm getting my history degree. Our University is in the planetary development plan for four years time. I've a position arranged to teach history there when I've got my degree.'

'It's a big contrast to Alpha sector,' said Dalmora. 'We normally marry at somewhere near 30, though individual planetary customs vary hugely because they were settled from different regions of Earth.'

'There's a general rule,' I said, 'that the older the sector, the longer people wait to marry. There's a historical theorem about it.'

'Quin's theorem.' Playdon unexpectedly joined in the conversation. 'It applies to periods back in pre-history too. People marry younger in newly settled areas, and where less education is available.'

'But what about Beta?' Joth asked in a blatant attempt to divert the subject away from any mathematical lectures.

Everyone laughed.

'Lolia and Lolmack are 24,' said Dalmora, 'and they've been married for two years. Until I talked to Lolia, I just thought of Beta sector as being casual about sex, but it's far more complicated than that, with a rigid clan and class structure. Betans have no nudity taboo, which gives other sectors the wrong idea about them, but actually only the lower class plebeian clans are involved in the sex vid industry. It's profitable, so Lolia and Lolmack's clan cluster is wealthy, but they have to struggle hard for social status, and few clans will intermarry with them.'

'Deltans often marry when they're still at university,' said Fian. 'I suppose that fits Quin's ideas.' He looked at me. 'What's the Military custom?'

A gale of laughter swept the dome. Even Playdon looked amused.

I hoped I wasn't blushing as I replied. 'Ninety percent of Military are born into Military families, but we also recruit from all sectors, even Beta. We don't have our own marriage law, so the law of the sector where the marriage takes place applies. Generally Military marry relatively young, and often in Epsilon sector.'

'Because it's close to Kappa and the Planet First teams?' asked Dalmora.

'No,' I said. 'Lots of the Military are on solar power arrays nowhere near Kappa. It's because Epsilon allows instant marriages without prior Twoing contracts. Military marriages often happen at short notice, because people want to marry when family are on leave from Planet First, or they need to marry quickly to get posted on the same assignment.'

'It sounds like the elope to Epsilon jokes,' said Krath.

'If you may not see your family again for a year, or face being on different assignments for a couple of years, then it might be a sensible thing to do,' said Dalmora.

'Of course, anyone can do that sort of thing,' I said. 'Once you're married, that marriage is legal in any sector. It's just the Military are more used to moving between sectors, so it's quite natural to pick a sector with marriage law that suits us. There's nothing to stop any of you portalling over to Beta and having any sort of marriage you like.'

Playdon had changed back into his impact suit. 'I'm just taking a sled down the clearway to call on Earth 3,' he told us. 'I should be back in an hour. Please don't do anything dreadful while I'm away. Jarra, keep Krath in line!'

We all shivered in the brief icy draught as Playdon opened the door, went outside, and closed it again.

'Playdon picks on me because of my father's work,' complained Krath.

We all thought about this for a moment.

'Playdon doesn't like garbage collectors?' asked Fian.

I giggled.

'My father doesn't just have a refuse collection and recycling business,' said Krath. 'He helps run a newzie channel.'

'He does?' Dalmora looked interested. 'Which one?'

'*Truth Against Oppression*,' said Krath. 'He's a founder member and he has his own programme every week.'

'Forgive me,' said Fian, 'but I've never heard of it.'

'Well, it's a small channel,' said Krath, 'and of course the government try to stop people listening. They want to limit everyone to hearing official propaganda.'

There was a thoughtful silence. Finally Joth spoke. 'This is one of those nardle channels isn't it?'

'It isn't nardle,' said Krath. 'Of course the government say rude things about it, because we tell people the truth that the official lies try to cover up.'

'Such as?' Fian had a big grin on his face as he asked the question.

'That whole business about Artemis,' said Krath. 'That never happened, you know. It was a cover up. No power beam ever touched the surface of Artemis. What really happened was the Military invaded Zeus. They forced Beta sector to surrender and rejoin the other sectors.'

'How can you possibly believe that?' I asked. 'You can see the scars on Artemis from space!'

'There aren't any scars,' said Krath. 'Only the Military go into space, and they fake all the photographs.'

'Excuse me,' said Dalmora, 'but the Military kindly allowed my father to go to the Artemis solar array when he was making the vid I showed you. He took the images of Artemis from space himself.'

'Well, I can understand your father going along with the lies,' said Krath. 'I don't blame him. He would have a lot to lose if he stood up and told the truth.'

'My father is not going along with any lies,' said Dalmora.

'Well, naturally you believe him,' said Krath, 'but . . .'

'I believe him, because I was there too!' Dalmora stated, her usual calm voice becoming rather aggressive. 'I saw the scars myself.'

'Well . . . Maybe they faked the scars by digging trenches or something,' said Krath.

We all burst out laughing.

'You shouldn't laugh,' said Krath. 'They're covering up lots of things. That planet in Epsilon sector. Miranda. The Military messed things up terribly in the Planet First checks. There are no children on Miranda, because every baby born there is Handicapped and has to be portalled to Earth.'

Amalie stood up. 'My home planet is Miranda. I was born there, and grew up there, you brainless scum! Your father may believe all this rubbish, but you could at least try and think for yourself.'

'You called me a scum!' Krath gaped at Amalie in shock. 'That isn't polite.'

Amalie glared at him. 'Being polite isn't on Miranda's planetary development plan until next year!'

I stood up as well. 'Playdon said I should keep Krath in

line, and I think it's time I did that.' I grabbed Krath's sleep sack and stuck it over his head, while the class cheered.

Fian decided to start a new and much safer topic of conversation. 'When will we hear about the paintings we found?'

'It's usually a few weeks before you get the report back on a family memorial box,' I said. 'On something important like this, we should get an initial report faster than that, but the details could take ages.'

'It will be amaz to see the images of the paintings we found,' said Dalmora.

There was a muffled noise from Krath. I couldn't hear what he was saying, but I could guess.

'Yes, Krath,' I said, 'the bounty payment might be sizeable, but it'll take ages for them to work it out. First they'll need to search through historical images and do a lot of analysis to work out who painted the pictures. They can't estimate a value until then.'

'I have to admit,' said Amalie, 'that any bounty payments would be very welcome. My family can't afford to pay my degree fees, so I'm facing a lot of education tax later on. I chose history rather than literature partly because I'd heard bounty payments can really help towards your degree costs.'

There was some more mumbling from Krath. I leant forward to hear it. 'Krath says that's why he's going to specialise in pre-history,' I reported.

Everyone laughed.

When Playdon got back, he found Krath with the sleep sack still over his head, while Fian and I sat on him. Playdon sighed. 'Let him out.'

Fian and I stood up, and Krath yanked the sleep sack off his head and looked round angrily.

'What did you do?' asked Playdon, looking at him.

'He was a nardle,' said Amalie. 'His father helps run some

264

vid channel, and he was telling us ridiculous stories about Military conspiracies.'

'They aren't ridiculous stories.' Krath turned to give me a wounded look. 'You shouldn't have treated me like that, Jarra. I've been keeping your secret, haven't I?'

I giggled. 'Keeping what secret? I haven't got any secrets.'

His eyes narrowed. 'Oh yes you have, and I've worked out what you're hiding. I wasn't going to tell anyone, even my father, but if you're going to . . .' He turned to face the rest of the class. 'You're all laughing at me, but you're just too blind to see what's right under your noses. You think Jarra's just another student, but she's been telling us all a pack of lies.'

Fian took a step forward. 'This isn't funny any longer, Krath. I suggest you shut up right now.'

'I refuse to shut up,' said Krath. 'It's time I told you all the truth. Jarra's an undercover agent from Military Intelligence, and she's infiltrated our class!'

'What?' I stared at him in disbelief.

'It's obvious, isn't it?' Krath looked round at the class. 'Jarra knows far too much to be just a student from Military school. Think how she handled the Cassandra 2 rescue. Not only that, but she's a pilot. I did some checking up, and they don't teach kids to fly at Military school, so she must have been to the Military Academy. Admitting she was a pilot was a mistake, but she had no choice. She needed to fly an aerial survey of New York Dig Site because the Military are looking for something there. Fian wouldn't let me go up in the plane with her, so I don't know what she was looking for, but . . .'

An agent from Military Intelligence? Krath was truly crazy. I looked at Fian to share the joke with him, but he was staring at me with a very odd expression on his face. I looked round at the crowd of grazzed faces. They actually believed the idiot. Honestly, civilians have no sense at all!

Playdon finally broke the silence. 'No, that can't be right. It still doesn't explain why Jarra applied via . . .'

'I'm not an undercover agent from Military Intelligence,' I said, wearily. 'I didn't get my pilot's licence at the Military Academy, but on New York Fringe last summer. If you don't believe me, just give them a call and ask. This secret agent is now going to bed.'

The class reluctantly abandoned thrilling daydreams of covert Military Intelligence operations and joined me in heading for sleep sacks. We all stayed awake for a while as we tried to find the *Truth Against Oppression* newzie channel on our lookups. Normally, it seems entirely wrong to be out in the wilds watching vids, but this was a special occasion. Sadly, the channel wasn't broadcasting at the moment, though breathtaking news about a government cover up was promised tomorrow.

'Pity,' said Fian.

I shook my head at him. 'You actually believed the idiot Krath. You thought I was from Military Intelligence. How could you be such a nardle?'

Fian blushed. 'It was just for a minute.'

I put away my lookup and prepared to sleep.

'So,' Fian whispered, 'it would be in keeping with Military tradition for us to elope to Epsilon.'

I giggled. 'Yes,' I said. 'Military Intelligence agents elope to Epsilon all the time. We could take Krath with us, and I could have a triad marriage with both of you.'

'I'm going to sulk now,' said Fian. 'Just like your ex, Cathan.' He pulled a face. 'Sulk, sulk, sulk!'

Playdon turned the lights out.

The next day, Playdon didn't rush us into getting up early. He let us have a leisurely breakfast and then got us to pack our bags. This seemed a bad sign to me, because it probably meant he wasn't going to let us have a break out of our impact suits between the morning's work and heading back to the dome in the afternoon.

We headed outside, clutching bags and sleep sacks, and I stopped as I saw the sky. 'That's looking a bit . . .'

'Something wrong?' Fian asked.

'I just saw the sky. If I was Playdon, I'd . . .'

Playdon spoke over the team circuit. 'Team 1, I'd like you to start packing the mobile dome. I didn't like the look of the weather yesterday, so I went to have a chat with Earth 3 in the evening. We've had a run of good weather for several weeks, but we think there's snow on the way. We don't want to risk having to abandon equipment and use the emergency evac portals, so we're packing up to head off site. Earth 3 had an hour or so of work they wanted to finish this morning, but they'll be along soon and we can drive out together in convoy.'

All right, I thought, Playdon was definitely good at his job.

We'd just finished loading sections of mobile dome onto its special transport sled, when the hover sleds of Earth 3 appeared. Half of them went ahead of us, and half followed behind, so that we novices were safely shepherded along the clearway. That seemed to be rather overdoing things to me, but Playdon obviously wanted to play safe with snow coming.

I giggled suddenly.

'What's funny?' asked Fian.

'Playdon popping down to the neighbouring dome to ask them what they thought the weather might do next. In pre-history, they had lots of space satellites monitoring and predicting weather patterns on Earth. That's all gone now. No weather forecasts. We all just message the Earth Rolling News about any extreme weather where we are, and pop down to the neighbouring dome to see what they think.'

'Well, the weather doesn't usually matter that much now,' said Fian. 'People wouldn't live anywhere with dangerous weather, and you could just portal out anyway. Dig sites like this are one of the few places affected by weather, and we could use emergency evac portals if we had to.'

I laughed. 'Playdon doesn't want to leave his sleds and mobile dome behind, and I don't blame him. It would be a lot of effort to collect them afterwards.'

We'd been driving along the Grand Circle for about half an hour when a voice came over the broadcast channel. 'This is Dig Site Command. Earth Rolling News has reports of heavy snow moving in our direction and New York Dig Site is now closing. Pull out your teams now, please. I repeat: we have heavy snow incoming. Pull out your teams. New York Dig Site is closing immediately. New York Fringe is closing and will be evacuating domes. All teams, clear the area now!'

'Sounds like the snow is definite then,' said Fian. 'Why are they evacuating the New York Fringe domes?'

'New York Main is for the professionals,' I said, 'but New York Fringe is for amateurs, clubs, schools, that sort of thing. There won't be many people working Fringe in winter, and most of those will go home when the site closes for snow. They don't want to have to keep Fringe Dig Site Command manned just because half a dozen people are stubbornly sitting in a dome, so they're evacuating.'

After ten minutes, the voice came on again. 'This is Dig Site Command. I have five teams who have not confirmed departure, and their sled signals are still stationary on our screens. New York Main Dig Site is closing, team leaders please confirm you're on your way out.'

After another five minutes, the voice was back again and

faintly aggressive. 'This is Dig Site Command. I've still got two teams pinpointed on my screens that aren't moving out. Ajax 3, Prometheus 1, I'm waiting.' There was a pause. 'Ajax 3 is confirmed and moving. Prometheus 1 has a problem.'

I frowned. Snow was coming, and most of the teams must already be nearly out of the dig site. If Prometheus 1 had trapped team members, they would be in real trouble.

Another voice cut in. 'This is Earth 22. I think we were working near Prometheus 1, should we turn back and assist?'

'This is Dig Site Command. Thank you Earth 22, but Prometheus 1 have now made it to emergency evac portal 39. They are abandoning sleds and portalling out. It appears they forgot to recharge their sleds' power overnight before entering the dig site.'

I burst out laughing.

'Did that mean what it sounded like?' asked Dalmora on the team circuit.

'Oh yes,' said Playdon. 'Their team leader is never going to live this down. The entire dig site knows he forgot to plug his sleds in. Even now, his team are arriving in a Hospital Earth Casualty unit, suffering from a chronic outbreak of embarrassment. I'm just thankful it wasn't one of University Asgard's teams . . .'

By the time we turned off the Grand Circle, on to the clearway that led to our base dome, snow was starting to fall. Just a few tiny flakes at first, but they gradually grew thicker and more numerous, until the landscape was lost in whirling snow. The glows marking the edge of the clearway were suddenly very welcome.

Fian and I were riding on one of our transport sleds near the front of the convoy. Peering ahead through the snow, I could just see the leading sled turn its lights on. The brightness echoed down the line, as all the other drivers turned on their own lights in turn.

'This is incredible,' said Fian. 'I've never seen snow before. I had no idea . . .'

'This is awful,' muttered Joth. 'I'm scared I'll lose the clearway.' He was driving our sled, and grimly concentrating on following the one ahead of us.

Playdon's voice came over the team circuit. 'Earth 3 have kindly offered to escort us all the way back to our base. I've invited them in for refreshments, but they say that given the rate it's snowing they'd better not stop. They'll carry on and circle round outside the dig site to reach their own dome. I've told them we're very grateful for the escort, and I hope you all appreciate it.'

'I don't know about the others, sir,' I said on the team circuit, 'but given the visibility at the moment, I'm very pleased to have Earth 3 guiding us.'

26

Next morning, there was a mail on all our lookups from Playdon. Heavy snow had continued to fall overnight and New York Dig Site would be closed for at least two days.

I'd been expecting that, and hoping I could spend the morning in bed, but I couldn't. Playdon was giving us extra lectures instead. Oh joy.

Since we didn't have any windows in the dome, Playdon promised us a peek out of the dome door so we could admire the snow before we started lectures. 'I normally don't allow this without everyone wearing impact suits,' he said, 'just in case some fool wanders off alone, but I don't think anyone would get far in this.'

He opened the dome door with a dramatic flourish. A wall of waist high snow blocked the doorway, and a few flakes were still falling.

'Is it safe to touch it without an impact suit?' asked Fian, wide eyed. 'We've never had snow on Hercules. It doesn't get cold enough for it.'

'We've got Winter in Gamma sector,' chorused several voices. 'All of the schools have annual trips to Winter so we can play in the snow.'

'That's a really confusing name for a planet,' said Krath, the perpetual critic. 'Winter is a season not a place.'

We ignored him.

'Why did Gamma sector get a planet that was so cold?' asked Amalie, staying well back from the dome door. 'Surely Planet First couldn't have made that big a mistake.'

'They wanted a cold planet for some special manufacturing processes,' said one Gamman.

'But we go there to play as well,' said another.

'The manufacturing story is just a cover up,' said Krath. 'They originally intended it to be used for experiments creating mutated forms of humanity, but the mutants turned on the humans and had to be slaughtered. My dad says that . . .'

'Oh shut up, Krath,' we all told him.

'I've been to Winter and it's wonderful,' said Dalmora. 'Alpha sector has requested Planet First find them one too. Several sectors have requests in for useful specialist planets, but we have to wait until they finish checking the new Kappa worlds of course.'

Thirty minutes later, I could see that Playdon was regretting ever opening the dome door. By then, the saner members of the class had gone and put extra warm clothes on. The Betans were hiding in their rooms, because they were scared of the snow, but we couldn't get the Deltans to tear themselves away from it. They kept telling us it was white, it was magical, it was amaz! The dome corridor was all slushy from them throwing snowballs at each other, and I was having an argument with Fian.

'Oh go on,' whined Fian. 'Please.'

'No,' I said, firmly. 'Absolutely not.'

Finally, Playdon had had enough. 'Time to shut the door and do some work,' he said.

'Just one more thing,' pleaded Fian. 'There's lots of really soft snow, Jarra. Go on . . .'

'Now what?' asked Playdon.

'He wants her to throw him across the jungle clearing,' explained Krath.

'What jungle clearing?' Playdon gazed round at the lack of jungle.

Several voices explained about the vid series, *Stalea of the Jungle*. Fian was obviously not the only fan in our class.

'Oh, you mean at the end of every episode when she . . .' Playdon broke off, but he'd already given himself away. He obviously watched it too.

'Jarra won't throw Fian round in the dome in case she hurts him,' Krath continued.

'Very sensible,' said Playdon.

'The snow's nice and soft though,' said Fian, hopefully.

'No,' I said.

Playdon sighed. 'Jarra, please throw him across the jungle clearing or we'll be here all day.'

It was an order, so . . . 'Yes, sir.' I moved away from the crowd, and Fian came eagerly over. I gauged my attack, went in low, grabbed his waist, and hurled him over my shoulder.

Fian lay on his back in the snow, with a blissful expression. 'Totally, totally zan!'

The class bounced up and down cheering.

'You should really leap on him now,' said Joth.

'You should really listen to some lectures now,' said Playdon, and he finally drove them back inside and shut the door.

It took quite a while longer for everyone to change out of snowy clothes. We also had to persuade the Betans it was safe to come out of their rooms. There was a shock when they appeared. We stared at them, totally grazzed. Instead of the usual clinging clothes with holes displaying

273

patches of skin, they were wearing ordinary outfits like the rest of us.

Lolia looked at us bravely. 'Our daughter's advocate says it will be beneficial to her development if we attempt to follow Earth customs on behaviour and dress while on this planet. While we were staying at the Nursery, the advocate advised us on clothes to buy.'

'That's very wise,' said Dalmora. 'I think you look very nice.'

There was bad news awaiting the class as we finally settled down in expectant rows in the dining hall, and gazed at Playdon with our innocent, unsuspecting faces.

'I think this is a good time to tackle Granth's Mathematical Evaluations of Human Conflict,' he said.

I gave a faint scream.

'It's not that bad really, Jarra,' said Playdon.

Clearly my scream hadn't been faint enough.

'Now,' Playdon continued, 'as I'm sure you all know, Granth formulated a mathematical method that assesses various factors in society and calculates the likelihood of a war resulting. In fact it comes up with a set of probabilities for various scales of conflict. We are fortunate in being able to look at specific situations in pre-history and see just how well this mathematical model works out in practice.'

I thought assorted moaning thoughts, while Playdon droned on about Granth. He was interrupted after about ten minutes, when Amalie stood up. 'I'm sorry, I can't cope with this course any more. I'm leaving.' She burst into tears.

'Don't do that!' Krath hastily stood up too. 'Why leave?'

'I'm useless,' wailed Amalie. 'I don't understand any of this theorem stuff, and it's frightening, and there's no one else from Epsilon.'

'You're a fine student, Amalie,' said Playdon. 'Epsilon is still building up its education system, so you were admitted to this course under the special access scheme, but you're doing as well as, or better than, most of the highly qualified students.'

'I can't do this,' Amalie repeated. 'I wanted to study here and go back to teach at the university we're building back home, but I can't . . . It's frightening . . . There's snow outside!'

I felt guilty. I'd been aware of the Betans screaming noisily about the snow, but I hadn't realized Amalie was silently terrified.

Dalmora stood up. 'I'm sorry. I should have noticed you were . . . I was so occupied with my own worries. I've been scared too, being away from home, and the dome is so . . . well, basic. I'm just not used to living like this.'

'I would really hate you to give up your plans, Amalie,' said Playdon. 'Epsilon needs its new teachers.'

Amalie sniffled.

It was just the wrong moment for everyone's lookups to bleep, bing, chime, and play suggestive music.

'Solar storm warning!' said Dalmora.

'Again?' Fian checked his. 'We've got an eight-hour warning this time. Portals out for . . . three days!'

Playdon was reading his lookup urgently. 'There's a bad solar storm coming. I'm afraid they seem to have some link with the weather, so it's not entirely coincidence that it arrives at the same time as the snow. Portals will be out of operation for three days.'

'Three days!' All the class, Alpha down to Epsilon, were screaming it.

Hysteria was spreading round the class faster than I could say Arrack San Domex. Honestly, civilians, terrified of being away from their portal lifeline! Humanity survived

275

for thousands of years without portals, and the prospect of three days without them reduced this bunch to total jelly.

Our Alphan clearly summed up the feelings of the whole class when she wailed. 'Three days here, with no portal, thick snow outside, and packs of wolves!' Dalmora completely lost it. 'I want to go home!'

I was impressed by Playdon. He was going to have a mass walk-out unless he did something fast, and he did it. 'Pack your bags. I'm not keeping the class stuck here in the dome for three days when we can't work the dig site. Even if the snow melts, Dig Site Command won't open the site while the portals are out.'

Everyone ceased panicking and looked at him with sudden hope. 'Where are we going?' asked Dalmora.

Playdon clearly felt this was no time for half measures. Taking them somewhere else on Earth might get rid of the snow and the wolves, but it wouldn't give them a functioning portal. 'We're going to Asgard!'

They all cheered.

'I give you fair warning,' Playdon said, 'it might mean camping on a lecture room floor. I'll have to call the university and see what accommodation is free. You all go and pack. Meet up back here when you're ready.'

They all charged off at high speed. I didn't understand what the big hurry was. They had eight hours before the portal was due to go into lockdown. Was it really likely to take them eight hours to pack?

Playdon suddenly turned to look at me. 'Jarra, do you have any problem with going to Asgard?'

'No, sir,' I said. 'Personally, I wouldn't be worried staying here, but I'm happy to go.'

'That's fine then. You really had me confused when you arrived. I'd been given the ridiculous impression . . .'

He broke off, and started making his call to University Asgard.

I went off to pack. The others seemed to be packing all their possessions, but I was more selective. I should only be on Asgard for four days.

27

I was the last to go to pack, and I was the first back to the dining hall. That's civilians for you. I'm not including Lecturer Playdon in this criticism. He was back only five minutes after me, despite being delayed by arranging accommodation.

The room gradually began to fill up with people and vast amounts of bags. I had one. Fian had three. Dalmora had seven. It got too crowded to count soon after that. The first nervous comments about portalling before it was too late were already beginning to start, and we still had seven hours before the Earth portal network was expected to go into lockdown.

'We have to wait for everyone and go as a group,' said Playdon. 'I'm not leaving people alone here.'

The Betans were the last to arrive. Lolia went up to Playdon. 'Lolmack and I feel we should be with Lolette. We can stay in a parent room at her Nursery, as we've done before.'

'Stay? During the solar storm?' Dalmora looked really impressed. 'That's so brave.'

'All right,' Playdon said, 'they'll take care of you at the Nursery. I can vid any classes you miss and . . .' Playdon's lookup bleeped. He glanced at it and frowned. 'There's a message for us from Cassandra 2. They expect we'll be pulling out soon for the portal outage, and if our rescue squad would like to portal over to their dome before leaving, they'd really like to say thank you. Apparently, they have a special gift for Jarra.'

'Now?' asked Dalmora. 'But the network is going down.'

'Not for nearly seven hours,' said Playdon. 'You can call over there and catch us up on Asgard.'

Dalmora gulped. 'I think I'd rather go with the group.'

Amalie and Krath nodded. Fian looked uncertainly at me.

'I'd love to meet them,' I said.

'Then I'll go too,' said Fian, bravely.

'I have to stay with the main group,' said Playdon. 'I wouldn't leave you two here alone, but you can't get into trouble at the Cassandra 2 dome. Portal from there straight to America Off-world, and then follow us on to Asgard. I'm sending everyone the portal codes now.'

Lookups did their usual blips, bleeps, and chimes.

Playdon led us off to the portal room. 'Fian and Jarra had better go to the Cassandra 2 dome first, then Lolia and Lomack can go to America Transit. After that, I'll count the rest of you through to America Off-world.'

Fian and I came forward, with our hover luggage following us. Playdon put in the portal code for the Cassandra 2 dome and we stepped through. A tall man of about 30 was waiting for us. He had an engaging smile, and a face like an elegant ebony sculpture, but there was an odd patch of distorted skin on his left temple. After a moment, I realized it had to be scar tissue, but I didn't understand why anyone would have a scar when a simple fluid patch treatment would cure it.

'Welcome,' he said. 'Just the two of you coming?'

'The others are heading off to Asgard right away. They're

a bit nervous about the portal outage,' I explained. 'I'm Jarra, and this is Fian.'

He nodded. 'Portal outages can be worrying until you get used to them. Welcome, both of you. I'm Rono Kipkibor, senior team leader, but people just call me Rono. Everyone else is in the dining hall.'

He led the way and made introductions. I've never been that great at remembering names, so I missed most of them. They were divided into two dig teams. A woman, Jerez, doubled as leader of team 2, or an extra heavy lift operator, whichever was needed. Their team 1 tag leader was a man called Keren.

'As you would expect, we're still short two people,' said Rono. 'Our team 2 tag leader, Stephan, is making a great recovery in Hospital Earth America. His wife, our team 2 tag support, is staying over there with him. They both send their thanks. We really thought we'd lost Stephan back there.'

'We were glad to help,' I said.

Fian gave a shy mumble.

'It's a bit embarrassing of course.' Rono grinned. 'People with our experience, being rescued by a team who hadn't been on a dig site for more than two days. Normally, we have our two teams working independently near each other, so if one gets in trouble then the other can dig them out, but when a whole tower comes down and buries the lot of us . . .'

He broke off and pulled a graphic face of pain. 'Well, you certainly did a great job saving us. Now, there's a tradition that a rescued team give a thank you gift to the tag leader who took the risks to save them. We checked the size with Playdon, just shout if it isn't quite right and we can swap it.'

He looked round, and a couple of the others came forward with a big box.

'You didn't need to . . .' I said.

'We must follow the tradition.' He smiled. 'Open it.'

I took the box and opened it, wondering what the chaos was inside. I gasped when I saw the contents and lifted it out reverently. My own brand new impact suit. Not one of the standard dome issue, but one of the proper ones the professionals buy themselves.

'This is . . .' I hugged it, completely overwhelmed. 'This is totally zan. I'll only ever have my own smell in there with me.'

They all laughed, including Fian.

'You can get special sprays to customise the colour,' said Rono. 'That makes it easier to recognize people.'

Keren grinned. 'You can spot Rono from a whole sector away. No one else would wear purple and silver.'

Rono aimed a mock punch at him, and shook his head sadly. 'Ignore Keren. He has no taste at all.'

'The suit is wonderful,' I said. 'Thank you so much. I'm afraid we have to go now and catch up with the rest of our class. They'll be on Asgard by now, and . . .'

'Of course.'

The whole group went back to the portal room with us. As we entered the room, all the portal lights suddenly flashed on green, then rapidly amber and red, as it ran through the lockdown sequence in less than five seconds. The red lights went out and the portal sat there, totally inert.

28

We all stared at the portal in disbelief.

'We were supposed to have another six hours,' said Rono in confusion. 'I've never known the forecasts be more than an hour wrong before. Why did it go through lockdown so fast anyway? It usually takes at least five minutes so people can finish sending stuff through open portals.'

'We're stuck?' asked Fian.

'I'm afraid so,' said Rono, 'but don't worry. You won't be in trouble with Playdon. I'll mail him myself and explain what happened. We've got several spare rooms, and it'll be a pleasure to have you stay with us until the network is back. I expect your class will be back soon after that as well.'

Fian was still looking worried, but I gave him an encouraging smile. 'We'll be fine, Fian.'

'The mystery is how the warning could be six hours wrong, and why lockdown was so fast . . .' muttered Rono. 'We'll sort some rooms out for you two in a minute, but before that I must see if there's any information on why the portals went out early.'

Everyone went back to the dining hall of the dome,

and suddenly there was a chorus of lookups screaming for attention.

'That has to be a solar storm update,' said Rono.

We all checked our lookups. 'A Carrington event!' Fian yelled. 'It's a Carrington event!'

The rest of us were just standing there, open-mouthed.

'Well, we're certainly going to be right in the middle of some history,' Rono said thoughtfully.

My head was trying to absorb what was happening. This was incredible. I'm no scientist, but everyone knows the effect that solar storms have on portals and the arrays out in space that supply power to all our planets. They're only a real problem on Earth, because Planet First chooses worlds in systems that only suffer infrequent solar storms. This time Earth wasn't just being hit by a solar storm, but a Carrington event, which is a massive solar super storm.

'That's why the leading edge of the storm hit earlier than expected and took the portal network down,' I muttered. 'It's the same as the original Carrington event back in 1859, when the solar super storm came in much faster than a normal storm.'

'How bad is this going to be?' asked Fian.

I waved my hands to indicate ignorance. 'According to the surviving records, Earth hasn't had another solar super storm as bad as the one Carrington observed in 1859. It wasn't much of a problem then, because there were no portals to be affected and very little other technology either. About all they had was a very early electronic communication system called the telegraph. It did something really primitive involving sending electrical signals down wires. The storm made those fail, some parts even caught fire, but it didn't really matter.'

'But now we have lots of technology,' said Fian, grimly.

Rono had turned on the dining hall vid, and set it to show

283

Earth Rolling News channel. A news presenter, looking a bit shocked but also thrilled to be presenting the story of the century, was in mid sentence. '. . . evidence that such a solar super storm occurred on Earth on average about every 500 years. Since then, Earth has prepared and waited for another Carrington event. It's happening now.'

The news presenter's eyes flickered, and he paused for a moment. He was obviously getting new information. 'The Carrington event in 1859 was estimated at seventeen times as powerful as a moderate solar storm. Experts are expecting the current super storm to be even stronger, peaking at eighteen times more powerful than a moderate solar storm.'

He paused again. 'We are receiving advice . . . The Earth portal network is already locked down. Earth Power is telling us they expect to lock down and fragment the power grid in one hour to prevent damage. Check your home's power is fully charged now, also any vital equipment and hover sleds.'

I frowned. They'd learnt as early as the twentieth century what big solar storms could do to a power grid on a planet surface. Fragmenting the grid was standard procedure for a major solar storm, but it might not be enough to defend against a solar super storm.

Rono vanished off for a moment and then reappeared. 'I've just done a triple check. We're on full power.'

After yet another brief silence, the presenter was talking again. 'The comms net is remaining open, but we can expect communications to be hit hard. Local data net lookup will be limited to priority system access, and we will probably lose off-world comm links entirely at some point. We're going to be using multiple redundancy techniques to try and keep the vital links open. This means sending out a lot of simultaneous copies of each transmission, so there may be some interference but they do arrive. This is a huge extra load on the system, so Earth Entertainment is closing down all vid channels other than the Rolling News. We apologise for any interference on the Rolling News channel, which may be reduced to sound only.'

'No vids,' said Fian. 'No data access from lookups. No pictures on the news channels. This is like going back to the dark ages!'

'The messaging system is expected to go into multiple redundancy within two hours,' said the presenter. 'Public information and emergency messages will take priority over private messages which may not be transmitted for several days. Do not abuse the system by flagging private messages as emergencies unless they are. Abuse could delay vital messages to and from the emergency services, endangering life, and culprits will face serious charges.'

'I'd better call Playdon before the system is out,' I said. I took out my lookup. 'I've got an error saying there are no free call slots. I've never seen that before.'

'The messaging system must be swamped,' said Rono. 'If you can't get through, then he'll find out what happened soon enough. This is going to be on all the newzies in every sector.'

I stared at my lookup, waiting for a free call slot. The news presenter was talking in the background.

'Schools followed standard procedure and closed down immediately they received the warning, so we've only a few reports of children stranded. Education Earth wants us to reassure parents and ProParents that all schools are prepared for this situation. Stranded children will be well cared for, and there is no cause for concern.'

My lookup flashed something new. 'I've now made it into the queue for an available call slot,' I reported. I knew that message. You often got it when you tried to call all your friends to wish them a happy Year Day.

The presenter was chatting again. 'I've just had an update from Hospital Earth. They report that significant numbers of at risk patients did not make it to hospital in time.'

'That's bad,' muttered Fian. 'That's very bad. People could die.'

'If you are an at risk patient, who did not make it to your designated hospital area,' said the presenter, 'please go to any medical building in your settlement. If you need assistance to travel there, please contact your settlement services number now. Owners of hover sleds, please contact your settlement services number if you are able to assist with providing emergency transport.'

'Pity we can't help,' said Keren. 'We've got lots of hover sleds, but the nearest settlement is miles away.'

'I've got a call slot!' I cried.

Rono turned the volume down on the Earth Rolling News and came over to join me. There was some interference on the picture on my lookup, but I could see Playdon. He seemed to be in some sort of hall, with the rest of the class.

'Jarra!' said Playdon. 'I was getting worried. We're on Asgard and I've managed to get rooms for everyone. We're just waiting for you and Fian.'

As they heard my name, the class gathered up, heads bobbing in and out of the screen view.

'We won't be able to make it, sir,' I said. 'The Earth portal network went into lockdown six hours early, and we're still with the Cassandra team. Earth is being hit by a Carrington event, so we won't be able to call you for several days.'

My words were being sent out from Earth, relayed through Alpha sector, and then on to Asgard in Gamma sector. There was a second of delay before Playdon reacted.

'What!' Playdon almost yelled the word, and there were gasps from the class.

'What's a Carrington event?' asked Krath.

'We made it out just in time,' said Dalmora.

Playdon ignored them both. 'Jarra, will you and Fian be safe? How bad will the situation be?'

'We'll take care of them,' Rono told him. 'Earth is trying to keep the Rolling News and emergency messages operating through the storm, but personal messages will be out, so don't worry if you don't hear anything for a few days.'

'I wish there was something I could do to help,' Playdon said.

'We'll be fine, sir,' I said. 'The call system's overloaded, so I'd better clear this call slot now.'

'I suppose so,' said Playdon. 'Good luck, Jarra, Fian, everyone.'

I could hear a vid come on in the background, and the class turned to look at it. '. . . is that a Carrington event is occurring on Earth. Scientists in every sector will be watching to see how technology designed to . . .'

I ended the call just as all the lookups yelled at us about priority incoming mail. It was emergency information, mostly what we'd already heard on the news. Rono studied it carefully. He was team leader, so our safety was his responsibility.

'They recommend everyone finds out the location of their nearest available medical centre now in case of emergencies,' he said. 'It's possible the messaging service fails entirely, so people may not be able to ask for advice.'

There was a strange crackling sound from overhead. Fian leapt nervously in the air, and even the Cassandra team seemed a bit worried.

'What was that?' Fian asked.

'No idea,' said Rono, looking upwards. 'The storm shouldn't be bad enough yet to affect the . . .'

'This is Dig Site Command,' said a disembodied voice.

'What?' We all looked round in bewilderment.

287

The voice continued speaking. 'Due to the imminent Carrington event, we've brought the old inter-dome communication system on line. This is Dig Site Command. If you're hearing this, please locate the dome communication system controls in your dining hall. They're probably located behind the food dispensers but it depends when your dome was built. Some domes may have them in the portal room or even the store room.'

Rono was already on his knees behind the food dispensers. 'All I can find here is dust.'

'You're looking for a grey control box,' said Dig Site Command. 'The cover is marked I.D.C. If you flip up the cover, you'll see a control unit similar to the suit ones. If you're really lucky one of the old handsets is in there as well.'

'Still no box,' said Rono. 'Team 1 search in here. Team 2 check the store room. Jarra and Fian, take a look in the portal room.'

'Yes, sir.' I acknowledged the order.

Rono blinked at me. 'Why are you calling me that?'

'Sir, since Lecturer Playdon is on Asgard and out of contact, you're now my commanding officer.'

Rono laughed. 'Oh yes, you're the Military Honour Child the dig site was talking about. That was the first Honour Ceremony they've ever had at New York Dig Site.'

Fian and I headed out of the hall door. We could only faintly hear Dig Site Command in the corridor, but they were loud and clear in the portal room.

'This is Dig Site Command. When you've found your control units, can team leaders please call in your team numbers, dome, and status. The messaging service is going to be limited to emergency messages and may fail entirely. A lot of teams decided to go off world for a break rather than sit out a three day portal outage. We're not sure who actually managed to get off world, and who got caught by the portal lockdown.

We want to know who is here, and where you are, so we can help each other out in emergencies.'

'This is Beowulf 4,' said a voice. 'Six people here. Our team was in the middle of portalling out when the system locked down.'

'This is Earth 19. There are twenty-nine of us.'

'Found it!' I cried. The box was hidden away on the wall behind the portal control system. I flipped open the cover. 'This must be the remote unit.'

I took it out and headed back to the dining hall, where Rono was still searching round the food dispensers.

'I think this is the remote, sir.'

'Wonderful. Someone tell team 2 that Jarra found it.'

He peered at the remote, pressed a button and spoke. 'This is Cassandra 2.' His voice echoed from some speaker overhead, so it was clearly working. 'We have ten people here.'

Teams kept calling in for a few minutes, and then it went quiet.

'This is Dig Site Command. If anyone else is out there and can't find the control box, please call us over the usual impact suit system. We'll patch you in from that.'

There was about five minutes of silence, then the voice came over the speakers again. 'This is Dig Site Command. We're getting no calls on the suit system, and the team check is consistent with what we knew of everyone's plans. Surprisingly enough, the old inter-dome system is still working despite being abandoned fifty years ago. This is a situation that only happens every five hundred years, so I think we can relax the usual Dig Site communication protocols a little unless any emergencies crop up. Feel free to chat a little.'

'This is Achilles 1,' said a voice that sounded strained but deeply thankful. 'We'd like to thank whoever remembered the old dome comms system. I didn't even know we had it. I've got a class of thirty Foundation course students here, and we got caught just before we left for Achilles. My students were starting to feel a bit isolated, so this is reassuring them a lot.'

I could imagine what the Achilles 1 lecturer was facing. If Asgard 6 had been trapped at their dome, Playdon would have had blind panic on his hands.

'This is Dig Site Command. Remember you aren't alone. Our count says we have 238 people in the dig site domes, and there are five of us here at Dig Site Command. It was mostly the research teams that stayed, so there are a lot of highly experienced people nearby to help.'

'This is Earth 8. I think we're in the next dome to you, Achilles 1, so if you have problems we can reach you by hover sled in about fifteen minutes.'

'This is Achilles 1. Thank you for that Earth 8. It's reassuring but don't take unnecessary risks. My class is feeling rather happier now.'

'This is Earth 8. Just shout if you need company. We're an Earth team, we're all Handicapped and used to carrying on life as normal during a portal outage. I admit this one is a bit special, but the inter-dome system will help a lot.'

'This is Earth 19. We're happy to hover sled to anyone needing help as well.'

'This is Beowulf 4. We're only pathetic little scared exos, but we would try and help too.'

'This is Dig Site Command. We'd rather have everyone staying safe in their domes, but if anyone has problems then just call and we'll work out who is closest and can assist. Any other Foundation courses out there?'

Rono spoke into his handset. 'This is Cassandra 2.'

'This is Dig Site Command. You can't fool me, Rono, you aren't a Foundation course.'

Rono laughed. 'I've ten people here, but only eight are my team. As some of you know, Stephan is in Hospital Earth for a few more weeks yet, and his wife is staying with him. We had two visitors from Asgard 6 Foundation course with us when the portals went into lockdown.'

'This is Dig Site Command. Does that mean you have tag leader Jarra with you?'

'This is Cassandra 2. We have tag leader Jarra and her tag support Fian with us.'

'This is Dig Site Command. I hope you'll treat your guests extremely well. They did a very fine job there.'

'This is Beowulf 4. That was great work on the rescue. What we want to know is has Cassandra 2 paid their traditional debt yet?'

Rono held the handset towards me and I nervously spoke into it. 'This is Jarra. They gave me the most wonderful impact suit of my very own.'

'This is Dig Site Command. If they hadn't, then they'd have been banned from every dig site. It's a long standing tradition among the professionals who work the sites. If the tag leader who digs you out doesn't have their own suit yet, then you buy them one.' There was a short pause. 'While we're checking up on who is out there, do we have any medical experts?'

'This is Earth 19. We have a qualified doctor on the team, though obviously she has limited medical equipment.'

'This is Dig Site Command. That's good to know. All domes should have emergency medical supplies. Call on Earth 19 for advice if you need to give anyone any medication. The nearest settlement has a hospital unit but that's several hours away by hover sled.'

Fian tapped me on the arm, so I turned to look at him.

'Jarra, I was checking what was happening with the messaging system. It says absolute priority goes to the emergency messages, but they're going to try and keep some of the other services open for compassionate reasons. Contract Registry is one of them. I know our families aren't here to witness, but in the circumstances . . . It would be really romantic.'

I stared at him. I was grazzed.

'Jarra, can we Two? We could call up now and register . . .'

I hadn't expected it to happen this soon, but let's be honest. Ever since I pinned him to the floor of his room and kissed him, I'd intended to tag Fian with a Twoing contract one day. How could I say no to registering it now? Just imagine. One day, we might be telling our children how we registered our first Twoing contract during the Carrington event. Nothing could be more zan than that!

I grinned. 'Call them!'

Fian kissed me, and called Registry on his lookup. It was slow, desperately slow. Several minutes ticked by. They might be trying to keep Registry open, but Earth was heading into a solar super storm and maybe we wouldn't get through.

Dig Site Command and the other teams were still chatting away over the inter-dome system. We were cut off. Humanity's scientists were finally going to discover whether its technology, carefully designed to survive solar storms, could actually cope with a Carrington event. It was rather scary, but somehow the inter dome system had turned it into a sort of party. We weren't alone. The dig teams were facing the unknown together. I hoped Achilles 1 were feeling that too.

'I'm through,' said Fian. He entered codes fast, and placed his hand on the lookup screen to verify his identity.

By now the Cassandra 2 team had realized what was going on, and were clustered round us watching. We had another long wait before the system accepted the data. Every safety protocol they had was being used to protect equipment from the solar storm, so the system was literally down to crawl speed.

Fian thrust the lookup towards me. 'Quick before we lose connection.'

I entered codes, clumsy with haste, and placed my hand on the screen.

There was another painfully long wait. Fian and I exchanged agonized looks. Having decided to do this, we wanted it desperately. It would be the greatest let down in history if the connection failed now.

'Come on!' I ordered the lookup. 'It's stuck in the middle of verifying I haven't got a current contract registered.'

'You'd better not have,' Fian teased. 'That's an automatic fraud conviction.'

'Registry could have lost connection to the data net or . . .' A message popped up on the screen. 'It's through!'

Fian grabbed the lookup and read the message. 'Your Twoing contract is officially on record and valid for the next three months. Congratulations and best wishes from Registry.'

'Congratulations!' chorused the Cassandra 2 team.

Fian blushed. 'I suppose this seems a bit rushed to you.'

'Not at all,' said Rono. 'Tag leader and tag support often develop an intense relationship pretty fast.'

'I'm betting Jarra got buried,' said Keren.

Fian and I looked at him, startled. I'm not sure what our faces gave away, but everyone laughed.

'Don't worry,' said Rono. 'It's like tag point itch. It happens to a lot of people. When anyone gets buried or hurt, the rest of the team tend to react strongly. Just look at me!' He tapped the scar on his forehead, and there was another ripple of amusement from the Cassandrans at what was obviously a private joke.

'I'd suggest opening some wine to celebrate,' continued

Rono, 'but we need to keep clear heads during the Carrington event. Another dome might need help from us, and I don't want a drunken team making a journey by hover sled through the snow and the wolf packs.'

'Pity we couldn't actually get married,' said Fian. 'We haven't got the three prior contracts and the full year required.'

I giggled. 'I think actually getting married would definitely be rushing things too much.'

Rono spoke into the handset. 'This is Cassandra 2. Sorry to interrupt the conversation, but I'm sure you'd all like to know that Jarra and Fian just signed up for a Twoing contract.'

'This is Earth 19. That's a wise move, Jarra. Fian's a good tag support, so you want to hold on to him.'

Rono handed me the hand set for a moment. 'This is Jarra. I know that, and I've got Fian firmly tagged!'

'This is Dig Site Command. I want that officially confirmed by Fian. Let's hear from him.'

Fian blushed and spoke into the handset. 'I'm definitely tagged and pinned down.'

There was the sound of laughter and cheering from what sounded like several different teams.

Rono took the handset back. 'This is Cassandra 2. You'll have to excuse us for a few minutes now. We've got a lot of spare rooms in our domes, but they're all singles. I think it's time to move a wall.'

The Cassandra 2 team really did move a wall. They got a special gadget from the store room, dragged furniture out of the way, and unlocked the bolts securing the flexiplas wall between two of the bedrooms. Fian and I watched them shift the wall along and attach it to a neighbouring one. We were completely grazzed.

'I didn't know you could do that,' I said.

Rono tapped the side of his nose and winked at us. 'We keep it a little quiet, because we don't want students messing

294

about with the walls. You can never depend on them to put them back for the next poor person who has the room. However, since you two took part in a rescue, you count as fellow professionals.'

Keren appeared carrying a tray of food and drinks, and Rono grinned at us. 'Right, you've got food, drink, and a double room. There's a single room free next door as well, so you can arrange yourselves however you like. We'll give you a call when it gets dark outside, because they're predicting the sky is going to be incredible with auroras from a storm this size. Until then, we'll leave you to . . .' Rono's grin widened. 'Unpack.'

The Cassandra 2 team gave us a flurry of good wishes and headed off back to the dining hall. Fian shut the door behind them and looked at me.

'So . . .' he said, hopefully. 'Is this where I finally find out what happens after the end credits of *Stalea of the Jungle*?'

'That depends,' I said. 'Just how badly behaved are you by Deltan standards?'

He gave me a dreadfully wicked grin.

29

Fian and I joined the Cassandra team as night fell. We knew it would be bitterly cold outside, and the wolves might be roaming in the darkness, so we all suited up. I was wearing my new, beautiful, odourless impact suit. The Cassandra team had their own personal suits too, in a range of colours from Keren's sedate plain blue to Rono's spectacular design in purple and silver, but poor Fian had to settle for one from the store room. I felt a bit guilty.

When everyone was ready, we opened the dome door and we got our first glimpse of the sky. I'd never seen anything so amaz! It was filled with streaks of violet and crimson flame. The spectacle of the sky was reflected by the snow, turning the ground into ripples of fire. We stepped outside, wading through glowing snow. Night had been overwhelmed by the solar super storm and it was as bright as day.

Rono spoke in a mesmerized voice. 'It's . . . incredible. Stay together and close to the dome though. This is no time for accidents.'

We didn't need to go far to appreciate the splendour. The Cassandra 2 dome was on the top of a low hill, and we could look across the blackened ruins of New York Main Dig Site, and see the remains of skyscrapers silhouetted against a burning sky.

There must have been people everywhere on Earth, recording scenes like this for future vids, but seeing it on a vid could never match this. We were there, standing in a landscape more alien than any inhabited world, as dramatic as anything anyone would see on Planet First. We stood there, just looking at it, for an hour or more. Fian had his arm round me, impact suits rather reduce the romance of that, but the suits did stop us freezing to death while we were lost in the magic around us.

The voice that came over the communication channel made us all jump. 'This is Dig Site Command. I know a lot of you are outside admiring the view, but I think you might wish to check the Earth Rolling News channel.'

It was a calm, measured, professional voice, but we could tell something was horribly wrong.

We headed back inside, and Rono double checked we were all safely in before he closed the dome door. We didn't change out of our impact suits, just opened the hoods, and hurried into the dining hall to put the vid on.

The face of the news presenter was freckled white with interference, but his expression was clear enough to confirm he had something awful to say. 'This is Earth Rolling News, repeating main stories to try and reach you through the Carrington event. The story in everyone's hearts is the announcement from Military Command.'

'Military Command?' murmured Rono. 'What?'

The news presenter continued in a grim voice. 'Standard safety procedures for an incoming solar storm are to disconnect the solar power arrays out in space from their transmitters, turning off the beams supplying power to the planet below. The Military crews manning the solar arrays then portal out to avoid the increased radiation levels during a solar storm.'

I realized where this was going, and my mind went numb. 'Oh no . . . Please no.'

'The leading edge of the storm arrived at the Earth solar arrays six hours ahead of forecast, since this was not a normal solar storm but a Carrington event. The Military crews aboard the solar arrays had only five minutes warning before the portals were unusable. They chose to stay at their posts and complete disconnecting the arrays to avoid the power beams being overloaded during the storm, breaking free, and causing large scale loss of life on the planet surface. 352 Military personnel are now trapped aboard the solar arrays in lethal levels of solar radiation. Shields can protect them for only a few more hours.'

'We're all right down here,' said Fian numbly. 'We're safe down in the atmosphere, but the radiation is killing them.'

'They stayed there to save us,' said Rono. 'You know what that power beam did to Artemis. Think what one could do in a Carrington event . . .'

That beautiful sky, I thought, that wildly stunning sky, was solar radiation killing 352 people.

'Is there any chance if they portal?' asked someone.

Fian said what we all knew. 'What arrived at the other end wouldn't be . . .' He shook his head. 'They could receive signals from another system but that doesn't help them escape. They can't send themselves anywhere.'

'We've now been told that the Military have been sending equipment to the trapped crews,' continued the news presenter.

That sounded like they were trying something. We all listened frantically.

'The crews have been working against time, converting

their ships. They will be attempting to enter Earth's atmosphere in two hours from now.'

'What?' yelled Fian. 'They're trying to land on Earth!'

'Can that possibly work?' asked Jerez.

'The solar array ships are just used to move sections of solar sail, they aren't designed to enter an atmosphere,' I said, totally grazzed. 'Nothing is. Fighters and dart ships use conventional or drop portals to reach their destinations. Anything bigger has to be portalled in pieces, and assembled after arrival. We've nothing like the Apollo programme. We haven't had a spacecraft land on a planet for six hundred years!'

'I remember studying Apollo 13,' said Rono. 'They were stuck in space too and made it back. Maybe some of these will make it.'

'They've nothing to lose,' said Fian. 'It's better to try this, than just sit and wait for the shields to fail.'

'They're fighting,' I said. 'It's the Military way. We don't just give up, we go down fighting. They'll try this even if they don't believe anyone will make it.'

'Sorry, Jarra,' said Rono. 'This news had driven everything out of my head, but of course it's especially hard for you. These are your people.'

We listened to Earth Rolling News repeat the same story several times. Finally some more details came in. The interference was worse now, but it was the same news presenter, looking overwhelmed by what he was reading.

'We have more details now from Military Command. The Military personnel will be coming down in five ships, one from each solar array. These ships are only designed to operate in space. They've modified the screens to protect them while they enter the Earth's atmosphere, but they will have very limited control during the descent and have no way to land other than crashing. They are hoping that the combination of ship shields and impact suits will mean some people survive the crash. Military Command states that crews will, at all costs, avoid endangering Earth settlements. They will not risk civilian loss of life.'

The news presenter paused for a moment. 'The ships will be attempting to land at White Sands, New Mexico, in Earth America. Earth Rolling News will update you with any information we receive. Our thoughts are with the Military ships in this desperate bid, and we ask all Earth America settlements in the New Mexico area to prepare to receive injured Military personnel. Military Command is receiving messages of best wishes from all sectors.'

Everyone had been absorbed by the news reports, so the voice that came over the inter-dome communications startled us. 'This is Dig Site Command. We expect some people will want to watch the skies as the ships try and land. New Mexico is quite a way south, and it depends on their approach path whether we'll see anything. I'm patching Earth Rolling News commentary into the impact suit comms channel, so you can listen to news updates if you want to try watching outside.'

'Jarra, will any of your relatives or friends be on those ships?' asked Rono.

I tried to work out where everyone was, but something strange was happening to my mind. I couldn't remember where my brother Keon was, or my friend Issette. It was as if my head didn't want to think about them. Was that because they were up there on those solar arrays? I tried to force myself to remember.

'The Colonel who led Jarra's Honour Ceremony will be on one of them,' said Fian. 'He's the commanding officer of the solar arrays. What about your brother, Jarra?'

I was getting muddled by panic. I had to make myself think logically. Keon was only 18, the same as Issette and me, so he must be training somewhere, but . . . No, that couldn't be right. My brother and sister were a lot older than me.

Sister, what sister? My head whirled in confusion.

'Jarra, are you all right?' Fian asked.

My parents. I focused on thinking about them. I knew they couldn't be on the Earth solar array, because they were safely on Planet First assignment in Kappa sector. Something seemed to thunder in my head. My parents weren't safe. I remembered the face of a Military General breaking the news. Telling me . . . Telling me my parents were dead.

'Jarra?' Fian's face was in front of me, he was staring into my eyes, but I couldn't be distracted by him. I had to think.

Fian was talking to Rono now, but I didn't hear what they were saying. My real parents were dead. I still had Candace, but she wasn't Military. I had a ProDad too, but we didn't get on too well. Candace wasn't just being a ProMum for the money, she really cared about me, but I didn't think that my ProDad did and . . .

I had ProParents . . .

Fian had tugged me out of the hall and was guiding me into our room. 'Jarra? Is someone important up there? Your brother, Keon? When you were talking to him and Issette at the zoo, I couldn't see any routing lag at all, so I guessed they couldn't be further away than Alpha sector. They weren't wearing their uniforms though, so they surely couldn't have been up on the Earth solar arrays.'

I sat on the bed. Keon wasn't my brother. He was a friend. One of the other kids from my year in Next Step. We'd been a sort of family.

Fian sat down next to me. I was working things out now. I slowly disentangled the three sets of reality, and worked out what was true and what was false. My fake Military background. My real Military background. My Earth background.

301

It took me a while to get it all sorted out, get past the pain of my parents' death, and realize what I'd done. I was an ape. Fian was a norm. Fian and I had a Twoing contract. I should never have registered that contract, but I'd been lost in fantasy land, believing I was a norm as well. I had to tell him the truth now, but it was going to be hard to make him understand.

'Fian, when I started on the pre-history course here, there were some things I didn't tell people.'

'You mean about being an Honour Child?' he asked.

'I didn't know about that then. I found out when I asked for the information on my parents.'

'What?' Fian shook his head. 'Jarra, just tell me, is Keon up on that solar array? Is that why you're so . . .'

'No,' I said. There was no way to explain this sensibly. I gave up and just said it. 'Keon is studying art at University Earth.'

'What?' Fian stared at me. 'Your brother is Handicapped?'

'Keon is Handicapped, but he isn't my brother.'

'You said he was adopted.'

'There were nine of us at my Next Step on Earth,' I said. 'Keon was there, and my best friend Issette, and Cathan, and Ross and Maeth and . . .'

Fian interrupted. 'Next Step on Earth? What are you talking about? You're Military.'

'I'm Handicapped. I grew up as a ward of Hospital Earth. I pretended to be Military so the class wouldn't find out I was from Earth and Handicapped, then I asked for information about my parents. I found out my family really were Military, and there was the Honour Ceremony, and . . . Then I got some really bad news, and my head just caved in. I started believing the lies myself.'

'You . . .' Fian stood up and stared down at me. 'You let us register a Twoing contract, and you didn't tell me! What in chaos will my family think when they find out I'm Twoing with an ape?'

I winced. When someone says leg, you know which bit they mean by the way they say it. When someone says ape, the way they say it means a lot too. I'd never heard Fian use the ape word before, and now he had, and in the worst way.

Sometimes it only takes one word to say everything. I got up and walked out of the room.

'Where are you going?' asked Fian, sharply. 'We need to talk.' He followed me down the corridor.

'I think we finished the talking,' I said. 'Yes, I'm an ape, a nean, a throwback, and the garbage of the universe. You can call me all the names you like, because I know I deserve them, but you'll just be wasting your breath. I know them all already and I've been hearing them all my life.'

'Jarra, we have to . . .'

I kept walking. Somehow the sheer extent of the disaster left me feeling weirdly calm. 'I'm very sorry, Fian. I know I've done something dreadful. It was bad enough telling you and the rest of the class all those lies, but the Twoing contract . . . I can only apologize for the mess I've got you into. My parents died a few days after the Honour Ceremony, and that made me go a little crazy. I'll do anything I can to fix things later, anything at all, but right now . . . right now I can't do anything except worry about those Military ships.'

'Jarra, stand still and talk to me!'

He caught my arm, but I tugged it free. 'No, Fian. There's nothing I can possibly say except that I'm terribly sorry, and I've said that. Now, I'm going to take off this impact suit for a few minutes and have a shower. Then I'm going to put it on again, go outside to watch the sky, and pray that whatever deity runs this universe will guide those Military ships down safely. I'm only an ape girl, but they're my people,

303

and they're in trouble. My parents didn't make it back, but there's still a chance that some of these will.'

I went into the bathroom, locked the door behind me, and stripped off my impact suit. Fian hammered on the door and tried to talk to me, but I went under the shower, turned it on full blast, and let the sound of the water save me from hearing him. Fian and I were finished, and I couldn't blame anyone but myself. I should never have let myself get involved with him. Fian had every reason to scream abuse at me, but I didn't want to hear it, and I didn't need to hear it. I was screaming enough abuse at myself. The dumb ape had set out to get revenge on the evil exos, and she'd destroyed herself instead. She deserved that, but she'd messed up Fian's life too, and that was unforgiveable.

I'd do anything I could to make things right for him, but how the chaos could I even start to do that? I'd buried both of us in an avalanche of my own lies, and there was no way I could dig us out from it. We couldn't even hush up the Twoing contract, since the whole of New York Dig Site knew about it. The only thing I could do was get out of Fian's life as fast as possible, and I couldn't even do that until the Carrington event was over. I couldn't portal, I couldn't even message anyone, but the minute I could then I'd collect my stuff from the Asgard 6 dome and leave. I had no idea where I'd go, but I'd have time to work that out before the portals were back.

I turned off the shower. Fian was still there when I came out, but a couple of the Cassandra team were queuing for the bathroom, so he didn't try to talk. I had my impact suit on properly now, glad to have my face safely hidden from the world. The two Cassandrans insisted on Fian taking his turn in the bathroom ahead of them, and I went off to join Rono who was already waiting by the dome door.

30

Dig Site Command had patched the Earth Rolling News channel into the suit broadcast circuit. Interference kept drowning out their words, but they were repeating each sentence in an attempt to help people hear.

Fian and the rest of the Cassandra team arrived, and we went outside into the aurora that changed night into day. The sky was shades of green with a few streaks of fuchsia now, and the snow took the colours, blending and distorting them together, and reflected them back, returning the borrowed light to the sky.

It was far too early for the ships to be landing yet, so we stood there waiting in silence for long minutes. Over in the dark ruins of New York, a chain of fire suddenly flashed.

'What's that?' Rono asked.

'Probably part of an old power net or pipe or girder,' said Fian. 'A bad solar storm can induce electrical currents, so a Carrington event . . .'

'Earth Rolling News reported a few fires,' muttered Rono.

Fian had sounded grim but calm, while I was alternating between numb despair and panic. Most of my head was thinking about the Military ships, but the rest was trying to

305

face up to the consequences of my own actions. Earlier today, I'd had everything I wanted. Now I'd lost not only the dream but the reality. My relationship with Fian had been based on fantasy and that was gone. My future as a historian was based on reality, but I'd lost that too. I had to be fair to Fian, get out of his life, and hide the fact that Jarra Tell Morrath, the pre-history student, was an ape. Achieving that meant vanishing from the class, from the dig sites, and from studying history.

Earth Rolling News had been repeating advice on coping with the solar storm, and announcing it was going to sound only. Now it finally went back to the story of the Military ships. I forgot my own concerns and listened.

'. . . landing at White Sands . . .' said the Earth Rolling News through the interference. '. . . launching Solar 1 in three minutes . . . closest settlements . . . lose contact during entry . . .'

We stood under a lurid green sky and waited.

'. . . launched. Solar 1 launched . . . Solar 1 . . .' said the voice of Earth Rolling News, drifting in and out of the static. '. . . lost. Contact lost. Contact . . .'

'They've crashed then,' said Rono, his voice harsh with emotion.

'I hope it just means they're entering the atmosphere,' I said. 'We'd lose contact during that.'

We waited for what seemed ages.

'. . . Sands. Solar 1 reports . . . landed at White Sands, with . . .' the Rolling News commentator said.

'What's he saying?' asked Fian.

'. . . Sands, they report seven injured . . . sleds to assist. Solar 1 has landed at White Sands, they report . . . settlement sending sleds to . . .'

'They made it!' I shouted.

We all cheered.

'Did anyone see anything in the sky?' asked Rono. 'I might have seen a white streak, but with the aurora . . .'

'. . . 2 is launching. Solar 2 is . . .' the Rolling News said.

'One made it,' said Fian. 'Let's hope . . .'

'Even one person making it down would have been a victory,' I said. 'It sounds like most of a ship load made it.'

'Five ships all together,' said Rono. 'So about seventy people on each.'

We waited again, struggling to hear the words of the Rolling News.

'Did they say Solar 3 had launched?' asked Fian. 'Solar 2 isn't down yet.'

'I don't think they can afford to wait,' I said. 'They'd want to let the first ship land in case that gave them extra information, but they may not have time to send the rest one by one.'

'. . . Solar 4 . . . launching Solar 4 . . . still working on . . . working on Solar 5 . . .' said the Rolling News.

'They've launched three more ships, but they're still working on Solar 5,' said Rono.

'They must be running out of time,' I said. 'When the shielding up there fails, the solar radiation . . .'

'. . . landed. Solar 2 has landed . . .' Earth Rolling News vanished under a torrent of crackling sound for several minutes before we got another clear spell. ' . . . ships landed. Four ships landed. 2 deaths. 27 injured. 2 deaths. 27 injured . . . sleds to medical . . . Alamogordo. Solar 5 still . . . further . . .'

'Will Solar 5 make it in time?' asked Rono.

'It's not looking good,' I said. 'If they launched the others so close together, it was because they had to.'

'. . . 5 launching now. Solar 5 . . .'

The voice of Earth Rolling News was conquered by static, and we waited, tensely listening to meaningless crackling and hisses.

'Look!' Fian pointed upwards and yelled the word.

I saw the white bolt shooting overhead across the green sky. 'It's too low, much too low . . .' I broke off as I saw flames flare up among the black ruins of New York.

There was dead silence for thirty seconds, before the static of Earth Rolling News vanished and was replaced by Dig Site Command talking on the broadcast channel.

'This is Dig Site Command. This is Dig Site Command. Solar 5 has crash landed on New York Dig Site.' There was a long pause. 'We think they're out near intersection 3 of the Grand Circle and the Loop. If that's right, then we can expect that they've hit some towers. We've got someone trying to contact them now. Teams willing to assist in rescue please call in. Be aware the solar storm will affect equipment and conditions will be extremely hazardous. Keep this off broadcast channel; we don't want anyone feeling pressured into volunteering.'

'Are we in?' asked Rono.

'Yes!' I said.

'Not you two,' said Rono, 'you're only on your Foundation course. I meant my team.'

'We're in,' chorused the rest of Cassandra 2.

'I am the Honour Child of Jarra Tell Morrath,' I said, 'and I'm in.'

'You're not as experienced as us,' said Rono.

I wasn't being left out of this. My parents were dead, and I could do nothing to change that, but I could try and help the Military in Solar 5.

'With respect, sir, who was it that dug you experienced people out from under that tower block?' I asked, fiercely.

'You know,' said Rono, 'I have to admit that argument is hard to counter. Playdon will kill me for this, but if you want it . . .'

'We're both in,' said Fian, quietly. 'Your team 2 need a tag leader and tag support, and we're it.'

'Fian, you don't have to do this,' I said. 'It's different for me.'

'Fian, you're sure?' asked Rono.

'I'm in,' said Fian. 'The solar array crews stayed at their posts to save us, and now it's our turn to save them. If you're taking Jarra, then you have to take me as well. She's totally crazy, and I'm the only one who can possibly keep her under control.'

Rono laughed. 'I'll let Dig Site Command know.'

He called in. We were all standing close together, so I could hear his side of the conversation. 'This is Cassandra 2. We're in. Jarra and Fian from Asgard 6 insist on filling the gaps in our team 2, so we can run a double team.'

Rono paused for a moment. 'Yes, I've already been through that with them, but you try telling the people who rescued you that they aren't experienced enough to . . .'

He paused again and then spoke on the team circuit. 'Dig Site Command say we're to take two sensor sleds, two tag support sleds, three heavy lift sleds, and the special transport sled with the mobile dome.'

We were halfway through getting sleds out, when Dig Site Command started talking again. 'This is Dig Site Command. We have contact with Solar 5, and they have 67 people aboard, 21 of whom are injured. They're definitely near intersection 3, and they seem to be buried.'

Rono groaned. 'If they're buried, we'll never reach . . .'

'They have ship shields protecting them, which they estimate will last for between 18 and 27 hours,' Dig Site Command continued, 'so we stand a chance of reaching them. Thank you everyone for volunteering to help. We've had the whole dig site calling in, even Achilles 1. We appreciate the courageous offer, Achilles 1, but we feel a Foundation course class had better stay in their dome during this.

'We have a lot of partial teams out there,' continued Dig Site Command. 'We know a couple of teams have already arranged substitutes. Remaining partial teams call in on channel 9 and we'll help you fill gaps. We're giving individual instructions on what sleds to bring, but also pack anything else that's useful. Food. Medical supplies. Spare impact suits. We expect to have equipment failures due to the solar storm, so take your time packing and bring as many spares as you can. Drive slowly because the storm may affect the hover sled controls, and head to intersection 3 by your safest route. We'll be setting up a base camp there. Call in as you arrive at intersection 3, and don't try heading directly for the crash site. We'll be selecting a couple of teams to make the first site inspection.

'Achilles 1 are being stubborn, so they will be helping drive sleds and run the base camp for us. Just load everything you've got into your sleds, Achilles 1, and head to intersection 3. Since the whole dig site will be there, and the interference is getting worse, we're transferring Dig Site Command to our mobile command sleds and heading to intersection 3 as well.'

I don't know why, but somehow the news that Dig Site Command was moving to mobile command sleds brought home just how incredible this all was. My head reeled for a moment as I realized what we were trying to do. 'So we're going to dig up a buried spaceship instead of a stasis box . . . This is crazy.'

Fian gave a sudden laugh. 'Things always seem crazy around you.'

For a moment, the crisis had driven everything personal out of my head. 'I'm sorry,' I said.

'I'm getting used to it,' said Fian.

Rono got us all loading supplies on to sleds. I carried across boxes of packaged food, and wondered what Fian had meant by that, if anything. Maybe he hadn't meant anything significant at all.

When the sleds were loaded, Rono stood in silence for a moment. 'Charges. Guns. I don't think we've forgotten anything vital. We've got eight sleds, so my team each drive a sled. I'll lead the way on the mobile dome transport sled, and Jarra and Fian can ride on the back of that. Let's go.'

Everyone climbed on the sleds and started them moving. Fian and I sat on the row of seats at the back of the transport sled. There was a mountain of mobile dome storage sections, neatly packed under an orange cover, in front of us. We looked out sideways as our sled entered a snow covered dig site and then stopped.

'We're just waiting for Thor 3 to join us,' said Rono's voice on the team circuit. 'There are only two of them left here, and Dig Site Command doesn't want us travelling in groups of less than four sleds.'

Fian and I looked back, and saw two large sleds bobbing their way along to join the back of our convoy. 'What sort of sled are those?' asked Fian. 'They look a bit like transports but . . .'

'Dumper sleds,' I said. 'You use them when you have to shift rubble around by sled for some reason.'

We started moving again. 'How long will it take us to get to intersection 3?' Fian asked me.

'Probably a few hours. I'm not sure where we are now, so . . .' I hesitated. Rono was the other side of the mound of mobile dome parts, and couldn't possibly hear us unless we spoke on the team circuit. I could safely mention personal matters, but it was hard to work out what to say. In the end, I said the obvious thing. 'You didn't have to do this.'

'I didn't have to do this. I chose to do it,' said Fian.

There was a long silence. The hover sled seemed to be jolting much more than usual. I was sure Rono could drive a hover sled perfectly well, so I assumed that the solar storm was affecting it.

'What were you planning?' Fian asked suddenly. 'What the chaos were you going to do when the class portalled to Asgard? You didn't know that Cassandra 2 would invite us over here, you couldn't have known there would be a Carrington event, so what excuse were you planning to make at the last minute?'

'I didn't have a plan,' I said. 'I didn't know what I was doing. I'd contacted my parents, they were going to come to Earth and meet me, and . . . and when the General called to say they'd been killed I just couldn't handle it. My head went off into fantasy land, and nobody else knew there was anything wrong. Even Playdon believed I was normal by then. I thought my parents were still alive. I thought I could portal to Asgard. I thought you and I could be . . .'

I broke off. Fian and I couldn't be anything any longer, and that hurt.

'You'd have walked through the portal?'

'Yes.'

'But . . . that's insane,' Fian said. 'You'd have died within minutes, unless people realized what was happening and sent you back.'

'It would have been worse than just dying,' I said bitterly. 'Portal networks have lists of the genetic codes of people who aren't allowed to portal off world because they're criminals. On Earth they use the same system for both criminals and apes, to stop us apes doing stupid things. If I'd stepped into an off-world portal, it would have scanned me, seen my genetic code was forbidden access, and shut down. Alarms would have gone off, and I'd have been arrested. After a bit, they'd have worked out I was a crazy nean not a criminal, and then they'd have sent me to a hospital secure unit for compulsory psychological treatment.'

'That still wouldn't be as bad as dying,' said Fian.

I sighed. 'That's a matter of opinion. I hate talking to

psychologists. My only chance would have been if I could convince Candace to get me out of there, and in the circumstances that would have been pretty hard.'

'You really believed it.' Fian wasn't asking a question. He seemed to be talking to himself and working things out. 'That first evening we spent with the wine and watching the silly vids. I was sure you liked me then. I was sure you felt just the same way I did, but the next morning you froze me off. I couldn't work out what I'd done wrong.'

'I couldn't get involved with you,' I said. 'I was lying to you. You were a man and I was an ape. I knew that you'd hate me when you found out the truth.'

'You kept me at arm's length after that, until a few days after the Honour Ceremony, when you suddenly changed. You were crazily happy, like you were floating on air, and you were smiling at me. Everything was so zan. I couldn't believe my luck, it was . . .'

He broke off, and I didn't dare to say anything. My face was safely hidden inside my impact suit hood, but if I spoke then my voice would give me away. I'd been living in a wonderful, wonderful dream, but now I'd woken up, and the real world was looking grim.

We both sat in silence for a few minutes, and then Fian spoke again. 'You'd gone into fantasy land, and you stayed there until we heard the news about the Military?'

'Yes,' I said. 'When I tried to remember where Keon was, my head didn't want to think about it, but I forced it and suddenly . . . My mind was going crazy. I was remembering several different realities. The lies I'd made up didn't fit my real Military family. My real brother is a lot older than Keon, and I have a sister too, and then . . . Then I remembered the General telling me my parents were . . .'

Fian was silent for a moment. 'Incredible. You seemed such a strong and capable person, that I felt you didn't need me or anyone else, but you have your breaking point like the rest of us.' His voice suddenly became businesslike. 'So, we have to decide what to do.'

'I've been thinking about that. I've already decided I'll leave the course. The whole dig site knows we're Twoing, so we can't stop the class from finding that out, but it's best for you if no one discovers I'm an ape.'

'I wish you'd stop calling yourself that.'

'I'm a smelly ape, an ugly nean, and a dumb throwback,' I said, bitterly. 'It doesn't matter what anyone calls me, but it's better for you if the class don't find out what I am. My plan is this. We go back to the class. I tell everyone the truth for once, and say that my parents have been killed. Then I pack my things and dash off. They'll all think I've gone to Kappa sector. I never come back and you make up any story you like about what happened to me. Pretend I'm dead and whatever happened is classified, or that I've joined the Military and gone to the Academy.'

'But what would you really do?'

'My ProMum can probably get me transferred to a University Earth course. Literature or something where I'll be safely out of the way.'

'But you love history,' said Fian. 'The look in your eyes when you talk about it . . . No one could fake that.'

'I can't go to another pre-history course,' I said. 'I've attracted far too much attention on New York Dig Site, and someone would spot me as the girl from Asgard 6.'

'You aren't leaving the class,' said Fian.

I shook my head. 'I can't just go back and carry on lying to them all. I can't face that again, and it would never work anyway. Even if I didn't trip myself up with my own lies, people would still find out I'm Handicapped. It's been pure luck that I haven't already run into someone who knew I was Handicapped because they'd met me on New York Fringe

314

or one of the other sites. I suppose the change of surname at the Honour Ceremony helped, but flying that plane was inviting disaster.'

'Why was flying the plane so bad?'

'Fian, don't you realize how few pilots there are? When I was at New York Fringe seven months ago, there was one professional pilot covering both New York Main and the Fringe. At any time, there would probably be two or three amateur pilots on dig site teams to help him out. The professional pilot was about to retire, and he was running a final full survey of the Fringe before leaving. I got him to teach me to fly while he did it.'

I shook my head. 'Think about the situation. Dig Site Command haven't found a replacement professional pilot yet, and they're going to be even more interested than usual in the amateur pilots on the dig teams. Someone is going to look at the Fringe records to check my flying history, or mention my name to people on New York Fringe. Guess what? Fringe never heard of a Military girl called Jarra Tell Morrath learning to fly there. The only person to learn to fly on Fringe in the last three years was an ape girl, and by a strange coincidence her name was Jarra as well. It'll take them about two seconds to work out what that means.'

'So, we have to assume people will find out you're Handicapped,' said Fian, thoughtfully.

'Exactly. That means I have to leave as fast as possible. If the new pilot vanishes then perhaps no one will bother asking Fringe about her. I can't guarantee it, but it's the best I can do.'

'I already told you that you aren't leaving,' said Fian.

I stared at him. Of course, that did me no good at all. You can't tell much about what someone is thinking when they're inside an impact suit. The face is just a vague blur behind the impact suit material, and because impact suits are so restrictive even body language doesn't really work.

'Fian, I have to leave. That's the only fair way. I tricked you into signing up to a Twoing contract with an ape. I can't undo that. The only thing I can do to help is leave.'

'But I'm not sure I want you to do that,' said Fian. 'Of course I was angry when I found out. I'm still angry for that matter. You lied to me right from the start. Maybe later you believed what you were saying, but . . .'

He paused for a moment. 'Jarra, I need time to think about this, and I need to understand exactly what happened. Tell me the whole story, right from the beginning. I'm confused about which people are real, and which were made up, and what you knew at the start and what you found out later. I need to get it sorted out in my head, so please explain.'

'What's the point? It won't change anything.'

'Jarra, a few hours ago I was incredibly happy, and now my life has fallen apart. I think you owe me a proper explanation, don't you?'

'It's a long story.'

He shrugged. 'This is a long sled ride.'

So I told Fian all of it, starting with the crazy ape kid in her room in Next Step, and he just sat there listening. By the time I finished, the broadcast channel was beginning to get busy. Teams were arriving at intersection 3, and Dig Site Command sent two of the Earth teams to take an initial look at the crash site.

'Sounds like we have quite a few Earth teams here,' said Fian. 'That makes sense I suppose.'

That was it? I'd just told him my whole mad story, and he wasn't strangling me, he wasn't yelling at me, he wasn't saying a word about it. He was doing the dig site equivalent of discussing the weather. What the chaos did that mean?

It took me a second before I realized it meant Fian was doing the right thing, the sensible thing. We were here to rescue people, and that meant playing our part as tag leader and tag support, not fighting with each other. When the Military trapped on Solar 5 were safe, Fian could yell at me all he wanted, but not now. I forced myself to answer him.

'Well, obviously us apes don't run away off world during a portal outage,' I said.

'Stop calling yourself an ape, or I'll start calling myself an exo,' said Fian. 'Plenty of expert Earth teams is good news. How will we manage to dig in all this snow? You won't be able to see the rocks to tag them.'

'I think a crash landing spaceship, with hot shields from entering the atmosphere, might have melted the snow a bit,' I said.

'Good point,' said Fian.

'I've just reported that we're approaching intersection 3,' said Rono on the team circuit. 'Dig Site Command already has enough teams assembling mobile domes, so we're to park our sleds and take a break from the impact suits at the base camp. There should be some food there when they've got things organized.'

Fian and I peered round the side of the orange cover, and saw what was ahead. A line of sleds that looked like a vid scene of a pre-history traffic jam, and a bunch of domes that were either complete or half assembled.

'That's a lot of mobile domes,' Fian said in awe. 'I make it ten. We're building our own settlement here.'

'That's a lot of sleds,' I said. 'We'd better remember where we park ours.'

Rono pulled our sled in at the side of the clearway, and the rest of Cassandra 2 parked neatly behind us. The dumper sleds from Thor 3 drove straight on. They seemed to have instructions to head somewhere specific.

We hiked along the uneven surface of the clearway, to reach the gaggle of domes. Someone was helpfully writing on the doors in large letters. Medical 1, Medical 2, Food, and three Rest Rooms were already labelled.

'Food first,' Rono led the way into the dome marked 'Food', and we lowered the hoods of our impact suits.

Inside, several people in suits labelled Achilles 1 were unloading boxes of packaged food. Upturned boxes were being used as counters holding trays of drinks and food. I noticed masses of standard food dispenser cakes among the packaged stuff. Presumably someone from Achilles 1 had had the bright idea of getting those from their food dispensers and bringing them along.

There was another team ahead of us, so we formed an orderly queue. Fortunately, there was no risk of the cake running out before we got there. There were more teams arriving in the dome and joining the queue behind us, so once we had the food we took it across to one of the domes labelled 'Rest Room', and joined a crowd of people who were already sitting on the floor and eating. The heat panels were on maximum and there was a stack of thin metallic emergency blankets. It was blizz to take off my impact suit and wrap myself in a blanket. You learn not to be too modest on camping trips, and none of the people in this dome were leering Betans, but the blankets were still nice for more than just warmth. It's a bit embarrassing wearing just a skintight in front of a crowd of strangers.

Fian had come to sit next to me, and I looked nervously at his face. He seemed strained, but quite calm and a bit thoughtful. He spotted me looking at him, and his eyes flickered round the members of Cassandra 2 sitting around us. He leaned across to whisper in my ear. 'We can't talk here, but you aren't leaving. We're going to find a way to sort this out.'

That was nice, but unrealistic. I whispered back. 'We can't. I'm an ape.'

Fian frowned at me, and I got another whisper in my ear. 'Shut up. The clueless exo is in charge now. You got yourself in trouble as usual, and your tag support has to rescue you.'

I suddenly wanted to giggle and cry at the same time. Things were too big a mess to sort out, but at least Fian didn't seem to hate me anymore. I couldn't cry in front of all these people, and important things were happening on the broadcast channel, so I tried to concentrate on that.

'This is Dig Site Command. The crash site is five minutes east along the Loop from our base camp, and then a short distance due north across the rubble. We're marking the safest route with glows, so stick to it. No taking short cuts in any circumstances. We're running this rescue under the same procedures as a multi team dig, though we've obviously got more teams involved than any previous operation. Pereth of Earth 2 has handed over team command to his deputy and will be our Site Leader. I think most of you will know Pereth.'

I glanced across at Rono. 'Pereth is good,' he said simply.

'This is Site Leader Pereth,' said a new voice on the broadcast channel. 'Dig Site Command are just parking their sleds at the base camp and getting properly set up, so I'll give you a situation report while they do that. Bear with me if I go quiet occasionally, I'm running a site as well as talking to you.'

There was a short pause before he continued. 'We can't get a proper sensor net up yet, and naturally sensors are being badly affected by the solar storm, but we've located where the ship is buried. They seem to have hit a tower cluster and brought down two towers on top of them. There are two further towers making the area very hazardous, so our first step is taking those down. Earth 2 and Earth 8 are setting charges at the moment.'

'He sounds so relaxed.' Fian shook his head in amazement.

'When the towers are down,' said Pereth, 'we can start organizing the main rescue work. We have a lot of teams with substitutes from one, or in some cases two other teams, which is potentially confusing. Since the most urgent instructions are likely to be going to the tag leaders I'll be addressing teams by the team designation of their tag leader. Make sure you know what that is and remember it.'

Rono laughed. 'Team 2, that means you're designated Asgard 6 for the rescue.'

'I'm going to have twenty-four working teams on the site,' said Pereth, 'and this is going to be a clock excavation. You'll be working as double teams, and obviously I'll keep people together where possible. As usual for the clock, positions are based on the ancient clock face. Earth 2 teams 1 and 2 are together at one o'clock. Cassandra 2 and Asgard 6 are at two o'clock.' He ran through a whole list of team names.

'What's a clock excavation?' Fian asked me in a whisper.

I shrugged. I didn't know either.

Rono pulled a face. 'Twenty-four tag leaders on site . . . I'm glad I'm not running this. We usually do a clock with six, and the previous highest ever was twelve.'

'I think Dig Site Command are back with us now,' said Pereth, 'so over to them.'

'This is Dig Site Command. Solar 5 are you on our broadcast channel yet?'

'This is Solar 5, Colonel Riak Torrek commanding.'

Fian raised an eyebrow at me. 'The Colonel who did your Honour Ceremony,' he said in a low voice.

I nodded.

'This is Dig Site Command. Is your ship still level and the

320

shields green? We need to blow up two ruined skyscrapers near you and your area will be hit by shockwaves and rubble.'

'This is Solar 5. We're within five degrees of horizontal, and the shields are stable, but you shouldn't attempt this. It's our job to protect civilians, not put them at risk rescuing us.'

'This is Dig Site Command. We aren't civilians, we're archaeologists! You've already breached site regulations by entering New York Main without proper clearance, so we expect you to quietly follow instructions.'

The Colonel laughed. 'We apologize for failing to get clearance. We were far off our planned flight path, losing control, and didn't know where settlements would be. I'd been on your dig site for an Honour Ceremony recently, and the ruins are obvious from the air. I knew no one would be in them during a solar storm, so I aimed for the middle.'

Rono gave me a startled look. 'Solar 5 crashed here because of Jarra's Honour Ceremony!'

I was grazzed, but Fian gave a sudden laugh. 'Crazy things always happen around her.'

Pereth was back on the broadcast channel. 'Earth 2 and Earth 8, status check please.'

'This is Earth 2, charges set and withdrawing from site.'

'This is Earth 8, final charge just set.'

'This is Site Leader. Withdraw to Loop everyone.'

'I've got to see this,' said Rono, and he started putting his impact suit on.

Rono wasn't the only one. Everyone in our dome started putting on suits. When we got outside there was a crowd standing there. I spared a moment to look at the bulky enclosed sleds labelled 'Mobile Command', and then joined the rest in staring north east at the two nearest ruined towers.

'This is Site Leader. Solar 5, seal your suits, check shields, and report when braced for impact please.'

'This is Solar 5. We're ready.'

'This is Site Leader. Earth 2, fire charges.'

One of the great ancient giants crumpled and fell in a thick cloud of dust. Even at this distance, I could feel the ground shake under my feet.

'This is Site Leader. Solar 5 status please?'

'This is Solar 5. We got shaken a little, but no damage. Ready for second one.'

'This is Site Leader. Earth 8, fire charges.'

The second tower seemed to hesitate and think about it for a moment, but then it too toppled to the ground. A second dust cloud billowed up to mingle with the first.

'This is Site Leader. Solar 5, how are you?'

'This is Solar 5. No damage. That felt closer though.'

'This is Site Leader. Site teams get your working sleds and head out along the Loop in clock face order, one o'clock first. I'll guide you to your positions.'

Fian and I followed the others back to the sleds, and Rono pointed us at a tag support sled. We climbed aboard, Fian went to the controls, and we started moving with the other Cassandra 2 sleds. We were going to dig up a spaceship!

31

We drove along the Loop for a few minutes, and then turned north through the ruins, following a path marked by twin lines of glows. I could see the crash site ahead, marked by the thick pall of dust still hanging in the air. The rest of the ruins had their white blanket of snow, but here it had melted or been buried in falling rubble. We reached the end of the marked path, and Rono led our group of sleds around a curve marked by occasional single glows until we parked by one.

'This glow marks our position at two o'clock,' said Rono. 'There's a vid bee hovering above each glow, recording images and transmitting them so the Site Leader can view the site from any of the team positions.'

I looked across the crash site, counting the other eleven glows that marked the circle of the huge clock face. Another single glow marked the centre of the circle. After a few minutes we heard Pereth speaking on the broadcast channel.

'This is Site Leader. Set up boundary glows in red, and start with ten markers per clock point please. As you can all see, we have a huge area to cover. Solar 5 have to take their shields down to use their escape hatches, but they can't do that until we shift the rubble off the top of the ship, and they're buried pretty deeply. To prevent dangerous landslides, we're aiming to dig out a gently sloping crater within our clock face that will be deep enough at the centre to uncover the whole top of the ship.'

Rono unpacked two red glows, and a set of markers from one of the sensor sleds. He set up one of the glows on each side of us, showing the boundary points between us and the neighbouring teams at one o'clock and three o'clock, and then placed evenly spaced numbered markers along our section of the circle.

'This is like a cake?' Fian asked me. 'We have to dig out the slice of the cake between the red glows?'

I nodded. 'I think so. We dig out one twelfth of the cake.'

The Site Leader was talking again. 'We've already encountered problems because the solar storm is causing lift beams to flux erratically. That means a lot of rocks will get dropped by the lift sleds, and there'll also be problems with tag support lifelines. Everyone on tag support, remember when you pull your tag leader out of trouble, keep them quite low in case the beam drops them. I've had to rethink plans a little, to try and keep everyone working as much as possible while still keeping risks to a minimum. Normally we double team by running two independent teams near to each other, but we're going to try something a little different today.'

He paused. 'All teams call in when you're positioned and markers are set.' The various teams around the clock face called in that they were ready, and Pereth continued. 'Tag support sleds for your first and second teams move to markers one and two respectively. Team leader and sensor sled for first team will be working with the tagging crews. Everyone else is the lift crew and should wait at your clock positions.'

'I've no idea how this is going to work,' said Rono on

the team circuit, 'but I'm betting Pereth knows what he's doing.'

Fian drove our tag support sled round to marker two. The other tag support sled was a short distance away at marker one.

'That's looking good,' said Pereth. 'Our sensor net is up, but people on sensors will already see that interference from the solar storm will be making their job really hard. Team leaders please look for dangers visually as well. At least the aurora is helping us there by turning night into day. Tag leaders should tag rocks working along the line between you and the centre glow. You'll need to mark smaller rubble than usual because we're going to have to load everything into dumper sleds and shift it away from our dig area. Contact me with any questions, otherwise we're ready to start.'

'This seems complicated,' said Fian on the team circuit.

'It's going to be very complicated,' said Rono, 'but only our Site Leader needs to understand the whole plan. The rest of us just trust him and follow directions.'

I tagged rocks, while nervously aware the rubble beneath me wasn't just unstable, but still actively moving in places as it settled under its own weight. Visibility was difficult too, with the weird coloured light from the aurora, and the fog of fine dust in the air. I was deeply thankful for the impact suit air system, which saved me from having to breathe the filthy stuff.

I was a fair distance into the circle when Pereth started talking again. 'Tag leaders return to your tag support sleds please. When they're back, I want the tagging crews to shift round the circle to markers five and six and start work there.'

I headed back to the tag support sled, and Fian drove it round to marker six.

Pereth was giving instructions again. 'Everyone else is lift crew, and should go to markers one and two to shift tagged rubble. There'll be a dumper sled either there already or arriving. Only lift rubble when the dumper sled driver is safely clear of the site on the nearest sensor sled. I don't want people getting rocks dropped on their heads.'

That lot of instructions didn't really concern me and Fian. For us, it just meant that the rubble I'd tagged was now being shifted, and I was working at a safe distance from any falling rocks. I concentrated on my tagging, moved position when ordered, and let our Site Leader worry about who he was shuffling to where and why.

We shifted to and fro sideways several times, and I suddenly realized this was reminding me of something. When I was a kid of about 7 years old, I was in Home with Issette, and Keon, and everyone, and the staff used to get us doing dancing. We'd all be in a circle, holding hands, and one of the staff would call out the steps to us. Two steps left, then two steps right.

This was similar in a crazy sort of way. The Site Leader was calling out the steps, and the circle of tag crews and lift crews danced to his bidding. After a while, we started to learn the dance, and could guess where he would move us next. When he had us all move in towards the centre glow, mark out another smaller circle and work there a little before moving us back out again, I nearly laughed. That was so like the dances in Home as well. Boys step in and out. Girls step in and out.

The dance was working. We were starting to dig out our crater, moving in and out so that we didn't have any dangerously high banks of rubble. There were problems of course. At any point in the dance, some tag team would be struggling with a huge boulder or girder that sprawled across the areas of two or even three markers.

We had our turn at that of course. 'We'll have to cut that up into small pieces to get them on a dumper truck,' said

Rono, as I approached a vast length of diamene. 'Our two tag leaders had better work together. Keren get a laser gun and do the cutting. Jarra follow him along and tag please.'

I wasn't surprised Rono preferred the experienced Keren to be handling the laser gun, rather than handing it to a novice when the solar storm was causing random effects on equipment. I might be a crazy ape, but I preferred things that way too.

At one point, our team reached a section of wall that had stubbornly clung to life and was still dangerously high. Rono called in the problem. Pereth took a look using the vid bees that monitored the dig, and then came round in his red Site Leader sled to take a look in person. The entire dance was halted, the teams pulled back, Solar 5 warned to brace themselves, and we blew up the wall with charges.

Then it was back to the dance, but others had their share of incidents too. There was a sudden cave-in, which briefly buried two tag leaders over near eight o'clock on the circle. A hazardous power storage unit was spotted and had to be dealt with. An old underground cellar actually had to be filled with rubble because it was dangerously deeper than we wanted at that point in our crater. An over eager dumper sled driver managed to get hit by a jagged piece of metal sufficiently hard to damage his impact suit and get him ferried off back to the base camp for medical checks. All of these things called for the attention of our Site Leader, and I wondered how Pereth could cope with it all.

I'd totally lost track of time in the weird cross between night and day, when our Site Leader stopped the dance. I know the aurora colours had shifted from green to pink, and Rono had offered stims to anyone on our team who needed them. The sensor sled operators accepted, exhausted by the strain of trying to distinguish real danger warnings from the crazy images caused by interference. The rest of us

327

were buoyed up by the adrenaline of the situation and didn't need meds.

'This is Site Leader. We're going to mark out a third, even smaller circle, and work directly over the ship for a while. Solar 5, please let us know immediately if you have any shield issues, because our tag leaders will be working directly above you. We'll only have space for half the teams to work safely, so teams at two, four, six, eight, ten, and twelve o'clock go back to the base camp for an hour break. Leave your working sleds where they are, because I've got transport sleds arranged to ferry you to base camp and back. Everyone else, I'm afraid your rest break is an hour and a half away.'

A transport sled pulled up at the two o'clock marker and we piled aboard. 'Welcome aboard the Achilles 1 ferry service,' said the cheerful driver. 'We deliver you to the door of your luxury dome accommodation, where you'll find food, drinks, blankets, sleep sacks and superior individual washing facilities awaiting you.'

We were exhausted, but we managed a laugh anyway.

'What are the superior individual washing facilities?' asked Rono.

'Well,' our driver admitted, 'they're just bowls of water, but we did our best.'

Achilles 1 had indeed done their best. We were delivered to the door of a dome that was now labelled 'Rest Room Two o'clock', and staggered inside to find the heating panels on maximum, sleep sacks and blankets laid out, a makeshift table of upturned crates loaded with food and drinks, and the promised bowls of water.

'I love Achilles 1,' said Rono, with deep feeling.

There was a chorus of agreement.

We all stripped off our impact suits, washed, and ate and drank like the starving people we were. Then we stretched out on sleep sacks. After being confined in a heavy impact suit for hour upon hour, this was blizz, complete and utter blizz.

It was ten minutes before I realized I'd forgotten to be embarrassed about being half-naked among strangers. I was just too tired to care. Besides, Fian was lying on the sleep sack next to mine, but the Cassandra 2 team were right over the other side of the dome, ostentatiously not looking in our direction. We were a newly Twoing couple, so they were giving us as much privacy as they could.

Fian rolled on his side to look at me. 'So,' he said, 'we should discuss plans.'

I whimpered. 'I'm exhausted. I've been tagging rocks, while you just had to sit on a sled.'

'True. I just had to sit on a sled, and tensely wait to yank you out of trouble, while knowing that the solar storm could mean the sensors missed major hazards, or my tag support beam failed at the crucial moment.'

'Eleven times, thank you.' I said, wearily.

'What?' he asked.

'You yanked me out of trouble eleven times, including two major landslides and a falling girder that I hadn't even seen coming. Thank you. Now let me scream quietly in peace.'

'I want to discuss things now. I'm in a better physical state than you are, so this is my best chance to talk you into submission.'

I sighed. I'd been trying to blot out the personal nightmare and concentrate on doing my job, but now I forced my fuzzy brain to think. 'The plan is I leave.'

'Not an option. We entered into a Twoing contract. We have a commitment to try and make this relationship work.'

'You didn't know I was Handicapped. I'd lied to you, so you've no obligation to honour that commitment.'

Incredibly, the mad norm grinned at me. 'No I don't, but you do. I didn't lie to you about anything, so you've got no excuse to walk out on me. I've decided to hold you to your contract. You signed up with me for three months and you're staying with me for them.'

I sat up and stared at him. 'You don't want to Two with an ape. You said so. Are you planning some sort of revenge?'

Fian laughed. 'I'm not the revenge type, and as for comments about apes . . . You can't blame me for being angry after all the lies you told me. You lied, I called you an ape, and we're both sorry. Now, let's move on and work out how to fix things.'

'The only thing I can do is leave.'

'I've said that I refuse to let you,' said Fian, happily, 'and I mean it. I have legal rights here. I might have grounds to terminate our Twoing contract, but you don't. I didn't get you to agree to the contract under false pretences. I haven't walked out. I haven't been violent. I didn't exactly force my attentions on you earlier today. I might have called you an ape once in the heat of the moment, but you can't really claim that was unreasonable behaviour given the circumstances.'

I was grazzed. 'You're threatening to go legal? No one goes legal over a Twoing contract!'

'Watch me do it,' said Fian. 'If you don't already know how stubborn I can be, then you'll soon find out. I have rights and I will enforce them. I can demand that we both attend a relationship course including psychological counselling.'

'That's evil! I told you I hate psychologists.'

'At the risk of being thrown across this dome, I must say that I think recent events indicate a bit of time with a psychologist might help. However, I'll let you off legal action and psychologists, if you agree to carry on with our relationship.'

'You're serious? I'm an ape girl!'

Fian frowned. 'Don't call yourself that! You're as human

330

as I am. You're just . . . an Earth girl. And yes, I'm perfectly serious. I was furious that you'd lied to me, Jarra. Now I understand you didn't let us get close to each other until you were in shock after your parents' death and living in your dream world, and that makes a big difference. The lies you told before that . . . Well, I could wind myself up to be angry about those again, tell you to get the chaos out of my life, and you'd go off and martyr yourself taking some other course, but would that make either of us happy?'

He pulled a face. 'I've been asking myself how I'll feel if I do that. How will I feel tomorrow, and the next day, and in the weeks and months after that? After the anger and resentment wears off, I'm going to remember just how good we were, and I'm going to wish . . .'

He shook his head. 'Jarra, I thought you were a crazily brave Honour Child from a Military family, who could throw me across the room, and take me places that were utterly zan. I thought you shared my love of history, and enjoyed my stupid jokes, and you cared about me. Now, despite the lies, aren't just about all of those things still true?'

'Yes, but I'm . . .'

'You're an Earth girl,' he said. 'You're Handicapped, so you can't walk through a portal and go off world. That does change the situation. It causes some problems, and solves others. I've wasted a lot of time worrying what happens if you decide you want to go combat Military and join Planet First. It's quite funny when you stop and think about it.'

'I'm afraid I still can't see it as a joke. What about your family?'

Fian shrugged. 'My sister exists off in a mental universe of her own, concentrating on wave particles, so she won't care. My parents won't like it when they find out you're Handicapped, but they didn't like me going history either. They know me

331

too well to think they can stop me when I'm determined to do something. Did I mention I was stubborn?'

'I don't think you're stubborn, I think you're insane,' I said. 'What about the rest of the class? Do you really think I can keep lying to them?'

'No, I don't think you can keep hiding your Handicap. Thinking back, you really weren't very good at the lies, Jarra. You constantly made mistakes, and I would have guessed the truth if it hadn't been so unbelievable. Even if you didn't tangle yourself up in the lies, you're probably right that someone would find out because of you being a pilot, but it doesn't matter because I want Playdon and the class to know the truth.'

'What? Why?'

'Because I'm not risking you having any more fantasy spells and thinking you can walk into off-world portals. You may have faith in the alarms going off and stopping you, but I don't want even the remotest chance of you dying.'

I frowned. 'I'm not going to do that again, Fian. My parents' death hit me like . . . Well, it was like being buried by rocks, and going into impact suit blackout, but I'm fine now.'

'It's still best if we tell the class.'

'Seriously? Just stop and think what they'll say.'

Fian shook his head. 'It can't be that bad. They've already been through something similar with Lolia and Lolmack.'

'That's different,' I said. 'Lolia and Lolmack kept things hidden, but they didn't tell a lot of deliberate lies the way I did. I told the class all those things about being from a Military family.'

'But as it turns out, you really are from a Military family. You've got a brother and sister, rather than just a brother, but I expect I'm the only one who was interested enough to remember details. Your parents really were on Planet First,

332

and they've just been killed. You didn't tell the class immediately that happened, but no one will yell at you because of that.'

I pointed out the obvious. 'They'll be too busy yelling at me for being an ape.'

'They may say a few things in the initial shock, but when they calm down I expect the fear of being thrown across the room may make them watch their words. I'm pretty sure Playdon will be on our side as well, and threaten them with code warnings.'

Fian really seemed to mean it. He was sticking with me despite the lies, and despite me being an ape. If it wasn't so hard to believe, and if I hadn't been so exhausted, I'd have jumped up and down to celebrate. If we'd actually been alone in the dome, I might have done even more.

Fian was studying me intently. 'You do still want us to be together? Liking me wasn't just part of the fantasy was it? You do still care?'

I blushed. 'I do still like you.'

'You wouldn't like to upgrade that statement?' asked Fian. 'There's another word you could use.'

I've never been good at making declarations of affection. Back when Cathan and I were boy and girling, he'd try to push me into saying stuff, but he never managed it. I'm much better at expressing hostility than affection.

'Not just now . . .' I said. 'It's . . . not the right place.'

I was a bit relieved when Rono picked this moment to stand up and call across to us. 'Time to start getting suits on.'

Fian sighed heavily, stood up, and pulled a face at me. 'I know I'm not much to look at . . .'

I stood up as well, groaning at the effort, and stared at him. He really seemed to mean it. He looked like Arrack San Domex, and he didn't think he was attractive? How nardle brained was that?

'A lot of us on Hercules are slim and blond,' Fian said sadly, as he struggled with his impact suit. 'I know girls find that boring.'

It's a mistake to giggle when you're putting on an impact suit. I nearly fell over. 'We do? Maybe the girls on Hercules find blond men boring, but personally I like them.'

Fian didn't seem entirely reassured. 'There's the muscles issue too. Hercules is at the low end of the gravity criteria for Planet First. I know that's only three percent less than Earth standard, but I still feel whoever chose our planet's name was poking fun at us, and when I came here . . .' He pulled a face. 'I barely noticed the higher gravity when I was just walking round the dome, but then I put on an impact suit and . . .'

I felt horribly guilty. 'I knew Planet First excluded planets with a higher gravity than Earth, but I didn't think it through. Stupid of me. No wonder everyone was complaining about the impact suits so much. I'm sorry.'

'Oh I've adjusted to wearing an impact suit now,' said Fian, 'but there are still times like earlier today. We were in a dome packed full of people, and it was really demoralizing seeing the men take off their impact suits and show off their muscles. Just look at Rono.'

We both managed the final tricky phase of getting our arms into our suits, then did the easy bit of sealing the front and pulling up and closing our hoods. I glanced at Rono. 'What about him?'

Fian turned to look towards Rono, as he answered. 'Well, he's really good-looking, and he's got all those amazing muscles. I could understand if you preferred someone like Rono to me.'

The echoing sound of Fian's words in my ears, told me the hideous truth even before Rono's amused voice spoke over the team circuit. 'I'm deeply flattered, but would like to point out I'm not only already tagged, but also scared of Jarra and the way crashing spacecraft follow her around. It's a terrifying thought that Solar 5 aimed for New York Dig Site because it's where Jarra had her Honour Ceremony. By the way, Fian, you'll find that a couple of years working on a dig site in an impact suit will do wonders for your muscles. At 18, I could barely lift a glass of Fizzup.'

Fian made a sort of strangled noise, and spoke in horror. 'I said that over the team circuit?'

Rono laughed. 'It's frighteningly easy to put your suit on and forget that you've left it set to speak on a channel.'

Keren's voice spoke on the team circuit. 'Don't worry, Fian, we've all done the same thing. Rono once declared undying love over the broadcast channel.'

Rono groaned. 'It's been seven years, you might let me live it down.'

Keren continued mercilessly. '"My heart is yours until the end of time itself." Not only did the whole of London Dig Site hear him, but Ruth was duty Dig Site Command Officer that day and she said . . .'

There was a chorus of Cassandra 2 voices. 'This is Dig Site Command. Tempting though the offer is, Rono, I'm afraid I'll have to stay with my husband for the sake of our children.'

Rono sighed. 'My only consolation is that it wasn't as bad as what happened last time we were at the California Rift. That couple from Thor 2 . . .'

Keren laughed. 'Yes, that was unforgettable. Just like a Beta vid soundtrack.'

The dome door opened. 'Your Achilles 1 ferry service awaits,' said a familiar, chirpy voice.

We headed outside, and rode on the transport sled back to the crash site. The centre area had been nicely flattened out while we were away.

'This is Site Leader,' said Pereth's voice on the broadcast channel. 'Welcome back to the first shift. We're moving back to the middle circle to do some more work there for a while, and after that the second shift will take their rest break.'

We spent five minutes getting everyone positioned and settled, and then started work again. As I was tagging rocks, I noticed a lone snowflake, followed a moment later by two or three more. I didn't like the look of that. It would be impossible to work if it really started to snow.

I was just wondering whether to mention it to Rono, when Pereth's voice came over the broadcast channel.

'This is Site Leader. Yes, thank you, I'm aware of the snow. Earth Rolling News have struggled on through the interference and organized a weather watch for us. Selected settlements across the continent have been messaging emergency priority weather reports every half an hour. I was expecting slight snowfall about now. It shouldn't last long, and we can expect clear weather for at least six hours after that.'

I relaxed and ignored the snow. Pereth was right. The sporadic snowfall stopped within fifteen minutes, and just after that there was a call on the broadcast channel.

'This is Earth 19. We know this isn't our main purpose today, but we've accidentally found a stasis box.'

Everyone laughed.

'This is Site Leader. If you think Solar 5 is inside then open it, otherwise a transport sled will be over shortly to collect it.'

We moved from the middle circle to work on the inner one after that. At least, those of us who'd already rested started work on the central circle, while the others went for an hour break. While we were moving sleds, I had a good look at the crater we were making. It looked as if we'd finished work on the outermost circle now, and just needed to dig deeper at the middle and centre. It was strange working at the centre, knowing somewhere beneath my feet was a spacecraft.

The other teams returned after their hour, and we worked the middle circle again. After about twenty minutes there was a call on the broadcast channel. 'This is Earth 19. Unfortunately, not a stasis box this time. We've found a young mountain of what seems to be a very tough diamene compound.'

'This is Site Leader. Sounds like I'd better come and take a look.'

Pereth presumably took a look and didn't like what he saw. He moved the teams on even numbered clock positions to work on the central circle, while the rest dealt with the problem chunk of diamene.

So I was back working directly above Solar 5, tagging rocks, when something dazzling white and spraying sparks seemed to streak across the rubble in front of me. About three sensor sled alarms went off, I felt Fian's lifeline yank me backwards, and there was an explosion.

32

The next thing I remember was that my suit was totally rigid, I was struggling to breathe, and my left leg was hurting like chaos. The suit started relaxing, and Fian was yelling in my ear.

'Jarra? Jarra?'

The broadcast channel was urgently talking as well. 'This is Site Leader. Everyone out of the central circle and stay out. I've reports of five injured tag leaders. Earth 1, Asgard 6, Earth 19, Beowulf 4, Hera 6. Medical advice is do not remove their suits. I repeat, do not remove their suits because we expect electrical burns. Our doctor is coming round on a transport sled to assess and move casualties.'

'Jarra?' asked Fian again. 'Are you all right?'

'I'm in slight discomfort,' I said, calm and stoic in the face of agony. No, to be honest, once I got my breath back I screamed.

'This is Hera 6. Our tag leader is in a lot of pain. Can we give painkillers?'

This seemed a good question to me. I was in a lot of pain too.

'This is Site Leader. Our advice is open the suit enough

338

to give one standard painkiller shot. Make sure you don't open the suit near a burn.'

'Where does it hurt, Jarra?' That was Rono. I still had my eyes closed, in the strange theory that it would make my leg hurt less, but it sounded like Rono was next to me. There were several other people talking in low voices as well.

'Left leg,' I said. I somehow wasn't in the mood for long conversations.

'Nowhere else?'

'No.'

I felt someone take down my hood and open the front of my suit a fraction. Amid the chill of New York winter air, there was the slightly different chill of an injection, and then they closed my suit again. I'm not normally keen on meds, but I was that time. The pain in my leg stepped down several levels from acute agony to merely hurting quite a bit.

'I got you out as fast as I could,' said Fian, miserably. 'It wasn't fast enough.'

'You did great,' I said. 'It would have been a lot worse than just my leg otherwise. What happened?'

'We're still working it out,' said Rono. 'The storm induced a current in some wiring, which triggered an old power storage unit, but the explosion was somehow magnified by Solar 5's shields being so close.'

'This is Site Leader. I think we have to thank our tag support people there. We have five nasty injuries, but it could have been much worse. Tag supports had better accompany their injured tag leaders to base camp. We're getting close to Solar 5 now, so the rest of us can proceed extremely slowly and carefully to remove hazards and complete the dig. We need hospital treatment for both Military casualties and our own, so once the rescue is complete, we'll drive in convoy to the nearest settlement with medical facilities.'

A strange female voice was talking to me. 'Jarra, where does it hurt?'

'Left leg.'

There was the sound of a scanner and I felt something odd. I finally opened my eyes to see Fian, the hood of his impact suit down, and his long blond hair in tangles round his anxious face. Next to him, was the purple and silver figure of Rono, and a yellow clad stranger who was writing on the front of my suit.

'Hey! That's a new suit.'

'You can wash it off with solvent later, Jarra.' Rono sounded amused. 'It's the best way to make sure a record of your treatment stays with you at all times.'

'My suit is all right, isn't it?' I asked, panicking in case it had been damaged in the accident.

'If it isn't, you can bill the Military for a replacement, but it should be fine,' he reassured me. 'It's just completed a successful self diagnostic.'

'Oh good.' I relaxed.

'She's crazy.' Fian sounded close to panic. 'Is she going to be all right? We can't portal her to hospital and . . .'

'Fian, I promise we'll get her there by sled,' said Rono.

'I can stabilize the injury for now,' said the strange female voice. 'Jarra, I'm setting your suit controls to keep your left leg a little cooler than usual, and I'm giving you some meds to help with the shock and prevent infection. They'll make you feel relaxed and possibly a little sleepy.'

They opened my suit again briefly for another injection. Fian and Rono strapped me to a stretcher after that, and moved me on to a transport where there were already three other tag leaders on stretchers with worried tag support in attendance.

'I want to stay and watch the rescue,' I complained.

'Tough,' said Fian.

'The vid bees are recording it,' said Rono. 'You can watch it later. Take care of her, Fian. We'll soon catch up with you at the base camp, but call me on the team circuit if you need anything at all before then. Playdon is going to kill me for letting Jarra get hurt . . .'

We bobbed our way off on the transport, and picked up the fifth injured tag leader. There was a brief argument, since the tag leader concerned wanted to keep working despite having a burnt arm. His tag support expressed his opinion on this pretty forcefully, and the tag leader was strapped to a stretcher and loaded in near to me.

Fian was sitting next to me. He listened to the argument, and shook his head in disbelief. 'He's as mad as you are, Jarra.'

'They're all mad,' said the other tag support bitterly. 'Tag leaders are all totally, utterly, stark raving mad. Are you the two from Asgard 6?'

'That's right.' Fian nodded.

'I've heard about her. You have my sympathy. We're Earth 19, by the way.'

'Pleased to meet a fellow sufferer,' said Fian.

'I was all right after the pain killer,' grumbled the Earth 19 tag leader. 'I could go back now and . . .'

'Nuke it!' yelled his tag support savagely.

Fian jumped nervously. I couldn't, since I was firmly strapped to a stretcher.

'Sorry,' the Earth 19 tag support apologised to us. 'I find the only way is to be firm.'

The Earth 19 tag leader kept grumbling all the way back to base camp. Our stretchers were carried in to the dome labelled 'Medical 1', and the doctor came round and checked us again. I was allowed to have the front of my suit slightly open.

'You mustn't take the suit off that leg under any

circumstances,' the doctor lectured me as she gave me another shot of meds. Either this one was a lot stronger than the previous one, or they combined and ganged up on me, because within a few minutes I started feeling woozy.

I would like to state right now, that I was not entirely responsible for anything I said after that point. In fact, the next thing I said was more a noise than a real word. 'Wheee.'

'Are you all right?' asked Fian.

I considered the point carefully. 'I don't know what they put in those meds, but I think I'm a bit powered.'

Fian brought me a drink of water, and then mopped my brow with a wet cloth. I think he'd seen someone doing that in a vid. It felt quite nice.

'You really want us to stay together?' I asked.

'Yes,' said Fian. 'I can write it on your suit if you like.'

I giggled for ages.

He gave me a worried look. 'Was it really that funny a joke?'

'It's the meds,' I said.

I peered around at the other patients. I was on the end of the line, and the next stretcher was the Earth 19 tag leader. He and his tag support had stopped shouting at each other, and were now talking in low voices. I didn't know whether they were lovers, married, friends, or brothers, but they were totally absorbed in each other. I checked that my suit definitely wasn't broadcasting on any channel at all, and decided that Fian and I had relative privacy.

'Fian,' I said cautiously. 'You don't want me to vanish?'

He shook his head. 'I really will have to write this on your suit. Listen to me carefully. I'm a poor panicky exo. I'm scared to death because you're hurt and I can't portal you to a hospital. If there was any lingering doubt in my head about what I wanted, then this situation has made things totally clear. I don't want to lose you. I don't want you to vanish. That is not an option under any circumstances. We get you to a hospital, we get you well, and then we tell the class.'

'It's not fair on you if . . .'

'Nuke it, Jarra!' Fian was obviously under the influence of the Earth 19 tag support. 'If the class yell at you because you're Handicapped, then we'll cope with it. If they yell at me, then we'll cope with it. If Playdon yells at both of us, then we'll cope with it. If it's really impossible, because the class are too chaos prejudiced, we'll both transfer to a University Earth course. The Handicapped can call me an exo all they like because I don't care. Do you understand me? Yes or no?'

'Yes, but I really don't deserve to have you sticking by me like this.'

'I know you don't,' said Fian, 'but I'm your tag support. Getting my crazy tag leader out of trouble is my job.'

'Fian,' I said, 'you're a totally zan tag support, much better looking than Rono, and I don't just like you, I really . . .'

I don't remember exactly what I said after that, but I have a feeling it was something incredibly embarrassing. I'm not good at saying affectionate stuff, but I was under the influence of the meds and . . .

So, things got a bit silly for a while, but then we spared some attention for what was happening on the broadcast channel. We'd worked on that rescue until nearly the end, but we could only listen to the comments on the broadcast channel during the big exciting finish. I eventually saw the coverage from the vid bees about a week later. Solar 5 lying in the bottom of the giant crater with its shields glowing against the rubble. The shields going off, and the escape hatches opening. The Military coming out, carrying some of their people on stretchers. Amaz.

It was about fifteen minutes after that, when someone gave a gentle cough, and we discovered Rono had come to visit.

'Gah!' I said, wondering what he'd overheard.

Rono read the latest medical report on the front of my suit, while I watched the arrival of a group of people in Military blue impact suits, some of them towing hover stretchers. They must be bringing their injured into the Medical domes, to be checked over while everyone else packed sleds ready for the trip across to the settlement. There were two Military doctors as well, and one of them came over, scanned my leg, and read the notes written on my suit.

'This is silly,' I said.

'It is?' he asked.

'I was supposed to be rescuing you, and you're treating me.'

'You did rescue me,' he said, 'and I very much appreciate it. How are you feeling?'

'Drunk,' I said, happily. 'It's the meds.'

'Good. We want you relaxed and pain free.'

Another figure appeared to join the group round my stretcher. I already had one Fian, one Rono, and one Military doctor. I was startled to discover I'd added a Military Colonel to my collection. 'Sir!'

Colonel Torrek had his left arm strapped across the chest of his impact suit, and his hood was down to show the face I remembered from my Honour Ceremony. 'Jarra Tell Morrath,' he said, thoughtfully. 'Well, I might have guessed. Your grandmother always had to be in the thick of the action as well.' He paused. 'Jarra, it was tragic news about your parents. Your brother said he'd had no contact from you, and I didn't feel I had the right to bother you with personal messages, but . . .'

I bit my lip. 'Thank you, sir. I needed a while to recover from the news before . . .'

The Colonel nodded and looked enquiringly at Fian and Rono. I pulled myself together and introduced them.

'Jarra and I are Twoing,' said Fian.

'I was less lucky,' said the Colonel. 'Hold on to her. She seems almost as unique as her grandmother.'

He headed off to talk to the other injured tag leaders, and Fian and Rono looked at each other and then at me.

'The Colonel was an admirer of your grandmother?' asked Fian.

'I don't know,' I said. 'He served with her on Planet First.'

Fian and Rono grinned at each other.

I didn't have much time to think about the Colonel, because someone gave me yet more meds, my suit was sealed, and I was carried out and loaded on to a transport sled. Rono went to check on the rest of Cassandra 2, while Fian stayed with me. After a few minutes, a huge convoy of sleds started moving. Mostly transports, though I spotted the odd mobile dome and work sled being taken along in case we got stuck somewhere. We were taking a lot of sleds with us, but a lot of domes and other sleds were being left behind.

'Someone's going to have an awful job getting all this equipment back to the right dome,' I said.

'So long as we get through to the hospital, I don't care what happens to the sleds,' said Fian.

'There'll be wolves,' I fretted as we headed off through snow covered ruins. I didn't like lying there, strapped to a stretcher and helpless.

'We've got plenty of people with guns,' said Fian. 'There's an armed member of the Military on every sled. They insisted it was time they did some of the work.' He lay down next to me. 'Relax and let me distract you.'

345

He murmured distractions into my ear for the next three hours, until someone came and gave me yet more meds and I passed out entirely. I'd missed the final exciting climax of the rescue, and I missed our convoy arriving at the settlement as well.

33

I woke up in a bed that felt strange. I was in a room with a white ceiling and walls. There was a white table by the side of the bed with a jug of water, a glass, and a bunch of grapes. It was exactly like when I was in hospital back when I was 14, except there was also a Fian sitting in a chair next to me.

'Hello Fian,' I said. My mouth was dry and my voice sounded a bit odd.

He smiled at me. 'Hello Jarra. How are you feeling?'

I tried moving my legs. I seemed to have two functioning ones, which was reassuring. I reached down and counted toes with my fingers. 'Fine. My left arm itches a bit.'

'They had a monitor on it earlier.'

I shifted my pillows, struggled into a sitting position, and reached for the jug of water. Fian beat me to it, poured out a glass of water, and handed it to me.

I sipped water for a minute before speaking. 'We made it to the settlement then.' It was a pretty stupid thing to say. We obviously weren't in a grey flexiplas dome, so we must have made it to the settlement. I wasn't sure what else to say though. Fian had had time to have second thoughts about us staying together and I didn't want to assume anything. It would be horrible if I tried to kiss him or something and he pulled away.

'We made it to the settlement a week ago,' said Fian.

'A week!' I squeaked in shock.

'If you're feeling well enough, I can tell you what's been happening.' He grinned. 'I'm afraid I had to make a few decisions, and you're rather stuck with them.'

'What sort of decisions?'

Fian took out his lookup. 'I've been making a list of things to tell you. First of all, the settlement medical centre got all our casualties stable, but they weren't equipped for serious reconstructive therapy. They decided to keep the worst cases, including you, sedated. On the . . .'

'I've still got my old leg, haven't I?' I interrupted anxiously. 'Surely I must have. Growing new ones takes longer than a week.'

'It's the same leg,' Fian reassured me. 'It was a mess but they could fix it.'

'Good.' I knew a new leg would be indistinguishable from my old leg, but I had an irrational attachment to the original. We'd been getting on well together for eighteen years.

Fian glanced at his lookup. 'On the second day at the settlement, messaging and the vid channels started coming back. After another day and a half, the portal network came back. The settlement medical centre transferred all our casualties to Hospital Earth America Casualty for proper treatment in regrowth tanks, and I came along with you.'

'How did all the settlements cope during the solar storm?'

'A few lost their protective barriers, and there were a lot of fires, but on the whole not too badly. Everywhere is still running on stored power, but about a thousand Military personnel portalled in to the solar arrays two days ago and they're working on repairs. Stored power should last for another two weeks, and they expect the power beams to be back on well before that.' Fian paused. 'Now for the more personal stuff.'

'Personal stuff?' I waited nervously.

'When the vid channels came back, all the newzies were going crazy about the Carrington event, and the Military ships landing, and the rescue. They were interviewing everyone they could get hold of, and they were especially interested in you of course. You were only 18, an Honour Child, injured . . . You can see why they focused on you.'

'Oh . . .' I had a bad feeling.

'They mentioned you in the first detailed reports of the rescue, and got coverage of your Honour Ceremony from Military archives. They mentioned me as well, and that we were Twoing. Then lots of messages came in. Ones from Playdon and the class of course, but there were also ones from Candace, Issette, Keon, Maeth, Ross . . . You can imagine.'

I could. I gulped at the thought of Fian facing a torrent of messages from worried strangers.

'Well, I sent mails explaining the situation to all your Earth friends and your ProMum.'

'You mailed Candace!'

'Of course.' Fian smiled down at me. 'Candace was very worried. Now there's a lot more you need to know. The day after the portals started working again, Playdon brought the class back to Earth, and I portalled over to the dome to tell them you were Handicapped.'

'What? I should have done that.'

'Tough,' said Fian. 'I did it. I thought there might be a few shocked comments that you were better not hearing. On the whole, they took it pretty well. By that point, we were being mentioned on the newzies, and most of the class were willing to overcome any prejudices and forgive heroic,

349

wounded Jarra just about anything. Playdon, of course, was on your side already, though totally confused about the whole Military and Handicapped thing. So, the good news is there should be no trouble when we rejoin the class. The bad news is Playdon has been helpfully recording all the classes we missed, so don't think we'll get excused any work just because we're heroes.'

I laughed.

'The next thing was the newzies found out you were Handicapped. Some of the class think Krath sold the information to them, but I don't believe that. Krath is far too occupied having a major fight with his father. Apparently, his father thinks the ships landing on Earth, and the crash, was made up by the Military to get publicity. Even Krath can't accept that one. He's seen the crash site himself. Dig Site Command got a full size freight portal set up at intersection 3 to shift out all the sleds and equipment we left there, and Playdon portalled the class over so they could help out.'

Fian shrugged. 'The newzies probably found out you were Handicapped when they were researching your background. They'd already been talking about you as a heroine, so I can imagine there was some fast thinking. Some of them instantly dropped you from their news stories, but the others decided to go for it.'

'So, brace yourself.' Fian grinned. 'You are now the heroic Military Honour Child who was tragically born Handicapped. I'm your off-world lover who is willing to sacrifice the universe for the sake of true love.'

I felt a need to double check the basic situation at this point. 'You haven't changed your mind? You still want us to stay together.'

Fian sighed. 'Weren't you listening to the things I said to you before they knocked you out with all those meds? Yes,

I still want us to stay together. I'm your off-world lover who is willing to sacrifice the universe for the sake of true love. Watch the newzies if you don't believe me.'

I giggled, but sobered up rapidly. 'But what about your family?'

'Well, they were a bit shocked at first, but all the romantic stuff about us on the vids got my mother on our side. She's talked my father round now, which makes life a lot easier. My sister still thinks I'm mad, but she doesn't really care what I do. She's too obsessed with her research to worry much about her kid brother.'

Fian checked his lookup. 'I think that's most of the news. Everyone knew when the hospital would let you wake up from the meds, so there's a queue of people waiting to visit you. I thought we'd better start with your ProMum and ProDad, because they're outside having a huge argument in the corridor.'

'My ProDad came?' I stared at Fian. 'I haven't seen him in over a year.'

'That's exactly what your ProMum keeps saying. I gather they haven't met before, and they aren't getting on too well. Your ProMum thinks he's irresponsible for not having regular contact with you. Your ProDad thinks she's irresponsible for letting you apply to University Asgard.'

I giggled. 'I bet Candace is winning.'

'She is. Now, after your ProMum and ProDad, your next scheduled visitors are Issette and Keon. Then there are a bunch from your school and Next Step over in the cafeteria. Playdon and the class are planning to visit this evening. I thought you'd need a little more recovery time before you meet my parents, so they're down for tomorrow afternoon.'

I gulped. 'Your parents are here on Earth?'

Fian nodded. 'The hospital thinks they'll discharge you

tomorrow morning, so I thought we could spend the afternoon with my parents at the zoo. Please try not to call yourself an ape in front of them. After that, we'll head back to the dig site. Playdon says you'll have to sit around in the dome for several days, because he wants to make sure you've fully recovered before you try tag leading.'

'But . . .'

Fian held up a hand. 'You can argue that with Playdon if you like, but it won't get you anywhere. Now, we'd better get on with the visitors, and let in your ProParents before they try and kill each other.'

He opened the door. I could hear Candace talking in a voice icier than a New York winter. 'You seem very eager to criticize my lack of control over Jarra's recklessness. Allow me to point out that you've only seen Jarra three times in seven years, and have had no influence over her at all!'

'Jarra is able to see you now,' said Fian, in a determinedly cheerful voice, 'but the doctors say that your visit has to be limited to fifteen minutes at maximum because she's still extremely weak.'

I hastily lay back on the pillows and tried to look weak.

34

A month later, I was sitting on one of a group of 243 chairs in the centre of Earth Olympic Arena. On one side of me was Fian. On the other side of me was Rono, with the rest of the Cassandra 2 team filling up our row. The Earth 2 team were in front of us, so I'd worked out we'd been seated in the clock sequence from the excavation. Dig Site Command and other oddments seemed to be at the back with Achilles 1.

I glanced at Fian and saw that he was looking terrified. I don't think it was the size of the audience sitting around the arena that was bothering him, as much as the vid bees floating around covering this for all the newzies.

I was trying not to look at the audience to my left. There was a bank of seats over there packed with Playdon, the rest of the class, a bunch of my friends, Candace, Fian's parents, and his friends. Most of them were behaving themselves, but Issette was wild with excitement. Whenever I looked towards her, she would bounce out of her seat to wave at me, and Keon had to grab her and drag her back down again.

My brother and sister were on Planet First assignments,

so they couldn't be here in person, but they'd be watching the vids either now or later. Their friends would see this too, so I hoped I didn't embarrass them by doing anything silly. I kept my eyes firmly forward, and tried to look suitably calm and serious.

In front of the massed dig teams was a podium, and on the other side of it, facing us, were another bunch of chairs. These ones were filled with members of the Military. There would be 350 of them. There had been 352 on the solar arrays, but two had been killed when the ships landed.

The Military suddenly seemed to straighten up, and everyone else picked up the signal and quietened down. There was a moment of silence, and then the anthem started to play. Around the arena the huge flags unfurled, and then the anthem ended and the arena screens came to life. They were showing clips of vids, some that I'd already seen and some that were new to me. Scenes from the solar arrays, on board the ships, views of the ships crash landing, and coverage of the rescue of Solar 5.

That must have lasted for ten minutes, and then the screens swapped to show the flag of humanity and the hymn began to play. Everyone stood to attention as it played through to the high note, and then we saluted, sat down and relaxed. The screens started showing images from the vid bees around the arena.

A Military General stepped up to the central podium, and there was a rustle of expectation from the audience. I'd been expecting Colonel Torrek to do the presentations, but now realized that was a silly idea. He couldn't present his own medal.

'The Thetis and the Earth Star,' said the General's hugely magnified voice. 'Solar 1.'

The first batch of Military stood and came forward to collect their medals as the crowd applauded. I knew the

Thetis was traditionally awarded to Military risking their lives to save civilians. The Earth Star was the beginning of a new tradition, and it looked like it was intended to be both a Military medal and a civilian award.

The crews of Solar 2, 3, and 4, followed. It was the last group that really interested me.

'Solar 5, Colonel Riak Torrek commanding.'

I leaned forward eagerly to see Colonel Riak Torrek lead the crew of Solar 5 to collect their medals. I also spotted the doctor who'd helped treat me at the crash site.

'The Earth Star,' said the General. 'Earth 2.'

Earth 2 dig team went up for their medals, and I applauded madly.

'Cassandra 2 and Asgard 6.'

That was us! I heard Fian gulp as we stood up and went to be presented with the little medal boxes. As I turned round with mine, I caught sight of Issette. She was going nuts again. My magnified face was being shown on screens all round the arena, and those images would be going out live on the vid stream, so I forced myself to stay looking serious rather than give in to a fit of giggles.

Dig Site Command were the last to pick up their medals. Their round of applause died down, the General stepped down from the podium, and his place was taken by Colonel Riak Torrek. He spoke two words that changed the mood of everyone.

'The Artemis.'

Everyone stood in solemn silence as the flags around the arena dipped in salute. Two members of the Military had died when the ships crash landed, and they were giving them the highest Military honour of the Artemis. I approved of that. Its roll of honour began with the four Military who died at the Artemis solar array, so it was more than appropriate.

'Lieutenant Uri Ray Ivanov. Solar 3.'

For two minutes, the screens around the arena showed us the face of a young man who couldn't be here to collect his medal.

'Captain Marra Leonie Meyer. Solar 3.'

For the next two minutes, an older woman smiled at the crowd from the arena screens. They went dark for a second after that, then swapped to showing the Colonel standing at the podium, and the flags returned to normal. The audience started to sit down, but hastily stood again in confusion as another name was announced.

'Davide Jenning of Earth. Tag leader Earth 1.'

The arena screens showed chaos among the ranks of dig team members, as everyone turned to look at a shocked young man. The rest of Earth 1 pushed him to his feet, and he staggered his way out from among the chairs and across to the podium. The Colonel pinned on the Artemis and shook his hand. The audience had realized what was happening now, and went crazy applauding.

Next up was the tag leader from Hera 6. I just sat there, watching in disbelief. You had to be dead or wounded to receive the Artemis. It was the highest Military honour, and had never before been awarded to civilians.

Fian turned to look at me. 'Jarra. It's the tag leaders! The tag leaders who got hurt.'

I was still sitting there with my mouth open. The Military were used to being the ones doing the rescuing, not being rescued themselves by civilians. They were making a point here, and they were doing it in style. They were giving us the Artemis. They were going to give me the Artemis!

It was fortunate that I was fifth and last to be called, because I needed every second to get in a fit state to move.

'Jarra Tell Morrath of Earth. Tag leader Asgard 6.'

I went up and Colonel Riak Torrek pinned the Artemis

356

on my left shoulder next to the Earth Star. This time he didn't need to say my grandmother would be proud of me, but I knew he was thinking of her. He'd shaken the hand of the other four tag leaders because they were civilians. I was an Honour Child, and the granddaughter of Colonel Jarra Tell Morrath, so he caught my eye and we went for the salute simultaneously.

His eyes flickered sideways after that, signalling the next move to me, and I realized they'd called me up last for a reason. The Colonel and I turned to salute the group of other dig team members, and the crews of the Solar ships stood to salute as well. The Artemis wasn't just for the tag leaders. It was the Military saying thank you to all of the rescuers, and at that moment I was counted as both rescuer and Military.

So that's about it. There's been a lot of silly stuff on the vid channels about me, and about Fian too. That's why I've been writing this, to tell you what really happened, to tell norms what it's like to be the one in a thousand who's born Handicapped. I may not seem all that nice in places, but at least it's the real me, not some saccharine invention of the newzies. I'm Jarra, I'm an Earth girl, and I'm proud of it. You can laugh at me for being an ape if you want, but there are only eleven living people entitled to wear the Artemis, and I'm one of them. I'm proud of that too.

Issette says they may finally be researching something that will lead to a treatment for our handicap. She says they think the mistake was trying to find what was on the other worlds but not on Earth. They now think the problem is something they screen out in Planet First. Something that seems bad but is actually vital for some of us, and they've been deliberately picking worlds that don't have it. If they can find what it is, then maybe they can find a way of treating us to get round the problem.

Issette is excited, but personally I don't believe a word of it. They've been looking for hundreds of years and I expect they'll keep looking for hundreds more. I'm Handicapped, and I always will be.

I can't join the Military, but I've got history and Fian, and I think they're the most important. There's a very old saying that dates back to pre-history, and I think it sums up the way I feel. Two out of three ain't bad. In fact, two out of three can be pretty good.

Fian says that two out of three can be even better than chocolate ice cream, so I'm going to stop writing this now and let him prove it.